## Marie Force is beloved by readers:

'There is never any doubt that Marie Force will deliver!'
**Sarah Walford**

'Marie Force never disappoints with her writing. I have read all her books… Her writing is first class'
**julie redpath**

'She is a fantastic author and draws you into her world of characters and weaves wonderful love stories for you to live alongside'
**karen1859**

'As soon as I had finished I instantly wanted to re-read and experience this wonderful story all over again… A truly delightful, heart-warming and at the same time emotional read. This novel is so beautifully written, it drew me in instantly and had me captivated'
**Megan (*ReadingInTheSunshine*)**

'I loved this book. I feel bereft now I have finished… and cannot wait for the next instalment in the series'
**Miss C H Normally**

# By MARIE FORCE

## Green Mountain Series

Your Love Is All I Need
*(published in the USA as All You Need Is Love)*

Let Me Hold Your Hand
*(published in the USA as I Want To Hold Your Hand)*

I Saw You Standing There
*(published in the USA as I Saw Her Standing There)*

And I Love You
*(published in the USA as And I Love Her)*

You'll Be Mine
*(A Green Mountain Novella)*

It's Love, Only Love
*(published in the USA as It's Only Love)*

Ain't She Sweet

# MARIE FORCE

# Ain't She Sweet

**headline**
ETERNAL

The right of Marie Force to be identified as the Author of
the Work has been asserted by her in accordance with the
Copyright, Designs and Patents Act 1988.

Published by arrangement with Berkley,
A division of Penguin Group (USA) LLC,
A Penguin Random House Company

First published in Great Britain in 2016
by HEADLINE ETERNAL
An imprint of HEADLINE PUBLISHING GROUP

1

Cataloguing in Publication Data is available from the British Library

ISBN 978 1 4722 3445 2

Printed and bound in Great Britain by CPI Group (UK) Ltd, Croydon, CR0 4YY

Headline's policy is to use papers that are natural, renewable and recyclable
products and made from wood grown in well-managed forests and other controlled
sources. The logging and manufacturing processes are expected to conform to the
environmental regulations of the country of origin.

HEADLINE PUBLISHING GROUP
An Hachette UK Company
Carmelite House
50 Victoria Embankment
London EC4Y 0DZ

www.headlineeternal.com
www.headline.co.uk
www.hachette.co.uk

# Ain't She Sweet

Aunt She Sweet

# CHAPTER 1

◄►

*This might be the stupidest thing I've ever done*, Charley Abbott thought as she jogged up a steep incline covered with snow and ice. But God forbid she back down from a direct challenge from her sworn nemesis. Said nemesis was trudging along next to her, smoothly navigating the hazardous trail and barely breathing hard when she was about to die from the exertion and the cold. Not to mention her face was numb, and she suspected her numb face was covered in frozen snot. But since backing down was not an option, she kept plugging along, uphill, in the snow, determined to see this through to the finish even if it killed her.

The way he'd looked her in the eye and said, "If it's too much for you, I'll go alone. One week off from training won't derail you." Feeling like a bull that'd had a red flag waved in front of its face, Charley had picked up that gauntlet and run with it, straight up an icy hill with no end in sight. Surely her lungs would explode or her legs would fall off before they reached the peak. And then there was the matter of getting back down . . . *One thing at a time, Charley.*

Whose freaking idea had it been to train for a marathon

anyway? As she ran through the frigid tundra that had kept every other member of their running club home today— except for *him*, of course—she couldn't remember a single reason why she'd wanted to run a marathon in the first place. A stupid, ridiculous, painful goal. But Charley didn't do easy, so naturally she'd picked a challenge that required her to run in weather like this.

Next to her, Tyler Westcott made it look easy. That was just another thing to hate about the man who drove her crazy with his insistence that she should go out with him when she had zero interest in him. Sure, he was good looking and fit, and he had a decent job or so it seemed from the top-of-the-line Range Rover he drove, the stylish clothes he wore and the way in which he carried himself. Too bad none of that impressed the woman who'd already dated her way through Butler, Vermont, and found every man she met lacking in some way or another.

Why Tyler thought he would be different was beyond her, as was the top of this hill. With her eyes now officially frozen open, Charley decided enough was enough. Even if it meant having to look less than capable to him, she was calling a stop to this workout from hell.

As she opened her mouth to speak, the ground fell out from under her. She screamed as she fell down a steep embankment, smashing against trees and rocks and other obstacles before landing with her right leg wrenched under her at an awkward and painful angle. Her chest heaved from the effort to draw air into her lungs, and everything hurt.

From far off in the distance, she heard Tyler calling her name, but since she couldn't breathe, she couldn't reply either.

"Charley, *oh my God!* Say something or do *something* to let me know you're alive."

Weakly, she raised an arm in acknowledgment.

"Thank God. I'm going for help. I'll be back as fast as I can. Do you hear me?"

She raised her arm again.

"You're going to be fine. I promise. Hang in there until I get back."

Charley waved her hand, hoping he'd get the message to

just go already. She shivered so violently that her teeth chattered, but oddly she didn't feel cold. Trying to remember what her paramedic brothers had taught her about shock and cold-weather survival, her mind wandered to worst-case scenarios. What if Tyler fell or hurt himself on the way back or he couldn't find the place where she'd fallen? What would happen then? Was it already getting darker, or was something wrong with her eyesight, too?

The uncontrollable shivering and the pain coming from her knee were so intense they required almost all her attention. This was bad. No way around it, she was in big trouble here. And her life depended on a man she'd rejected so often it was a wonder he didn't have a complex. The irony would be funny were it not for the awful pain coming from her knee.

Her stomach heaved, and she turned her head to vomit, noting a speck of blood in the snow. Did that mean she was bleeding inside?

Charley had no idea how long she lay in the snow, shaking and aching and vomiting repeatedly, aware enough to know she was drifting in and out of consciousness. The ever-present pain dragged her out of blissful unconsciousness.

It could've been hours or days for all she knew before she heard activity above her, and the sound of Tyler's frantic voice as he screamed for her. "Charley! I've brought help. We're coming down to you. Just hang on."

She couldn't manage to raise her arm to acknowledge him, which made her feel bad. In the deep recesses of her mind, she knew he had to be panic-stricken, and she was sorry to have put him through such an ordeal. He might not be the man for her, but he was nice to be so concerned.

Then she heard her brothers Landon and Lucas above her, screaming orders and getting closer to her. She shifted her gaze up and saw them dangling on ropes, rappelling down the side of the steep hill. Above them, she could hear Tyler arguing with the person in charge of stopping him from coming down, too.

"Charley, honey," Lucas said when he reached her. "Talk to me."

"Hey," she croaked.

"Where does it hurt?"

"Everywhere."

"Can you move everything?"

She forced her fingers and toes to move. "Yeah."

Landon came down on the other side of her. "That's one hell of a drop, sis. Leave it to you to do it up in style."

"Mmm, hurts."

"I know. We're going to give you something for that. Hang on."

The next hour was a blur of pain and agony and movement and people. They strapped her to a backboard and then got her into a litter that they used to haul her back up the way she'd come. It had taken far less time to come down the mountain than it did to go back up.

Landon had given her a shot to take the edge off the pain, so she floated between awareness and darkness. Nothing seemed real, except for the anguish on Tyler's face as he ran alongside her, holding her hand as the paramedics worked to get her down the mountain while the snow continued to fall.

She wanted to shake him off, to tell him she didn't need him to hold her hand, but she couldn't seem to make her limb cooperate with the message from her brain. So she endured attention from him that she'd never wanted. Then it occurred to her that he'd saved her life, and she ought to cut him some slack. She'd see to that after she stopped hurting so badly.

They bounced along the trail, every bump sending pain rocketing through her body. The worst of it was in her knee, which was now braced and iced, as if any part of her needed to be colder. Her teeth continued to clatter from the uncontrollable shivering that made her feel like she was connected to something electrical.

Mercifully, she blacked out for a big part of the trip down the mountain, coming to as her brothers and the other firefighters pulled Tyler away from her so they could load her into the ambulance. In the background, she could hear him yelling at someone, begging to be allowed to accompany her to the hospital.

"Let him in," Landon said, apparently overruling the objections of others because he was her brother and knew best. How could he know that Charley didn't want to encourage Tyler's misplaced affection? And with an oxygen mask now covering her face, it wasn't really the time to clue Landon in on the true nature of her "relationship," such as it wasn't, with Tyler.

The man in question sat on the bench across from her. Glancing over at him, she was shocked to see him disheveled and spent from the ordeal. He was always so supremely well put together. It was one of the things she'd found off-putting about him—he usually smelled and dressed better than her or any woman she knew. He was like her brother Hunter in that way. It would be weird to be attracted to a man who reminded her of her older brother.

At the moment, however, Tyler bore no resemblance whatsoever to his usually well-put-together self. He seemed frazzled and frozen and on the verge of an emotional breakdown. Keeping his hand over his mouth, he stared at her while her brothers tended to her on the way to the hospital. She thanked God that her younger brothers hadn't needed to remove her clothing.

They started an IV that had her whimpering from the pain of the needle stick.

Tyler was right there, brushing the hair back from her face and wiping up her tears with a tissue. "You're going to be okay, Charley. I know it hurts now, but the doctors will fix you right up, and you'll be back to your usual ball-busting self in no time."

"Please allow us to enjoy the break while it lasts," Lucas said dryly, making her smile. If he was joking, the situation must not be as dire as she'd feared.

"Seriously," Landon added. "Enough with our older siblings falling off things."

His comment served as a reminder to Charley about the harrowing accident Hunter had had while rock climbing last fall. He'd broken something. She couldn't recall what inside the fuzziness of the drugs they'd given her. But the pain had let up somewhat, and the heat blanket they had wrapped her in was the best invention since sex. However, she could live without the burning sensation in her frozen feet and hands as the blood began to flow once again.

When they arrived at the emergency room, things happened fast. Her brothers and Tyler disappeared from view, and she wanted to ask if Tyler was okay after spending hours in the freezing cold. Was someone looking after him, too? But her tongue was too big for her mouth, or at least that was how it felt.

The doctors and nurses worked quickly to free her from her clothes, to assess her injuries, to clean cuts and treat bruises. She floated along on a sea of drug-induced tranquility until someone tried to move her injured knee, and she heard herself screaming, as if she were outside the room watching from somewhere else.

Then blissful darkness sucked her down and under, giving merciful relief.

"I heard her screaming," Tyler said to the nurse whose sole job, or so it seemed to him, was to keep him away from Charley. "You have to let me back there. She needs familiar faces."

"Dude." Lucas took him by the arm. "They won't even let *us* back there, and we're her brothers. Take a chill. They'll let us know as soon as they have any kind of news."

"The fact that she's screaming is actually a good thing," Landon said. "It means she's alert."

"It means she's in pain," Tyler said through gritted teeth.

"Did you get in touch with Mom and Dad?" Lucas asked Landon.

He shook his head. "I tried to call the airline, but they couldn't do anything. They said the plane had already boarded."

"Where're they going?" Tyler asked.

"London," Lucas said. "They've had this trip planned for a year. They were due to fly out of Boston this morning sometime."

"Just as well," Landon said. "There's nothing they can do for her that one of us can't do while they're gone."

"Mom will want to turn right around and come back home when she hears about this."

As he listened to them, Tyler ran scenarios in his mind. He'd call in nurses, he'd order the equipment she'd need to get by at home—and he'd take her to his home, which was all one level and easy to navigate if she was temporarily in a wheelchair or on crutches. He'd tend to her every need himself. After all, it was his fault for taking her up on the mountain when the weather was so shitty. The run uphill had been his idea. In truth, he'd been certain she'd decline the challenge he laid out to her after they were the only two who showed up for the weekly run.

When she'd given him her trademark mulish look and taken off up the trail, he'd had no choice but to go with her into the foothills of Butler Mountain, pushing himself to his limits right along with her. And then she'd disappeared off the side of the hill in the single most terrifying moment of his life. He'd thought for sure that she had to be dead after taking a fall like that. Until she'd lifted her arm to let him know she was alive but injured—badly so, if her brothers' reactions to seeing her at the bottom of the ravine were any indication.

"Tyler, you need to let the doctors look at you to make sure you don't have frostbite or exposure injuries," Landon said. "You were out there a long time."

The run back to his SUV where he'd left his phone had taken forty minutes that'd felt like forty hours. Thinking of her, alone and broken at the bottom of that sheer drop-off, had fueled him to run faster than he ever had before, risking his own safety on the icy trail as he pushed through the cold and the pain and the fear to get help for her. All he could think about during the interminable wait for rescue to arrive and then the arduous trek back up to where she'd fallen was what if she died without ever knowing he was crazy about her? How would he live the rest of his life without having told her that? Things were going to be different from now on. He'd make sure she knew how he felt, even if she didn't return the sentiment.

He paced the waiting room, needing to hear she was going to be okay.

Ella Abbott came rushing in with her fiancé, Gavin Guthrie, in tow. "Landon! Where is she? What're they saying?"

"Hey, El." Landon hugged her and then Lucas did, too. "We haven't heard anything yet, but she was awake and alert when we got to her, so that's a good sign."

"Mom and Dad . . ."

"We tried to call the airline," Lucas said, "but they were already gone."

Gavin put his hands on Ella's shoulders, offering what comfort he could while Tyler continued to pace.

"Tyler was the hero of the day—he ran back for help and led us right to her," Landon said.

"Don't call me a hero," Tyler said more harshly than he'd intended. "It's my fault she was up there in the first place."

# CHAPTER 2

———◄•►———

This had to be what it felt like to go crazy. Waiting for news of Charley's condition had Tyler more anxious than he'd ever been before, and he didn't officially have the right to be anxious about her—yet. Her siblings hadn't allowed him to take the blame for her fall, but he still blamed himself. He had to do something to make this right for her, which had him placing a call to his mother, who had tuned in to his affection for Charley a long time ago. His friends and family had later picked up on his "crush," or whatever you'd call it, and teased him endlessly about how many times she'd shot him down. He'd been called everything from a masochist to a chump, and still he went back for more.

"Hi, honey," his mom, Vivienne, said. "Can you believe this snow?"

"Mom, I need a huge favor."

"Of course. Whatever you need."

He filled her in about running with Charley and how she'd fallen down a steep ravine.

"Oh my goodness! Is she okay?"

"We're still waiting to hear, but she was awake and talking to the paramedics."

"That's a good sign."

Tyler had wanted to hear her say that. She'd worked as a registered nurse for a home-health service until she retired and took a part-time job at the store owned by Charley's family to stay busy. She loved that job and the Abbott family, too. "Do you still have friends at the nurses' office?"

"I sure do."

"I need you to call in some favors for me." He gave her a list of what he needed and asked that she have the equipment delivered to his house. "You've got my card. Get anything else you think we might need."

"I'm sure her insurance will cover it."

"We'll worry about that later."

"Tyler . . ." When she said his name in that particular tone, he knew he was about to get mothered—and lectured. "What about her family? Aren't they going to want to be involved in her care?"

"Her parents are in England on vacation, and her siblings are all working crazy holiday hours at the store and the Christmas tree farm. It's my fault she was up in those hills on a day like this to begin with. This is the least I can do to make it right."

"It's not your fault that she fell."

"Will you take care of getting the stuff for me?"

"Yes, of course I will," she said with a sigh. "Just tread lightly, will you? If you alienate her family, you won't have much of a chance of winning her over. They're a tight-knit clan."

"I know that, and I have no desire to alienate anyone. I feel responsible for what happened to her, and I'm just trying to make it right." The door from the exam rooms swung open, and two doctors appeared, wearing scrubs that had blood on them. Charley's blood? The thought of that made his eyes swim. "I've got to go, Mom. The doctors are here."

"Keep me posted."

"I will."

"Charlotte Abbott's family?" one of the doctors said.

Ella, Gavin, Lucas and Landon rushed over to the doctors. Tyler followed them, unwilling to wait for secondhand information.

"Your sister is stable and responding well to treatment," one of them said. "She's up at X-ray for scans of her knee and head. We'll have more information after we get the results."

"Do you think she has a head injury?" Landon asked.

"We don't think so, but we're not ruling it out until we see the scan. There's a good chance the knee injury will require surgery to repair."

Hearing that, Tyler took a couple of deep breaths as the dots in front of his eyes continued to swirl.

Gavin happened to glance at him and moved quickly to get him into a chair, pushing Tyler's head between his knees. "Breathe."

Tyler did as directed, forcing air into lungs that didn't seem receptive. It took a few minutes, but eventually his head stopped spinning.

"Let's get him looked at," the lead doctor said.

"No, I'm fine."

"You were exposed to the elements for hours," Lucas said. "Let them check you out, Tyler."

"You'll let me know what's happening with Charley?"

"Yeah, we'll keep you posted," Landon said.

Because that was the best he could hope to hear, Tyler allowed the doctor to lead him to an exam room where he was attached to all sorts of monitors and given an IV to replenish his electrolytes. Settled in the hospital bed with nurses in and out of the cubicle, Tyler tried to stay awake but something they put in the IV dragged him under. He'd take a short nap and then get back to making sure Charley had everything she needed—including him.

\* \*\*\*

Charley woke to darkness and pain. Everything hurt. She moaned, which started a flurry of activity around her. She forced her eyes open to find Ella, Gavin and her brother Wade looking down at her, their faces tight with concern. Where was she, and why did everything hurt so badly?

"She's in pain," Gavin said. "Push the button."

Ella did something that led to almost immediate relief. Whatever that was, Charley wanted more of it.

"Charley," Ella said. "Open your eyes."

Charley would've sworn they were already open. She forced her lids to move when they felt too heavy to lift.

"Do you remember why you're here?" Ella asked.

"Something about a fall . . ."

"Yeah," her sister said, breathing a sigh of relief. "The good news is you don't have a head injury, and the only serious damage is to your knee. You got very lucky."

"What happened to my knee?"

"Torn ACL and MCL. You really did a number on it. You've been in surgery for the last few hours to fix it. That's why you're so groggy."

The whole thing came flooding back to her—marathon training, Tyler Westcott's annoying challenge, the run in the snow, the ground dropping off beneath her, the long wait for help, the bumpy trip down the hill, the ambulance ride, Tyler fighting to go with her.

"I was down to see Tyler a few minutes ago," Wade said. "They've admitted him."

"Why?" Charley's tongue still felt too big for her mouth and didn't want to cooperate with her need to know everything.

"He's being treated for exposure. He was in the cold for hours getting help for you and leading them back to where you fell."

"He's okay?"

"Except for being pissed off that he has to stay down there rather than up here with you where he wants to be,"

Wade said. "You should know . . . He feels responsible for what happened, and he intends to take care of you when you get out of here."

"No."

"He's quite determined, Charl."

The thought of Tyler taking care of her sent her into a panic that far surpassed any fear she'd experienced after the fall.

"The whole Abbott crew was here earlier, but they wouldn't let us all be in here with you, so the others went home and said they'd be back tomorrow," Ella said. "Everyone is worried about you."

"Tell them I'm fine." Her eyelids were so heavy. She couldn't keep them open.

"Do you want us to call Mom and Dad?" Wade asked. "We haven't yet. We waited to see what you wanted us to do."

Charley forced herself to focus. "No, don't call them. They've been looking forward to this trip for a year. We'll tell them when they get back."

"And we'll let you take yet another fall with Mom when she flips out that we kept this from her," Ella said.

"Don't call them. Tell Gramps and Aunt Hannah not to tell her either."

"We will," Wade said. "Get some rest. One of us will be here."

"Mmm, go home. I'm fine. No need to watch me sleep." Charley gave in to the pull of sleep and stopped trying to fight it. The next time she awakened, the room was still dark, and she could only see a tall silhouette standing by the window. She couldn't tell if it was Wade or one of her other brothers, so she cleared her throat to let him know she was awake.

He turned, and Charley bit back a gasp at the sight of Tyler Westcott.

"What're you doing here?" Her voice sounded rough even to her own ears. "I thought you were admitted."

"I was. I am." From behind him, he produced an IV pole that came with him when he sat in the chair next to her bed. "How're you feeling?"

"Great. Never better. You?"

"Same."

"Liar."

"So are you." He released a shuddering deep breath. "Charley, I'm really sorry—"

"Thanks for what you did up there—"

They spoke on top of each other.

"What're you sorry about?" she asked.

"I never should've laid down that challenge with the weather we were having. It was dangerous and foolish, and I was only trying to push your buttons. I never expected you to go along with it. I should've known you'd be too stubborn to back down from a challenge. I'm so sorry you got hurt."

"It's not your fault the ground disappeared from under me. You couldn't have planned that even if you wanted to get rid of me."

"I don't want to get rid of you. That's the last thing I want to do."

Charley was too drugged up to properly process that information. "What's this I hear about you making decisions for me after I get out of here?"

"Before you dismiss my plan, hear me out. I have a one-story house with a ton of space. I work from home, so I'm always there. Your entire family is dealing with Christmas season at the store or they work weird hours like Lucas and Landon, they're out of the country or they have stairs in their homes. You can't very well recuperate on Colton's mountain or at Hannah's house when she's getting more pregnant by the day. You can have your own room with lots of movies and your own remote control. I've got state-of-the-art Wi-Fi *and* I can cook. Once upon a time, I'd planned on being a chef, so I can *really* cook."

Charley couldn't believe she was actually tempted to take him up on his kind offer, but the thought of living with him when she could barely stand to run with him had her shaking her head. "It's too much to ask of you. We hardly know each other—"

"Don't give me that bullshit, Charley. We know each other. We've known each other for years. Let me do this for you. It's the least I can do after challenging you to run up that trail when neither of us had any business being up there today."

"I knew that as well as you did. I could've said no."

"You'd never have said no to a challenge from me. I might see it as a sign of weakness or something equally ridiculous."

It was frightening—and rather unnerving—to realize he understood her so well, when she'd like to think they didn't know each other at all. It was also intriguing that seeing him like this—undone by her fall, vulnerable and desperate to make it right—made him attractive to her in a way he never had before. She wanted to see more of this Tyler, the less-than-perfect Tyler. And he could cook. Charley loved to eat and hated to cook.

He was also right about her siblings—and their schedules. They were extra busy with the holiday season underway at the store, and most of them had stairs in their homes that would require her to recuperate on a sofa rather than the comfy bed that Tyler had offered her. Her own apartment was on the third floor of an old Victorian, and it bummed her out that she wouldn't be seeing her cozy place for a while. Her siblings would raise a fuss about her going with him, especially Ella and Hannah, who'd object to anyone but them caring for her.

"My sisters are going to want to help."

"They can do whatever they want. I'll give them keys."

"What if it doesn't work out . . . me being there?"

"I'm not going to shackle you to the bed, Charley, as appealing as that sounds."

What the hell? How was it possible when she was drugged to the hilt that his suggestive comment made all her girl parts stand up for a closer look at him? The words he'd said to her last month, when they'd danced together at the Grange, came rushing back to her. *I'm not giving up on you, Charlotte*, he'd said then. *And P.S., I don't buy all your abrasive bullshit. Underneath all that bluster, there's an interesting woman lurking. I'd like to get to know that woman.*

At the time, and every other time he'd asked her out in the past, she'd encouraged him to give up, but now . . .

"You'd be my guest, not my prisoner," he said with a small grin that only added to his new appeal. "You'd be free to come and go as you please." He surprised the hell out of her when he took hold of her hand and ran his lips over the back of it, setting off another of those reactions that registered in her most important places. "I really want to do this for you, Charley. I hate that you got hurt because of me. Let me help you get back on your feet."

For the first time since she'd known him and had been aware of his interest in her, Charley wasn't annoyed by him. No, she was too busy being aroused and intrigued to be annoyed. Blame it on the drugs and the trauma of the day, but she found herself saying, "Okay."

The smile that lit up his face when she agreed to his plan had her hoping she wouldn't live to regret being taken in by the man who'd driven her nuts for years. But that was before he saved her life, revealing a whole new—and intriguing— side to his too-perfect-to-be-believed self.

# CHAPTER 3

❧❧❧

Charley spent a week in the hospital, mostly because of an infection that set in after her surgery that left her weak and drained from the ordeal of fighting it off. Her brothers, sisters, grandfather, aunt and cousins came by every day after work, between shifts, whenever they could, bringing books, movies, flowers, chocolate and anything they could think of to cheer her up and help pass the time. Hunter loaned his laptop to the cause, and she used it to watch movies.

While her family was in and out, Tyler was there all the time. He'd appointed himself her ambassador of sorts with the doctors who did rounds when she was asleep and the nurses who came and went throughout the day and night. During the worst of the infection, when she'd been gripped with a fever, he added blankets when she shivered with cold and bathed her forehead with cool cloths when she was sweltering.

It took far longer than it should have for Charley to come to the realization that her siblings, particularly her sisters, had to be in collusion with Tyler for him to have such unfettered access to her. She waited until he'd gone to get some food before she pounced on Ella.

"What gives?" she asked.

Ella paused in the midst of folding a blanket. "What do you mean?"

"*He* is here *all* the time. Morning and night. The nurses even let him sleep here. How did that happen?"

"He offered to stay with you, and he was so nice and sincere and worried about you that we couldn't say no to him."

"Yes, you could have."

Ella averted her gaze and bit her lip, a classic Ella "tell."

"You're *lying!* What's really going on? You'd better tell me, or I'll kick your ass the second I'm out of here."

Ella rolled her eyes. "What*ever*. You won't be kicking anyone's ass for months."

"I'll remember this, and I'll kick yours the minute I'm able to."

Ella draped the blanket across the foot of Charley's bed and then sat, gingerly, so she wouldn't jar Charley's injured leg. "We like him, Charley. He's a really good guy, and he cares a lot about you. Plus, when you said you agreed to go to his place after you get out of here, we thought *you* must like him, too, or you never would've gone along with that plan."

She wasn't sure how to reply to that, because it made far too much sense.

"Do you like him?" Ella asked.

Charley would've squirmed under Ella's intense gaze, but squirming led to pain. "He's okay."

"How can you be so nonchalant when the guy has put his whole life on hold to be here for you when you needed him?"

"I never said I needed him. *He* decided that." As she said the words, Charley felt guilty for downplaying his help. He had been amazing and selfless and wonderful. She couldn't deny that.

"I have something I want to say to you, and I want you to listen to me, all right?"

The unusually serious tone of Ella's voice put Charley on alert. "What?"

"Tyler is a good man who cares about you for some strange reason. He's incredibly handsome and adorable and devoted. Will you please be nice to him and show some gratitude for what he's done for you? Vivienne said he's got a room set up for you, including everything you'll need to do physical therapy at home rather than having to go somewhere."

In need of something to do with her hands, Charley played with the blanket, letting it slide through her fingers. "When could he have done that when he's been here so much?"

"Apparently, he had it done. Called people. Hired them. Whatever. He's gone to a lot of trouble—and expense—to make things easy for you. All I'm asking is that you be nice to him and give him a chance."

"He overwhelms me."

Ella stared at her, agog. "I've never once heard you say *anything* or *anyone* overwhelms you."

Charley scowled at her. "Well, he does. He's so . . . I don't even know what the word is."

"Devoted?"

"Yes! And *why* is he so devoted? Before this happened, I'd never given him any encouragement. I don't get it."

Ella began to laugh, her body silently rocking.

"What the hell is so funny?"

"You are. He *likes* you, Charley. He *really* likes you."

"*Why?* Why does he like me? I don't know if you've noticed but I can be somewhat unlikable at times."

"I have no idea what you mean," Ella said with a smirk. "And you're not unlikable. You're exacting. There's a difference."

"Exacting . . . Is that what it's called? Men like me are considered badasses. Women like me are bitches."

"You're not a bitch. You've got a great big heart, and you'd do anything for anyone. You know what you want and what you don't, and there's nothing wrong with being true to yourself. All I'm saying is it might be okay to let down your guard a little with Tyler. He genuinely cares. Even when you were shooting him down, he still kept trying. You've got to give him props for that."

"Maybe," Charley conceded. He had been determined. She'd never deny that. "Let's talk about you rather than me. How's it going with Gavin?"

"Fantastic," Ella said with a happy, dopey smile and a deep sigh. "It just keeps getting better all the time." She glanced over her shoulder and then lowered her voice. "We're moving in together after the holidays."

"Wow, that's huge news! When were you going to tell me?"

"You've been a little busy being injured and feverish."

"Still . . . You know how I need to know everything."

Ella laughed. "My apologies for holding out on you. Won't happen again."

"See that it doesn't."

"Same to you—I want to know everything that's going on with Tyler."

"There's nothing going on except in your imagination."

"Yet," Ella said with the knowing smirk that set Charley's nerves on edge.

"Still talking about you, not me. Which one of you is moving?"

"I am. He owns his place, and it's way bigger than mine—and far more private. Mrs. Abernathy has big ears," Ella said of her landlady, who'd been their math teacher in high school.

"You must be giving her plenty to hear."

"Maybe," Ella said with a wink.

"I'm happy for you, El. You've got it all figured out, and you got the guy you always wanted."

"It wasn't easy. You know that better than most people. But it was worth the hell and heartache to get to where we are now."

"When's the wedding?"

"I don't know yet. We've talked a little about the summer, but we haven't made any solid plans. We're not in a huge rush."

"I thought you wanted to have a baby like yesterday."

"I do, and so does he. If the baby comes before the wedding, we're both fine with that. I'm going to be thirty-two soon, and we want to have a nice wedding that'll take time to plan. If I get pregnant before then, so be it."

"Wow, have you told Mom that?"

"Max sort of paved the way for the rest of us by having Caden when he wasn't married."

"That's true," Charley said. "Have you talked to him at all? He was in to see me the other day, but he couldn't really talk with Tyler here and nurses in and out."

"I haven't seen much of him since the baby was born. Colton said Max is back to work on the mountain when he doesn't have Caden."

"And the baby will still be in Burlington with Chloe the rest of the time?"

"I guess. Not sure how that's going to work."

"I can't imagine how hard it must be for them to have broken up right before the baby was born."

"I know," Ella said. "Gavin and I were talking about that the other night. Max has a lot on his plate."

"He knows he's not alone, not with this family surrounding him."

"Still . . . He has to be going crazy trying to figure out how he's going to work here with Colton while taking care of his son who lives two hours away."

"Maybe he can talk Chloe into moving over here."

"Doubtful. She doesn't seem willing to do anything to make his life easier."

"I hate this for him. It totally sucks."

"Yes, it does, and you might want to think about how lousy Chloe has been to him while Tyler is waiting on you hand and foot."

"You need to work on your subtlety."

"I'm just saying . . ."

"Yeah, yeah, I heard you the first two hundred times. I know he's a nice guy. That's not the issue."

"Then what is?"

Charley was saved from having to respond when the doctor entered the room with the usual entourage of interns and residents who sucked up to him every chance they got. It had been a source of endless amusement to her and Tyler, who'd been great about taking notes every time the doctor came by on rounds.

"How're you feeling today, Charlotte?" the doctor asked as he perused her chart.

"Much better and ready to get the hell out of here."

"Your blood work came back great this morning. If you feel up to it, I don't see any reason why we can't spring you today. What's your plan for recuperation?"

"My, um, friend Tyler, who's been here with me, has set me up at his house. It's all one level, and he's brought in everything we'll need to do PT at home."

"That's one heck of a friend you've got there."

Ella shot her an I-told-you-so look that put Charley's hackles up. Just because she was letting him help her didn't mean she was going to marry the guy.

The guy in question came into the room and immediately began questioning the doctor about her progress. Since he'd been there with her all week, the doctor had sought her permission to speak to him directly when he asked questions she never would've thought of.

Tyler quizzed the doctor on every aspect of her return home, from medication to possible side effects to physical therapy and how soon it could start.

Charley's head spun with information, but Tyler listened intently, taking notes on his phone as the doctor spoke.

"The nurses will take it from here," the doctor said. "I'll see you in the office next week. Keep a close eye on the incisions, and let me know right away if you see any swelling or redness." He handed Tyler his card. "My cell number is on there. Call me day or night."

Tyler shook his hand. "Thanks so much for everything."

The doctor then shook hands with Charley. "It's been a pleasure. Charlotte, take it easy and get plenty of rest. Do what this nice young man tells you to."

*Really?* He *had* to say that? "Thanks, Doc," she said through gritted teeth while Ella beamed with amusement.

"I'll take good care of her," Tyler said.

Charley was already having buyer's regret on this plan of his, and they hadn't left the hospital yet.

Ella stayed to help the nurses get her up and dressed to

leave the hospital. By the time she was seated on the bed, clean and dressed in a sweatshirt and a pair of sweats of Tyler's that he'd brought in hoping they'd fit over the leg brace, Charley was completely wiped out. She'd never felt more depleted in her life. Between the injuries she'd sustained in the fall and the infection she'd battled after the surgery, she was weak as a newborn.

So much for her grand plan to run a marathon in the spring.

By the time they got her to Tyler's waiting Range Rover, she was seriously doubting she'd ever move again under her own power, let alone run a marathon.

"Don't do a thing," Tyler said. "I'll do it all with the nurses."

Because she had no choice, she ceded to his wishes even when her first impulse was to tell him to stop being so bossy with her. He was only trying to help her, and there was no place in the midst of all that devotion for her to be bitchy. Besides, bitchiness would take resources she just didn't have.

After he buckled her into the car, Tyler produced a wad of keys that he handed to Ella. "These are for my place. You all should come and go as you please while Charley is there."

"This is so nice of you, Tyler. We really appreciate what you're doing for Charley."

"It's no problem. Least I could do."

Charley wanted to tell him—again—that none of this was his fault. She'd gone on that run knowing it was dangerous and risky, and she'd done it fully aware that he'd challenged her because he wanted her with him and knew she'd never back down. But telling him that would require energy she just didn't have.

She'd tell him later. When she could keep her eyes open long enough to form a sentence—or two.

Tyler's nerves were shredded as he drove Charley home to his place up in the Butler Mountain foothills, not far from where she'd fallen. He'd built the house three years ago and had spared no expense or attention to detail since he worked from home and was there more often than not.

He hoped she liked it as much as he did, and he hoped she'd be comfortable there while she recovered.

However, he also worried that she would take one look at the place and jump to conclusions about him that weren't that far off. He'd made a lot of money in the stock market and had a comfortable lifestyle as a result. That was just one of many things she didn't know about him.

Charlotte Abbott had repeatedly dismissed him because she thought she had him figured out. She thought he was like every other guy in Butler who pursued her relentlessly because she was gorgeous and sexy and fun and mouthy and challenging. Until Tyler met her, he'd had no idea that those qualities were a huge turn-on for him.

She'd rejected him more than any other woman ever had, and he still wanted her. His friends said he was a masochist to be stuck on a woman like Charley, who led with her mouth and her fists.

Tyler chuckled softly at that image of her, knowing she'd love that he thought of her in such graphic terms. She didn't need to know that he also pictured her in sexy lingerie with her mouth and fist wrapped around his cock. The second that thought registered, he hardened. Great . . . Because that was just what she needed—him lusting after her when he'd brought her home to recover from a serious injury.

*Put some ice on it, Westcott. This arrangement is all about rest and recuperation. Keep your mind out of the gutter.* Throwing the car into park in front of his three-car garage, he kept repeating those instructions to himself over and over again until the throbbing in his lap let up.

Then he made the mistake of looking over at her, and his resolve flew out the window. She was so damned gorgeous, especially asleep with her claws sheathed. Her cheeks were flushed from the heater, her lips puckered in repose and her hands folded peacefully in her lap.

He wanted to reach out and run a fingertip over that perfect face, to see if her skin was as soft as it looked, but he didn't dare. If she caught him, she'd call a halt to everything and he'd lose the chance he'd been given to prove to her that she belonged with him. Tyler couldn't say exactly when he'd decided that. It had happened over a period of years and many, many rejections. He'd lost count of how many times he'd asked her out and how many times she'd said no. The number had to be in triple digits by now.

He took a lot of abuse about Charley from his friends and family, who'd been urging him lately to accept defeat and move on. But that wasn't how he rolled. Defeat only made him dig in deeper and try harder. That was how he'd managed to accrue a fortune working from a home office with a couple of laptops and several TVs set to financial news channels.

Giving up wasn't an option, not when he was convinced they could have something special, if only she'd give him a chance to show her what was possible. When he began to shiver from the cold, he realized he'd been sitting there staring at her for far longer than he should've been.

He pressed the button on the garage door opener and then went around to open her door. Though he hated to disturb her, he didn't want to touch her without her permission or her awareness. The last thing in the world he wanted to do was cause her any further pain or distress.

"Hey, Charley," he said softly.

She didn't budge.

"Charley."

Wow, she was really asleep. Probably because of the pain-killers the nurses had given her to make the trip home more comfortable. Shit, what to do. Since leaving her in the cold wasn't an option, he went in through the garage to open the doors to the house so he could carry her in without obstruction. He went back to the SUV to get her, reaching over her body to unclip her seatbelt. Then he carefully and gently lifted her into his arms, taking care to keep her injured leg supported.

Though her personality packed a big wallop, she was a compact package that fit easily—and comfortably—in his arms. He moved slowly because God forbid he should slip on unseen ice or jostle her. Inside, he went directly to his room, which his mother had set up for her.

Charley didn't need to know that he'd given her his room,

and she wouldn't see much of the rest of the house for a few days, which bought him some time until she learned things about him he wasn't quite ready to share. Not that he thought Charley or any of the Abbotts were materialistic. He didn't think that at all. They were a nice, hardworking, well-grounded family.

He placed her on the bed, propping her leg on a stack of pillows as the nurses had instructed him to do, put an ice pack on her knee, and covered her with a down comforter.

She never stirred, which told him she'd be asleep for a while yet. Ella was coming over shortly with Charley's prescriptions, so he would leave her to sleep while he did some work to catch up from the week he'd spent at the hospital.

As he walked out of the room, he couldn't help but smile. Charley Abbott was sleeping in his bed. The scenario that had brought her here wasn't exactly ideal, but he hoped to make the most of their time together to show her what might be possible for them.

He no sooner had that thought than another more disturbing one intruded to remind him that it was entirely possible—even probable—that she would leave here as soon as she was able with no more desire to be with him than she'd had before.

"I can't let that happen," he said out loud, almost as if saying it would make it so. "She has to see that no other guy is ever going to care about her the way I do."

The sound of his mother's voice jarred him out of the disturbing thoughts. "Sweetheart? Are you here?"

"Come in, Mom."

Vivienne bustled around his kitchen, plugging in the Crock-Pot she had brought and depositing a basket of home-baked bread on the counter. "I brought some stew for you and Charley. I hope she eats meat. Do you know if she does?"

The innocent question was a reminder of how much he still had to learn about Charley. But he wanted to know her—really know her. What she liked and didn't like, her favorite food, her favorite music, color, movie. "I, um, I think she does." She'd been on a mostly liquid diet in the hospital, so he wasn't entirely sure.

"Well, if she doesn't, she can eat the vegetables. How's she doing?"

"She's asleep. Whatever they gave her for the trip home really knocked her out."

"Just remember to stay on top of the pain meds. You don't want to let them wear off."

"Her sister is picking up her prescriptions and bringing them here."

"You look exhausted, sweetheart."

"It'll be nice to sleep in a real bed tonight."

"I hope Charley appreciates all you're doing for her."

Tyler laughed. "Who knows if she does and who cares? You can feel free to tell me I'm totally foolish for using an injury to get closer to a woman."

"The last word I'd ever use to describe you is *foolish. Loyal, devoted, thoughtful, smart, savvy, handsome.* I'd use those words before *foolish* any day."

"You have to say that stuff. You're my mom."

"When have you ever known me to say something because I had to? I mean it. You're a catch, Ty. And if she doesn't realize that, she's the foolish one."

"She's not like other women." Blame the oversharing on the exhaustion and the emotionally charged days that had followed her surgery. The infection had scared the hell out of him.

"No," Vivienne said with a chuckle, "she certainly isn't. She's a tough nut to crack that one, but I like her. She's feisty and knows what she's about."

"Her siblings tell her—to her face—that she's a pain in the ass. She takes that as a compliment."

Vivienne laughed. "Of course she does. And her siblings may be right, but at the end of the day, she's a good person. She does the right thing and cares about the people she loves. Not too many people know that she regularly delivers meals to Mildred Olsen and does her grocery shopping and errands for her."

Intrigued to hear of Charley's kindness to the Abbotts' oldest employee, Tyler said, "Who's going to do that while Charley is laid up?"

"The ladies in the store have it covered. Don't worry." After a pause, she said, "In case you were wondering, Charley also volunteers at the animal shelter and mentors young girls at Butler High School about career opportunities."

"You just doubled what I already knew about her."

"My point is that no one is as simple or as complex as they appear on the surface. There's always more to the story."

Tyler wanted Charley's full story. He wanted to know everything about her. "What does it say about me that I'm so gone over a woman I barely know?"

"Attraction is half the battle, my dear. When I first met your father, I remember thinking he could be a garbage man for all I cared. He was so handsome and so kind." She fanned her face with her hand and flashed a suggestive smile his way. "In fact, I might go see what he's up to."

"Please, Mother," Tyler said groaning. "Stop."

"What? Aren't you happy to hear that your parents still got it going on after forty years together?"

"No, I am not happy to hear that. Not one bit happy."

Laughing at the scowl he directed her way, she went up on tiptoes to kiss his cheek. "I shall hope that you, too, are still hot and bothered for the woman you marry after forty years."

He covered his ears and closed his eyes. "Make it stop."

Laughing again, she said, "Stop being such a baby."

"Whaaaa."

She chuckled at the face he made at her. "You know, son, her siblings must really like you for her to have agreed to this plan of yours. If they weren't on Team Tyler, they would've figured out a way to have her at one of their homes."

Tyler dropped his hands and opened his eyes. "I suppose that must be true."

"I work for them. I know how tight they are. They like you, or she wouldn't be here." She zipped up her coat and pulled on gloves. "I'll be by tomorrow to check on you guys, and call me if you need anything."

"I will. Thanks again for everything, Mom."

"Happy to help you any time. You know that." She placed her hand flat against his chest. "Tread lightly with this kind heart of yours. I like Charley very much, but don't let her hurt you, Ty. You hear me?"

"Yeah, I hear you." He kissed her cheek and sent her on the way to God knows what with his father.

# CHAPTER 4

————◄►————

S haking off unimaginable thoughts about his parents, Tyler unpacked the bag that Ella had put together for Charley, tucking sweats, flannel pajamas, T-shirts and lacy underwear that he tried unsuccessfully not to notice into a drawer that he cleaned out for her.

Ella had enclosed some family pictures, including a framed photo of their new baby nephew Caden that Tyler put on the bedside table for her. He stacked her e-reader and several paperbacks next to the photos and took her cosmetics bag into the bathroom and placed it on the counter, leaving that for her to unpack when she felt up to it.

The doorbell rang, and he went to answer it.

"Hey," Ella said, when he let her in. "*This* is *your* house? Oh my God, Tyler! I love this place! It has the best views of any house in Butler!"

"Thanks, I like it. Feel free to come in through the garage any time you want."

"I will, thank you. So the whole town was talking about

this house when it was being built, and everyone wondered who the owner was."

"I bought it under my corporation so people wouldn't be talking about me. You'll keep my secret, won't you?"

"My lips are sealed, but only if you give me a tour."

"You got it." He opened the blinds so she could get the full impact of the view from the huge great room in the middle of the house.

"I have total house envy," Ella said. "This is *awesome*."

Through the big bay windows, they could see the deck he enjoyed in the summer as well as the town of Butler nestled in the snowy hills below. From this vantage point, the town looked as if it belonged on the front of Christmas cards. He led her down the hallway where there were four bedrooms, each of them with adjoining bathrooms. "Charley is asleep in there," he said, pointing to his room. "Come see my office." Tyler opened the door to the room he'd designed to maximize the view of the mountains. Multiple computer monitors and flat-screen TVs lined the interior wall that also housed a built-in desk with several laptop computers.

"What exactly do you do up here?"

"I run the world," he said with a sly smile that made her laugh. "I buy and sell stock."

"For who?"

"Myself primarily."

"So you . . ."

"Manage stock with a goal of increasing my portfolio." It had been days since he'd logged on to the computer to check his accounts. For all he knew, the market could've crashed while he'd been standing guard over Charley in the hospital.

"Ahhhh."

"You don't get it, do you?"

"Not even kinda."

"I'll put it more simply—I make money."

"*That* I understand."

"I don't tell people too much about what I do because it sounds pretentious if you don't really understand it. I hope you don't think I sound pretentious for saying it that way."

"If you're worried about that, it's probably safe to say you aren't. Pretentious people want others to know they've got money."

"I suppose that's true." He jammed his hands in his pockets. "Could I ask you something kind of weird?"

"Um, sure," she said with a laugh. "Go for it."

"Why did you guys go along with letting me bring Charley here?"

"You went to a lot of trouble to help her out."

"Still, if you all weren't in favor of her being here, she wouldn't be."

"*She* went for it, which is half the battle with Charley. The other half is that we like you with her. My grandfather was delighted to hear you've stepped up for her. In fact, if you two end up together, he'll probably find a way to take the credit."

Tyler felt like he'd been electrocuted at the thought of being "together" with Charley. "You think that'll happen? That she'll actually give me a chance?"

"I think she already has by letting you bring her here, Tyler. If she didn't want to be here, she wouldn't be. That's one thing you can be sure of. You earned some big points with her and all of us by the way you stepped up for her after the accident."

"I feel so bad that it happened in the first place. When I suggested we run up the mountain, I never thought she'd do it."

Ella laughed. "Charley *never* backs down from a challenge—ever. We grew up with seven brothers who were always challenging us to do something we shouldn't do. If you don't really want her to do something, don't challenge her."

"That's good to know." He filed away the information for future reference. Perhaps someday he'd want something from her that he could only get by challenging her to do the opposite. "She's a contrary sort, isn't she?"

"That's putting it mildly, but she's also the most fiercely loyal person you'll ever meet. There's nothing she wouldn't do for any of us. There might be some lip involved, but she always comes through."

Tyler glanced at the clock on his desk. "She's due for pain

meds in a few minutes. They said we should keep on top of it, so I'd better go wake her up. Unless you'd like to do it."

"Ahhh, nope. I'll leave that special joy to you."

"Why do I feel like I'm being set up here?"

"Is *that* the time? Wow, I've got to go. Gavin will be home any minute now, and I promised I'd make dinner."

"I'll remember this."

"Call me if you need anything! You have my number. I'll be back tomorrow."

Tyler shook his head in amusement at Ella's quick departure. Steeling himself to do battle with Charley, he took the prescription bags into the bedroom along with a glass of ice water. He turned on the bathroom light and sat on the edge of the mattress, careful not to go anywhere near the injured leg he'd propped up on pillows.

He gazed down on her face, angelic in sleep. "Hey, Charley? Time to wake up and take your meds. Charley?"

From far, far away, a voice beckoned. Once again, her eyelids felt too heavy to move and the sweet comfort of sleep too lovely to abandon just yet. From the vicinity of her leg, a throbbing ache made its presence known. If she just kept her eyes closed, she wouldn't have to deal with what hurt.

"Charley, I know you can hear me."

*Him! Ugh, what now?* "Go away, Tyler. I'm sleeping."

"The nurses said you don't want to get behind on the pain meds. You're overdue."

"I'm fine."

"Charley."

She forced her eyes open and immediately saw the exhaustion that clung to him. Then she looked beyond him to the unfamiliar room. On quick inspection, she saw that the walls were painted a dark beige color, the furniture was made of a rich, dark wood and the bed was huge—and comfortable. "Where are we?"

"My house."

"How long have we been here?"

"A little while. Ella was here and brought your prescriptions."

He was trying to help her, and she needed to remember that none of this was his fault, even if he wanted to blame himself. With that thought in mind, she pushed herself up onto her elbows and blanched from the pain that ricocheted through her body from even that slight movement.

"Easy," Tyler said as he put pillows behind her shoulders. His dark hair was messed up, his jaw sprinkled with whiskers and his blue eyes were rimmed with red that she chalked up to fatigue. The poor guy had been a trooper.

She sank into the pillows, gritting her teeth from the unrelenting pain. "You said something about meds . . ."

"Right here." He doled them out and handed her a glass of water.

Charley choked down the pills. "Freaking horse pills."

"They're big ones."

"Let's hope they work fast." She handed the glass to him and confronted the next challenge—the fact that she needed to pee urgently. "I, um, what's the bathroom plan around here?" For the first time since she was hurt, she desperately wanted her mother right then. Or Hannah. Or Ella. Anyone but Tyler Westcott, who'd been so amazingly amazing to her since her fall.

"I'll carry you."

"You can't be carrying me around. You'll throw your back out."

"How do you think you got here in the first place? I'm much stronger than you think, and you're light as air."

"Whatever. You're not going to the bathroom with me."

"I'll take you in there and leave you to do your thing in private." He stood and crossed the room, returning with crutches.

"Where'd those come from?"

"The nursing company my mom used to work for set us up with everything we'll need." He disappeared into an adjoining room and returned a minute later. "Crutches are in place waiting for you. Do you want to wait until the meds kick in or go now?"

"I need to go now."

"Okay then, I'll go as slow as I possibly can. Tell me to stop if it hurts too much."

Charley gritted her teeth in anticipation of agonizing pain that materialized as he gently lifted her from the bed. By the time he got her into the bathroom, tears were streaming down her face. The infection had left her body weak, and after he set her down, she wavered precariously.

"Hold on to me."

She had no choice but to do just that.

He wrapped his arms around her and held her until the room stopped spinning and the pain retreated somewhat.

Charley breathed in the appealing scents of soap and fabric softener. "I'm getting your shirt wet," she said after they stood there for a couple of minutes.

"I don't care about that."

"I shouldn't be here. This is way too much to ask of you."

"God, Charley, are you serious? There's nothing I'd rather do than take care of you. I've been trying to tell you that for a long time now." He drew back from her and brushed the sweaty strands of hair off her forehead and wiped the tears from her cheeks with his thumbs. Then he kissed her forehead, leaving her breathless for reasons that had nothing to do with pain and everything to do with him.

Though she needed to pee urgently, she found herself asking, "Why? Why me?"

"Because you're incredible. You're gutsy and fearless and gorgeous and mouthy and challenging. You just do it for me." He followed the revealing statement with a deep sigh. "And that's probably way more than you wanted to know, but it's the truth. All of it."

Charley had no idea how to respond.

"Anything you need, just tell me. There's nothing you could ask of me that I wouldn't do for you."

"Could you maybe help me get these sweats off?"

He smiled and winked. "With pleasure."

"No looking."

"I'll be a perfect gentleman."

And he was. He helped her drop the oversized sweats, easing them over the huge brace around on her leg, keeping his gaze fixed on her feet rather than the part of her that was now only covered by a thin strip of lace. Her sexy-underwear fixation was rather impractical in light of current circumstances, but it was all she owned.

"I think I can take it from here."

He handed her the crutches and pointed out the special seat with rails that had been placed over the toilet. Tyler—or someone—had thought of everything she might need, and his thoughtfulness touched her deeply. "I'll be right outside. Don't do anything heroic, you hear?"

"I don't think I could even if I wanted to."

Tyler waited until she was relatively steady on her good foot and the crutches before he left the room, seeming hesitant to leave her.

*Agony* was the word of the hour as she tried to gingerly lower herself onto the raised seat. If only the pain were contained within her knee, she might be able to cope, but it was a full-body kind of ache that wouldn't subside until the meds kicked in. *Any second now, please, dear God . . .*

For a long time after she took care of business, Charley focused on breathing through the queasiness caused by the pain and the medication. She couldn't remember ever feeling quite so shitty, but the nurses had told her it would be a week or more before she started to feel like her old self. And she was on some hard-core antibiotics that they said made the cure worse than the ailment.

"Hey, Charley?" Tyler said through the closed door. "Are you okay?"

"Um, well, sort of."

"What's wrong?"

Since she couldn't exactly tell him she wanted her mother in the worst possible way, she said, "I could use a lift if you're not doing anything."

"Are you decent?"

She hiked her underwear up as high as she could get it without standing. "Sort of."

"Is it okay if I come in?"

"Since the alternative is spending the night here, I guess so."

"Don't worry, I won't look."

Like before, he kept his gaze on her feet as he helped her to stand and got her back into her clothes, keeping his arms around her, which was the only thing that stopped her from falling over when a dizzy spell hit. "Hold on to me," he said. "I've got you."

His arms were strong around her, his scent appealing and his T-shirt soft against her face.

"In case I forget to say thanks for all this, thank you. From the bottom of my injured knee."

"It's my pleasure, Charley. I'm glad you're here."

"Tell me the truth."

"Always."

"Did you push me down that ravine so you could get into my pants?"

Laughter bellowed from him, making her smile. She liked the way he laughed. "If only I were so devious—and clever—I could've saved us both a lot of time by doing that a year or so ago."

"I wouldn't have agreed to this then."

"Why did you agree to it now?"

"You've worn me down with your persistence. And you saved my life. That counts for something."

"You shouldn't give me credit for that when it was my fault you were up there to begin with."

"You need to let that one go. No one is blaming you except for you."

"I'll let it go when you're back on two feet and getting around like normal."

"That's going to be a while."

"Good thing I'm a patient kind of guy. Do you think you're ready for a ride back to bed?"

"So ready."

This time when he picked her up she didn't hurt quite as much, which she took to mean the meds were beginning to do their magic. He set her down gently, giving her time to catch her breath before he removed his arms, settled her injured leg on the stack of pillows and replaced the ice pack with a new one. They'd been told that controlling the swelling was critical the first weeks after surgery.

"You're very good at transporting injured people."

"I'm good at transporting *you*." He pulled up the down comforter and tucked her in. "You have to be getting hungry. Mom made some stew and homemade bread for us that she brought over while you were sleeping."

"I love Vivienne. That sounds delicious."

"I'll bring it to you."

"You don't want me eating in bed."

"Why not?"

"I don't know. What if I spill it?"

"You won't, and if it makes you feel better, I'll eat in here, too, so we can both make a mess. Okay?"

"If you're sure you don't mind."

"I don't mind. Be right back."

Charley watched him go, taking a good long look at the back of him, which more than lived up to the front. Tyler Westcott was hot when he wasn't all put together. She loved the way he looked in basketball shorts and appreciated the broad shoulders under a gray Dartmouth T-shirt. Had he gone to Dartmouth? She had no idea. Hell, she didn't know where he went to high school, but suddenly she wanted to know that and anything else he might want to tell her.

*This is crazy*, she thought. *It has to be all the drugs that have me looking at him in a whole new light. Or maybe I'm looking at him differently because he's been so nice to me since the accident.* Whatever the reason, something had changed. That wasn't to say she wanted to date him or anything, but she couldn't deny that she wanted to get to know him better.

Beyond that? Who knew?

He returned a short time later carrying a tray that held

two steaming bowls of stew, a basket of bread, a beer for him and more water for her.

"No fair. I want a beer, too."

"Not with that cocktail of pills you're taking."

"I know. Gonna be a while before I can drink anything other than water or do much of anything else that's fun."

"We can still have fun. Your family brought tons of movies, and I've got access to all the online movie channels. I've got Monopoly, but I should warn you that I'd kick your ass in that and then feel guilty for taking advantage of you in your injured state. I've also got Scrabble, but I'm crazy good at that, too. And then there's Clue . . ."

"Let me guess. You rock that, too."

"I probably should've been a detective."

"Do you have Risk?"

"My all-time favorite."

"Great. The one game I'm actually good at is your favorite."

"You like Risk?"

"I love Risk. None of my brothers could ever beat me. Used to drive them crazy."

He fanned his face. "That's so hot."

"Shut up," she said, laughing.

"No really. It's hot. I've never met a woman who liked that game."

"Well, I'm not your average woman."

"No, Charlotte Abbott, you certainly are not."

# CHAPTER 5

---◆◆◇◆◆---

It was as good as Tyler had always known it would be to have her in his home—and in his bed—even if the leg brace and crutches hadn't figured into the scenario he'd had in mind when he pictured her there. But the laughter and the teasing and the good-natured bickering were a nice surprise. He liked the way her laugh lit up her entire face and made her golden-brown eyes dance with glee. Despite her ordeal and the paler-than-normal face, she was gorgeous— and never more so than when she laughed.

They watched a romantic comedy her sister Hannah had given her that made Charley sigh more than once when the guy did something particularly cheesy. Tyler made a mental note that cheesiness made her sigh in a good way. He enjoyed cataloging each new discovery he made about her.

"What would you be doing tonight if you weren't playing nursemaid to me?"

"Nursemaid? Really?"

"What would you call it?"

"At least make me an orderly. It's much more manly."

"That's sexist. There're tons of male nurses out there. I had a few myself—and they were studly."

"So you were checking out your male nurses while I was sacrificing sleep and sanity to tend to your every need? Good to know."

She giggled at his outrage, and Tyler experienced a profound sense of rightness that he'd only ever felt with her, despite her repeated rejections. That feeling was why he'd come back time and again for more, hoping she'd eventually change her mind and give him a chance. "So you never answered my question about what you'd be doing tonight."

Tyler ran his fingers through his hair and stifled a yawn. He had to get out of there soon before he made the "mistake" of falling asleep next to her. "My brothers and I play poker with some guys one Saturday night a month. On the other nights we might hit a bar or hang at one of our houses to watch some sort of game. We follow the Bruins, Patriots, Red Sox and Celtics, so depending on the season, we're watching one of those teams."

"How many brothers do you have?"

"Three, and two sisters. Sometimes on Saturdays I've been known to babysit for one of my sisters."

"How many kids do they have?"

"My sister Cheryl has three boys, and Paula has two girls. They're all under the age of eight, so they keep me busy."

"Aww, I bet they love their uncle Tyler."

"We have fun together. They're great kids. When I stay with the boys, all we do is wrestle until they conk out. With the girls, it's all tea parties and dolls and make-believe."

"I'm picturing you wrapped up in a pink feather boa all of a sudden."

"I can neither confirm nor deny that there may have been boas at one time or another."

"How about tiaras?"

"Stop. You're unmanning me."

She laughed so hard that tears filled her eyes.

God, he loved this. He loved being with her and seeing the

softer side to her that he'd always suspected was in there somewhere behind the abrasive exterior she showed the world. Unfortunately, she'd had to fall down the side of a ravine for it to emerge.

"I know your parents moved here after they retired, but I don't know where you grew up."

"Rutland. We used to ski at Butler all the time and we loved it, so they bought a retirement home here a year or two after I got out of college. Most of us have gravitated here, but two of my brothers still live in Rutland. I moved into this house about three years ago." He glanced over at her. "You know what else?"

"What?"

"Every time we came to Butler, we had to stop at your family's store. Highlight of our weekend was always getting candy from the store."

"That's so cool. I like hearing that. So no date nights in the midst of all this Saturday evening revelry?"

Was she fishing or was that his imagination? "Not recently. The only girl I like keeps shooting me down. So I've been hanging out with my family an awful lot."

She averted her gaze, and he hoped he hadn't made her feel bad. "It's not you," she said softly. "You're a nice guy, and I've always known that, even when I was saying no to you."

"If it's not me, then what is it?"

"Me. I'm so over the dance, you know?"

"What dance?"

"Dating and all the bullshit that goes along with it. The false charm, the bravado, the boasting, all of it. Guys will say *anything* to get what they want."

"And what do they want?"

She shot him a withering look. "Seriously? Do I really have to spell it out?"

"Nah," he said with a grin. "I got ya."

"That's all they want—a quick *wham, bam, thank you ma'am*. After that, they're different. The charm stops, and they don't even bother with the bullshit anymore. It's all about getting more of what they've already gotten, and if you hold out, looking for something more—some *substance*—they move on to someone willing to give them what they want."

"You paint a rather dismal picture of mankind."

"My experience with mankind has been rather dismal."

Without taking even a second to contemplate the wisdom of what he was about to do, he took hold of her hand and linked their fingers. "We're not all like that."

"Everyone I've dated has been like that."

"You should've said yes to me if you wanted something different."

"How would you be different? What would a first date with you entail?"

"Oh, you want like details? Right here and now?"

"Details would be good."

He rubbed at the stubble he'd allowed to accumulate on his jaw during the long days in the hospital. "Wow, that's a lot of pressure."

"Something tells me you know exactly what we'd do."

He smiled at the certainty in her tone because she was spot on. He'd had their first date planned in his mind for more than a year. "I'd take you to Boston for the night. We'd go to a show of some sort, something you've been dying to see. We'd have dinner in the North End at an Italian place and stay at the Ritz-Carlton—separate bedrooms, of course."

"Of course."

"But I'm sure you've already done all that with the many dates you've been on."

"Never."

He raised a brow. "Never?"

"Nope."

"Huh. So my first date sounds sort of good to you?"

"Sort of," she said with a teasing grin. "It sounds sort of fantastic."

"Yeah?"

"Uh-huh, but you knew that. It's probably your go-to first date."

"I've never taken anyone on that particular date. I've been saving it for the day when Charlotte Abbott finally said yes to me."

Her mouth opened and then closed, as if she'd thought better of whatever she'd been about to say.

"What? You don't believe me?"

"I'm sorry if I hurt your feelings all the times I said no to you. I mean it when I say it was more about me than you. Although . . ."

"Although what?"

"Part of it is about you."

"Ah-ha! I knew it. Now we're getting to the truth of the matter. What part of it is about me?"

"The part where you act like you know me better than I know myself. That's irritating. And you remind me of my brother Hunter, which is worrisome."

"I remind you of *Hunter*? How?"

"You're always so . . ." She pulled her hand free of his clasp, seeming to just realize they'd been holding hands for a while now. "Perfectly put together."

"And that's a bad thing?"

"It's like you're *too* perfect or something."

"Do I look too perfect right now after not shaving for three days and barely combing my hair in that time?"

"No, you look good right now. Normal."

"Got it—so by not shaving or combing my hair I gain points with you. Good to know."

"That's not what I said."

"That's what I heard. Now about me knowing you better than you know yourself, what's that supposed to mean?"

"I don't know. It's just the way you look at me . . ."

"I *see* you, Charley. Not just the pretty package or the smart mouth or the endless attitude. I see *you*."

"What do you see?"

"That there's more to you than what you show the rest of the world, and I've been endlessly curious about that other side you keep hidden."

"How do you know I do that?"

"Because no one could be as abrasive as you are and still have so many people love you if there wasn't another side to you."

"See? There you go acting like you know me better than you should."

Tyler shrugged off the predictably acerbic comment. "Am I wrong?" She glared at him, and he laughed. "I didn't think so." As much as he didn't want to end this intriguing conversation, it was time for her to take more meds. Though it was the last thing he wanted to do, he got up to dole out her pills and get her some more water.

"Thank you," she said after she'd taken them.

"No problem. How about another trip to the bathroom before we call it a night?"

"Okay."

Like he had several times already, he carried her into the bathroom, helped her out of her clothes and left her to do her thing while he waited outside the door feeling optimistic about his chances with her for the first time ever. They'd covered a lot of ground just now. At least he understood why she'd shot him down so many times and that it was less about him than it was about her certainty that he was like every other player she'd had the misfortune of dating.

*That's all they want—a quick* wham, bam, thank you ma'am. *After that, they're different.*

She'd been looking for substance and not finding it. He could do substance, because he wanted much more than her delectable body. He wanted her heart and soul, too. She wanted substance? He'd show her substance.

Propped up on crutches, Charley brushed her teeth and thought about the revealing conversation she'd had with Tyler. It had to be the drugs that were making her spill her guts. How else to explain the way she'd opened up to him?

Despite her discomfort, she'd had fun tonight, eating dinner in bed with him, watching a movie that had probably bored him and then talking about things she rarely talked about with anyone, even her sisters. It hadn't escaped her notice that he'd taken hold of her hand at one point and that she hadn't immediately pulled hers back. No, she'd let him touch her, and she'd liked it. She couldn't deny that, even if she might want to.

Her feelings for him were one big ball of confusion. She'd spent so much time and energy fending him off that she almost didn't know how to let him in now that things had changed between them. And when had things changed exactly? Did it happen the day he'd saved her life? Or was it the many nights he'd tended to her while she was in the hospital and fighting off an infection? Maybe it was when he arranged for everything she needed to come home with him or how he'd put his own life on hold to take care of her?

There was a lot to like about this man, including the romantic first date he'd saved just for her despite frequent rejections.

He knocked on the door. "You okay in there?"

Charley had zoned out into her thoughts. "Yep." She finished brushing her teeth and hobbled to the door using the crutches. The small effort took most of the strength she had, which made her realize how weak she really was. Opening the door, she found him leaning against the far wall, the T-shirt stretched across his broad shoulders and chest. He'd put on black-framed glasses and was checking his phone when she emerged.

Tyler looked up at her, and her breath caught at the yearning she saw in his gaze. Then he blinked, and it was gone. He pushed himself off the wall, stashing his phone in his pocket. "Ready for a lift?"

"I'd better get used to doing this myself. You can't carry me forever."

"Why not?"

"Because you'll throw your back out."

"Haven't we already had this fight? You're a cream puff to a stud like me."

"Easy, stud. Don't trip over your ego."

"I'll try not to."

And he was funny, she thought, a quality that was always attractive to her. She managed to get herself back to bed, painfully, and sat on the edge of the mattress to catch her breath. "This totally sucks."

"Yes, it does, but the doctor said you're going to feel a little better every day, and you'll be back to busting balls in no time."

"Can't happen soon enough for me."

He helped her settle her leg on the pile of pillows and made her comfortable in the bed with the ever-present ice bag. "What else do you need?"

"I think I'm good."

"I'll be right across the hall if you need me during the night."

"This is your room, isn't it?"

"Yeah."

"It's a big bed. You could probably sleep here if you wanted to."

His brows lifted in surprise and what might've been pleasure.

"Don't act like I just offered to bang you or something."

He rested a hand over his heart. "Please don't talk dirty to me, Charlotte. My fragile heart can't bear it."

She snorted with laughter. "If you can manage to control yourself and your fragile heart, feel free to sleep in your own bed. That's all I'm offering tonight."

"Tomorrow night, on the other hand—"

"Shut up, Tyler, and go to bed."

"Shutting up now." He went into the bathroom and closed the door.

She heard water running and the toilet flushed before he emerged wearing a pair of flannel pajama pants and nothing else. And oh damn, he was cut. Seriously, beautifully cut with those V-shaped muscles on his hips that only the fittest of guys had. She licked her lips and told herself she shouldn't stare, but damn, she was only human, and he was smoking hot.

Who knew? Sure, she'd known he could run for miles without seeming to break a sweat, but she hadn't suspected he was hiding *that* under his starched dress shirts.

He slid into bed next to her, and she tried to ignore the insistent beat of attraction that trumped the pain for her attention. When he was settled, he reached for the light and with the click of a switch, the room descended into darkness except for a night light.

"Is that for me?"

"What?"

"The night light."

"Uh-huh. I know where the bathroom is."

"Thank you for everything, Tyler. I mean that sincerely. You've made this so easy for me and my family—and don't say it was the least you could do after you dragged me up that hill. I went up that hill with my eyes wide open."

"I'm happy to help you out, Charley."

"This was fun tonight."

"For me, too. Way better than poker night with the guys."

"Gee, thanks. I'm honored."

His hand came across the bed and somehow found hers in the darkness. "You should be honored. There's no one else I'd rather hang out with on a Saturday night than you."

"If that's true, you probably need to get out more."

"Ha-ha. I've gotten out plenty. I know a good thing when I see it. Or her."

"Many would call you a masochist for feeling that way about me."

"Let them say what they will," he said on a yawn. "I can take it."

Feeling oddly contented to be holding hands with Tyler Westcott in his bed in the dark of night, Charley drifted off to sleep, wondering what tomorrow might bring.

# CHAPTER 6

—◆—

Sunday began with a shower that took a tremendous amount of coordination by both Charley and Tyler, who wrapped her brace in a huge black trash bag to keep it dry. He set out everything she needed to sit on the bench in his big shower with her leg propped on a stool outside the open door.

She fidgeted with the knot on the robe of his he'd lent her for the cause. "I'm going to flood out the bathroom if I leave the shower door open."

"No worries," he said, laying down several big beach towels to soak up the water. "Do you need any other help?"

"I think I can do it."

"Remember what I said yesterday—no heroics. Believe it or not, I've seen a naked woman before, and the sight of your fine body won't shock me senseless or anything."

"How do you know that? My body is better than most."

His Adam's apple bobbed in his throat. "I have no doubt about that."

"Be gone with you. You're not seeing me naked today."

"She gives me so much hope for the future," he muttered as he left the room, closing the door behind him.

Charley removed the robe and turned on the water in the shower before taking a seat on the wide bench. Tyler had already adjusted the showerhead to direct the water where she needed it, allowing her to wash her hair and body somewhat effortlessly despite the awkward position of her leg.

For the first time since the fall more than a week ago, she took a good look at the rest of her body, which was covered in bruises, scrapes, cuts and swollen lumps. As she took inventory of her many wounds, it came down hard on her how much worse it really could've been. Hell, she could've been killed if her head had connected with a rock or the right artery had been severed.

The realization made her weak with relief that she'd *only* torn up her knee and not the rest of her.

She blew out a deep breath, as her limbs quivered from the delayed shock that rippled through her body. Such a huge wake-up call that precious life can be snatched away at any moment without warning. Tipping her face up to the warm cascade of water, Charley made a silent vow to start living more completely, to try not to be so cynical and jaded, to stop holding Tyler at arm's length and let him in. Not so far that she couldn't get out if need be but enough to ascertain what might be possible.

Moving slowly, she managed to stand on her good leg, shut the water off and reach for the towel he'd left hanging on the shower door. He thought of everything, and it wouldn't take much to fall for a guy like that, a guy who paid attention to the little things and stayed focused on what he wanted even in the face of frequent rejection.

*God, I've been a stone-cold bitch to him, and he still likes me.* The thought made her huff with laughter. What was wrong with him anyway?

A soft knock on the door dragged her out of her thoughts. Speak of the devil himself.

"How're you making out?"

"No disasters yet."

"Let's keep it that way. Do you need me to dry your back or powder your unmentionables?"

The teasing question restarted that surprising hum of desire she'd experienced last night. "My unmentionables don't require powder, but thank you for the offer."

"I also do lotion and excellent massages, should the need arise."

As the thought of him rubbing oil on her body registered, the tingle between her legs intensified. "Also good to know."

"Breakfast is ready when you are."

"I'll be out in a few."

"Take your time. It'll keep."

In the short time she'd been in the shower, he'd made breakfast. Most of the guys she'd dated were long gone by the time breakfast rolled around. The shower had worn her out, so she settled for combing out her wet hair and leaving it to air-dry rather than using energy she didn't have to blow it dry. She brushed her teeth, then found her favorite moisturizer in the bag Ella had packed for her. Other than deodorant, she skipped the rest of her usual beauty ritual because it would take strength she simply didn't have.

She put on a bra and a long-sleeved University of Vermont T-shirt that often doubled as a nightshirt. Good thing, because the underwear and sweats wouldn't be happening without some help. "Hey, Tyler?"

"Yep?"

"I could use a bit of assistance here."

"Can I come in?"

"Uh-huh."

When he opened the door and stepped into the room, she saw that he, too, had showered—and shaved. He looked more like he usually did except for the clean T-shirt and basketball shorts he wore rather than the starched dress shirts she'd become accustomed to. "What? Do I have something on my face?" He rubbed his cheek. "Did I cut myself shaving?"

"No," she said, embarrassed to realize she'd been caught staring. Again. "You shaved." *Duh, Charley. Obvious much?*

"I couldn't take the scruff anymore. It was starting to itch."

"You look good."

"So do you. But then again, you always do."

"Right. Especially lately."

He came into the room, stopping a couple of inches from her. In the mirror, she noted the way his hands rolled in, as if he were trying to control the urge to touch her. "Never more so than lately. I'm so damned glad you didn't die on me last weekend."

"That would've been a bummer."

Tyler raised his hand to skim his finger over her cheek where a fading bruise remained. "A huge bummer. I never would've gotten to do this if you'd died on me."

Before she could ask what *this* entailed, his lips were sliding over hers. Oh. *That. That* was quite nice. Just as she decided to lean in to get more of *that*, it stopped.

"Sorry," he said, his thumb continuing to stroke her face as he stared down at her. "Didn't mean to do that."

"No?"

He shook his head. "You called me in for help, not that."

"That wasn't *bad*, per se."

His bark of laughter made her smile. "I can do better than *that*, but not when we've got Abbotts lined up at the door wanting to see you."

She wanted to ask when he planned to do better, but instead she said, "We do?"

Nodding, he said, "Four phone calls while you were in the shower. Hope you're feeling social today."

"I will once I get some pants on. I seem to have hit a snag there."

"More than happy to help, although, for the record I'd like to say that I'd much prefer to *remove* your pants than put them on."

She playfully slugged his shoulder.

"Too much?" he asked, raising that brow of his as he dropped to his knees before her, putting all sorts of salacious ideas into her addled brain. The drugs! It had to be all the damned drugs that were making her horny for Tyler West-cott. That little voice inside her head chose that moment to weigh in, reminding her she was horny for him because he'd been flat-out incredible to her since her injury—and because when she took the time to really *look* at him she'd discovered he was sexier than hell.

"No."

"Feel free to say so if harmless flirting ventures into the land of harmful. I don't want to do anything to hurt my chances of actually having that first date in Boston."

"I'll keep you posted."

"You do that."

With her hands propped on his shoulders, he helped her into underwear and sweats with a minimum of fuss. At critical moments, he looked up at her rather than sneak a peek at the goods, which earned him more points with her. He was really racking them up.

"All set," he said, standing.

"Thank you."

"You want breakfast in bed or do you feel up to a short walk?"

"I'll do the walk. The more I lie around, the worse I feel."

"Just take it slowly."

"No choice about that." It took ten long minutes to make her way to his dining room table, which he'd set with navy-blue dishes and coffee mugs.

Tyler held a chair for her and took the crutches as she eased into the seat.

Charley closed her eyes for a long moment, catching her breath from the arduous trek. When she opened them, he was watching her with concern.

"You okay?"

"Yeah."

"You don't look okay."

"I can't believe that short walk totally wiped me out."

"You've been through a lot. It's going to take a while to feel normal again. No need to rush yourself."

"I couldn't if I wanted to."

"Physical therapy starts tomorrow. That'll help you regain your strength."

"Something tells me there won't be anything fun about that."

"Probably not, but it'll expedite your recovery."

Charley shifted her gaze toward the window, doing a double take when she saw the extraordinary view. "Whoa. Where the hell are we anyway?"

"About halfway up the mountain, looking down at the town."

"I remember when this house was built! Everyone wondered whose it was."

"Ella said the same thing—and she promised to keep my secret."

Before she could ask why it was such a big secret that he lived here, he went into the kitchen and returned with coffee that he poured for both of them. "I made eggs, bacon and toast, but I have other stuff if that doesn't work for you."

"That sounds delicious." Her stomach let out a loud growl that made them laugh.

"The lady is hungry."

They enjoyed delicious scrambled eggs, crispy bacon, wheat toast and coffee.

"These eggs are amazing. What's the secret?"

"I'll tell you if you're nice to me."

She stared at him. "Not sure what you think is possible, but this is as nice as I get."

Laughing, he leaned in and whispered, "Half-and-half."

"Like the stuff you put in coffee?"

"Yep. Makes the eggs fluffy and light."

"Wow, that's a new one on me."

"I learned that in cooking school."

"How did you go from cooking school to doing what you do now? And what is it exactly that you do now?"

"I buy and sell stocks."

"For a company?"

"Sort of." Was it her imagination or did he squirm? "I do it for my company."

"Oh. So you . . ."

"Manage money."

"Whose money?"

"Mine."

"And that's a full-time job?"

His low chuckle came off as a nervous laugh. "You could say that."

"Oh."

"What does that mean?"

"It's what people say when they don't know what to say."

He gazed at her over the top of his mug. "Is it a big deal that I have money?"

"No, of course it isn't."

"Good, because if it was, that would be disappointing."

"How much are we talking?"

"Enough to keep myself and any family I may have some-day very comfortable for a long time to come."

"Oh."

"I'm going to level with you, Charley." He pushed his plate aside and put his arms on the table. "After we get you through all of this, I want to take you on that first date to Boston. I want that to be the first of many things we do together. But if the fact that I have money is going to be a problem for you, I'd rather know that now than later."

"Has it been an issue in the past?"

"It's always an issue in some way or another."

Charley wanted to hear more about how it had caused him trouble. She wanted to know how'd he accumulated such a vast fortune and what it took to manage it. But her questions were put on hold by the arrival of her grandfather and her mother's sister, Hannah, who came bearing cider donuts from the store.

Elmer Stillman walked right over to Charley and kissed her cheek. "How's my granddaughter today?"

"A little better, Gramps. Thanks."

"Darned glad to hear it—and see it. You gave us a heck of a fright for a few days there, sweetheart."

"Sorry about that."

"Your mother is going to kill us for keeping this from her," Hannah said bluntly.

"I'll take all the blame," Charley said, tipping her face up to receive a kiss from her aunt.

"Nice place you've got here, Tyler," Hannah said.

"He doesn't want people to know he owns this house," Charley said, drawing a curious glance from her aunt.

"It's okay," Tyler said. "I didn't want the whole town up in my grill when I was building it, but it's no big deal now."

"Heck of a view," Elmer said.

They spent half an hour visiting, during which Tyler helped her move to the sofa, propping her leg up on more pillows and producing a fresh ice pack. While Tyler showed Elmer his office, Hannah sat on the oak coffee table.

"What're you doing up here with him, Charley? Are you two dating?"

"We're friends," she said, suddenly defensive of her relationship, such as it was, with Tyler. "He's been really great to me since the accident."

"Just be cautious. No man does all this without an ulterior motive in mind."

Her aunt had earned the right to be bitter toward men in general after her husband, Charley's uncle Mike, left her alone to finish raising eight children. "I'm always cautious, Auntie. Don't worry about me. So is this the weekend Grayson is due to move home?"

"He got here yesterday with a moving truck," she said with a sigh.

"You're not happy to have him home?"

"Oh no, I'm thrilled. But I worry that he'll regret giving up that plum job in Boston."

"From what I've heard, that job wasn't making him happy."

"So he says. Everyone sends their regards. I talked to Izzy yesterday, and she said she'll be by to see you at some point when she's back in town. She's at a shoot up north this weekend and then she'll be home until Hunter's wedding."

"That's nice of her. So how mad is Mom going to be that we kept this from her?"

"On a scale of one to furious? I'd venture to say furious. You'll find out for sure on Tuesday when they get home."

Her aunt and grandfather left a short time later, and

must've passed Will and Cameron coming in with Max and baby Caden.

"Oh my God," Charley said of the baby Max placed in her arms. "He's grown a ton since I last saw him."

"He's doing great," Max said with obvious pride.

"How're you?" Charley asked her youngest sibling while Will and Cam visited with Tyler.

"I'm fine compared to you. How's the leg?"

"Great as long as I stay on top of the pain pills. But don't blow me off on the other thing."

"I'm doing the best I can in a shitty situation. We're dividing time with the baby for now. I've got him for the weekend, so I brought him over here."

"That's a long ride by yourself with a new baby."

"I stopped every fifteen minutes to make sure he was still breathing," Max confessed. "He slept the whole way."

"I'm sorry it's been so hard for you."

Max shrugged. "Wasn't meant to be with Chloe, I guess. I just wish she would show a little more interest in her son."

"You show enough interest for both of you."

"I guess. I worry about him when I'm not with him."

"You don't think she'd ever . . .?"

"No, nothing like that, but it's pretty obvious that she wants nothing to do with him—or me."

"Have you thought about asking her for full custody?"

"God, no. I couldn't handle it by myself. No way."

"Yes, you could."

"No, Charley. I really couldn't."

Cameron came over to gaze down at Caden, whose lips moved adorably in his sleep. "He's so cute. So, so cute."

"Thanks," Max said. "I think so, too."

Will put his arm around his wife and took a turn at gazing. "I think he looks like me."

"He does not," Max said. "He looks like *me*. Mom says he looks exactly like I did as a baby."

"He really does," Will said as Charley nodded in agreement. "Poor kid."

Max laughed at Will's good-natured ribbing. It was nice to hear him laugh again after the upheaval of the last few months with Chloe.

"Do you think it's over for good with Chloe, Max?" Charley asked.

"It is for me. The way she's acted about him . . . The only thing I feel for her anymore is disgust."

Cameron put her arm around Max and rested her head on his shoulder. "She's going to wake up someday and realize she let the best guy in the whole world get away."

"Hey!" Will said, making the others laugh.

"Thanks, Cam," Max said. "I should get him home because he's going to wake up hungry."

"Are you staying at Mom and Dad's while they're away?"

"They're staying with us this weekend," Will said. "No need for them to be alone when they could have company."

"I've made this all about me and Caden," Max said. "We should be talking about you, Charley."

"I'd rather talk about Caden," Charley said.

"You're feeling okay?" Cameron asked.

"Better today than yesterday, but still weak as a kitten."

"That'll get better every day," Tyler said.

"How's the pain?" Will asked.

"Manageable as long as I take my horse pills on time."

"You're not missing anything outside," Cameron said. "It's snowing like crazy. That's all it seems to do lately."

"Welcome to your first winter in Vermont, babe," Will said.

Cameron smiled up at her husband. "Nowhere else I'd rather be than in the midst of your snowy winter."

"And it's not even officially winter yet until the twenty-first," Tyler said.

A collective groan greeted his statement, making him laugh.

The foursome left and over the course of the day, they saw Hannah and Nolan, Colton and Lucy, who had her sister, Emma, and niece, Simone, with her, Hunter and Megan, Ella and Gavin, Lucas and Landon and then finally Wade.

"Bringing up the rear, little brother," Charley said from her perch on the sofa. Tyler had started a fire in the huge fireplace, making the room toasty warm and cozy. He'd tended to her quietly throughout the day of visits with her family, making sure she ate and took her pills and stayed hydrated, without interfering in her time with her loved ones. More points.

"Hannah had a schedule," Wade said. "I got the last slot."

"She actually *scheduled* everyone?"

"She didn't want us to overwhelm you or Tyler."

"She's too funny," Charley said, imagining her sister organizing the rest of them. "Mom will be back on Tuesday to relieve Hannah of her need to be in charge of everything."

"Thank God for that."

They chatted until Charley's eyes got heavy, and Wade took his leave, promising to be back soon. "Sorry to pass out on you."

"No worries." Wade kissed her forehead, shook hands with Tyler and headed out into the snowy late afternoon.

"You want to go to bed?" Tyler asked when they were alone.

"Nah. This is delightful. I love the fireplace."

"I do, too. I designed the entire house around it." He covered her with a light blanket that he tucked in around her. "Take a nap while I make dinner."

"Spoiling me," she said.

"Am I?"

"Mmm." She thought she felt his lips on her forehead, but she couldn't summon the energy to open her eyes to confirm it. But the suspicion was enough to fill her with an unusual sense of contentment as she drifted off to sleep.

# CHAPTER 7

------ ◄►◄► ------

T he torture began on Monday with the arrival of Debbie, the physical therapist sent straight from hell. She was young, blond and peppy, and Charley hated her on sight. First, she removed Charley's brace and bandages to check the incision, and she was a whole lot less gentle than Tyler had been when he'd checked the incision the night before.

"Looks good," Debbie declared. "You've been icing it?"

"Religiously."

"Excellent. You'll need to keep using the crutches for another week or so, when we'll want to start working on some weight bearing. For today and this week, we're going to do some basic stretches to work on strengthening your quadriceps."

What sounded simple enough was anything but once the "basic" stretching began. Five minutes in, Charley was bathed in a cold sweat and whimpering pathetically from the agonizing pain.

"You're doing great," Debbie said. "You've got excellent muscle tone to begin with. That'll make for a speedier recovery."

Charley couldn't reply because she was desperately trying not to puke up the pancakes Tyler had made for breakfast. By the time Debbie left ninety minutes later, promising to be back for more of the same the next day, Charley was contemplating murder for the first time in her life.

"How'd it go?" Tyler asked when he emerged from his office wearing well-faded jeans, a brown sweater and those sexy glasses.

"Fantastic," Charley said from the sofa where Debbie had left her to recover from therapy. "Best time of my life."

He took a closer look at her. "You're all pasty and pale. What the hell?"

"She freaking tortured me. That's what the hell."

"She *hurt* you?" His lips flattened with what might've been fury.

"I think that's her job," Charley said begrudgingly.

He sat on the coffee table and took her hand, giving it a gentle squeeze. "Are you okay?"

"I will be. Eventually."

"I'm sorry you have to go through all this. I hate to see you hurting."

He'd slept next to her again during the night, holding her hand the way he had the night before. Lying next to him in bed, Charley had relived that brief, fleeting kiss he'd given her in the bathroom, wondering if he would do it again. And yes, she was well aware that she'd gone from fending him off to wishing for more of the all-too-brief taste he'd given her the day before.

She took a good long look at his lips.

"Charley."

His voice snapped her out of the stare fest. "Yeah?"

"What're you doing?"

"Nothing." She couldn't very well say she was staring at his lips thinking about what it had been like to kiss him. It hadn't lasted long enough to get a full impression. Would he kiss her again or had that been a onetime thing? Did she want him to kiss her again? Well, yeah . . .

"Why're you staring at me?"

"I'm just thinking."

"About?"

"Nothing."

"I wish you'd just say whatever's on your mind. Is something wrong?"

"Other than the therapist straight from hell and the surgically repaired knee?"

"Other than that."

"Nothing is wrong."

"Do you need anything before I go back to work?"

"No, thank you. I'm good."

He gave her hand another squeeze and released it when he stood. "Yell if you need me."

"I will." Charley watched him go, noting the superior fit of his faded jeans, and wondered when exactly she'd stopped pushing him away and started wanting to pull him closer.

Tyler was losing his mind. Having her in his house, sleeping next to her at night, holding her hand . . . It was too much and not enough at the same time. He'd made a critical error by kissing her in the bathroom yesterday. The instant his lips met hers, he'd panicked, fearing if he moved too fast she'd run away as soon as she could.

And with her parents returning from their trip tomorrow, she'd have no good reason to stay with him anymore. He ached at the thought of her leaving already. If he had his way, she'd stay forever and they'd live happily ever after in the house he'd built for the family he hoped to have someday.

He shouldn't have kissed her. He knew that in the moment, but it happened anyway, and he wanted to do it again—as soon as he possibly could. But he couldn't move too fast or push her for things she wasn't ready for, especially when she was recovering from such a serious injury.

Propping his elbows on the desktop, Tyler dropped his head into his hands. He was in so deep with her and had been for a while now. Every time she dismissed him or snapped back at him with a sassy retort, he wanted her more.

And when she'd joined his running club, he'd praised the god of kismet for ensuring that he'd see her weekly for months.

She'd wanted to quit when she realized he was a member. Remembering the look of utter disdain she'd sent his way that first day drew a small smile to his lips. The more she disdained him, the more he wanted her. Crazy, right? More than one person had said as much to him, but none of that changed the way he felt about her. Those feelings had only deepened in the days since her fall. He would never forget the sight of her at the bottom of that ravine, or the bone-deep fear he experienced as he ran for help, praying with every step that she wouldn't die down there, that she wouldn't leave him before he had a chance to hold her or kiss her or make love to her.

He blew out a ragged deep breath. It didn't matter that she was injured or laid up or prickly. He wanted her madly, desperately. She'd been staring at his mouth earlier. Was she thinking about the kiss in the bathroom, too? He should say something to her about that. If they talked about it, maybe they could address the awkwardness and move on. But how did he go about starting that conversation? *So about that kiss in the bathroom . . .*

His computer chimed with new e-mails and stock updates and other things he should be paying attention to, but all he could think about was how badly he wanted to kiss Charley Abbott again and when—or if—he'd get the chance.

Hannah decided that Hunter should be the lucky one to meet their parents as they arrived home from their trip. As he navigated the one-lane covered bridge that led to his parents' home, the melting snow they'd gotten over the weekend splashed against his car in an icy slush that would leave a mess behind.

Ahh, winter in Vermont. Good times. And speaking of good times, he couldn't wait to tell his mother about how they'd kept Charley's fall and serious injuries from her while she was on vacation. At least he could place all the blame on Charley, who'd insisted they not spoil their parents' long-awaited trip. And what was up with pregnant, bossy Hannah deciding *he* was the best one to loop their parents in on Charley's situation? He expected better from his twin and closest friend than that.

Prepared to take one for the team, he hung a right onto Hells Peak Road and pulled into the long driveway that led to the red barn where his parents had raised ten children and still lived with their dogs, Ringo and George. The dogs were frolicking in the yard, which meant his parents had stopped to pick them up at his grandfather's house on their way home.

Hunter parked and got out of his Lincoln Navigator, ignoring the nasty sludge caked on the car as he would until after mud season in the spring. There was simply no point in trying to keep a car looking nice during winter and spring in Vermont. He went in through the mudroom, the dogs in hot pursuit. They ran by him into the kitchen, where his mom was standing watch over a kettle on the stove.

"Hey," he said. "Welcome home."

"Hi, honey." Molly greeted her eldest child with a warm smile and a hug. "This is a nice surprise."

He returned her hug and kissed her cheek. "How was it?"

"Fantastic. We had the best time. I've got lots of pictures."

"I can't wait to see them."

"So what's going on here?"

"Usual stuff plus a few other things."

"What other things?"

Before Hunter could reply, his dad came into the room. "Hey, son. How's it going?"

"Good." Hunter hugged his dad. "Nice to have you back."

"Good to be home. How're things at the store?"

"Busy, the way we want it this time of year."

"Excellent."

Molly crossed her arms. "Hunter was just about to tell me what's been going on around here while we were gone, and something tells me I'm not going to like this."

"Before I say anything, this was all Charley's doing, so you can take it up with her."

"What am I taking up with her?"

"So a week ago Saturday—"

"The day we left."

"Yes, and before I say anything else—she's okay—or she will be eventually. She was running up on the mountain in the snow with Tyler Westcott when the ground fell out from under her."

Molly sucked in a sharp deep breath.

Lincoln's hand landed on her shoulder.

"What happened?" Linc asked, his complexion gone ashen.

"She took a bad fall. A really bad fall down a ravine. Tyler ran for help, and thankfully, the only thing she injured was her knee. She had surgery—"

Molly let out a cry of distress. "My *child* had *surgery* and no one thought to *tell* me that?"

"Charley told us not to. She didn't want to mess up your vacation."

"Why did she need surgery, son?" Linc asked.

"She tore the ACL and MCL in her knee, and then there was an infection—"

"Where is she now?" Molly glared at him as if it had been his decision to keep this from her.

"At Tyler's place. He felt responsible for her getting hurt and insisted on helping her out afterward."

"You all let her go with him rather than one of you?"

"It's what she said she wanted."

"Charley—*my Charley*—said she wanted to go home with Tyler Westcott, who she's been avoiding for ages, instead of one of her own siblings?" Molly asked, incredulous. "Did she hit her head, too?"

"Her head is fine."

"Take me to her right now, Hunter. This minute."

"Okay—and if you could please keep in mind that I'm only the messenger."

Molly took him by the arm and marched him through the mudroom the way she had when he was in trouble as a kid. She was still as freakishly strong as she'd been then. "Drive. Now."

*    *    *

Charley's second session with Debbie went much like the first, only this time there had been tears—a lot of them. The more Charley cried, the harder Debbie pushed her. As he had the day before, Tyler came out of his office to check on her. Today he wore a white Dartmouth T-shirt with another pair of deliciously faded jeans.

She couldn't work up any enthusiasm for the jeans or the hot guy in them because she couldn't stop crying.

"Charley." He took his usual seat on the coffee table and reached for her hand.

She yanked it back.

"What's wrong?"

"What *isn't* wrong? Everything I own hurts like hell, and that *woman* will be back again tomorrow to *torture* me some more. *That* is what's wrong." Using the sleeve of her T-shirt, she mopped up her tears.

"What can I do for you?"

"Nothing! There's nothing you can do, so stop being so freaking nice to me and go back to work!"

To which he calmly replied, "Are you hungry?"

"No, I'm not hungry. In fact, I'm afraid I'm going to puke all over your sofa."

"If you do, we'll clean it up."

"Go away, Tyler. Leave me alone. I mean it."

"I'd rather stay here with you so you don't have to be upset alone."

"I want to be upset alone. I want to go home. I want my bed and my stuff and my life. I'm supposed to be at work right now, and the store is probably crazy busy, and I have Christmas shopping to do. And . . . And this . . . it . . . It *blows!*"

"I know it does. But you're in luck—I can help with at least one of those things." He got up and walked away, disappearing into his office for a few minutes that she used to chastise herself for lashing out at him when none of this was his fault—despite what he might think.

Tyler came back carrying a laptop that he put on the coffee table next to him when he returned to his perch.

"What's that for?"

"I've got the best Internet connection in town up here, and that laptop gives you access to every online retailer in the world. Get your shopping done. Have it all sent here, and I'll help you wrap it."

"As the co-owner of a brick-and-mortar store, online shopping goes against everything I believe in."

"I understand, and I hereby grant you a onetime, special-circumstances exemption. You know you want to go crazy shopping for your nephew, so have at it."

Charley stared at the computer for a long moment before extending her hand. She had been looking forward to shopping for Caden. That was true.

Tyler put the computer in her hands and then went to answer the door after a pounding knock interrupted them.

Charley heard her mother before she saw her.

"Where is she? Where's Charley?"

"Come in, Mrs. Abbott, Mr. Abbott," Tyler said. "She's on the sofa. Right this way."

"Hi, Mom." Charley smiled up at her mother, who came rushing over to hug her, taking Tyler's spot on the coffee table.

"Oh my goodness, Charley!" Molly touched Charley's face, her arm and then her hand as if to confirm she really was fine. "*How* could you tell them to keep this from me?"

"I was fine, and I didn't want to mess up your trip. Nothing to worry about."

Charley's dad came over to kiss and hug her as best he could with Molly crowding him out. "What's all this, my love?"

"A little fall, a little surgery, nothing to be concerned about. How was the trip?"

"Never mind about that," Molly said. "Tell me everything that happened."

While her dad wandered off to talk to Hunter and Tyler, Charley recounted the entire incident—or as much as she recalled of it—for her mother. "Lucas and Landon were amazing. Turns out they're good for something other than driving us all nuts."

"That's good to hear." Molly glanced over to the kitchen, where Tyler was pouring coffee for Linc and Hunter. *"What're you doing here?"* she asked in an exaggerated whisper.

"That's another long story. He's been . . . He's been really great, Mom. Amazing, in fact."

"Charley . . ."

"Can I get you anything, Mrs. Abbott? Some tea or coffee?"

"I'm fine, thank you, Tyler." When he had returned to his conversation with Hunter and Lincoln, Molly continued to whisper. "I thought you said you weren't interested in him."

"I wasn't. I'm not."

Molly raised a brow that let Charley know she needed to do better.

"We're having a good time together, believe it or not, and my craziness doesn't seem to faze him."

"I've always thought he was a very nice boy."

Thinking of his spectacular chest and abs, Charley said, "He's a *man*, Mom. Not a boy." *All man*, she thought but didn't say. "I don't want you to worry about me. I'm going to be fine. Another week of crutches and a few months of PT, and I'll be back to normal. I can even run again in about six months."

"You could've been killed. Hunter said it was a bad fall."

"It was. I was pretty scared, and so was Tyler, but he ran back for help and everyone says he saved my life. He blames himself for me being up there in the first place."

"Why?"

"Because when only the two of us showed up for the Saturday training run, he basically dared me to run up the mountain."

"And you never back down from a dare."

"I have seven brothers, Mother," Charley said dryly. "Backing down from a dare is a sign of weakness."

"And God forbid anyone ever think Charley Abbott is weak."

"Indeed, although this last week has been a bit humbling in that regard."

"I imagine so."

The men came to sit with them, and Charley glanced at Tyler. "Are we keeping you from your work?"

He waved off her concern. "It'll keep."

"Why don't we get you packed up so you can come home with us?" Molly said.

Charley looked at Tyler, whose expression was unreadable. "Oh, um . . ."

# CHAPTER 8

with me?" Molly said.

T yler could barely breathe while he waited to hear what
Charley would say to her mother's suggestion. Should
he ask her to stay, in front of her parents and brother, or would
it be better to say nothing and let her decide? She knew he
wanted her to stay, didn't she?

*Stay, Charley*, he thought. *Stay and spend this time with
me. Let me be the one to help you recover.* He stared at her,
hoping he'd done enough to show her how much he wanted
her in his home and in his life.

"I'm sort of settled here, Mom," she said.

Tyler's chest loosened and air began to flow freely to his
lungs again.

"And Tyler was gracious enough to get everything I need
to get by here."

Molly looked at him and then returned her gaze to Charley. "If that's what you want."

"I hope that doesn't hurt your feelings."

"It doesn't," Molly said. "I understand, and thank you, Tyler, for everything you've done for Charley. Hunter said you've been great."

Tyler looked at Charley when he said, "It's been my pleasure."

Her face burned with awareness of him, of his feelings for her. She wasn't ready for her time with him to end. Not yet, anyway.

He pulled a set of keys out of his pocket and handed them to Molly. "Please come and go as you please. My home is your home."

"That's very kind of you," Molly said. "Thank you."

"The whole Abbott family has keys to this place," Hunter said. "He'll live to regret that."

"Nah," Tyler said with a good-natured smile. "It's fine. Charley needs her family around her."

"I'll make sure to collect all the keys when I go home," she said, directing a warm smile in his direction.

His heart sank at the thought of her leaving, which he knew was ridiculous. Of course she'd want to go home at some point. He was in way over his head with her if he was depressed over the thought of her eventually leaving.

"I'm not worried about it," he said.

Her parents and brother left a short time later with promises to check in later.

"How're you feeling?" he asked Charley when they were alone again.

"Concerned."

Taking his favorite seat on the coffee table, he said, "What're you concerned about?"

"I turned down my mother's offer to go home with her without even checking with you. You're probably tired of having me around. I should've let them take over."

"No."

"No?"

"Just no—to all of it. I'm not tired of having you around, and you shouldn't have let them take over. Unless that's what you want."

"It's not."

Two little words had never packed a greater punch or given him more hope. Then she took it a step further by reaching for his hand for the first time. "I like being here with you."

Her words and the shy way in which she said them sent a shock wave of heat through his body. "I'm glad you do," he managed to say.

"Could I ask you something?"

"Anything you want."

"What happened in the bathroom—"

"I'm so sorry about that, Charley. It shouldn't have happened. I brought you here to rest and recover, and I didn't mean to take advantage of you."

"Oh. You didn't?"

"No, of course I didn't."

"It's just that I, um . . . I kinda liked it, and I was sort of hoping you might do it again. If you want to, that is."

"If I want to." Shaking his head, he laughed at the ridiculousness of the statement. "You have no idea how badly I've wanted to kiss you—among other things—for a really long time now."

She looked up at him, expectantly.

He acted before he could take the time to think, sliding his arms under her and picking her up—carefully.

Judging by the expression on her face, her gasp had nothing to do with pain and everything to do with surprise.

Tyler carried her into his room and put her down on the bed. Then he crawled in next to her. "There," he said. "That's better." He cupped her cheek and turned her to face him. "Much better angle."

"For?" she asked, sounding breathless.

"This." He started slow, with just the slightest brush of his lips over hers, making sure she was with him before he kissed her the way he really wanted to—hard and deep.

The catch of her breath encouraged him to add his tongue in teasing strokes against her lips, which were still tightly closed. Tyler was about to pull back to gauge whether she was enjoying this as much as he was when two things happened at the same time—her hand curled around his neck and her mouth opened to his tongue.

*Go time.*

He felt like he'd waited forever for the opportunity to kiss her the way he really wanted to, and it more than lived up to his vivid Charley Abbott fantasies. Her tongue twisted with his, making his blood boil. But he had to remember she was hurt and he needed to take it easy. With that in mind, he softened the kiss.

"Mmm, I knew it," he said.

"What did you know?"

"Underneath all that bluster you show the world, there's a ton of sweetness waiting to be found."

"I am *not* sweet."

He dragged his tongue over her bottom lip. "Yes, you certainly are."

"No, I'm certainly not—"

"Charley?"

"What?"

"Less talking and more kissing." Before she could argue with him, he kissed her, reminding himself once again to go slow, to not let his hands wander, to not push her for too much too soon. But she didn't make it easy to go slow, not when she sucked on his tongue and bit down on his lower lip, making him harder than he'd been for any woman ever.

He was about to say to hell with going slow when a voice called out from the other room. "Hello? Tyler? Charley? Where are you guys?"

Tyler froze. Christ, it was Ella.

Why was he stopping when it was just getting really, really good?

"Charley?" She startled at the sound of her sister's voice.

Tyler pulled back from her abruptly. "I can't see her right

now," he muttered before he got up and disappeared into the bathroom, closing the door behind him.

"In here, El," Charley called, her voice wavering. She pushed herself up to a sitting position and hoped Ella wouldn't take one look at her and see that she'd been making out with Tyler Westcott.

Holy shit, she'd been *making out* with Tyler Westcott. Charley reached up to touch her lips, which were still tingling. Her cheeks felt like they were on fire, as did her neck where his whiskers had rubbed against her skin. Ella was going to take one look at her and know exactly what'd been going on before her arrival.

"Hey." Ella poked her head into the room. "Is it okay if I come in? You weren't sleeping, were you?"

"Nah, I was reading."

Ella had brought a vase full of lilies and other gorgeous flowers.

Hoping to keep her sister's attention on the flowers rather than obvious signs of vigorous kissing, Charley said, "Wow, they're beautiful."

"I know! I couldn't believe the grocery store had them this time of year. I had to buy them."

"I'm glad you did. They smell awesome." How long exactly did Tyler plan to hide out in the bathroom? And then it occurred to her *why* he was hiding out. She stifled a laugh by coughing.

Ella eyed her with concern. "You okay?"

"Yep. Choked on my own spit." That was better than saying *I'm laughing because I kissed Tyler Westcott into a hard-on that he's now hiding from you.* Right?

Ella handed her the cup of water Tyler had gotten for her earlier.

Charley took a sip.

"So what's really going on around here? Where's Tyler?"

"Oh, um, he was taking a shower, I think. I was napping."

"I thought you were reading."

"I was. Before I fell asleep." *Please let Tyler be listening through the door.*

"You're acting weird."

"You woke me up. How am I supposed to act?"

Before Ella could reply, Tyler came out of the bathroom. "Oh hey, Ella. How's it going?"

"Fine. How are you?"

"Great. I'm, ah, going back to work. Let me know if you ladies need anything."

Ella watched him go and then shifted her gaze back to Charley. "Did I interrupt something?"

"No. Stop. I told you I was sleeping."

"With him?"

"Not with him." Charley fisted handfuls of the comforter. "By myself. Don't you have a job to do?"

"Two of them, thanks to your tumble down the mountain."

"Sorry to put you out."

"No problem. You covered for me the week after Thanksgiving, so I owe you."

"Yes, you do."

Ella laughed at the saucy reply.

"Is the store busy?"

"It's insane. Even the snow over the weekend didn't keep them home. And it's supposed to snow again tonight."

"I feel so out of the loop with everything—work and weather and all the usual stuff."

"I heard Mom and Dad came right here when they got home. Did you get yelled at?"

"As much as you'd love to hear I did, I'm afraid I have to disappoint you. She was so relieved to see me alive that she quickly got over the fact that we didn't call her."

"Too bad she can't ground you anymore the way she used to. Ahh, those were the days."

"You always did enjoy seeing me get into trouble, didn't you?"

"I enjoyed getting to use the car without having to share it with you while you were grounded."

"Nice," Charley said, chuckling.

"So what were you reading before you fell asleep?"

Charley glanced at the bedside table for her e-reader, which was of course in the living room. "I . . . um . . . My reader is out there. I came in here to nap."

"You're so full of shit. What were you really doing?"

"None of your business."

"I knew it! I knew there was something! Is it none of my business like it was none of yours when I was first with Gavin?"

"Just like that."

Ella busted up laughing and then leaned forward, lowering her voice. "Tell me."

"I don't want to."

"Come on, Charley, you *know* you want to."

"I just said I *didn't* want to."

"That's a lie. Tell me."

If she told Ella, it was no longer hers and Tyler's alone. But this was Ella, and they told each other stuff. "There might've been some kissing."

*"Ohhhhh,"* Ella said on a long exhale. "And?"

"And what? That's all it was."

"That's not all. Was it just lips touching lips or were tongues involved?"

"There might've been some tongue action."

"Oh my God."

"What? Why are you oh-my-God-ing?"

"Because!" Her whisper was more like a hiss, or at least that was how it sounded to Charley, who was becoming increasingly more uncomfortable the longer this conversation went on. "That's why he was in the bathroom! He was turned on!"

"Shut up. He was not."

"He was, *too*! He didn't want me to see."

"Ella, you need to go home now. Go worry about your own fiancé's Johnson and stop speculating about Tyler's."

"I bet he's got a *good* Johnson. He's all lanky and muscular. The lanky guys have always got it going on down there."

"And how do *you* know that?"

"Hello, Gavin isn't the first guy I ever slept with, as you well know."

"Go away and don't come back unless you call first."

"Why? Are you afraid you'll be spending time with Tyler's Johnson, and I'll interrupt something?"

"No, because I'm afraid if you don't *shut up* and *leave* I might levitate out of my sickbed and *punch you in the face!*"

Ella, that bitch, laughed her ass off. "Go ahead. Make my day."

"I'm writing down all your transgressions for when I'm recovered. Your ass will be grass then."

"I'm not scared of you."

"You should be. Go home to your man and leave me alone."

"Are your lips getting lonely?"

"I hate you right now."

"You do not."

"No, I really do."

"I'm taking my flowers back."

"If it means you'll leave, have them."

"Too bad. I was going to share some family gossip with you, but if you're gonna be that way, I'm outta here."

"Don't you dare leave without telling me the gossip."

"You have to promise not to say anything. It's total speculation at this point."

"I'm listening."

"I think Cameron is pregnant."

"Really? Why do you say that?"

"She's spending a lot of time in the bathroom at work, and I heard retching noises. Will hovers outside the door when she's in there. And she's late for work sometimes, which is new."

"I thought they were going to wait a while."

Ella shrugged. "Babies happen. I'm hoping it happens to me soon."

"I hope so, too." Charley was well aware of how badly Ella wanted to be a mom, whereas she had almost no desire whatsoever to procreate. "It's a regular baby boom around here. Mom will be thrilled."

"I know. I bet Hunter and Megan won't wait long either. He's going to be thirty-six soon. No time like the present."

"True. How're the wedding plans? Have you heard?"

"From all reports, they're keeping it simple. Family and a few close friends. Megan's sister will be home this weekend for the shower and she's staying for the wedding."

"I doubt I'll be able to do the shower."

"Let's wait and see what the weekend brings. You may feel better by then."

"Hope so. I'd hate to miss it, and I feel bad that I can't help at all."

"It's fine. Hannah is all over it, like the drill sergeant she's become since she got pregnant."

"I much prefer drill sergeant Hannah to decimated Hannah."

"I do, too. Very much so. Speaking of Hannah, she and Nolan got into a huge fight yesterday because she's worried that no one has seen Fred in town or at any of his usual hangouts in more than a week. She's afraid he's hurt and wants to go looking for him."

"To which Nolan totally freaked out and told her she's going nowhere near the woods in her condition."

"You got that right. She told him she's pregnant, not feeble, and if he doesn't chill out, this kid will be an only child. He said if *she* doesn't chill out where Fred is concerned, he's going to have him captured and sent to a zoo."

"*Ohhh*," Charley said. "Wrong thing to say, Nolan."

"Yep. She's furious with him from all accounts, and she's trying to recruit the boys to go looking for Fred. Of course they're not that inclined to put their rescue skills to work for a moose, so they're at a stalemate."

"Wow, let me know if anyone hears from Fred and how long it takes for Nolan to sweet-talk his way back into Hannah's good graces. I miss all the fun being stuck in bed."

"Not all of it, from what I've seen." Smiling, Ella leaned

over to kiss her forehead. "I'll turn you back over to your studly keeper. Happy kissing."

Charley swung wildly at her sister, who was well out of range by the time the punch would've landed. "I'm adding that to the list!"

"See ya! Try to behave yourself!"

"Ella!"

She turned back, raising a brow in inquiry.

"You won't say anything, will you?"

"Get real, Charley. You and me? We could ruin each other, and we never have. And P.S. He's a nice, sweet, sexy guy. Enjoy yourself a little, why don't you?" Ella left her with that unsettling thought.

Charley thought about what her sister had said. It mattered that her family liked Tyler. Hell, they loved him for stepping up for her so they wouldn't have to. Not that any of them wouldn't have helped her out if it had come to that, but she wasn't known for being the easiest Abbott to get along with. No, that honor probably went to Ella, who was normally easygoing. Today being a notable exception.

Charley couldn't say why she was so annoyed that her sister had tuned right in to the fact that she'd interrupted something between her and Tyler. Normally, she didn't care if her sister knew who she was kissing or sleeping with or anything else for that matter. There were few secrets between her and Ella, but this . . . This felt different, and damned if she could say why.

The conversation with Ella had left her cranky and out of sorts, which was how Tyler found her when he returned to the room half an hour after Ella left.

"Did Ella go?"

"Yeah, a while ago."

"I'm going to make some lunch. You ready to eat?"

"No, thank you. I'm fine." She turned away from him as best she could without jarring her leg, which was suddenly hurting like a bastard. Tears stung her eyes, and the last thing she wanted was to cry in front of him so she closed her eyes. She thought he'd gone, but when she felt the bed sink down next to her, she found out otherwise.

"What's wrong?" The whisper touch of his fingers on her cheeks was her undoing.

"You shouldn't like me the way you do."

"Why not?" he asked with a low chuckle.

"Don't laugh at me. I'm spoiling to punch someone."

He laid his hand over her fist, as if that could stop her. "What did your sister say to make you so mad?"

"Nothing."

"Must've been something because you were in a pretty good mood before she showed up."

Charley couldn't very well tell him that she'd told Ella what they'd been up to when she arrived.

"Did you tell her you were kissing me and that you liked it?"

Her eyes flew open to find his dancing with laughter.

"I *knew* it!"

"I never said I liked it."

"Ouch. I can see I'm going to have to work much harder to make sure you like it enough to keep doing it." He leaned in slowly, probably to give her time to tell him to stop. "You aren't mad enough to bite, are you?"

"I might be."

"I'd better be careful then." This time there was no soft persuasion and no gentle preliminaries. This time, he went straight to where they'd left off before Ella's ill-timed arrival.

Charley's brain couldn't seem to catch up. Surely she needed to tell him they shouldn't be kissing like this. She'd never intended to let this happen. But another minute or two wouldn't hurt anything, would it? Just as she was about to turn away from the kiss, he went gentle on her, seducing her with sweet strokes of his tongue against hers and soft bites of his teeth on her bottom lip that set off a wildfire of undeniable desire.

*Good God, the man could kiss.* She hadn't had nearly

enough when he pulled back to stare down at her, seeming as poleaxed as she felt.

"I knew that, too."

"What did you know?"

"That if I kissed you, even once, I'd never want to kiss anyone else ever again."

# CHAPTER 9

T yler's sweet words stayed with her throughout the rest of that day and into the evening. He made a delicious dinner with pasta and vegetables and crunchy bread. They ate in the living room while they watched another of the many movies that had been delivered by her siblings. Outside the wind howled and snow pinged against the window, but inside . . . Inside was warm and cozy thanks to the fire Tyler had built and the down blanket he'd tossed over their laps.

Charley couldn't concentrate on the movie because she was too busy wondering if there'd be more kissing. The waiting and wondering took her back to high school, when boys and men were still a mystery to her. In recent years there'd been nothing all that mysterious about the men she'd dated.

She actually couldn't recall the last time she felt unsure of herself around a man. The feeling was new and not altogether welcome.

Tyler laughed at the movie.

Charley had lost track of the plot twenty minutes in.

He caught her watching him and smiled before returning his attention to the movie.

She wanted to scream with frustration, which had her laughing to herself at how things had changed. A few weeks ago, the thought of kissing Tyler was unimaginable. Now, she couldn't wait for the chance to do it again. Which led to another, much more disturbing thought. Since when did she, Charley Abbott, wait for any man to make a move? What the hell was wrong with her? Had she lost her mind on the way down that ravine?

A flutter of nerves overtook her belly. It took a moment for her to recognize the flutter for what it was, since she had rarely been nervous about anything. Nerves were for wimps, or so she'd always thought. No one had ever accused her of being a wimp, but she sure felt like one at the moment because the thought of reaching out and taking what she wanted from Tyler made her nervous as hell.

Her hands rolled into fists as she stemmed the urge to touch him. She gritted her teeth and tried to focus on the movie, but it was hopeless.

"What's the matter, Charley?"

Startled by the question, she went on the defensive. "Nothing's wrong."

"Does your knee hurt?"

"Not at the moment."

"Are you hungry?"

"No, I'm not hungry." He'd fed her to within an inch of her life since she'd been staying with him. "If you keep plying me with food, I'm going to be nine hundred pounds by the time I leave."

"Something's got you wound up."

"I am *not* wound up." Yes, she sounded shrewish, but there he went again acting like he could read her mind.

"Whatever you say." He got up, taking the popcorn bowl with him, and returned with a fresh beer. Sitting a foot from her on the sofa, he propped his sock-clad feet on the coffee table, his body relaxed as if he didn't have a care in the world.

To hell with it. She struggled to her feet, nearly falling in her haste.

"*Whoa.*" Tyler jumped up. "Slow down."

"I don't want to slow down." She made her way, awkwardly and painfully, toward the bedroom, trying to figure out how she could slam the door to his own room in his face. But he denied her the opportunity to carry out her plan when he darted around her, walking backward in front of her.

"Will you please stop and tell me what's wrong? Please?"

Something about the way he said *please* the second time infuriated her. She swung her crutch at him, and he darted out of the way. "You kissed my face off earlier and then . . . Nothing. Not so much as a look or a . . . a . . . *Nothing!*"

He took a step and closed the distance between them, until he was so close that she could count the whiskers on his jaw had she been so inclined. She wasn't. "You want *something*?"

Setting her chin, she forced herself to look up at him. His eyes were on fire, and if she could have, she would've taken a step back out of sheer self-preservation. "What if I do?"

"You have to say it." He was suddenly closer than he'd been before, and how was that even possible? "You have to tell me what you want."

If asked under oath, Charley wouldn't be able to say what made her do it. One minute she was seething and the next her crutches were crashing to the floor and her hand was around his neck, dragging him into a kiss. She clung to him, hoping he would keep her from falling over and reinjuring her healing knee.

Once again, he came to her rescue, wrapping his arms around her as his lips crashed down on hers. Every muscle in her body turned to liquid and only his tight hold kept her from falling. He kissed her as if his entire life depended on this kiss and this moment.

"If you wanted me to kiss you," he said between kisses, "all you had to do was say so." He kissed her again, his tongue delving deep into her mouth, triggering the sort of intense desire she'd heard about but hadn't experienced personally before. In fact, before him, before now, she would've said this kind of desire was a myth.

His hand slid down her back to cup her ass, pulling her in tight against the hard ridge of his erection.

Charley rubbed against him shamelessly, looking for relief from the need that throbbed through her body like a live wire.

And then she was in his arms. He never faltered, and he made sure to protect her leg as he settled her on the bed and came down on top of her without missing a beat in the kiss that had gone from crazy to downright insane. She'd never kissed anyone with such unrestrained lust before him. She'd never wanted to tear the clothes from a man's body and fully experience him the way she did now.

Her hand found its way under his T-shirt. She loved the moan that came from him when her skin connected with his. It was a huge turn-on to know he wanted her so badly. Other men had wanted her, but not like this. Not like Tyler did. When she tried to get closer to him, her knee fought back, making her wince from the bolt of pain that took her out of the moment.

"Easy, honey," he said, softening the kiss.

"Tyler . . ."

He nuzzled her neck, setting off another wildfire that traveled straight to her nipples and clit. "What? Tell me."

"I need . . ."

"Say it, Charley. Tell me what you need."

"Touch me. I want you to touch me."

"Where?" His lips continued to do crazy things to her neck and ear while his hands stayed stubbornly still by her sides.

"Everywhere."

The low groan that came from him was about the sexiest thing she'd ever heard. Charley reached for the hem of her T-shirt and worked it up and over her head, exposing her bare breasts to his greedy gaze. Then she went to work on his shirt, tugging on it until he took the hint and removed it with one hand, while the other arm held him up.

She trailed her fingers over the bulging muscles in his arm, fascinated by the way he was built.

He came down on top of her slowly, carefully, bringing his chest into contact with hers.

Charley wrapped her arms around him and closed her eyes, absorbing the exquisite pleasure. It was almost too much, which was another first. She had always enjoyed sex, but this was something else altogether. This was attraction on a whole other level, and it scared the hell out of her.

"I'm afraid to hurt you," Tyler said, his voice tense from the effort it was apparently taking to hold back.

"I'm fine. I won't break."

He moved slowly at first, rubbing his chest over hers. The feel of his chest hair on her aching nipples made her desperate for more.

She hooked her good leg around his hips to bring him in tighter against the part of her that ached.

"Christ, Charley," he muttered as he latched onto her nipple, making her cry out from the heat of his mouth and the pinch of his teeth. "You're so gorgeous and so sexy. I love to watch you move." As he spoke, he continued to tease her nipple with his tongue and teeth. "I always run behind you at workouts." His hand worked its way under her to squeeze her bottom. "Ah, God, I've wanted to grab hold of your sweet, sexy ass for so fucking long."

The dirty talk electrified even as it shocked her in the best way possible. Who would've thought that prim and proper Tyler Westcott could get down and dirty?

He moved against her, touching her in all the right places, but even that much wasn't nearly enough.

Charley wanted to toss aside any thoughts of caution or hesitation and give herself over to the desire that had overtaken every cell in her body. It didn't matter that one of her legs didn't work the way it was supposed to or that this was Tyler, who she'd held at arm's length for so long. Nothing mattered but the need.

His hand moved from her breast to her belly, sliding down the front of her.

Charley's breath caught while she waited to see what he

would do next. Would he take it further or stop? She didn't have to wait long for him to make up his mind. His fingers ducked under the waistband of her flannel pajama pants and straight into the lacy scrap of fabric that covered her. *Dear God . . .* His assertiveness was hot as hell. Guys who asked permission before they acted turned her off. Tyler didn't ask. He just took, which was wildly arousing.

And he knew exactly where to touch her.

Charley gasped and then moaned as his questing fingers pressed against her clit before sliding into her, filling her completely and then retreating to do it again. Her fingers dug into the dense muscle that covered his broad shoulders.

"Tell me to stop," he said in a low growl.

"Don't you dare stop."

"Your leg . . ."

"Is fine."

He took her mouth in another of those kisses that quickly spun out of control while his fingers continued to play her like a maestro. No direction needed. He just knew. He knew her.

Charley tore her lips free of the kiss to scream out the pleasure that overtook her entire body, her muscles seizing from the force of her orgasm, which was cut short by the sharp pain that lodged in her leg when she forgot she couldn't move it. The pain brought tears to her eyes.

"Ah crap," he said. "That hurt."

"Only for a second. It was worth it." She forced her gaze up to meet his. The way he looked at her, as if she'd just handed him the one thing he wanted more than anything else . . . It was almost too much. She turned her attention to his finely muscled chest. "What about you?"

"I'm fine. Don't worry about me."

"I don't believe in leaving my partner wanting."

"Oh, um, I . . ."

Charley laughed at his fumbling reply.

"I don't like to think about you with other guys."

The stark statement surprised her. "I'm not exactly a virgin, Tyler."

"Neither am I, but still . . . I don't like to think about you with others. That time I saw you and Tim Burke at Kingdom Pizza?"

"What about it?"

"I wanted to lure him outside and beat the shit out of him."

"Tim Burke is a logger. He could've killed you."

"Still . . . The thought of his hands on you . . ." Propped up on one elbow, he ran his finger over her collarbone and down to the valley between her breasts. Her nipples were immediately back on duty, standing up to see what else he would do. He watched them with that hungry gaze of his before taking a taste of one and then the other. "I could've killed him."

Charley sank her fingers into Tyler's hair. "He never got his hands on me."

He lifted his head to look at her. "No?"

She shook her head. "Not for a lack of wanting."

"The poor guy is only human."

"You were wanting to kill that poor guy a minute ago."

"I've lost interest in killing him now that I know he never touched you."

"Others have."

"I'll need a list of names and addresses." His teasing smile made her heart do a funny flip. Jealousy had never been much of a turn-on for her, but under the right circumstances . . .

"I want to touch you," she said. "The way you touched me."

A muscle in his cheek twitched from the tension that tightened his jaw.

"Can I?"

"Yes, God, yes, but only if you feel like it."

"I feel like it." She felt like she'd expire from wanting to if he didn't let her. "Come here." Holding out her hand to him, she brought him over to straddle her hips and then she set about freeing him from the pajama pants he'd put on earlier. She was intrigued to find nothing between him and the pants, but then he fell hard and hot into her hand and all thoughts were erased except for giving him the same pleasure he'd given her.

"Scoot forward," she said.

"Charley . . ."

"Just do it."

He moved up, bringing his long, thick erection closer to her mouth, which watered at the sight of him. Ella had been right about the lanky guys packing heat below. At least this one was, and she filed that fact away for her ever-growing list of ways that Tyler had surprised her.

She stroked him with her hand and teased the tip with her tongue.

His head fell back and his eyes closed, which left him unprepared for her to suck him into her mouth. He inhaled sharply, and she smiled to herself, loving the effect she was having on him. As she redoubled her efforts, he fell forward, his hands propped on the headboard, his hips moving in time with her strokes.

"Charley," he said on a low growl. "Honey, stop. I'm gonna . . ."

She didn't stop. Rather, she moved faster, enjoying the view of him above her, lost to what she was doing to him. His muscles tightened and his body stiffened as he came with a cry of completion that thrilled her. He came hard, and she took everything he had to give and didn't let up until he sagged into her, breathing raggedly.

"Fucking hell, Charley," he whispered. "You amaze me."

"I amaze myself sometimes."

He laughed and then moved to stretch out beside her, keeping his head on her chest and his hand flat on her belly. "That was the hottest thing ever."

"Ever?"

"*Ever.*"

"Mmm, that's a pretty good compliment."

"You and me," he said, "this . . . It's gonna be something big. Are you down with that?"

The statement and the question left her reeling. "I, um . . . I don't really do big."

"What's that supposed to mean?"

"If you're looking for white picket fences and two-point-two kids, I'm not your girl."

"You *are* my girl. You're absolutely my girl."

"Because I sucked your dick once? That makes me your *girl*?"

He barked out a laugh that infuriated her. How dare he laugh when she was dead serious? "You're a piece of work, Charlotte Abbott."

"Don't patronize me. How in the world have you made it so I'm your 'girl'? I'm nobody's girl but my own."

"I want you to be mine. I want you in my life and in my bed."

"I'm not the kind of girl you marry, Tyler."

"Why in the world would you say such a thing? Of course you are."

"No, I'm really not. Despite what you think you know about me, that much is true."

"I don't buy it. I think you tell yourself that so you won't have to risk that carefully guarded heart of yours."

"There you go again with the insight into Charley. Here's a news flash for you—so we're hot for each other. Big deal. That doesn't mean there has to be hearts and flowers. Why can't two people just have sex and call it what it is instead of making it into a big hairy deal?"

"No reason at all, I suppose. It's just that if I hadn't felt the evidence to the contrary, I'd wonder if you were the guy here."

"Why? Because I don't want what other women do? I don't dream about the big white wedding and the Christmas cards with my cute little kids on them?"

"What's wrong with cute little kids?"

"Not a thing, as long as they belong to someone else."

His mouth opened and then closed as if he'd thought better of whatever he'd been about to say.

"Don't know me as well as you think, do you?"

"Maybe not, but that doesn't change anything."

"You've been amazing to me, but you're the kind of guy who needs a nice girl to marry and settle down with. I'm nowhere near ready for any of that, so we probably ought to take a step back before someone gets hurt."

Rather than take a step back, he cupped her breast and tweaked her nipple, which was all it took to get her motor running again. How did he do that so easily? "I don't want to take a step back. I want you any way I can get you. If you tell me all it can be is sex, I can live with that."

"For how long?"

"For as long as you want to have sex with me."

"And you aren't going to start pressuring me for things I told you I don't want?"

"When have I ever pressured you into anything?"

"I seem to recall a run up an icy mountain . . ."

"Pressuring is different than challenging."

"I'm not going to change my mind about these things, Tyler."

"Okay."

She eyed him skeptically.

"What?"

"That means a month or two from now, when you've had your fill of me and I move on, you're going to be fine with it."

"Okay."

"Just okay?"

He shrugged. "What else would you have me say?"

"You could repeat after me and say, 'I, Tyler Westcott, have not only heard Charley Abbott say she doesn't want a serious relationship, but I have *listened* to her when she says she means it.'"

Tyler looked her in the eye as he recited the words back to her. "Satisfied?"

"I'll be more satisfied when my stupid leg works right again and we can do a hell of a lot more than we did tonight."

Other than his Adam's apple bobbing in his throat, he had nothing to say to that.

# CHAPTER 10

L ong after Charley had fallen asleep, Tyler lay awake staring up at the ceiling thinking about the way she'd come apart in his arms and then made him see stars when she returned the favor. He'd never come so hard in his life, and he was dying for more of her. She'd no sooner given an inch, however, when she took back the mile in progress he'd thought they'd made since her accident.

She didn't want a husband and kids and a life committed to someone else, or so she said.

He'd said what she wanted to hear tonight, because he was nowhere near done with her or done trying to convince her that they could have something special. So he'd bought himself some time by saying what she wanted him to. He hadn't lied so much as stretched the truth to accommodate her needs. That didn't really count as a lie if his intentions were honorable, did it?

He was convinced—*absolutely, positively convinced*—that they could be magic together if only she allowed herself to at least try. And he wasn't about to give up on her before they'd had a chance to see what might develop. In the back of his mind was the voice of his mother warning him to be careful to guard his heart, his siblings saying he could've chosen an "easier" woman, his friends teasing him about being a masochist. Those voices were drowned out, however, by the sound of *her* voice asking if she could touch him.

His body reacted predictably to that memory, hardening to the point of pain as he recalled the exquisite pleasure of her lips and hand wrapped around his cock as she sucked him to completion. It would be a very long time, if ever, until that memory didn't rank at number one on the list of things he never wanted to forget.

The only thing that could top that memory was more of her. Despite her warnings, he was falling harder for her every day and night they spent together. And while she hated when he acted as if he knew her better than she knew herself, he suspected he'd hit a bull's-eye with his comment about her well-protected heart. Her eyes had hardened and her lips had tightened with displeasure that told him he was spot on.

Someone had hurt his darling Charley—and hurt her badly enough that she'd convinced herself it was easier not to bother than it was to put herself on the line for a man. He was determined to show her how wrong she was about that. But he'd have to proceed carefully. He'd have to keep his own feelings hidden until she was ready for all the things he wanted to give her.

That might be the most difficult challenge of all, because he was definitely in love with her. He'd suspected he might be a long time ago, but the day she'd disappeared down the side of that ravine and he'd had all that time to wonder what he'd do if she was dead . . . Any doubt had been erased during those interminable hours. He loved her, he wanted her, he desired her—and only her.

As long as she was living in his house and sleeping in his bed—with him—he had a chance to convince her to let down her guard. He'd show her romance and affection and friendship and passion that would leave her dazzled. And if he went to all that trouble and still came up short?

Well, he'd cross that covered bridge when he came to it.

* * *

After taking his son back to Chloe's in Burlington, Max Abbott returned to Butler feeling out of sorts, the way he did whenever he was separated from his son by a couple of hours. Chloe had very little to say to him when he picked up or dropped off Caden, which left Max wondering what she was thinking and constantly on edge whenever he was not with his son.

It wasn't that he thought she would mistreat the baby, but her general apathy toward their son was worrisome. That worry had brought Max to his aunt Hannah's house, where he let himself in through the mudroom door that was always unlocked. He took off his boots and hung up his coat before venturing into his aunt's cozy kitchen, where she was sitting at the table with his cousin Grayson, who Max had come to see.

"Max!" Hannah jumped up to hug and kiss him. "What a nice surprise."

He returned her embrace. "Sorry to barge in on you guys."

"Not at all," Hannah said. "Can I get you a cup of something warm?"

"I wouldn't say no to that."

"Have a seat, honey. I'll get it for you."

"Thank you." He shook hands with Grayson, who eyed him shrewdly, already aware that this wasn't a social call.

"How's the baby?" Hannah asked.

"He's great." Like the proud father he was, Max whipped out his phone and showed them the new photos he'd taken during the last few days he and Caden had spent with Will and Cameron.

"He's absolutely gorgeous," Hannah declared.

"I think so, too."

"He looks just like you did as a baby," Grayson said.

"My mom says that, too."

"Poor bastard," Gray said with a sly grin that made Max laugh for the first time all day.

"Save it. My brothers have already said the same thing."

"They're all just jealous, Max," Hannah said, putting a steaming cup of hot chocolate on the table in front of him. "The youngest cousin is the best looking out of all of you."

"Gee, thanks a lot, Mom," Gray said.

"You're not ugly and you know it, Grayson."

"I think he's kind of ugly," Max said with a smile for his cousin. "There, now we're even."

"What brings you out in this weather, Max?" Hannah asked as she continued to move about the kitchen.

"I was hoping to talk to Gray about a few things."

"Sure," his cousin said, all kidding aside now. "Whatever you need."

"I'll leave you two to talk," Hannah said.

"You don't have to, Aunt Hannah."

She hugged Max from behind. "Talk to your cousin. I've got some work to catch up on. And bring me that baby to snuggle the next time he's in town."

"I will. Thanks for the hot chocolate."

"Any time, honey."

When they were alone, Gray looked at him expectantly. "What's on your mind?"

"My son is on my mind twenty-four-seven."

"As well he should be. I heard you and Chloe broke up."

Max nodded and stared down at his hot chocolate. "We called it quits between us a couple of weeks before he was born. It just wasn't working, and there was no sense in staying together for his sake when we'd only make each other miserable."

"Sounds like you made the best decision for yourselves."

"I guess."

"Did you not want to break up with her?"

"No, I did. By the time she finally said she was done, I'd been done for a while. She turned into someone totally different after she got pregnant. She was really pissed off about it, and took most of it out on me, as if she hadn't been a willing participant when it happened. I got tired of her crapping on me for something we did together."

"From what I've heard and seen, you've done the best you could throughout this entire situation."

"I've tried, but she isn't making it easy."

"How do you mean?"

"She's being really weird about him. About Caden."

"In what way?"

"She's very . . . detached, I guess you could say. I worry about whether she's taking proper care of him when I'm not there."

Grayson sat up a little straighter in his chair. "Like you think she's neglecting him?"

"Not technically, but if he has to cry for a while before his bottle, she doesn't think there's anything wrong with that, whereas I can't stand to hear him cry. I feed him right away when he cries. She takes her own sweet time getting to him. Stuff like that. And I noticed he had diaper rash when I picked him up this time, which was new. That leads me to wonder how long she's letting him sit in dirty diapers. It's making me crazy, Gray. I know she has rights, but so does he and so do I."

"Are you thinking about asking for full custody?"

"God, no. As much as I want to be with him every day, there's no way I could do it on my own."

"Yes, you could, Max. In our family, no one is ever alone. You'd be surrounded by help."

"Still . . . He needs his mother, too."

"Not if she doesn't want him."

"What do you think I should do?"

"We need to have a talk with her."

"*We* do?"

"You and me as your lawyer. Since you two have broken up, your custody arrangement needs to be formalized."

"We were just going to share custody."

"Which you can still do, but you need to make it legal, Max. What if she were to get a wild idea about moving out of state or overseas and taking your son with her?"

The very thought of such a scenario sent Max into a panic. "She can't do that!"

"If you don't have a legal agreement in place that prohibits either of you from moving or taking him overseas, she can do it—and so can you."

"Will you help me with this, Gray? I'll pay you for your time. Whatever it takes—"

"Of course I'll help you, and you won't pay me."

"You've just left your job to open a practice. You have to let people pay you."

"I'll let people pay me. I won't let *you* pay me."

His cousin's generosity nearly reduced Max to tears. "Thanks, Gray. I really appreciate this."

"Give me a couple of days to get my head around the details, and then we'll go to Burlington and talk to Chloe, okay?"

The thought of having that conversation with her made Max feel sick. "Are you sure that's the right thing to do?"

"I'm absolutely positive."

On Sunday morning, Tyler shoveled the driveway so he could take Charley to Megan's bridal shower at the Abbotts' barn. All morning he waited for her to ask for his help packing up so she could stay at her parents' place after the shower, but she didn't ask, and he certainly didn't offer.

She was getting around much better, and he'd be surprised if she wasn't off the crutches within the next few days. While he celebrated her progress, each milestone brought them closer to the day when she would return to her life already in progress—most likely without him a part of it.

He helped her put the brace on over a pair of jeans that did miraculous things to her ass. Her face was flushed from the effort it took to shower and dry her hair and make herself presentable. She wore a gray turtleneck sweater that clung to curves he now knew were as generous as they looked. It took all he had to not let his thoughts stray in the direction of the hot make-out sessions they'd had every night this week. He couldn't think about that or he'd be a walking, talking hard-on, and Charley would definitely notice.

So he thought about innocuous things like stock market fluctuations rather than the pale pink color of Charley Abbott's nipples.

"Tyler?"

Oh damn it, had he zoned out on her? "Yeah?"

"I was just asking if you were ready."

"Whenever you are."

"Are you going skiing with the guys?"

Her brother Will had called to invite Tyler along on the ski trip the guys were taking to get Hunter out of the way for Megan's shower. "I was planning to go. Is that all right with you?"

"Of course it is. Why wouldn't it be?"

"I wasn't sure if hanging out with your brothers counted as getting too involved with you."

She gave him a disparaging look. "You're more than welcome to be friends with my brothers."

"Good to know." Taking that as a positive sign, Tyler loaded up his skis, boots, poles and the clothes he needed for a day on the slopes and walked the equipment out to the Range Rover. In truth, he had a million things he needed to do for work, but he wasn't about to miss out on an opportunity to gather some more insight into Charley and what made her tick.

He went back to help Charley into her coat and to stand watch as she attempted to navigate the two steps that led into the garage. She bit her lip in concentration, which naturally led him to think about her biting his lip the night before. Running his tongue over the spot in question, he could still feel the pleasurable sting.

She reached the side of the SUV and looked up at the passenger seat the way a novice skier would eye the black diamonds.

"Give you a lift?"

"I suppose you'll have to." She sounded defeated, and he didn't like that.

"You'll be doing it by yourself in no time." When she had her balance on her good leg, he took the crutches from her and stashed them in the backseat before returning to lift her into the passenger seat.

Once he had his hands on her, though, he didn't want to let go.

"Tyler," she said, sounding as breathless as he felt.

He was trying to give her the space she'd said she needed.

But damn, it was tough now that he knew how sweet she tasted and the noises she made when she came. He didn't think. He acted, capturing her mouth in another of the heated kisses that he could easily become addicted to.

At first, he didn't think she was going to respond, but then she was kissing him back the way she did in bed every night lately. Tyler had no idea how long he stood there, kissing her as if kissing were about to go out of style or something equally awful. He wanted to pick her up and carry her back inside. He wanted to strip her bare and sink into her wet heat. He wanted to make love to her until day became night and night became morning. And then he wanted to do it all again.

A huge shudder traveled through his body as the salacious thoughts registered one on top of the other. Her hand on his neck calmed him and reminded him of where they needed to be. He withdrew slowly from the kiss. "Wow," he whispered.

"Mmm."

Tyler opened his eyes to find hers still closed, her lips damp and swollen from their kisses. She'd never looked more beautiful. "Charley . . ."

"We should go."

It took a moment for her words to register and for him to climb out of the fog of desire he'd slipped into while kissing her. He stared at her, wanting to etch every detail of how she looked in that moment into his memory bank.

"Do I have something on my face?" she asked, seeming unnerved by his inspection.

"No. You're just . . ."

"What?"

"Beautiful."

A flush overtook her cheeks, giving Tyler pause to wonder if that was the first time in her life that Charley Abbott had actually blushed.

"Thank you."

Tyler pulled the seatbelt across her and snapped it into place and then forced himself to withdraw, closing the door behind him. Walking around to the driver's side, he ached from the discomfort of unfulfilled desire. Every time he went near her, he ended up in this condition.

The ride downhill from his place to town was dicey, thanks to the snow that had fallen overnight. He took the hairpin turns with care, thankful for the four-wheel drive that was a staple of winter in Vermont.

"What do you do when it really snows?" she asked, breaking a long silence.

"I stay home. I've got everything I need up there, including a generator if the power goes out."

"Oh, fancy."

"It's more a necessity. Without power, I can't run my business."

"We've got one at the store, but it's only enough to keep the refrigerators going and the heat on so the pipes don't burst."

*Speaking of pipes bursting*, he thought, as he adjusted himself to make room for the erection that wouldn't quit when she was close by. Her scent filled the air around him, making him wish it had snowed enough to keep them at home today. Not that he'd want her to miss out on time with her family, but he was feeling greedy for more of her. Today was going to be a very long day as he anticipated what would probably happen when they got home again later.

Twenty slow minutes after they left his house, he pulled into the driveway at her parents' big red barn. Sturdy SUVs and pickup trucks were parked outside and a number of dogs frolicked in the snow. Tyler eyed the path to the door and surmised that Charley wouldn't be able to navigate the mud and slush with her crutches.

He got out of the car and went around to help her. "You'd better let me give you a lift, honey. Otherwise, you're apt to slip and fall."

She rolled her bottom lip between her teeth as she surveyed the terrain and came to the same conclusion. "Okay."

Tyler kept waiting for her to snap at him, to tell him not to call her honey because she wasn't his honey. But she didn't. Rather, she released the seatbelt and went willingly—or so it seemed to him—into his arms for the ride inside. Her brother Will appeared at the mudroom door as they approached and opened it for them.

"All hail Queen Charlotte," Will called over his shoulder. "Make way for Her Highness."

"Bite me," Charley said to her brother, who laughed.

"I'll pass. The last guy who bit you broke a tooth."

"That is not true," she said with a meaningful smirk that immediately put Tyler's hackles up. The thought of another guy *biting* her . . . Ugh.

"Take her in there." Will pointed the way for Tyler, who'd never been inside the charming home before. As a man who appreciated architecture, he wanted to take in every detail of the restored barn. It had been lovingly decorated for Christmas and looked like something you might see in a magazine.

Though he wanted to linger for a closer look, he had precious cargo in his arms that needed to be delivered. He followed the sound of voices to the great room, where a raging fire in the stone fireplace was one focal point. The other was the massive Christmas tree that occupied the other end of the huge room. In the center of the room, an easy chair had been decked out with white balloons and streamers and other decorations.

"Anywhere but there," Hannah said, pointing to the chair that had been reserved for the bride.

Tyler carried Charley to the sofa and put her down carefully before dragging an ottoman over so she could rest her leg on something. "You want a pillow, too?"

"Nah, the footstool is fine." She unzipped her coat, and he took it for her. "Thanks for the lift."

"No problem. Pick you up after?"

She glanced up at him, doing that uncertain thing with her lip again, and he decided he rather liked making her uncertain. He suspected that didn't happen very often. "Sure."

"Great." His entire system flooded with an unreasonable amount of relief. "See you then. Have fun."

"You, too."

Tyler knew he should walk away, that he should leave her to enjoy the shower while he went skiing. One afternoon apart wasn't going to change anything, but even knowing that, a pang of anxiety struck him anyway.

"You ready to roll, Tyler?" Will asked.

"Yeah, whenever you are." He left Charley with one last smile and followed Will back to the mudroom, taking the anxiety with him as he went.

# CHAPTER 11

———◆◆◆———

C harley watched Tyler go, wondering what he'd been thinking as he stared down at her. He unnerved her with the intense way he looked at her, as if he had a million things he wanted to tell her.

Cameron plopped down next to her on the sofa. "Holy sexy hotness, Batman."

"Eww." Charley covered her ears. "I don't need to hear that about my own brother."

"I'm not talking about Will, although he is crazy hot. I meant *Tyler*. Whoa. He's totally into you." Cameron nudged her with an elbow. "What goes on in the love nest up on the hill?"

"Your imagination is working overtime."

Cameron took an assessing look at Charley that made her feel exposed. "I don't think it is."

Ella brought Charley a steaming cup of cider.

"Please tell me this is spiked," Charley said.

"Mine is," Ella said. "Yours isn't. Not while you're still taking painkillers."

"Did Tyler tell you to say that?"

"Nope. I figured that out all on my own." To Cameron she added, "Is she spilling any of the dirty details?"

"Not yet, but I think she was about to."

"Think again," Charley said dryly.

"That means there're dirty details to spill," Cameron said. "Come on! I'm an old married woman now. I'm living vicariously through you single girls."

"Are you *already* bored with Will?" Charley asked.

*"Hardly,"* Cameron said, waggling her brows.

Charley rolled her eyes. "I'll say again—ewww."

Cameron laughed at the face Charley made at her. "There's nothing *ewww* about it. More like *ahhhh.*"

"Make it stop, Ella," Charley said.

"Cam, I think Hannah said she needed your help in the kitchen," Ella said.

"I see right through this ruse, ladies," Cameron said as she got up. "I'll be back for the dirty details later."

"Thank you," Charley said to Ella when they were alone. Lowering her voice, she added, "I see potential pregnancy hasn't done anything to quell her need to know everything."

"I'm not even potentially pregnant—that I know of, anyway—and I need to know everything, too. What goes on up there on the mountain?"

"Oh, you know. This. And that."

"Charlotte Abbott—tell me everything right now."

She shifted her gaze down to her hands. "We've been, you know, fooling around. Some. As much as we can." She gestured to the leg brace that represented a world of frustration.

"This is *huge,*" Ella whispered loudly—too loudly for Charley's liking.

"Shush. I don't want everyone hearing."

"I think they've already figured out that something is up with him."

"Still, I'm not ready to confirm anything."

"You guys are like together, though, right?"

"No, nothing like that. We're just hanging out. And fooling around. That's it."

"Does he know that?"

"Yes," Charley said, beginning to feel exasperated by the inquisition. "He knows."

"What specifically does he know?"

"Ella! Seriously?"

"Dead serious. What did you say to him?"

"I told him I don't do serious and committed, and if he wants to hang out and have fun and fool around sometimes, I'm down for that. Anything more, not my vibe."

"You actually said that?"

"Something like that."

"And he actually went for it?"

Charley shrugged. "He was fine with it."

Ella eyed her skeptically. "Really?"

"Really. Is there food? I'm starving." She wasn't even slightly hungry because Tyler had once again fed her an elaborate breakfast, but she was anxious to get rid of Ella and her questions.

"Yeah, there's food. When is there not food at Mom's house?"

"How about you go get me some?" Charley asked with a saccharine smile.

Ella got up. "Yes, ma'am. I'll get right on that."

Her mother came into the room a few minutes later bearing a tray for Charley. "I hear you're hungry," Molly said as she set the tray on Charley's lap.

"Thanks, Mom." Though she didn't feel particularly hungry, Charley's stomach growled at the sight of chicken salad rolls, pickles, chips and two brownies. "This looks yummy."

Molly sat next to her on the sofa. "How're you feeling?"

"Better every day."

"It's weird that you're up there with him rather than here with us."

Charley laughed at her mother's blunt statement. "Gee, Mom, tell me how you really feel."

"I just did. What gives, Charlotte?"

"I don't know what you want me to say."

"As you well know, Vivienne and Dave Westcott are

friends of ours. It would be unfortunate if our daughter were to hurt their son in some way."

Charley wished it were possible to squirm without causing herself pain. "I'm not going to hurt him. We're friends. I've been very up-front with him about what I want—and what I don't want." Images from the last few nights chose that particular moment to resurface in her mind, setting off a low throb between her legs.

"From all accounts, he wants everything from you. If you're not feeling the same way, please don't lead him on. He's a very nice young man."

"I know he is, and I like him—a lot. I'm not sure of anything else but that right now, and I'm not going to be pushed into calling this something it's not just to make everyone else happy."

"That's fair enough I suppose."

"Whatever it is, it's new, and we'll figure it out."

The arrival of Megan and her sister, Nina, extricated Charley from the uncomfortable conversation. Why did everyone care so much about what was going on with her and Tyler? Why were they all so invested? And then another more unsettling thought took root—what would her brothers say to Tyler today while they had him up on the mountain?

Fresh powder, bright sunshine and fast runs made for a great day on the slopes of Butler Mountain. The Abbott brothers and their cousin Noah were a bunch of crazy bastards, though, so Tyler hung back with Gavin Guthrie, who had confessed to not being much of a skier. "My brother was like them." From their vantage point on the chair lift, Gavin used one of his poles to point to Will, Hunter, Colton, Wade, Lucas and Landon Abbott, who flew down the mountain with Noah, all of them traveling at breakneck speeds.

"I've never seen *anyone* ski the way Will does," Tyler said.

"He was *this* close to the Olympics in snowboarding when he blew out his knee."

They took the lift up to the black diamond slopes, but

unlike the Abbotts, who did two runs to their one, Gavin and Tyler took their time navigating the difficult terrain. Tyler wasn't looking to injure himself when he had to take care of Charley.

"Speaking of blown-out knees," Gavin said as the lift took them back up again, "how's Charley doing?"

"Better every day. She'll be off the crutches soon, and the physical therapist says she's doing great. Of course Charley hates her guts."

Gavin laughed. "Of course she does. That's Charley for you." He glanced over at Tyler. "I have to be honest . . . I was surprised to hear she was going home with you after her accident."

"I think everyone was surprised to hear that, especially her."

"So you guys are together now?"

"I wouldn't say that. Yet." Tyler hesitated for a second, trying to decide if he should "go there" with Gavin, who he'd known since Gavin's logging company supplied the lumber for Tyler's house. That he was about to confide in someone he didn't know all that well was an indication of how desperate Charley had made him. "Let me ask you something."

"Sure."

"When a woman says she's not interested in a relationship, but she seems to be interested in everything that goes along with a relationship . . ."

"By everything you mean . . ."

"*Everything.*"

Gavin smiled widely. "Ahh, gotcha."

"What does that mean?"

Gavin tipped his head thoughtfully as he pondered the question. "Why doesn't she want a relationship?"

"She says it's not her thing. Apparently, she has no interest in marriage and kids and white picket fences."

"But she is interested in you?"

"To a certain extent."

"And you're into her?"

"Totally. Have been for a while now."

Gavin rubbed at his jaw. "Hmm. That's a tough one."

"I know, believe me. I have no idea what I'm doing here. She's like a puzzle that refuses to fit together in any way that makes sense."

"That's got to be kind of frustrating for you."

"It's maddening. We take a step forward, and then she takes three steps back, leaving my head spinning."

"It sounds like she's afraid to get hurt maybe."

"Charley's not afraid of anything," Tyler said with a laugh. "She's tough as nails."

"Everyone is afraid of something, Tyler. No matter how tough they may appear to the outside world." They got off the chair lift and skied to the side, out of the way of others exiting the lift. "Right now, I'm afraid of that," Gavin said, gesturing to the steep slope. "My brother used to tell me I was the world's biggest pussy when it came to skiing, but I never have been able to just say to hell with it and let go of the fear of crashing into something while standing on two sleds and going ninety miles an hour down a hill."

His commentary had Tyler chuckling. "Gotta say I agree with you."

"Caleb and the Abbotts and so many of the guys we grew up with never worried about crashing, but I always did. Still do. I guarantee there's something Charley is afraid of, too. You just have to figure out what it is."

Gavin had given Tyler plenty to think about, but the slope demanded all his attention as he followed Gavin down the steep trail. Despite what he'd said, Gavin was a more than competent skier, but he was right about the difference between those who were afraid of what might happen and those who weren't.

The metaphor wasn't lost on Tyler. Gavin's insight had helped to clarify a few things for him.

Much later, as the sun began to head for the horizon as it did far too early this time of year, Tyler joined the others for a beer in the lodge after the last run of the day. The Abbott brothers and their cousin Noah drank the way they skied, with hilarious abandon and nonstop bullshit.

"One more week, big brother," Landon said as he raised a mug to Hunter. "There's still time to run for your life."

"I'm not running anywhere." Hunter's small, satisfied smirk told the story of a happy man counting the days until he married the love of his life.

Tyler knew a moment of pure envy. What must it be like to finally have the woman you most desire and to know she'd be with you for the long haul? After what Charley had said to him the night before, Tyler had good reason to believe that would never happen for him. And that was a profoundly depressing thought.

"How's it going in your home rehab facility?" Wade asked Tyler, making him realize he'd zoned out.

"Good. Charley is getting better all the time."

"Dude, we're nominating you for a Purple Heart for taking her on," Lucas said.

"No kidding," Landon added. "Maybe a Purple Heart and an award for meritorious service, too."

While the others laughed, Tyler smiled and shook his head. "No awards necessary. It's been fun to take care of her."

They stared at him, slack-jawed and stunned.

*"Fun?"* Will finally said, breaking the silence.

"Well, yeah. Other than the surgically repaired knee that's given her some grief, she's been fun to have around."

"Wow," Colton said, "can we urge you to please marry her since there's not another man alive who will ever like her as much as you do?"

"That's not a very nice thing to say, Colton," Wade said. "She is our sister, even if she can be a pain. Have a little respect, will you?"

Tyler couldn't have said it better himself.

"I don't mean any disrespect," Colton said sincerely. "You know I love Charley. We all do. But we also know how she can be, and all I'm saying is it's going to take a special guy to . . . you know . . . take her on. Tyler might just be that special guy."

All eyes turned to him, and he wasn't sure if they expected him to say something or what.

"Leave the poor guy alone," Hunter said. "He doesn't need us piling on."

"Spoken by the love-drunk future groom," Lucas said, making gagging noises.

Hunter just smiled and flipped off his younger brother. "Someday, my friend. You just wait."

Lucas shuddered at the thought.

"Better you than me," Noah said with a bitter edge to his voice. It was well known in town that his wife had left him under mysterious circumstances a couple of years ago, and he'd thrown himself into his contracting business ever since.

"What he said," Lucas said, pointing his thumb at Noah as his eyes landed on a table full of young women who were watching their table. "As long as there're snow bunnies in need of company, there'll be no ring on my finger. Are you with me, Landon?"

"I'm so with you."

The twins got up and took their mugs of beer with them when they moved to the table full of women. Chairs were rearranged and the women could be heard asking if they were twins.

Tyler watched the scene unfold with a sense of detachment. Not that long ago, he might've joined them, but he was no longer interested in random hookups. They'd lost their appeal for him a while ago. He couldn't say exactly when he'd set his sights on Charley. It had been a series of encounters—once in her family's store, a couple of dances at the Grange, at a party for a mutual friend's birthday, at Kingdom Pizza when they'd both been picking up takeout, in the produce aisle at the grocery store. Every time he saw her, he wanted to see more of her until images of her and her many expressions had crowded out thoughts of any other woman.

"Don't mind if I join them," Wade said as he got up to leave the table.

"I'm with them," Noah said, decamping for the women's table.

"Ahhh, the single life," Colton said. "So overrated."

"Got to agree with you there," Gavin said with a satisfied smile that again sparked envy in Tyler.

He wanted to know what it was like to have the answers to life's most important questions. But even after all the time he'd spent with Charley lately, he was no closer to answers than he'd been at the beginning, which was another profoundly depressing thought.

"The secret to Charley," Will said, picking up the earlier conversation, "is to let her think she's in charge while you steer her in the direction you want to go."

"I don't know if I agree with that," Colton said. "She's apt to come out swinging if she figures out she's being managed."

"You have to manage her carefully," Hunter said. "Subtly."

Will nodded in agreement. "That's what I mean. You know what they say about kids—if you want them to do one thing, make them think you want them to do the opposite? Then they do what you want because God forbid they should go along with your plan. That's how Charley is."

Tyler drank in the insight, trying to make sense of it in the context of the woman he'd come to know quite well.

"Will is right," Colton said, nodding in agreement. "Child psychology. Make her think you want one thing when you really want something else altogether. Her contrary nature will make it impossible for her to go along with what's expected. She'll need to be, well, contrary."

"So you guys are suggesting he play games to get what he wants?" Gavin asked, his tone tinged with skepticism and maybe disapproval.

"Not games so much as *strategy*," Hunter said.

"What do you think?" Gavin asked Tyler.

"Knowing Charley, what they say does make a certain bit of sense, but I'm not really big on deceit."

"No one is suggesting you deceive her," Hunter said. "She is, after all, our sister, and we do love her even if we want to muzzle her sometimes. We're suggesting you approach your dealings with her the way you would a business deal. You negotiate terms and strategize to get the most favorable outcome. I assume you want her or you wouldn't have stepped up for her the way you have. Do I assume correctly?"

"You do."

"Then you have to play your cards carefully," Hunter said. "There's no way in hell Charley would be staying with you if she wasn't into you, too. So you've already won the first round. She's in your house. Now you have to figure out a way to keep her there without appearing to be desperate or anything."

"No desperation," Will said gravely. "That'll drive her right out the door. Charley doesn't like to be backed into corners. She comes out with her fists swinging."

"You guys make her sound like a feral beast or something," Gavin said with a laugh.

The brothers exchanged glances.

"There have been times," Colton said carefully, "when her behavior might be considered feral by reasonable people."

Tyler laughed at that. "She would kill you if she heard you say that."

"What happens on the mountain stays on the mountain," Colton said gravely. "Bro code."

"No worries," Tyler assured him. "Your sister will never hear from me that you used the word *feral* to describe her."

"Oh good, thanks," Colton said with obvious relief. "She's little but she's scrappy, and she fights dirty."

"Also good to know," Tyler said, more amused by this conversation with every passing minute. Then he took a glance at his watch and saw that it was approaching five. "I need to go. Charley is due for meds that are at my house, so I need to go pick her up. Anyone need a lift back to town?"

"I'll come," Gavin said. "I left my truck at the barn."

"Hey, Tyler," Will said. "We're having Hunter's bachelor party Thursday night up on Colton's mountain. Would love to have you join us if you're game for some cold-weather camping."

"I won't be able to camp, but I'll definitely come by. Thanks for the invite."

"Sure thing," Will said. "Good luck with Charley. Not that I think you'll need it or anything."

After everything they'd said, Tyler was quite convinced that it was going to take a lot more than luck to win Charley Abbott's heart. It was going to take military-level strategy, too.

# CHAPTER 12

Riddled with anxiety about the task before him, Max drove Grayson to Burlington to see Chloe on Sunday afternoon. He told himself that Caden would be there, too, which would make this difficult task bearable. This was for Caden. Everything was for him now.

Knowing he would soon see his son, Max pressed harder on the accelerator and cut thirty minutes off the trip.

"If you always drive this fast, you'll be needing a lawyer to bail your ass out of jail," Grayson said.

"Want to see my baby. I hate that he lives so far from me."

"Have you asked her to move to Butler?"

"I've mentioned it, but she's not interested."

"Even if it would make things easier?"

"She's not inclined to do anything to make things easier for me." Max tightened his grip on the wheel. "She wasn't like this before. She was fun, you know? Easy to be with and happy. After she got pregnant? Totally different story. And since he was born . . . Well, I don't know what's going through her head. She won't talk to me, even about him."

"What about her family?"

"We haven't heard much from them since she got pregnant. I guess her parents are really strict and they saw this as the worst thing that could've happened. Can you imagine that? He's a beautiful baby. How can that be anything other than a miracle?"

"One thing I've learned in my practice is that there's no telling why people are the way they are. Why would her parents turn their backs on her when she needed them most?"

"I don't know. I can't imagine my parents ever doing that."

"You got two of the good ones."

"And I know it after the last few months. Believe me. I know it."

"When my dad left," Grayson said, staring out the passenger window, "I remember thinking how *could* he, you know? How could he have *eight* kids and just walk away like we meant nothing to him? I'd never leave a kid of mine. Ever. Even if things didn't work out with the mother, I'd still be there for my kid." Grayson shook his head laughed, but there was a bitter edge to his laughter. "I never talk about this shit."

"I'm sorry if this is opening old wounds."

"It's okay."

They arrived at the tiny house Max and Chloe had rented near the University of Vermont campus. Every time he opened the gate and walked up the sidewalk to the front door now, his stomach knotted with tension because he never knew what to expect. He knocked softly on the door before he pushed it open.

Chloe was stretched out on the sofa. The small living room was cluttered with clothes and baby equipment. A box of diapers sat untouched on the floor where Max had left them the day before.

Aware of Gray behind him, Max resisted the immediate urge to go find his son.

"What're you doing back so soon?" she asked Max in a dull, flat tone.

"I was hoping we could talk. My cousin Gray is with me."

She tied her robe around her waist and sat up, pushing

blond hair back from her face. "What do you want to talk about?"

"Caden. Where is he?"

"Asleep in his crib, and please don't disturb him. He was up all night."

"He's too little for the crib, Chloe. We've talked about this."

"No, you've talked. I couldn't get him to sleep in the bassinet. I'm doing the best I can."

Max went to the doorway of the baby's bedroom and looked in on him, staring at him until he saw his chest move. Then he returned to the living room, where Gray stood awkwardly inside the door. "Come in," he said to his cousin. "Have a seat."

While Grayson took the used easy chair they'd bought at a yard sale, Max carried in one of the kitchen chairs. "I asked Gray to come with me today because he's a lawyer, and he suggested we consider some sort of formal custody arrangement for Caden."

"What's wrong with what we have?"

"We don't actually have anything in writing, and we should."

"Why do we need it?"

"Because, Chloe," Max said, his patience waning, "we're not together as a couple anymore, so we need a formal custody arrangement for the baby."

"You have a number of options." Gray handed both of them several papers he'd brought with him, outlining the pros and cons of each type of custody. "You can arrange for joint custody where you share in all the parenting decisions and costs, and determine a schedule for when each of you will have physical custody of Caden. It could be something like weekdays are Chloe and weekends are Max or whatever you deem suitable for the two of you. Once you've agreed to everything, I can draw it up for you in a legal agreement that you'd both sign."

"What are the other options besides joint custody?" Chloe asked.

"One of you could assign full custody to the other, with liberal visitation, of course."

"I'd never go for that," Max said firmly.

"You wouldn't want full custody?" she asked almost hopefully. What was that about?

"I want Caden to have *both* his parents in his life," Max said. "And I'd never sign away full custody. That's not an option for me. At the very least, I want joint custody."

Chloe turned her attention to the paperwork, seeming to read it over carefully.

"I took the liberty of drawing up a couple of different sample agreements that encompass a variety of options," Gray said. "You don't have to decide anything today, but I recommend you figure this out sooner rather than later. It's in Caden's best interest to get this done."

The baby monitor on the coffee table crackled to life.

Max was out of his chair at the first sound from his son. "I'll get him." He went into the baby's room and looked down at the little guy in the crib, his arms and legs bicycling. His eyes lit up when he saw Max there, and his arms and legs moved faster.

Smiling at the warm reception, Max lifted the baby out of the crib. "Hey, buddy. How you doing?"

The question was met with gurgling and other adorable baby noises that defied description. Max placed the baby on the changing table and removed the heavy diaper, relieved to see that the rash hadn't gotten any worse overnight. He applied the ointment his mother had recommended, stuff they carried in the store, and put a fresh diaper and sleeper on him.

Keeping the baby tucked into the crook of his arm, he carried him to the living room, eager to show him off to his cousin.

"There's the man of the hour," Gray said, smiling when Max entered the room. "Wow, he's so tiny."

"He won't be for long," Max said, gazing down at the little face that had taken over his life—and he wouldn't have it any other way. "The books say he'll be running around within a year. Hard to believe."

Gray reached out a finger, and Caden wrapped his hand around it.

"Look at that grip."

"He's already getting stronger."

Chloe watched them with the same indifferent expression she'd worn since the day the baby was born. It was nice to have Gray here to share in the wonder of the baby since his mother was unwilling—or unable—to do so. Or maybe she just didn't want to share in it with him. Max didn't know, and after months of beating his head against an unmovable wall, he didn't care anymore. All he cared about was Caden and what was best for him.

"So you'll take a look at the papers Gray gave us?" Max asked her.

"I said I would."

Gray handed her a business card. "My cell number is on the back. I don't have service in Butler, but I'm looking for office space outside of town so I'll have service. When you're ready to talk, leave me a message and I'll get right back to you. You can also call my mom's house. That's the second number on there."

"Okay, thanks." To Max she said, "Do you want to take him tonight?"

Surprised by the offer, he said, "I won't be able to get back here again for a couple of days."

"That's fine."

"My brother's wedding is Saturday."

"Why don't you keep him until Sunday, then."

"Are you sure?"

"I'm sure."

Max wasn't about to try to talk her out of it. "Would you mind holding him while I pack a bag for him?" he asked his cousin.

Gray hesitated but only briefly. "Of course." He reached for the baby and handled him carefully, which Max appreciated.

"Make sure you support his head."

"Got it."

Anxious to take his son and get the hell out of the house and away from the woman who had sucked the life out of him over the last few months, Max went through the dresser looking for clean clothes for the baby, but there wasn't much to be found. To hell with it, he'd buy him whatever he needed rather than argue with Chloe about why she couldn't be bothered to wash Caden's clothes. Then he noticed the bag he'd brought back the day before, which was full of clean clothes she hadn't unpacked. He picked it up and headed for the living room to grab the box of diapers, taking both to the car and then returning for Gray and Caden.

"I'll talk to you on Sunday," he said to Chloe after he'd bundled the baby into a lightweight snowsuit for the ride to Butler. He tried not to think about the logistics of six days with the baby in the midst of a family wedding at his parents' house. Whatever. He'd deal with it.

"Okay."

Max headed for the door, wanting out of there. He emerged into the fresh, cold air and took a couple of deep breaths. Being around Chloe these days left him off balance and out of sorts.

"How about I drive so you can ride in back with him?" Gray asked.

Max handed the keys to his cousin. "That'd be great. Thanks."

When they were on the road to Butler, Gray caught his gaze in the rearview mirror. "You think she's okay?"

"Hard to say. I've tried everything I can think of to get her to talk about what's wrong, how she's feeling. I even went so far as to contact the doctor to express my concerns about her mental state, but there's only so much I can do. She's made it clear that she doesn't want to be my responsibility, so what can I do?"

"Nothing more than you've already done, I suppose."

"I'm tired of feeling helpless where she's concerned. And I'm tired of feeling like she blames me for everything that happened, as if she wasn't right there with me when we made this little guy." Max paused before he said, "The funniest part is she pursued me. She was totally into me until she got pregnant, and then the whole thing became my fault."

Max stared down at his adorable son in the infant car seat. "I can't look at him now and see a mistake, Gray. I just can't do it. And that's how she wants me to feel." His voice broke and his eyes swam with tears. "He's not a mistake."

"No, he isn't. He's your destiny, and he's damned lucky to have you."

"I'm lucky to have him. I'm not quite sure how to describe what it feels like to know he's dependent on me for everything. It's like he's given my life meaning or something."

"You're doing all the right things, Max. As difficult as everything seems now, as long as you keep doing all the right things, it'll be fine. I promise."

Max took comfort in those words from someone he'd always looked up to and respected. As Caden wrapped his hand around Max's finger, he smiled, relieved to have the next six days with his son to look forward to. The rest would work itself out. Somehow.

While Megan opened a mountain of gifts and fully examined each one before moving on to the next, Charley was happily relegated to the sidelines as Nina and Hannah, her other attendant, tended to the happy bride. That would never be her. Not in a million years did she want what all the other women in her family seemed to want—home and hearth and husband and babies. The thought of it made her queasy.

Although, despite the queasiness, Charley was astonished to realize she'd actually missed Tyler during the afternoon with her family. Jeez, what was that about? When was the last time she'd *missed* a man?

A sharp pain in the vicinity of her heart was a reminder of the last time . . . Michael Devlin, the man she'd fallen hard for in college only to discover she was one of many women he was stringing along. His deception had hardened her heart, and she'd never forgotten the painful lessons learned during her sophomore year at UVM.

No one close to her had even known about him. He'd insisted on secrecy for reasons that became apparent after his web of lies was uncovered by one of the many other women he'd professed to love. Charley hadn't even told Ella about him, mostly because she'd been embarrassed and made to feel foolish by a man she'd thought she loved. Not only had he broken her heart, he'd stolen money from her, too. How sad was it that the only real "boyfriend" she'd ever had turned out to be a con artist of the highest order?

Ella had known about what Michael had done. The entire campus knew. But no one knew Charley had been one of Michael's victims. Others had pressed charges against him, but Charley had remained silently locked in her own private agony, too ashamed to speak up. She'd believed him when he said he loved her, that she was the only woman he'd ever love, that they were destined for a life together. Because he'd been the first guy she loved, she'd given him the gift of her virginity. Even hearing he'd been convicted on fraud charges a year and a half later hadn't soothed the ache she carried with her to this day.

Thinking about him now made her burn with rage, as if it had happened last week rather than years ago. Michael had been run off campus by a mob of angry women, and she'd never seen him again. But the damage he'd done hadn't been tempered by time. If anything, it had hardened her into the woman she was today—cynical, slow to trust new people and unwilling to risk more than she had to lose. He had stolen her belief in fairy tales and happily-ever-afters. Even seeing her siblings falling for their perfect partners hadn't softened her to the idea of love for herself.

Never again would she be in such a vulnerable position with a man, including Tyler. As much as she liked him—and she liked him a lot more than she'd ever expected to—she wasn't capable of loving him or any man.

That she was even thinking about shit from a lifetime ago was a sign that it had been the right thing—the *fair* thing—to put Tyler on notice about what wasn't going to happen between them. Thanks to what Michael had put her through, Charley handled her interactions with men with an overabundance of fairness and honesty. She never led anyone on. She never let them believe they were going to get anything more than a good time from her.

That was how she'd become a serial dater. Of course the fact that she didn't get "involved," so to speak, was how she'd also gotten a reputation for being easy when it came to sex, which wasn't necessarily true. Yes, she liked sex. She even loved it under the right circumstances, but she didn't give herself to just any guy who expressed an interest. There had to be some sort of interest on her part, too.

Despite what people liked to think about her, in the last five years, she'd had exactly three lovers—all guys she'd had long-term sexual relationships with. There'd been no dating, no promises, no talk of love or forever or any of the trigger words that sent her running. The first two sex-buddy relationships had died out over time. The third had been ongoing until she got hurt, and Tyler stepped up to care for her.

She wondered if man number three knew she'd been hurt or if he wondered why he hadn't heard from her. Probably not. Sex-only relationships didn't include checking in between hookups, which was how she liked it.

As if she'd conjured him from her musings, Tyler came into the room looking windblown and sexy in a black sweater and faded jeans. The sight of him had her questioning her own rules. Maybe just this once . . .

No. No. *No.* Never again.

As Tyler said hello to the others and crossed the room to her, Charley thought about the first date he'd saved for her and how much she wanted to let him take her on a romantic overnight trip to Boston. Maybe she'd allow that much in addition to whatever happened between them physically, but nothing more.

"Hey," he said when he reached her, right where he'd left her hours ago. His gaze drank in the sight of her, paying attention the way no one else ever had—except her mother, of course. "You're hurting."

"A little."

"Let's get you home to your pills."

"You make me sound like an addict."

"You're far from an addict." He retrieved her crutches and helped her up, putting an arm around her until she got her balance.

"Thanks."

"No problem."

Charley looked up to find every set of eyes in the room on her and Tyler, watching them with interest. She wanted to say, *Show's over*, but she held her tongue and walked slowly toward Megan. "Congratulations. You got some beautiful gifts."

Megan got up to hug Charley. "Thank you so much for the place settings and the crystal. I love them."

Charley didn't bother to mention that Ella had handled the gift buying for her. "You're welcome. I'll see you next weekend, if not before."

"Oh we'll be up to visit before then."

"Don't worry about me. Enjoy your big week."

Charley hugged the others on the way out, each of them promising to come visit her in the next few days. Her mom handed Tyler a basket. "You won't have to worry about dinner tonight."

"Thank you, Mrs. Abbott."

"Call me Molly." Watching her mother hug Tyler, Charley experienced an odd sense of concern over the way her family was taking to him as if he were already one of them.

"Thanks, Mom," she said when her mother kissed her good-bye.

"Call me if you need anything."

"I will." It took ten long minutes to reach the mudroom, where Tyler helped her into her coat.

"Let me put the basket in the car, and then I'll come back for you."

"Okay."

As she watched him dash out into the snowy darkness, it occurred to her that by continuing to stay with him she was giving him hope that he shouldn't have where she was concerned. A sense of panic overtook her. She looked back to see if her mom was nearby, but no one was there. Everyone was in the family room with Megan.

She shouldn't go with him. She should stay with her parents until she could return to her own place. It was the right thing to do despite how much she'd enjoyed the time she'd spent with him at his house.

Her brother Hunter appeared out of the darkness and stepped into the house. "Hey, Charl. How you feeling?"

She cleared her throat of the emotional lump that had settled there. "Good."

"I gotta tell you. I really like Tyler. He's a good guy."

"Oh, um, thanks."

Tyler came in the door. "Ready?"

She needed to talk to him, to tell him their time together had to end, but she couldn't do that in front of Hunter. She wouldn't embarrass Tyler after all he'd done for her. But they were going to talk tonight, and she would tell him it was time for her to go home.

"Yeah," she said, "I'm ready."

# CHAPTER 13

———◄◆►———

As they drove up the mountain in silence, Charley's nerves multiplied exponentially. The thought of telling Tyler she wanted to leave made her feel sick. This was exactly why she didn't get "involved" with men. Inevitably, she always wanted out, and it was much easier to escape when there were no feelings involved.

He had them for her, and she couldn't deny she'd begun to have them for him.

"What're you thinking about over there?"

His deep voice startled her. "I . . . um . . ."

"Did you have fun today?"

Grateful for the reprieve, she said, "I did. You?"

"It was great. Your brothers are insane on skis."

"They're insane off skis, too."

"I'm exhausted. That's what I get for trying to keep up with them. I hope I can move tomorrow."

"You're in good shape."

"Skiing always makes me sore the next day. Different muscles." He yawned loudly. "How do you feel about an early dinner and a movie in bed?"

Now would be a great time to tell him she wanted to move to her parents' home until she recovered enough to go to her apartment.

"Charley?"

"Um, sure, that sounds good." He was tired and hungry. What she had to tell him could wait until tomorrow.

When they got to his house, Tyler helped her get settled on the sofa, doled out her pills and then went to heat up the lasagna her mother had sent home with them. They ate that, salad and bread on the sofa in front of the fire he'd lit.

"Are you going to tell me what's wrong?"

Charley nearly choked on her bite of lasagna.

"And don't say it's nothing because something has been different since I got to your parents' house to pick you up."

She leaned forward to put her plate on the coffee table. Her heart beat fast, making her feel breathless. The last thing she wanted was to hurt him when he'd been so good to her.

Tyler took hold of her hand, running his thumb over her knuckles and setting off a reaction she felt everywhere. "Whatever it is, just tell me."

"I want you to know how much I appreciate everything you've done for me."

Groaning, he closed his eyes and leaned his head against the sofa. "Don't, Charley."

"Don't what?"

"Give me the gratitude speech before you tell me it's over between us. You said you were going to give me a chance, but you haven't."

"I'm such a cliché," she said with a sigh, wishing for just that moment that she could be someone different for him.

"What? Why in the world would you say that?"

"Because I'm going to say it is not you. It's me. It's most definitely me. You're great and handsome and sexy and so nice. You deserve so much more than what I can give you."

"I want to understand, Charley. I want to know why you think you're incapable of this when *this* is already happening. We're two weeks into it, and as far as I'm concerned, you're doing fine. I've never been happier than I've been since you came to stay here. I hate that you got hurt, but I love taking care of you."

"You can't love taking care of me," she said, her voice catching on a sob.

"Why not, honey?"

"Because! I told you! I don't do this. I don't do boyfriends or relationships and I *don't* do love. Any kind of love."

"And I told you I'm okay with that. You told me your rules, and I intend to play by them."

Charley shook her head. "I see the way you look at me."

"How do I look at you?"

"Like you want things I'm not capable of giving you."

He raised their joined hands to his lips, setting off a firestorm of sensation that flooded her senses with awareness of him. "What I want most from you, right now, is something you're perfectly capable of giving me."

"Sex."

His soft chuckle made her want to punch him. There was nothing funny about this conversation. "That's second on my list."

"What's first?"

"*Time*. I want to spend time with you doing exactly what we're doing right now—eating dinner in front of the fire, planning to watch a movie and turn in early. I want to take you on that date in Boston, but we don't have to call it a date if you'd rather not. I want to go to your brother's bachelor party on Thursday night—and yes, I was actually invited. I want you to ask me to come with you to his wedding next weekend. On Christmas Eve, I thought maybe you could come with me to my parents' house. My mom does a big dinner every year. Christmas Day is all yours to decide what we do. Whatever you want to do with your family is fine with me. So you see it's not really all that complicated unless we want to make it complicated."

"Everything about that is complicated."

"How so?"

"All that time together, families involved, important events." Charley shuddered. "It would be like having a boyfriend."

"You say the word *boyfriend* the way other people say *herpes*," he said with that adorable smile that set her heart to racing.

"I don't want a boyfriend."

"I don't want herpes, so we're on the same page."

"I fear you aren't taking me seriously."

"I take you, Charlotte Abbott, as seriously as it's possible to take anyone."

"That's exactly what I'm afraid of!"

With his free hand, he caressed her face, gently dragging his thumb over her jaw. "You have no reason whatsoever to be afraid of me."

"I'm beginning to think I have every good reason to be afraid of you."

Still smiling, he shook his head, leaned in and kissed her cheek on the way to her mouth as he brought both hands to her face, holding her in place so he could kiss her more intently.

How did he do this to her? How did he make her forget that she hadn't intended to kiss him again? How did he make her forget that she'd planned to tell him they couldn't do any of this anymore? When he kissed her, she forgot everything other than how he made her feel. Her hand found its way around his neck because she couldn't seem to get close enough to him.

Somehow he managed to arrange them so he was lying on top of her without breaking the kiss or causing her any pain. She wasn't sure how he did that either, but with his erection pressed tight against her core, she couldn't spare the brain cells to figure it out.

He stopped only to pull her sweater up and over her head before he kissed his way down her neck to nuzzle the tops of her breasts. "God, Charley. You're so sexy. You have no idea what you do to me."

She arched into him, wishing she had the wherewithal to tell him to stop. This had to stop. Soon. Soon she would say it, but not quite yet. Not when he was easing the strap of her tank top down her arm to expose her breast. Her nipple tightened immediately, and she held her breath, waiting to see what he would do.

Tyler cupped her breast and ran his thumb over her nipple, making her gasp from the sensations that rocketed through her. "Could I ask you something?"

"Now?"

"Right now."

"Um, okay . . ."

"When was the last time you had a real, honest-to-goodness boyfriend?"

She hadn't been expecting that question and had no idea how to answer it. Did she tell him the truth or make something up?

"Tell me, Charley."

Something about the open, honest way he looked at her made it impossible for her to lie to him. "Never."

"Not once ever?"

She bit her lip and shook her head.

"How have you gotten to age thirty without having had a boyfriend?"

"I've never wanted one before. Except for once, and there was nothing real or honest-to-goodness about that."

His brow lifted, which was when she realized she'd said too much. "What happened that one time?"

"Nothing I want to talk about now or ever."

"Is that why there's been no one else?"

"Partially."

"What's the other part?"

"I've told you before. I'm not cut out for relationships and all the crap that goes with them."

"What crap?"

"You know." She tugged her tank top back up. If he was going to force her to have this conversation, she wasn't going to do it with her breast hanging out. "The dance. The bullshit. The empty promises. I'm not interested in any of that."

"Someone hurt you, Charley." There he went again, pretending to see inside her. "Who was he?"

"Stop." She shook her head. "We're not going there."

"How can we move forward from here if I don't know what I'm up against?"

"I've told you I don't *want* to move forward from here." She cupped him intimately, making his eyes bug before he groaned. "Isn't where we are good enough for you?"

"Where we are is great for me, but it could be so much better if you'd just trust me when I tell you I'm for real here, Charley. I'm not out to hurt you. That's the last thing in the world I'd ever want to do." As he spoke, he caressed her face so tenderly and the way he looked at her, as if he'd give her anything if only she'd let him . . . Though he continued to throb in her hand, he drew back from her, forcing her hand to drop to her side. "Will you do something for me? Just one simple thing?"

"Nothing with you is ever simple."

That drew a grin from him complete with small dimples she hadn't noticed before now. Damn, they were cute and sexy, too.

"What is this one simple thing you want from me?"

"Your brother's wedding, the holidays, the night in Boston. Let me be your boyfriend for the next couple of weeks. If we do all that and you decide this relationship business isn't for you, I'll respect your wishes."

"By respect my wishes, you mean . . ."

"I'll leave you alone. But between now and then, though, you're all mine."

Charley swallowed hard at the implications behind his forcefully stated words. "Between now and when?"

"You want like an expiration date?"

"That's the only way you'll get me to agree to this harebrained plan of yours."

"Harebrained," he said with a laugh. "Ouch."

"Well, what would you call it?"

"Brilliant? Inspired?"

Charley rolled her eyes but had to hold back a smile that was bursting to get out. He was awfully cute when he negotiated a deal.

"You tell me. How long do I have?"

"Until the stroke of midnight on New Year's Day when you turn into a pumpkin."

Glancing up at the ceiling, he did the math. "Seventeen days. And in that time, I'm all yours and you're all mine. No restrictions, no limits."

"Why do I feel like I'm making a deal with the devil?"

His grin was positively devilish. "Baby, you have no idea what you're getting into."

Though his tone was teasing, her stomach knotted with nerves and a tiny bit of fear. In the years since Michael deceived her, she'd never come close to anything like what Tyler was proposing. But she was only potentially agreeing to a short-term arrangement with an expiration date and a get-out-of-jail-free card.

"If I go along with this harebrained scheme of yours, do you promise that you'll step aside on New Year's Day as promised?"

"If that's what you want, you'll never hear from me again."

"And when we run into each other around town?"

"I'll say, 'Hello, Charley, how are you?' And go on with my life."

"And you won't act all hurt and disappointed?"

"I'll be disappointed for sure, but you'll never see any sign of that."

"And I won't hear about your disappointment—or your hurt—from anyone?"

"I'll never speak of it to anyone. You have my word on that."

"What about the running club?"

"When you feel up to rejoining the club, I'll step aside. I've run marathons before. I know how to train for them. The club was about companionship during the training. You won't have to see me every week if you don't want to."

"I already feel like a jerk, and I haven't even dumped you yet."

Laughing, he said, "Has it occurred to you, even for a second, that maybe you won't want to dump me?"

"No, it hasn't."

Groaning, he flattened a hand over his chest and gasped from pretend agony. "You wound me, Charlotte."

"That's what I'm trying to avoid!"

"I know what I'm getting into, and I accept the possibility that you may dump me despite my very best efforts. Is that what you need to hear?"

"Seventeen days, and Tyler, I *will* dump you when our time is up."

"We'll see about that, Charlotte. We'll just see about that." He slid the tank top strap back down her arm. "Now where were we before we were rudely interrupted?" His lips encircled her nipple, stifling any protest she might've formed.

Charley buried her fingers in his hair and closed her eyes. When he touched her this way, he made her think anything was possible, even things she didn't want. Those frightening thoughts faded with the insistent tug of his lips on her nipple.

"Charley," he whispered. "Let's go to bed. Let me show you how much I care about you."

It had been a very long time—hell, it had been forever—since any man had made her *crave* the way this one did. As he lifted her off the sofa to carry her to bed, she realized she was going to have to be very careful not to give him more than she intended to.

In the past, she'd never had any problem keeping the emotion separate from the act. She was an expert at compartmentalizing, and those skills would come in handy now.

He set her on the bed, careful as always to ensure her injured leg was properly supported. Then he began helping her out of her clothes, starting with the tank top that left her bared to him from the waist up after it cleared her head. His greedy gaze took in every inch of skin as he removed the brace on her leg so he could help her out of the jeans she'd worn to the shower. He moved slowly and patiently to ease the denim down over her knee.

"Let's put this back on," he said of the brace.

"It's okay. Debbie said I can leave it off to sleep as long as I'm careful."

He laid his hands flat on her ribs and then slid them to the waistband of her panties.

Charley panicked, putting her hand down to stop him.

Pausing, he eyed her deliberately. "We'll leave them on," he said. "For now." He stood to pull the sweater over his head and then the thermal shirt he'd worn under it.

Charley watched him reveal himself to her, her mouth watering at the sight of well-defined pecs and ripped abs, covered by a nice bit of dark chest hair. A needy feeling overtook her at the sight of him reaching for the button on worn denim. He unzipped carefully, working around the huge bulge, and kicked off his jeans impatiently. While he undressed, he never took his eyes off her.

She had to fight the urge to squirm from the intense way he looked at her, as if he wanted to chain her to the bed and have his wicked way with her.

"Why did your whole body just turn a lovely shade of pink?" he asked as he crawled onto the bed next to her, placing his hand flat against her belly. He'd left his boxer briefs on for the time being, which was a relief. It gave her a minute to catch her breath. "What's going on inside that pretty head of yours?"

"All sorts of dirty stuff."

"Oh please. Do tell."

"I was thinking about how you look at me like you want to chain me to the bed and have your wicked way with me."

"That's exactly what I want. And you say we don't belong together. You're already reading my mind."

"You're a shameless opportunist."

"I have to take the openings where I can get them." His hand slid down the front of her, sliding over her panties and coming to a rest between her legs. "Mmm, it's getting warm down here."

There he went again, derailing her thoughts and making her tremble with desire.

His fingers delved deeper, finding the knot of nerves that tightened as he stroked her. "I want to taste you here, Charley." With his lips against her thigh, his words sparked an outbreak of goose bumps. "Let me taste you." He tugged at her panties, and this time she let him remove them.

She'd never been more acutely aware of her body than she was as he settled between her legs. He lifted her good leg and propped it on his shoulder.

"Tyler." His name sounded like a gasp. "Wait."

"Don't want to wait," he said as he nuzzled her most sensitive area.

"I don't really like . . . *Ahhh, God.*"

# CHAPTER 14

—◄►—

Tyler sucked her clit into his mouth and rubbed his tongue back and forth, which took her right out of her head and into the pleasure. She'd been about to say she didn't like receiving oral. Well, that was going to change. He would change her mind about every goddamned thing in the next seventeen days.

How it was possible that beautiful, sexy, contrary Charley Abbott had never had a real boyfriend was beyond him. She was the hottest woman he'd ever met, and he was determined to make her his forever. But it wouldn't be easy. He would have to overwhelm her on every level so there was no chance she would walk away from him.

And there was no time like the present to get started with the overwhelming, he thought as he slid two fingers into her, curling them forward until he found the spot that made her detonate. There was simply no other word for the way her body exploded under his lips, tightening around the fingers he drove into her repeatedly, riding the wave of her orgasm.

Hottest. Fucking. Thing. Ever.

"Do we need protection?" he asked as he withdrew from

her to remove his boxer briefs, kicking them off impatiently. Her eyes opened, and he saw a curious mix of desire and fear in them that put him immediately on alert. "Charley."

She blinked him into focus.

"Talk to me."

"I . . . I'm on long-term birth control." She pointed to a bump in her arm he hadn't noticed before. "And I'm clean. I've never had sex without a condom."

"Neither have I." He leaned toward the bedside table.

"Tyler."

The tone of her voice had him turning toward her, curious to hear what was on her mind.

"First time for everything?" she asked with a small smile that filled him with an unreasonable amount of hope. Not to mention what her words did to his already hard-as-a-rock dick.

"Are you sure?"

"We're in a committed seventeen-day relationship, right?"

"We are."

She reached for him. "Then I'm sure."

"Ah, Christ, Charley. First time with you and first time without a condom, too? You're not going to get my best work here."

She snorted with laughter that went straight to his overly committed heart. Dear God, he loved her. He loved every freaking thing about her, and he was determined to prove to her that she could count on him to be there for her long after their seventeen days were up.

"Your leg . . ."

"Is fine. Just be careful."

"I'll always be so careful with you." He started all over again with deep, desperate kisses that had her clinging to him. And when she sucked hard on his tongue, he saw stars and had to remind himself he wasn't allowed to come yet. Not until he'd blown her mind a few more times. His heart beat fast and hard, the way it did when he ran uphill. The metaphor wasn't lost on him. He was running an uphill race with her as the prize, and he was determined to win.

If he could focus on the things that worked particularly

well between them, he could gain an edge. The physical connection between them was nothing short of incendiary, so he used every tool in his arsenal to his advantage—lips and tongue and teeth and hands and fingers and hard cock rocking against soft, wet woman.

Her fingers dug into the dense muscles on his back, letting him know his efforts were having the desired effect. "Tyler . . . Please. *Please.*"

Nothing in his life had ever been sexier than the sound of Charley Abbott begging him to make love to her.

He lifted her good leg around his hips, opening her. Giving her just the head of his cock, he watched her face. "Is that what you want?"

*"Yes."* Her eyes widened when he pushed in deeper, her lips parting and her face flushing from the arousal that eased the way for him.

"God, Charley, you're so tight. You're on fire."

"Don't stop. Please don't stop."

Since that was the last thing he ever wanted to do, he continued to push into her in small increments until she'd taken all of him. Her internal muscles fluttered around him, milking him. To be surrounded by her tight heat with nothing between them but desire . . . Tyler couldn't begin to process it all in the moment, not when she was squirming beneath him and making mewling noises that had him wanting to hammer into her. Since he couldn't do that and keep his promise not to hurt her, he slid his hands beneath her to grasp her gorgeous ass, squeezing her cheeks as he began to move, slowly at first and then faster as her hips met his every thrust.

"Charley," he said on a long, tortured groan.

Just when he thought she couldn't turn him on any more than he already was, she reached down to where they were joined to finish herself off. "Fucking hell," he muttered the second before he joined her in the most explosive release of his life. It took every ounce of self-control he could muster not to tell her—right then and there—that he loved her, that he would always love her, no matter what happened at the end of their time together.

Thankfully, he managed to contain the rush of words that wanted out. She wasn't ready to hear them. Not even as her body quaked with the aftershocks of multiple orgasms. Not yet. He would save that for when he really needed it, and he had no doubt at all that at some point, he would really need it.

Her hands caressed his back, soothing trembling muscles.

Tyler raised his head so he could see her face, and the sight of her closed eyes, flushed cheeks and small, satisfied smile left him dumbstruck. He touched a soft kiss to kiss-swollen lips. "That was incredible."

"Mmm. Yeah."

"Charley."

"Hmm?"

"Look at me."

Her eyes opened slowly and looked up at him.

"Just making sure you remember who you're doing this with."

"How could I forget when you'd never let me?"

The husky tone of her voice had him hardening again, as if he hadn't just come so hard he saw stars. For a second, he thought she might stop him, but she didn't. Instead she began to move with him, showing him the second benefit to bareback sex—no time out between sessions. He could get used to this very quickly.

Okay, so sex with Tyler had been amazing. Or she should say it *is* amazing because apparently it wasn't over yet. She'd never been with a guy as big as he was, and had to give props to the person who coined the phrase *bigger is better*. But it was more than his size. It was everything about the way he absolutely possessed her, touching her heart as well as her body. It was his sweetness, his tenderness and the careful way he touched her, as if he were afraid to hurt her in more ways than one.

He was weakening her defenses, and seventeen more days with him weren't going to make anything easier. It would only make it harder to walk away. She'd been walking away for most of her adult life. Old habits died hard, but as Tyler made sweet love to her again, she began to wonder if it wasn't time for new habits.

For the first time since Michael crushed her heart and destroyed her belief in love, she felt a kernel of hope blossoming inside her. And as quickly as the hope appeared, her protective impulse kicked in to quash it before it could take root. She'd made promises to herself years ago—promises she intended to keep, no matter how wonderful Tyler might be.

As he moved above her, beautifully sexy and strong and intense in his devotion to her, Charley wished she were someone different, someone who could accept the things he wanted to give her. But that woman had died on a cold February night as she sat in the university library and overheard a sobbing woman tell her consoling friend that her boyfriend Michael Devlin was a cheating scumbag.

This was not the time for those memories, but they intruded despite her fierce desire to keep them in the past where they belonged. Charley's past was never far behind her, and she'd learned a long time ago that it was pointless to try to outrun it. The painful memories always caught up to her, no matter how far or how fast she ran.

"Where are you right now?" Tyler asked, jarring her out of her thoughts with his gruffly spoken words and the scrape of his whiskers on her neck.

"I'm here," she said, tightening her arms around him.

"You went somewhere else for a minute there, which makes me think I'm not doing this right."

"You're doing it right."

He raised himself up on his arms and picked up the pace, hammering into her with much more abandon than he'd shown her the first time, making it impossible for her to think of anything—or anyone—but him.

She lifted her good leg and curled it around his hips, wishing she could fully participate. It would be a while before she could do that, but in the meantime, he was more than compensating.

His fingers pressed against her core, and Charley arched her back, seeking the release that grew with every deep stroke of his hard cock. "Tyler . . ."

"I'm here, honey. Let it happen."

She came with a broken cry that was ripped from her chest. The powerful sensations brought tears to her eyes and took her breath away. He was right there with her, pressing into her and finding his own release.

"Charley . . . God."

The wonder she heard in his voice was matched by the wonder she felt after having the best sex of her life. Didn't it figure that she'd held him at arm's length for so long when they could've been doing *that* all this time?

"Are you okay?" he asked.

"I'm great. You?"

"Never better. That was . . . I can't think of the right word."

"Fantastic."

"That's a good word, but not quite what I had in mind." He withdrew and moved to her left side, away from her injured leg, but kept his arm around her. "Life changing is more like it."

"That's two words."

"They seem to fit the occasion."

"Tyler . . ."

"I know, I know. You told me I'm not allowed to change your life, but you can't blame a guy for trying, can you?"

She forced herself to look at his handsome face, which was even more so when flushed from exertion. "If I were going to make changes for anyone, I'd do it for you."

"I wish you'd tell me who hurt you and why you feel like you're not capable of being with me this way long term."

"I'm just not. It's not how I'm wired."

"Wiring can be upgraded, fixed, changed."

"Hard wiring can't be."

His hand moved over her body in a tender caress that told her how much he cared. This wasn't only about sex for him, and she had to keep that in mind over the next few weeks.

Trying to take the conversation in safer directions, she said, "Tell me about your business."

"What about it?"

"How did you start it?"

Pausing, as if he wasn't yet ready to abandon the other conversation, he finally said, "It actually started when I was in high school. I took an elective class that covered investing and the stock market. That Christmas, I asked for a subscription to *Money* magazine, and I've been addicted ever since. When I was in high school and college, I had a landscaping business cutting lawns, shoveling snow and doing odd jobs for people. I invested every dime I ever made, and over time my portfolio grew and multiplied."

"What about the crash a few years ago?"

"I saw it coming and made adjustments ahead of time. I was untouched."

"So you're crazy good at it?"

"I guess you could say that." He glanced at her. "I can see your wheels turning. What do you want to ask?"

"Just how much money have you made in the stock market?"

He hesitated but only for a second. "About two hundred."

"Thousand?"

Laughing, he said, "Million."

Charley felt like she'd been electrocuted. *"You've made two hundred million dollars in the stock market?"*

"Thereabouts."

"Oh my God, Tyler! That's insane."

"I've given a lot of it away to charitable causes."

"How does no one know this about you?"

"Because I don't tell anyone. My family knows, and now you know, too. But that's about it."

"Surely you've gotten attention from the industry."

"Some, but I keep it low key. I don't want to be defined by money. If people know, then suddenly that's all they see when they look at me—dollar signs."

"Aren't you in hot demand by other people who want to capitalize on your expertise?"

"My expertise isn't available to the public. I'm not a licensed broker, so I technically can't advise other people. Managing my own portfolio is a full-time job. I don't have the time to take on outside clients, and I don't want to anyway. The way it is now, I work when I need to, and I don't work if I don't have to. I don't answer to anyone, set my own schedule and follow my own rules. It's a pretty good deal."

"I'd say so. My mind is officially boggled."

"Is this going to change the way you look at me?"

"Are you afraid I'll see dollar signs when I look at you?"

"You wouldn't be the first. I've never told another woman the full extent of what I've made in the market, but when people hear what I do for a living, they jump to their own conclusions. It changes things . . . They treat me differently when they realize there's money, even if they don't know how much."

"I'm not going to look at you differently, but I am completely amazed by what you've accomplished."

"Thanks. It's been fun—and challenging. But mostly fun."

"I want to hear everything—how you got started, when you knew you were good at it, when you started making real money. Everything."

So he told her, starting with his initial investments in high school, through his one year of cooking school before he transferred to Dartmouth to pursue his true calling as a finance and economics double major, to turning down offers from all the top banks on Wall Street after he graduated, to running his own business for the last ten years.

Charley hung on every detail, realizing as he spoke that he was freaking brilliant, a prodigy of sorts. "I'm suitably astounded."

"I'm happy to brag about my financial prowess if it impresses you," he said with an adorable grin. "Anything I can do to further my cause."

As she returned his smile, Charley was unnerved by the admiration she felt toward him. Most of the guys she'd dated in the past had barely warranted anything resembling admiration.

"I can't believe your mom works as hard as she does in our bakery when her son is fabulously wealthy."

"My mom loves that job. She says it keeps her busy and active and engaged in the community. She doesn't do it for the money. I took care of my parents and siblings a long time ago. None of them have to work, but they all do anyway. We were raised with a healthy work ethic. I've been working since I was fourteen and started cutting grass and shoveling snow for the neighbors."

"And you're still working even though you don't have to."

"I'm too young to retire. I'd go out of my mind with boredom, and besides, my portfolio requires daily maintenance to remain profitable."

"So what do you do now that you couldn't do before you had the money?"

"Not much. My life is pretty similar to what it was before. Other than the house and a significant investment in the technology needed to run my business, I haven't really spent a lot on myself. I like to scuba dive, so I try to get to the Caribbean a few times a year. But like I said before, I give away far more than I'll ever spend on myself. If I have a family someday, my kids won't know we have money until they're adults. I refuse to raise overly privileged children."

Though Charley's heart fell at the word *children*, she admired his approach to parenthood.

"Why did your eyes just go dim when I talked about my future children?"

"Why do you have to watch me so closely?"

"Because there's nothing I'd rather look at than your gorgeous face."

She crossed her eyes and stuck out her tongue, making him laugh.

"Sorry, still gorgeous. Stop dodging and tell me why you don't want kids."

"I don't know. I've just never had that burning desire to procreate that some women have. Probably because I grew up in a madhouse full of kids, and I'm permanently scarred."

"Nah, I don't think that's it at all. I've seen you with your

siblings, and you love them. I think it's something else altogether, something you refuse to talk about with me or anyone, something that eats at you and has for a long time."

"Stop it," Charley said, far more harshly than she'd
intended. She turned away from him, bracing for the pain
as she swung her legs to the side of the bed, looking to
escape while she still could.

"Charley. Wait. Let me get your crutches."

He got up and came around the bed with the crutches.

Charley took them from him, trying not to look at him in
all his naked glory.

But of course, he didn't let her get away with that. His
fingers on her chin forced her to meet his gaze. "I'm sorry
if I upset you."

"You didn't."

"Why do you feel the need to lie to me?"

She wrenched her chin out of his grasp and hobbled to the
bathroom, feeling naked in more ways than just physically.
Reaching the bathroom, she slammed the door behind her
and immediately felt stupid for overreacting. So he struck a
little too close to home. Nothing like confirming he was getting too close for comfort by acting like an ass over it.

Charley was in way over her head in this situation, and
getting in deeper all the time now that she'd had sex with
him. She never should've agreed to this temporary boyfriend
arrangement of his. There was a good reason why she didn't
have boyfriends, and it was because she didn't want all the
drama that went along with commitment. She didn't want
someone else knowing her better than she knew herself.

After taking care of business, she hobbled to the sink to
splash cold water on her face and to brush her teeth. She ran
a trembling hand through her hair, attempting to restore
some order.

Tyler had left a T-shirt on the counter so Charley wiggled
her way into it, only to be assailed by his familiar sexy scent.
She sighed deeply, the confusion making her crazy. On the one
hand, she enjoyed spending time with him, and she'd certainly
enjoyed the multiple orgasms. Enjoyment wasn't the issue.

When she'd set her life rules for herself, she hadn't banked on a guy like Tyler coming along who would upend her orderly existence and want more than she was willing to give.

He'd asked for a fair chance, and she'd agreed to give it to him. But at the stroke of midnight on New Year's Day, she was done. She could only hope he would accept her decision and abide by her wishes.

Charley emerged from the bathroom to find Tyler wearing basketball shorts and sitting on the end of the bed.

He stood when the door opened. "Charley, I'm sorry if what I said upset you. I didn't mean for that to happen."

"I know," she said without looking at him. She crossed the room to the side of his bed that had become hers and lowered herself to the edge.

He took the crutches from her and propped them against the bedside table where she could reach them during the night.

She got into bed, realizing that it was finally getting easier to move around, which was great news.

Tyler got in bed and turned on his side to face her. "Can we talk about why what I said upset you so much?"

"I'd rather not."

"I get that, but if you help me understand, I could make sure I don't upset you that way again."

Charley sighed with frustration and a tinge of aggravation. "I don't know what you want me to say."

"I want you to tell me what makes you hurt."

"Has it ever occurred to you that you can't fix what's wrong with me?"

"I'll never be able to fix it if you don't tell me what it is."

"There are some things money can't buy, Tyler."

"*Wow*," he said slowly, drawing out the single word. "Low blow." For the first time, he sounded truly angry. "I'm not looking to buy you, Charley. I want to *understand* you, that's all." He turned off the bedside light, casting the room into darkness except for the night light he still left on for her.

Charley blinked back tears. "I'm sorry. I shouldn't have said that."

"No, you shouldn't have, but I forgive you. If you want to tell me what's got you convinced that you're not wired right, I'd be happy to listen."

She'd never told anyone what had changed her forever, and lying in the darkness with him by her side, her body still replete from his intense lovemaking, she wanted to tell him. She wasn't prepared to tell him everything, but she could give him the gist, and maybe that would help him to understand.

"There was a guy. Once." Her words were halting and stilted. She wondered if he could hear the hesitation in her tone. "He made promises he didn't keep. It made me see that certain risks are too big to take."

# CHAPTER 15

———◄◆►———

L ying in the darkness, Tyler finally saw the light. She'd resolved years ago to never get involved with a man again, and by falling for her, in all her prickly, perfect glory, he'd upended her carefully drawn plans. Telling himself to tread lightly, he reached for her hand and was relieved when she didn't immediately pull back.

"I can see how that might've influenced your thinking about certain things. How long ago did this happen?"

"College."

"That's a long time, Charley, and I'm sure the guy was young—more a boy than a man. Am I right?"

"I guess."

"Did you love him?"

"Yeah."

There was no hesitation in her reply, which told Tyler the man in question had done a number on her if the damage he'd left behind had lasted this long. "Will you tell me what happened?"

"It's not something I like to talk about."

"I know, honey, but if you keep it bottled up inside and don't let it out, how will you ever put it behind you where it belongs?"

After a long pause, she said, "Suffice to say I got fed a bunch of bullshit that I completely believed, and when I found out he was a liar, it about killed me. I never want to feel like that again."

"And so you haven't let yourself go beyond the surface with any guy since then?"

"No."

"Could I ask you something else?"

"If you must."

"When your brother Will married Cameron, do you think he intended for it to be a short-term thing before he moved on to someone else?"

"No, of course not. Will is crazy about her."

"How about Nolan when he married Hannah? You think he's going to bail when things get tough?"

"Nolan adores Hannah. He's not going anywhere."

"How about Gavin? Hunter? Colton? In it for the long haul, or are they looking to score and move on?"

"Long haul," she said in a small voice.

"Not all men are assholes, Charley. You happened to cross paths with one who is, but that doesn't mean all men are going to do to you what he did. Look at how long your dad has been with your mom. My parents are the same. My mom made me wish I were deaf the other day by talking about getting busy with my dad. They've been together more than forty years, and they've still got it going on. Your grandparents were married more than fifty years when your grandmother died."

She released a deep shuddering breath. "I didn't see it coming. That was the part that I couldn't understand. I grew up with seven brothers. It takes a lot to pull one over on me, and I had no idea he was stringing me along."

"I'm so sorry that happened to you, Charley, but by

holding on to what he did for all this time, you've missed out on so much."

"Have you been in love before?"

Surprised by the question, he said, "Twice."

"What happened?"

"One of them didn't feel the same way about me, which basically sucked. The other moved to California after we got out of college. I didn't want to go with her, and we tried to make it work for a while, but it burned out. Neither of us was very good at long-distance relationships."

"Why didn't you go with her?"

"My whole life is here—my family and friends. I didn't want to move that far away from everything and everyone else who mattered to me."

"If you'd really and truly loved her, you would've gone with her."

"I realized that myself about a year after she left when I started asking myself what the hell I was doing trying to make it work with three thousand miles between us."

"So maybe it's possible you've never been really in love?"

"Well, there's this third one who's sort of vexing but really, really sexy and cute, especially when she's telling me all the reasons she doesn't believe in love. I could really fall for her."

"You shouldn't do that. It wouldn't be wise. You've already had a one-sided relationship. You don't need another."

"I'm hoping she might fall for me, too. She's given me some time to prove to her that she can trust me to be everything she wants and needs. But she's been hurt really badly in the past, so it's going to take some finesse on my part to show her she's got nothing to fear where I'm concerned."

"You probably shouldn't be in bed with me when you're finessing another girl."

Laughing, he turned to curl up to her, pressing his body against hers. "As long as I have Charley Abbott in my bed, I don't need anyone else."

"You say that now."

"I'll say that forever."

"Forever is a really long time."

"I know, and if I had my choice of who I'd want in my bed forever, it'd be you."

"You can't possibly know that."

"I do know that. I've known it for a long time, actually."

"How does anyone know something like that?"

"How does Will know he wants to be with Cameron forever? Or Colton with Lucy or Hunter with Megan? How did Nolan know that he couldn't live without Hannah? People know, Charley. They just know."

"Tell me the truth . . ."

"Always."

"Did you push me off that mountain so you'd get the chance to tell me this stuff?"

Laughing again, he said, "While I'm not sorry to have the chance to tell you this stuff, I never would've pushed you off that mountain. I died a thousand deaths until I knew you were going to be okay. I'll never forget the terror of that run back to the car, not knowing . . ." His throat closed around a tight knot of emotion.

Her hand found his face in the dark. "I'm sorry I put you through that."

"I'm not sorry you ended up in my bed."

He loved the sound of her laughter.

Reaching for the hand she'd placed on his face, he pressed a kiss to her palm. "It's good between us, Charley. Maybe you can't see that yet, but I hope you will. I really hope you will."

"I want to try," she said in a small voice that told him a lot about what a big deal it was for her to admit that. Charley Abbott's voice was never small.

"That's a really good place to start."

Charley woke in the morning expecting awkwardness with Tyler after the intimacy they'd shared on multiple levels during the night. But it wasn't awkward. He was as sweet as always, making her breakfast and coffee before her session with Debbie the killer physical therapist. Before he left her to go to work, he kissed her forehead and then her lips.

"If you're a really good girl and work hard in your therapy session, I'll buy you lunch in town before your doctor's appointment."

"Oh boy. I've been craving a turkey BLT from the diner."

"Sounds good to me." He kissed her again, studying her in that intense way of his. "You okay?"

"I'm good. You?"

"Really good. Better than I've ever been in fact. I've got a new girlfriend who's sexy as hell and funny and challenging. Not sure how I'm going to think about anything but her today."

"I've heard she's a prickly pain in the ass who's making everything difficult for you."

He nuzzled her neck. "Not everything."

Charley leaned her head away from him, to give him better access to her neck.

"Some things with her are as easy as breathing."

"What things?"

"The way I want her and need her and think about her more than I think about anyone else. That part is easy."

"You need me?"

"Mmm, you've become quite necessary to me since you've been staying here. I can't imagine this place without you anymore."

"What about when I go home?"

"I don't want to think about you leaving. Too depressing." With his fingers on her chin, he held her still for a deep, sensuous kiss that made her wish the therapist wasn't due to arrive any minute.

As she had that thought the door to the mudroom opened and closed.

Tyler pulled back, smiling softly at her. "To be continued."

After he said hi to Debbie, Charley watched him cross

the room toward his office, noting again the superb fit of his faded jeans. When she thought about the things she'd shared with him, things she never shared with anyone, her heart kicked into overdrive, beating at a rapid, erratic rate. Had she said too much? Given him more insight into her than she'd intended? God, she was such a hot mess where he was concerned.

"That is one very sexy guy you've got there, Charley," Debbie said wistfully.

"Oh he's, um . . ." She'd been about to say he wasn't hers, but she stopped herself out of respect for him and the agreement they'd brokered the night before. "Yes, he is."

Over the next hour, Debbie took her through the pace of physical therapy, commenting repeatedly on how much progress Charley had made. "I'll be surprised if the doctor doesn't tell you to put down the crutches after today."

"That'd be nice. My armpits and hands would thank him."

"Just make sure you take it nice and easy at first," she said as she put on her coat to leave. "We don't want any setbacks."

"No, we don't. Thanks for everything."

"So you don't hate me anymore?" Debbie asked with a smirk.

"Oh no, I still hate you. Just not as much as I did at first."

Debbie was still laughing when she went through the door to the mudroom, after promising to be back for more of the same tomorrow.

Charley hobbled into the kitchen to put water on to boil so she could make some tea. She took a moment to fully appreciate the gourmet kitchen that had been designed by a true cook with extraordinary attention to detail. In addition to a huge gas stove, a double oven, spacious black granite countertops, matching black appliances and beautiful tile, the space boasted an incredible view of the mountains in the distance.

She poured boiling water over the tea and while it steeped she thought about how at home she felt here. It was more than the incredibly comfortable and luxurious house making her feel that way. It was him, too. He'd gone out of his way to make her feel at home, and it would be hard to go back to her tiny apartment after the spaciousness of his home.

Taking her tea with her, she took a trial run without the crutches, sitting at the table in front of the windows with the view of Butler nestled in the valley below. That was where Tyler found her when he emerged from the office a short time later.

"What's this? No crutches?"

"Test drive. I couldn't crutch and carry tea."

"How'd it feel?"

"Not bad, which is good."

"That's very good."

"How are things in the office of world domination?"

Laughing at her description, he said, "Humming right along."

"You know what just occurred to me?"

"What's that?"

"You haven't run since I got hurt."

"No, I haven't."

"That's no way to train for a marathon."

He shrugged off her concern. "There'll be other marathons."

"You shouldn't stop training because of me."

"It wouldn't be any fun to run with the group without you there glaring at me."

"I never glared at you."

"Um, yeah, you did. And P.S., you're cute when you glare."

"Well, that's disappointing. I was going for intimidating, not cute."

"Sorry to disappoint, but your claws have always been sexy to me."

"Has anyone ever told you that you might be a masochist?"

"Just about everyone I know has told me that since they figured out I'm into you."

Charley looked up at him, stunned by his confession. "So

they think you're crazy for liking me," she said, irrationally hurt by people she didn't even know.

"No one has ever used the word *crazy*," he said with the adorable smile that did weird things to her insides every time he directed it her way.

"But they think you're crazy for liking me."

He sat next to her and cupped her cheek, caressing her face with his thumb. "I don't care what anyone thinks, Charley. The only one who matters to me is you and what *you* think."

"But your family—"

Leaning in, he stole the words from her with a kiss that devastated her defenses. When he had kissed the fight right out of her, he said, "My family wants me to be happy. They like to tease me about my affection for a challenging woman. They don't think I'm crazy for wanting you."

"You are though. You have to know it's crazy to want—"

Again, he kissed her until she forgot what she'd been about to say.

"I'm crazy about you in all your prickly, difficult, sexy, funny, challenging, gorgeous perfection."

Stunned by an unexpected swell of emotion that seemed to come from the very heart of her, she closed her eyes.

He kissed her eyelids. "You're my dream girl, Charley," he whispered.

She reached for him, and he wrapped his arms around her as best he could with her leg extended between them, cupping the back of her head when she laid it on his shoulder. Regardless of her firm resolve not to get too involved, no man had ever cared for her the way he did. His tenderness set off a wild desire in her to forget the lessons of the past and leap blindly off the high dive into whatever this was with him. For once, she chose to let that desire run free, rather than immediately tamping it down.

While he held her, she focused on breathing, drawing deep breaths into lungs that were suddenly starved for oxygen.

"How about I take you into town to see what the rest of

the world has been up to while we've been in seclusion up here?"

Appreciating that he'd chosen not to focus on her emotional reaction to what he'd said, she nodded. "I'd love to stop in at the office, but I'm not sure I can do all those stairs."

"No worries. I'll get you up there."

# CHAPTER 16

C harley's emotions were all over the place on the quiet
ride down the mountain into town. Her mind raced,
her heart beat fast, her palms were sweaty. If she didn't know
better, she'd think she was coming down with the flu or
something. But it was him and the undeniable effect he had
on her with his tender sweetness, his refusal to accept her
bullshit at face value, his obvious desire for her and the
careful way he handled her. He took equally good care of
her emotionally as he did physically.

She was still trying to catch her breath after their intense
conversation.

*You're my dream girl, Charley.*

Would she ever forget those softly spoken words? Not in
this lifetime or the next. Those words had changed something in her, softening her, opening her to the possibilities.
As if he hadn't turned her entire world on its axis with five
words, Tyler hummed along to the radio as he drove, oblivious to the fact that he'd sent her reeling.

True to his word, he carried her up the stairs to the offices
above the Green Mountain Country Store. It was just her

luck that her family—or most of it anyway—was gathered in the reception area when Tyler carried her in.

Conversation stopped and all eyes landed on them. Awesome.

She tapped his arm. "You can put me down now."

He did as she asked, lowering her slowly to her feet and holding on to her until he was certain she was steady.

"Charley!" Their receptionist, Mary, came around the desk to hug her. "It's so good to see you. How're you feeling?"

"Better every day." Charley wanted to kiss Mary for breaking the awkward silence. "What goes on here?"

"We were just talking about you, Charl," Hunter said.

"How come?"

"We're having issues with the inventory system," Will said. "If you have a few minutes . . ."

"Sure, I'll take a look." She glanced at Tyler. "You want to hang out or do you have stuff to do?"

"I need to hit the post office and bank. I'll come back in a while."

"Okay."

He leaned in close to her, and for a horrifying second she thought he was going to kiss her in front of everyone. "Don't overdo it," he said before he turned and started down the stairs, leaving her reeling once again.

How did he *do* that?

"You okay, Charley?" her dad asked, watching her with that astute gaze that didn't miss much.

"Sure." Taking it slowly, she made her way to her office and flipped on the lights.

"Are you off the crutches?" Wade asked.

"Sort of. I have them in the car, but I'm starting to put a little weight on my knee. Got a doctor's appointment at two, and we'll see what he says. So what's the deal with the system?"

Everyone spoke at once, leading Charley to put her hand up to stop them. "One at a time."

"We added some new stuff," Will said.

"Wait, you *added* inventory to *my* system without talking to me about it first?"

"I wasn't aware that I had to ask permission," Will said dryly.

"Of course you do. You messed with it, and now it doesn't work, thus the need for permission. Come show me what you did."

Half an hour later, Charley banned Will from ever touching the system again.

"What was I supposed to do, with you out and stuff that needed to be added?"

"You could've called me. Nothing wrong with my ears or my mouth."

"Clearly."

"Out. Let me fix this mess you've made."

"She's fine," he said to Ella as she passed Will in the doorway.

"What did you say to poor Will?" Ella asked. "He looks devastated."

"Poor Will nearly crashed the whole system," Charley said, clicking away as she spoke. "And why's he adding stuff in the middle of the Christmas season anyway?"

"You know how it is with the Vermont Made line. Crafters show up with stuff to sell, and he has to roll with it."

"Maybe he could roll with it without screwing up my system."

Smiling at her cranky reply, Ella took a seat in Charley's visitor chair. "So how's it going up on the mountain?"

"Fine," Charley said without looking away from the screen.

"You two are awfully cute together. The way he carries you around."

The comment forced Charley to look directly at her sister. "He doesn't *carry* me around. He hauled me up that huge flight of non-handicap-compliant stairs that lead to our office. That's all."

"That's all?"

Charley hesitated, but only for a second. She needed to talk to someone about him, and Ella would always be her first choice. "Close the door."

"*Ohhh*, this is gonna be good," Ella said gleefully as she closed the door. "What's up?"

"He's very . . ."

"Devoted?"

"Yes. And . . . well, we kind of, well . . . had sex. Great sex. Amazing, unbelievably incredible sex."

Ella stared at her, agog. "How'd you manage that with your busted knee?"

"We were very . . . creative."

Fanning her face, Ella continued to stare. "So what now?"

"I don't know! I agreed to be with him until the end of the year and then . . . I don't know."

"You put a deadline on it?"

"Yes! I wanted a way out."

"*Why*, Charley? Why do you want out of it when you're having amazing sex and that sexy, adorable, *hot* guy is clearly stupid over you?"

"Because." Why did Ella's question make her feel like *she* was stupid for following her own instincts? "I don't do forever. I'm not like the rest of you. It's not what I want."

"And you told him that?"

"He knows how I feel."

Ella nodded, knowingly.

"What? What's that look about?"

"He agreed to your deadline because he's hoping to change your mind. You get that, don't you?"

"I've already told him I'm not going to change my mind."

*You're my dream girl, Charley.*

She wished she could scrub that sentence from her brain, but the words had been tattooed on her memory in permanent ink. Less than an hour after he said the words, she already knew she'd never forget them or the sound of his voice as he said them. "Everything is all jumbled up inside me. I'm turned upside down."

"You're falling in love, Charley," Ella said in a sweet, gentle tone that irked Charley. "That's what it feels like."

She rejected that notion with every fiber of her being—except for the one little corner of her heart that had liked hearing she was his dream girl. "I'm not falling in love. I don't do love."

Ella eyed her skeptically. "Maybe you do now. Have you considered that?"

"No, I haven't." *Yes, you have. Don't turn into a liar now on top of everything else.* She ran her hands through her hair roughly, tugging the strands together into a messy ponytail that she secured with a hair tie, putting at least one thing under her control. "I don't want that. I don't want to love him. I don't want him to love me. I just want to go back to the way my life was before I fell down that stupid mountain. I never should've gone home with him. That was a huge mistake."

"How can you say that after you just told me you're having amazing sex with him?"

"Had. Once. Or I guess it was twice. Whatever. That doesn't make for a *relationship*."

"Okay. So it's not a relationship. What is it then?"

"You want like a label?"

"A label would be good."

"We're friends. With benefits."

Ella clucked with disapproval and shook her head. "What're you so afraid of, Charley?"

*Other than everything?* "I'm not afraid."

"Something is holding you back from fully experiencing this *situation* with Tyler. Note I didn't call it a relationship."

"Thank you."

"So what is it? What's holding you back?"

"Nothing more than a lack of desire to commit to one man for the rest of my life. Just because that works for you doesn't mean it's right for me."

"Do you even know what that commitment entails?"

Resigned to hearing the dirty details of Ella's relationship with Gavin, Charley crossed her arms and set her face into her most mulish expression. "Why do I have a feeling I'm about to hear what it entails?"

"It's the most exquisite thing I've ever experienced in my entire life," Ella said, her expression an unsettling combination of wonder and awe and greedy desire that completely transformed her gorgeous face. "It's like the entire universe has fallen away, leaving only the two of us in this blissful state of unity. That's the only word I can think of to describe it. To know that he's thinking of me every minute of his day, and I'm thinking of him just as much. And at the end of the day, we get to go home to each other. That I get to sleep in his arms every night for the rest of my life . . . I honestly can't think of anything better than that. Can you?"

Unreasonably moved by Ella's impassioned words, Charley responded with humor to hide her emotional reaction. "Better than sleeping in Gavin's arms?"

Ella's withering look made Charley smile. "You know what I mean. Don't deny yourself that experience, Charley, because you're afraid to commit. The worst that could happen is it doesn't work out."

*That's not the worst that could happen*, Charley thought. *It can be so, so much worse than that.* "I hear what you're saying, and I appreciate why you're saying it. But just because that makes you happy doesn't mean I need the same thing."

"Fair enough. But it would be awful to look back someday and realize that by trying so hard to protect yourself you haven't really *lived*."

A stab of fear registered in her chest, forcing her to rub at the spot to ease the discomfort. The grim scenario Ella outlined would indeed be awful.

"I get it."

"But I need to shut up now?"

"Your words, not mine."

Ella laughed. "Even though you're still a pain in the ass, I'm so glad you didn't die that day on the mountain. I would've missed you terribly."

"Good to know someone would've."

"I'm not the only one. I wish you could've seen him that day, Charl. He was like a pent-up panther on the prowl waiting to hear you were going to be okay."

Ella didn't need to use names for Charley to know who she referred to.

"I hadn't seen him like that before," Ella continued. "He's

always so polished and put together and calm. He was a mess, and he was anything but calm. I thought he was going to rip the nurse's head off when she kept telling him he needed to relax and wait for the doctor."

Charley's skin prickled with that now-familiar feeling of hyperawareness at hearing how Tyler had reacted to her accident.

"Landon and Lucas tried talking to him, but he shook them off. He shook us all off until he finally got to see you, and then—and only then—did he relax ever so slightly. But he was still on edge. A guy like that, who cares about you the way he does . . . That doesn't come along every day, Charley."

She was too undone by the picture Ella painted to formulate a reply.

"Now, if you don't feel the same way he does, that's another story altogether. You're absolutely right not to string him along. But I think you do care. I think you care more than you want to, maybe more than you have before, and that scares the hell out of you. I know that feeling. I've been where you are, and I know how frightening it can be to want something so badly. That kind of want makes us vulnerable to getting hurt."

Charley was having trouble getting air to her lungs as Ella zeroed in on the heart of the matter.

"But if you don't take a risk, Charley, you may miss out on the most wonderful thing to ever happen to you."

Charley had to force words past the tightness in her throat. "What would you do if you found out that Gavin wasn't what you thought? That he'd deceived you in some way, made you think things that weren't true."

Ella stared at her, seeming dumbfounded. "I'd be demolished and shocked and . . . I don't know. I can't bear to think about such a thing. Are you afraid of that with Tyler?"

"No."

"Then what?"

"Sometimes things don't work out. That's all."

"That's very true, but sometimes they work out perfectly."

"More often than not, though, they don't."

"There aren't any guarantees. But you have to have faith that the person you've chosen to be with will do the right thing."

*Faith*. Michael had shaken hers to the core, and she hadn't gotten over what he'd done. She could see that now in the context of her "situation" with Tyler.

Just as she had the thought, she heard his distinctive deep voice in the outer office, and her heart lurched at knowing he was close by. She rubbed her chest, as if that could stop the emotional reaction from occurring almost against her will.

"Thanks for this, El. It helped."

"You know where I am if you need me."

Charley nodded, her heart beating fast as her urge to flee did battle with the powerful desire to see him again.

Ella scooted out of the office, leaving the door open. Because Charley didn't know what else to do with her sweaty hands, she returned to her work while trying not to listen to his conversation with one of her brothers.

Outside her office, Tyler found Charley typing away on the computer, her brows knit with concentration. Here was yet another facet of his dream girl, and he drank in the sight of her hard at work. Her fingers flew over the keyboard in a pattern that made sense only to her, and her lips moved as she typed.

Adorable. Sexy. Smart.

He knocked on the door frame.

"Oh hey," she said, her face softening at the sight of him—or was that wishful thinking on his part? "How long have you been there?"

"A minute. Maybe two."

"Stalker perv."

"You're sexy when you type. But then again, you're sexy when you breathe."

"Not here," she said through gritted teeth. "If one of my siblings hears you saying stuff like that, I'll be subjected to a lifetime of harassment."

"I'll try to behave."

"Do that."

"You ready for lunch?"

"Almost. I had to clean up a mess Will made in my inventory system."

"Do you have a laptop you could bring with you to work from home?"

"I don't have one, but maybe I could borrow Hunter's."

"You're welcome to one of mine if you can log in to the system remotely."

"I can. That would help, actually. You're sure you don't mind?"

"I don't mind, Charley."

He'd give her the moon on a silver platter if only she'd let him.

"Let's go, then," she said, shutting down her computer.

Tyler took her coat off the hook behind the door and held it for her. Then he put her hat on her head and tied the scarf around her neck.

"Nothing wrong with my hands, you know," she said with a spark of humor in her gorgeous eyes.

"I like taking care of you."

She had nothing to say to that and shifted her gaze away from his to head out the door. He matched his stride to hers as they moved slowly through the office, which was now largely deserted.

"Heading out, Charley?" Mary asked when they reached the reception desk.

"For now, but I'll be working from home if anyone needs me."

Tyler withdrew a business card from his wallet and handed it to Mary. "The phone number is on there. Feel free to share it with the others if they need to reach Charley."

Mary smiled up at him. "I'll do that. Thank you. Hope you continue to feel better, Charley."

"Me, too. I'm ready to get back to normal."

Her words struck a note of fear in him. The last thing he wanted was to return to the normal he'd known before she'd come to stay with him. Hell, he wanted her to stay forever, but in light of their temporary arrangement, he had to keep such thoughts to himself.

"Ready for a lift?" he asked at the top of the stairs.

She nodded, but he could sense her reluctance. His fiercely independent Charley hated being reliant on anyone for anything.

In what had become a familiar routine, Tyler picked her up, taking pains to protect her knee. "Hold on tight." As he started down the stairs, he caught her rolling her eyes at his shamelessness. But her arms tightened around his neck just the same, and he had to remind himself that this wasn't the time or the place to take a taste of her long, elegant neck.

"Should we go across the street while we're at it?"

"As long as you put me down before we go inside the diner, that's fine."

"Will do."

He carried her around to the front of the store and came to a halt at the sight of Fred the moose meandering down the middle of Elm Street as if he had all the time in the world. People and cars had come to a stop to let him pass, which led to half the town taking notice of Tyler carrying Charley.

That would set tongues to wagging if they weren't already. He had no doubt that it was all over Butler that she was staying with him. For his part, he couldn't care less if the town was abuzz over them, but she wouldn't like it.

Fred strolled past them, letting out a loud moo as he went.

Though Fred wouldn't hurt a flea, Tyler experienced a rush of protective adrenaline go through him as the large moose went by. He would, he realized, wrestle a moose if it meant keeping Charley safe from harm.

"Thank God Fred has reemerged," Charley said. "I'll have to make sure to let Hannah know he's been sighted. She was threatening to go looking for him because no one has seen him in a while."

"I'm trying to picture Hannah in the woods hunting for Fred."

"Now picture Nolan flipping his lid and them having a big fight over it."

"I can only imagine," Tyler said, chuckling.

When Fred had gone by, Tyler crossed the street to the diner and put Charley down outside, per her wishes. Following her up the small set of stairs, he hung back, prepared to catch her if need be. But she managed fine on her own, and he tried not to see that as a metaphor.

Everything with her felt so perilous. It had from that first day on the mountain when she'd disappeared from the trail. He'd been off balance ever since, trying to make sense of what she made him feel while navigating the obstacle course that surrounded her well-guarded heart.

Tyler helped her out of her coat and put it with his on a hook inside the door. They settled in the first open booth while everyone in the crowded diner took note of their arrival, which Charley couldn't see because her back was to most of the tables.

"Are they all looking at us?" she asked in that quiet tone she reserved for when she was uncertain.

Tyler helped her prop her leg on his side of the booth. "Not *all* of them."

"Hey, guys," Megan said as she came over with glasses of ice water. "This is a nice surprise. You're feeling better, Charley?"

"Better every day. How're you? I'm surprised you're working this week."

Megan's pretty face lit up with happiness. "I'm taking Friday off at Hunter's insistence."

"You wild child," Charley said, teasing her future sister-in-law.

"I feel like a wild child. I'm going to be off the week after Christmas, too, for our honeymoon. My sister is staying to help Butch while I'm gone."

"Where're you guys going?" Tyler asked.

"Bermuda. We wanted somewhere warm but close so we don't have to spend two days traveling to get there."

"Bermuda is beautiful," he said. "You'll love it."

"I'm looking forward to it. Do you need menus?"

"I don't," Charley said.

"You're having your usual then?"

"Yep."

"I'll have what she's having," Tyler said.

"Coming right up."

"You've been to Bermuda?" Charley asked when they were alone.

"Uh-huh." He hardly wanted to talk about a trip he'd once taken with an ex-girlfriend.

"Are people still looking?"

Tyler glanced around her shoulder. "Not really. Does it bother you that they know about us?"

"It would bother me if they start jumping to conclusions because we have lunch together at the diner."

"Yeah, because that would truly suck," he said with more bitterness than he'd intended.

"I don't want to have to explain anything. After."

In that moment, he realized she still planned to break up with him as soon as she possibly could. The thought left him deflated. "If you'd rather not do what we agreed to last night, you don't have to wait until New Year's Day to say so."

"Have you changed your mind?"

"Not at all, but if you have—"

"I haven't. I haven't changed my mind about anything."

Her meaning was received loud and clear. She still wanted to have a couple of weeks with him, and she still intended to leave him when that time was up.

Their lunch arrived, and they ate in uneasy silence—at least it was uneasy for him. The precarious nature of their arrangement reminded him too much of the day of her accident when things had been so uncertain. This wasn't all that different, really. That day her life had been on the line. Now he felt like his was. Regardless of all the time they'd spent together, and after the deep physical and emotional connection they'd shared last night, he was no closer to convincing her that he could be what she needed for a lot longer than the next sixteen days.

Somehow he managed to eat most of his turkey club and a few fries while Charley devoured her lunch, apparently unaffected by the disquiet that plagued him.

When they were finished, he paid their check and got their coats.

Megan waved to them on their way out.

On the sidewalk, he said, "Do you want me to give you a lift or go get the car and pick you up?"

"Save your back and go get the car."

"All right."

Disappointed to not get to hold her again, he jogged across the street to get the Range Rover where he'd left it behind the store. He'd known from the start that winning her over would be an uphill battle. After losing himself in her sweet body, he wanted her more than he had before. If only he could figure out what was going on inside her head. Then maybe he'd know how best to proceed.

# CHAPTER 17

CHAPTER 17

E lated after the doctor declared her recovery to be ahead of schedule, Charley wanted to celebrate being officially off the crutches. And she wanted to do something to thank Tyler for all he'd done for her, but she couldn't think of what would be appropriate. He'd been quiet since lunch, and though she wanted to ask him what was wrong, she refrained from posing the question out of fear of what he might say.

"Do you have time for a couple more stops?" she asked, staying in safer territory.

"Sure. Where do you want to go?"

"I'd love to stop in at the animal shelter to see my furry friends. I volunteer there when I can."

"That sounds like fun. Let's go."

The Butler Animal Rescue League was located on the northern outskirts of town, between the road that led to Colton's mountain and Gavin's lumberyard. Tyler let her off at the front door, and she hobbled inside while he parked.

"Charley!" The director, Dawn, greeted her with a hug. "It's so good to see you! We've been so worried about you."

"Thanks for the flowers you sent to the hospital. That was so nice of you guys."

"Least we could do for all the time you've given the shelter. You're not here to work, are you?"

"Not quite yet, but I was hoping I could do some visiting."

"Of course. The animals have missed their friend Charley."

Tyler came through the door, his face flushed from the cold and looking sexy with the sprinkling of dark stubble on his jaw.

"Um, this is my friend, Tyler. Tyler, Dawn. She's the director."

"Nice to meet you," Dawn said, shaking his hand.

"You, too," he said.

When he went to look at a bunny in a cage, Dawn fanned her face for Charley's benefit. "Holy smokes, girl," she muttered. "Come on back."

Amused by Dawn's reaction to Tyler, Charley made her way slowly down the corridor that led to the dogs' playroom, where several volunteer staffers were keeping an eye on things. Each of them greeted her with a warm hug and inquiries about her recovery. She introduced Tyler to them, and watched as they reacted to him the way Dawn had.

Since it wasn't possible for her to get down on the floor with the dogs, she took a seat on a folding chair and let them come to her. The first to greet her was a black lab puppy named Rufus, who'd been returned twice to the shelter because of his high energy level. Charley felt a bond with him. She knew what it was like to be rejected. When she picked him up, Rufus snuggled into her embrace.

"Tyler, this is Rufus."

"Hey, Rufus." He scratched the puppy's back.

Charley watched his fingers move and was reminded of how he'd touched her last night. The memory set off fireworks inside her, making her wish she could cross her legs against the insistent throb between them—all because he'd petted a puppy. Her physical reaction to him was unprecedented. That much she couldn't deny.

"This is Maude," she said of a white poodle that made her way over to give him a good sniffing.

"Hi, Maude."

Because she was female, Maude swooned with delight at the attention Tyler paid to her.

One by one, the others came over to see what was going on. Stud, the German shepherd. Duke, the Rottweiler. Maisy, the pug. Stewart, the bulldog. They pushed and shoved each other out of the way to get at Charley and then Tyler, when he paid them equal amounts of attention.

"They're so cute," he said, laughing at their antics.

"I love them all. I wish I could take them all home with me."

"Why don't you have a dog?"

"Landlord won't allow pets. Someday."

"If you could pick any one of them, which one would you choose?"

"Oh, God, I don't know. I want them all."

"One."

Rufus, who'd been sleeping in her arms, woke with a yawn and a stretch, before resuming the position. "Him, I guess, but he's a handful. He's been returned twice already because the people who adopted him couldn't keep up with his energy level."

Tyler signaled to one of the volunteers. "We'd like to adopt Rufus."

Charley gasped. "Tyler . . ."

"I can keep up with his energy level, and I don't have a landlord."

"You can't just . . . I mean . . . Adopting a dog is a huge responsibility."

"I know it is. I work at home, and I'm a runner. I can give him everything he needs."

As he said the words, he looked directly in her eyes, almost putting her on notice that he could do the same for her, if only she'd let him.

"You don't have to . . ."

"I know I don't." To the volunteer, he said, "When can I take him home?"

"Even though Charley could vouch for you, it's our policy to run background checks on potential adopters, and he's due for more shots at a vet visit later this week. Would next week be okay?"

"That would be perfect."

Charley couldn't believe he was doing this, but she absolutely loved knowing that Rufus would go to a good home. A great home, in fact. Here she'd wanted to do something for him, and he was clearly doing this for her. "You should go to your new daddy," she whispered to the sleeping puppy. But as she started to hand him off to Tyler, Rufus snuggled deeper into her embrace.

"He wants you to be his mommy," Tyler said with a sly grin.

"Are you using the baby to get to me?"

"Would I do that?"

"Yes, I believe you would. You absolutely would."

"Charley," he said in a teasingly disapproving tone. "You think so little of me."

"That's not true." In fact, she was beginning to think far too much of him, and that scared her more than anything had in a very long time.

They spent an hour with Rufus and the others before leaving the shelter with promises to be back next week to pick him up. Tyler had filled out the required paperwork and withstood a grilling from Dawn about how he would care for the energetic puppy. In the end, she'd declared him the answer to their prayers for Rufus.

"You've lost your mind," Charley declared when they were back in the Range Rover.

"Why do you say that?"

"Because! Who decides on the spur of the moment to adopt a puppy?"

"I've been thinking about getting a dog anyway. It can

get awfully lonely up on that mountain, and it would be nice to have a companion. Now where else do you want to go before we head home?"

"I'd like to stop by my place."

"Sure." He drove into town and headed for her house like he'd been there before, which he hadn't.

"How do you know where I live?"

"I don't know. I just do."

"Stalker perv."

"Hardly," he said with a laugh. "I pay attention to you. How does that make me a stalker perv?" He pulled into the driveway and turned off the engine. "Are you going to invite me in?"

"I sort of have to. I'm on the third floor."

"Ahhh, I *love* when you need me." He got out of the car and came around to her side, opening the door for her.

"Hey, Tyler?"

"Yeah?"

"Thank you so much for adopting Rufus. He needs a good home after being rejected twice before. I love him, and I'm so glad to know he'll be with you."

"Why, Charley Abbott," he said, his eyes dancing with mirth. "Is that a *compliment* you're giving me?"

She looked up at him and nodded. "He'll be lucky to have you."

Cupping her face in his big hands, he said, "You would be, too, you know." He lowered his head to brush his lips over hers. "I'd take such good care of you in every possible way, Charley. If only you'd let me."

He was chipping away at the wall she'd carefully built around her heart. One sweet moment at a time, he was making her forget all about why she'd tried to resist him.

"Ready to go in?" When she nodded, he helped her out of the car and carried her up two flights of stairs to her apartment.

"Don't expect too much," she said when he put her down on the third-floor landing. "This place is a mole hole compared to your house."

"It's your home, Charley. I can't wait to see it."

She used her key in the door and stepped into her apartment for the first time in weeks. "It smells musty in here."

"It's been closed up." His gaze encompassed her small living room and the adjoining kitchen and dining area. "This place is *so* you."

"How so?"

"It's eclectic and colorful and girly. Just like you."

She liked his description of her home. "The bedroom and bathroom are in there." While she went through the junk mail that Ella had left on her table, he went to see the rest of her small apartment.

"Charley, you need to come in here."

The way he said that had her thinking something was wrong. She hobbled across the living room to the doorway of her bedroom. He had removed his coat and was sitting on her bed. "What's wrong?"

He reached out to her. "Nothing at all."

Because she couldn't resist him when he looked at her that way, she went to him.

He pulled the hat off her head, unwrapped her scarf and unzipped her coat, pushing it off her shoulders.

Becoming unsteady on her feet for reasons that had nothing to do with her leg, Charley braced her hands on his shoulders. "What're you up to?"

Tyler wrapped his arms around her and held her tightly. "I needed this. Just this."

Charley cradled his head against her chest, running her fingers through his thick dark hair. Standing in his embrace in the waning afternoon light, she thought of something she could do to thank him for all he'd done for her. "Lie back," she said, her voice gruff with edgy desire that she no longer wished to deny. She wanted him physically. It was the rest she wasn't sure about.

Releasing her, Tyler looked up with curiosity. "How come?"

"Just do it."

He reclined on his elbows, propped up so he could see her. Hoping her leg would support what she had in mind, she began unbuttoning and unzipping his jeans, working carefully around the hard column of flesh that became more rigid when he realized her intent. "Charley," he said on a gasp when she freed him from his clothes. "You don't have to . . . Ah, *damn*." His elbows collapsed under him and his body arched, forcing him deeper into her throat.

Charley leaned over him, putting all her weight on her good leg and one arm, while she stroked him with her free hand.

"Holy Christ," he whispered when she sucked on the head before going deep again. "Charley, Charley . . ." His fingers dug into her hair, fisting the strands as he tried to gain some control.

But she didn't yield to him, taking him up nearly to the point of explosion before backing off and doing it again and again.

"Fuck, *Charley . . .*"

She loved the desperate, needy tone of his voice and decided to take mercy on him by cupping his balls and squeezing gently while she sucked him hard.

He came with a roar that echoed off the walls of her small bedroom and filled her with a feeling of feminine power she'd never experienced quite so intensely. She had owned this strong, capable, sexy man, and as wonderful as that had been, it had left her needy for more of him.

Pushing herself up on trembling legs, she pulled her sweater over her head and unclasped her bra. She removed her leg brace, unbuttoned her jeans and managed to fight her way out of them, her boots and her panties in the time it took him to open his eyes to see what she was doing.

She would never forget the way he devoured her with his eyes or how he rose up to remove his own sweater and kick off his jeans before bringing her, carefully, onto the bed with him.

"You never cease to surprise me, Charlotte."

"How do I surprise you?"

"I keep waiting for you to tell me we're done, and then you blow me to within an inch of my life before you get naked for me."

"I'm not going to tell you we're done. Not yet."

"Not ever."

"Not yet."

After setting her injured leg on a throw pillow, he turned over so he was on top of her, settled between her legs, gazing down at her with those eyes that saw her so completely. And while that had once terrified her, she was beginning to find comfort in being seen by him.

"I want to be with you here in my home for a little while. Can we do that?"

"Yeah, honey. We can do that." He brought his lips down on hers, devastating her with the desperation she tasted in his kiss. No one had ever wanted her the way he did, and she was captivated by the way he needed her. She opened her mouth to his tongue, sucking and biting and drawing a deep groan from him.

Then he got busy making her crazy with his hands, lips, tongue and teeth, kissing her everywhere except for the places that burned for him. Her nipples were so hard and so tight that they ached until he took first one and then the other into his mouth, turning the ache into an inferno of need. Her body ignited under his touch.

"Tyler . . ."

"Talk to me. Tell me what you feel."

"You. I feel you. I've never . . . Not like this."

"I know, baby. Me either. Not like this." He kissed her belly and moved lower, opening her to his tongue and fingers. "Sweet Charlotte . . . I can't get enough of you. I'll never have enough."

Just as he didn't hold back with his words, neither did he hold back with the deep thrusts of his fingers or the suction on her clit.

Charley exploded. She cried out from the sensory overload that gripped every cell in her body. She'd never come like she did with him and was still in the throes of it when he pushed into her, entering her in one deep, thick stroke that started a second wave of indescribable pleasure.

His fingers dug into her shoulders as he surged into her,

riding the waves of her release with deep, punishing thrusts of his hard cock.

Charley had never felt anything remotely like this. She came down from the incredible high to find him still hard and thick inside her.

"Hey," he said, smiling down at her.

"Hey."

"You all right?"

"Yeah, I'm good. Really, really good."

"That's what I want to hear. Ready for some more?"

"How can there be more?"

"Oh, baby, there's so much more." His lips skimmed her jaw, finding a sensitive place behind her ear that made her shiver. "I want to do everything with you. I want to touch you everywhere. I want to make love to you for entire nights and then the whole next day, too. I want to live inside you."

Charley trembled again, this time from the force of his words as much as the exquisite burn between her legs.

He began to move, slowly at first and then picking up the pace until he was surging into her and throwing his head back as he found his own release.

She held him tight against her, absorbing his aftershocks into her body.

"I'm too heavy," he said after a long silence.

"You're fine."

"Mmm, so are you." His hands found their way under her to squeeze her bottom. "I know I'm not allowed to say such things, but I've never in my entire life experienced anything that compares to making love with you."

Charley dug deep, looking for the courage she needed to be truthful with him. Didn't he deserve that much from her? "Neither have I," she said softly, so softly it was nearly a whisper.

# CHAPTER 18

———◄◗►———

Three little words . . . Other women had told Tyler they loved him, but never had three little words packed a greater wallop that that soft "Neither have I" did from Charley. He was making progress in convincing her that she belonged with him. But this was no time to get cocky. No, it was time to buckle down and get serious about the one thing he hadn't yet had a chance to give her—romance.

His Charley was jaded when it came to men and romance. It was up to him to show her that not all men were selfish jerks who said whatever it took to get what they wanted from a woman and then moved on when they'd used her up. He'd never been that guy, even in college when he'd had friends who epitomized that guy.

They'd teased him then about being too serious and too focused, but that was how he'd been then and how he was now. He was a one-woman-at-a-time kind of guy, and if he had his way he'd be a one-woman-for-all-time kind of guy before too much longer.

When Charley shivered in his arms, he used his foot to grab the throw blanket from the end of her bed and covered them with it. She snuggled deeper into his embrace, which was exactly where he wanted her. He took advantage of the opportunity to run his hand over the warm, soft silk of her back, letting his fingers learn the grooves of her backbone. At the base of her spine were two enticing dimples. He couldn't wait until she was able to move more freely so he could become intimate friends with those dimples.

His mouth watered at the thought of dipping his tongue into each tiny groove. And just that quickly, he was hard again. Christ on a stick, thinking about her got him hotter than actual sex ever had before her. When his cock hardened against her hip, she moaned. Naturally, that sound coming from her only added to the problem.

"You've got to be kidding me," she muttered.

"Excuse me?"

"You. *That*." She bumped her hip against his erect cock, making him hiss from the thrill of the contact. *"Again?"*

Tyler laughed at the disgusted tone of her voice. "I wouldn't dream of inconveniencing you again so soon after the last time."

Her snort of laughter was his new favorite sound. Well, one of several new favorite sounds. She lifted her head off the pillow to look at him. "What's got you all revved up again?"

He flattened his hand on her belly. "You do."

"And what exactly did I do?"

"I believe you were breathing next to me while naked. That's about all it takes."

"Has anyone ever told you you're kind of easy?"

"I've only ever been this easy with you."

*"Right . . ."* She rolled her eyes for emphasis.

"Charlotte."

Glancing up at him, she raised a brow.

"I've never wanted any woman the way I want you, which is pretty much all the time. Remember when I made you dance with me at the Grange?"

"How could I forget?"

"I had to leave after that because I was a walking, talking

hard-on." As he spoke, he moved back to his new favorite place—between her legs. "I had to go home and jerk off in the shower. All because I had the supremely sexy and exquisitely mouthy Charlotte Abbott pressed against me for five whole minutes."

"You ought to see someone about that."

"I am seeing someone." He cupped her breast and toyed with her nipple until it stood up tall and tight. "I'm seeing the cause of all my problems, and she's doing an excellent job of fixing what's wrong with me."

"What about all the things that are wrong with her? What'll you do about them?"

"I'll take them one at a time until she's no longer convinced there's a damned thing wrong with her. I think she's absolutely perfect exactly the way she is."

"You're a sex-drunk stalker perv if you honestly believe that's true."

He pinched her nipple tightly between his thumb and index finger, making her gasp. "I'm totally sober, and I honestly believe that's true." Before she could come up with another reason why he was crazy to want her, he replaced his fingers with his lips and sucked hard on her nipple, dragging his tongue back and forth across the tight tip.

While he tended to one breast with his mouth, he gave the other equal time with his fingers. He could easily become obsessed with her gorgeous breasts and the pale pink nipples that darkened to a deep rose color when she was aroused. Tyler loved knowing that about her. He loved knowing that when he sucked on her nipple he rendered her mute except for mewling notes of pleasure that came from the back of her throat.

He loved the way she fisted handfuls of his hair and tried to direct him. Always so bossy, his Charley. She was his, even if she wasn't yet willing to admit it to herself or to him. Though he knew she wanted him to move on, he kept up the sensual assault on her breasts until she was nearly sobbing from the unbearable tension that had her legs moving restlessly as she tried to seek relief.

"Tyler," she gasped after he sucked hard on her left nipple. "Come on!"

"What's wrong?"

Her broken laugh made him smile, but he hid that from her as he moved to the right side to continue "torturing" her.

"I want . . . I need . . ."

"Tell me," he said without letting up on her poor nipple. *"More."*

"We'll get there. Eventually."

Her protracted groan made his cock ache from the desire to give her exactly what she wanted, but he wasn't ready. Not yet. He tightened his teeth around her nipple while rocking his cock against her pelvis. Her wet heat coated his rigid flesh, which had him forgetting all about his plan to torture her.

Taking himself in hand, he surged into her with one smooth, deep stroke that made her come instantly. *God almighty* . . . Not only was she gorgeous and sexy and mouthy, but she was the most responsive woman he'd ever been with, too.

As her muscles clamped down on him, he lost his mind, hammering into her with no thought to her comfort or her injury or anything other than slaking the burning need she aroused in him every damned time he went near her.

When she came again, crying out from the pleasure, he went with her, drowning in her sweet sexiness.

"Ah, Charley . . . God, I'm sorry."

Her hand on his back soothed him ever so slightly. "For what?"

"I . . ."

"Fucked my lights out?"

The unexpectedly saucy comment drew a shaky laugh from him. "Something like that."

"Don't be sorry. I loved it."

"So did I, but I didn't hurt you or anything, did I?"

"No."

"Good," he said as relief flooded through him. The thought of hurting her in any way was unbearable to him.

"Can we stay here tonight?"

"What about your pain meds?"

"I have stuff I can take if I need it, but my knee is fine."

"We can stay put if you want to."

Her arms encircled his neck as her fingers continued to play with his hair. "I want to."

"Then that's what we'll do."


They never left her bed that night, except for the twenty minutes it took Tyler to cook a pizza he'd found in her freezer. Working in her small but tidy kitchen, he cut the pizza into slices that he put on a plate to carry back to her room where he kissed her awake.

"What time is it?" she asked as she blinked him into focus.

"After eight. I thought you might be hungry."

"Mmm, I'm starving, and that smells awesome." Keeping the covers tucked in over her bare breasts, she pushed herself up against a stack of pillows. The girl liked her pillows.

When she was settled, he handed her the plate and returned to the kitchen, hoping against hope that there might be a beer in her refrigerator. Pay dirt. She had an entire six-pack of Sam Adams. He opened one and took it as well as a glass of ice water for her back to the bedroom.

"Give me some of that," she said, pointing to the beer. "And before you can object, I haven't had pain pills in more than twenty-four hours."

He handed over the beer and watched her take a long, lusty drink that had his cock standing up in response to the movement of her throat.

Of course she noticed and up went her eyebrow. "Knock it off."

"What?" He laughed as he got back into bed and took a slice of pizza before she finished off the whole thing on her own.

"You know what."

"I'll stop getting hard every five minutes if you stop being constantly sexy."

"I'll work on that," she said dryly, smiling at him.

They ate the pizza and shared the beer, which was gone within minutes, so he got another one when he went to put their empty plate in the kitchen sink.

"That is *so* good," she said of the new beer.

"I had no idea you were such a beer lover."

"I'm not, really, but something about not being allowed to have it for weeks makes it extra good."

"Careful. It won't take much for it to go straight to your head."

She sent him a sly, sultry smile. "I get horny when I'm drunk."

"Then by all means, drink up."

Her lusty laugh was added to his new list of favorite sounds.

Then she surprised the shit out of him when she reached out to tug him closer to her. "What's that look?" she asked when he was curled up to her.

"What look?"

"I don't know what to call it. You just looked at me funny."

"I like that you want me right here next to you."

"Only 'cuz I'm cold."

"Ouch," he said with a chuckle.

"Ty?"

Those closest to him called him that, but to hear it from her . . . "Yeah?"

"I was kidding about being cold."

"Were you?"

"Uh-huh."

"So you wanted me for something else then?"

Her hand moved over his arm, restarting the slow burn. "Maybe."

"Do you think you could handle lying on your belly?"

"How come?"

"Just wondering."

"I could try."

Working together, they managed to turn her over. Tyler made use of the huge selection of throw pillows to put one above and one below her knee. "How is that?"

She looked at him over her shoulder. "Feels fine."

His gaze immediately zeroed in on the adorable dimples at the base of her spine. He wondered if she knew they were there.

"What're you doing?" she asked after a full minute of silence.

"Admiring the view." He ran his hands from thighs to supple cheeks, squeezing and shaping them to fit his hands. His thumbs delved into the dimples. "Did you know you have two sexy-as-fuck dimples right here?"

"Do I?"

"Mmm-hmm." He bent over her to touch his tongue to one and then the other, groaning at the sweet taste of her skin and the way she trembled under him. "I love the way you respond to what I do to you."

"I love what you do to me."

More words added to his list of favorites. Hearing her say she loved what he did to her gave him ideas about things he wanted to do. "Would you let me tie your hands sometime?"

"Are you into that?"

"Only if you are."

"What else do you like?"

He cupped her ass. "Have you ever been spanked?"

"Hardly. I haven't yet met a guy who thought it would be a good idea to spank me."

"Now you have, but again, only if it turns you on, too."

"What else?"

"Toys."

"What kind?"

"All kinds. You name it, I'd probably like it."

"To give or receive?"

"Mostly give, but I'm not opposed to experimentation." As he spoke, he continued to run his hands over her back and bottom, making her squirm. "Hold still."

"I can't."

"Why not?"

"Because! You're making me crazy."

"That's how I want you." His lips skimmed a path down her backbone. "Tell me what you like. I want to do everything with you."

"I . . . I don't know what I like. I haven't done that stuff."

"None of it?"

"No," she said on a long exhale that made him smile as he continued to kiss her back.

"Mmm, we're going to have so much fun." Cupping her cheeks, he let his thumbs delve between them to discover how wet their conversation had made her. "I think it's safe to say you like to talk about it."

Her soft moan was the only reply he got.

Moving her good leg farther away from the leg that was propped on pillows, Tyler lowered himself and guided his hard cock into her tight, wet heat.

Her head came up, and her hands fisted the comforter.

"Easy, baby. Nice and easy." The position made for a tight fit, which had him trembling to hold still until her muscles yielded to allow him in. "Is this okay?"

She groaned and pushed back against him.

"Words, Charley. Give me words."

"It's okay. It's . . . *Ahhh*, God. Don't stop."

"Those are good words." Wrapping his arms around her so she couldn't move and possibly hurt herself, he slid deep into her before retreating and doing it again and again and again until her entire body seized up and her internal muscles clamped down and finished him off, too.

His forehead dropped to her back as he fought to catch his breath while aftershocks from her release fluttered like butterfly wings against his sensitive flesh.

"Charley."

"Yeah."

"You okay?"

"Mmm, yeah. I'm good. Really good. You?"

"I'm great." He wanted to wallow in the scent of her, the feel of her soft skin, the heat of her. But he was afraid to put too much weight on her, so he lifted himself up and withdrew before helping her to turn over. Brushing the hair back from her face, he gazed down at her as she looked up at him, her expression one of wonder and disbelief.

"What're you thinking?"

"That I can't believe what a dirty dog Tyler Westcott turned out to be."

Her comment drew a huge smile from him. "I'm just full of surprises."

"Yes, you are."

"I hope these are good surprises."

"They're very good surprises."

Tyler caressed her face and leaned in to kiss her, loving how her hand curled around his neck to keep him there for a deep, searching kiss. Her tongue sought out his, and he hardened again, like he hadn't just come five minutes ago. That's what she did to him.

Rather than give in to the reawakened desire, he gathered her in as close to him as he could with her leg positioned on the pillows. "Comfortable?"

"Very."

"Tell me something about you that I don't know," he said, his hand moving from her belly to her breast, because he couldn't resist her gorgeous breasts.

She winced ever so slightly.

"Sore?"

"A little. You gave them a hell of a workout earlier."

"Want me to kiss them better?"

Laughing, she said, "That's probably not the best idea."

"I thought it was a great idea."

"You would. And I thought you already knew me better than I know myself?"

"I'm still finding out all sorts of new things."

"Like what?"

"I love that you do this cute little snore when you're asleep," he said, imitating the sound.

"I do not!"

"Yes, you do. It's not all the time, just once in a while, and it's so cute. And then there's the way you set your jaw when you're pissed about something, which seems to be often when I'm around." Again, he mimicked the expression to show her what he meant. "And let's talk about the sounds you make when you come." He shivered. "I love those."

"Let's not talk about that. Ever."

"Why not? They're on my list of favorite sounds in the whole world."

Charley put her hands over her ears, making him laugh. "Stop it right now, or you'll never hear them again."

"Never?" He slid his hand down to cup her, dipping a finger into the well of moisture between her legs. "Never, *ever*?"

"*Ugh*, stop. You're out to kill me, aren't you?"

Kissing her shoulder, he said, "Not even kinda."

# CHAPTER 19

————◄►————

On Thursday evening, the Abbott and Coleman women invaded Tyler's house so they could keep Megan entertained during Hunter's bachelor party. In addition to Molly, Hannah and Ella, Megan's sister Nina, Cameron, Lucy, her sister Emma and niece Simone, and Charley's aunt Hannah and cousins Isabella and Vanessa Coleman were in attendance.

Not only had Tyler invited the girls over, but he'd cooked for them, too.

"If you don't marry this guy," Izzy said as she devoured the pulled pork he'd made, "I call dibs."

"I'm not marrying him." *No, I'm just having astounding sex with him.*

"So he's fair game, then?" Izzy asked with a challenging look.

"I didn't say that."

Izzy pounced on that. "Ah-*ha!*"

Charley wasn't prepared to answer questions about her and Tyler, what they meant to each other or what the future held for them. She was taking things a day at a time, and so far that strategy was working for her. It had *really* worked for her yesterday when they spent the entire afternoon and night in his bed, getting up only to eat before going back for more.

"Her face is all flushed," Vanessa said. "What do you suppose she's thinking about?"

"Whose idea was it to invite the Colemans tonight?" Charley asked, making the others laugh.

"For what it's worth, I think Tyler is incredibly sexy," Megan offered.

All eyes turned to the bride-to-be.

"Not as sexy as Hunter, of course," she said, smiling. "Not even close."

"Ewww," Charley said. "He's *way* sexier than Hunter ever thought of being."

"*No one* is sexier than Hunter," Megan declared, drawing groans from his sisters and cousins.

"Will is *way* sexier," Cameron said to more gags from Will's family members.

"Let's call it a draw," Molly said. "This is a family full of good-looking men, particularly their father."

Charley covered her ears. "Tell me when it's over," she said to her sister Hannah.

Hannah patted her good knee. "There's nothing sexier than the smell of motor oil and sweat on a man after a hard day of work," Hannah said, fanning her face as the others screamed with laughter.

"I can top that," Lucy said. "Wood smoke and maple syrup. *Yum.*"

"Chalk dust," Nina said with a dramatic shiver that got everyone laughing again. Her husband, Brett, was a teacher at a school in France.

Charley's aunt Hannah got up and left the room, heading for the kitchen where she began doing the dishes. Charley got up and went after her, moving slowly on a leg that was getting stronger all the time. "You okay, Auntie?"

"Sure, just tending to some of these dishes."

Charley stood next to her aunt at the sink, drying as she washed.

"Don't let all the lovebirds push you into something you don't want," Hannah said after a long silence. "Marriage isn't for everyone."

"I agree. I'm not so sure it's for me."

"Nothing wrong with being single. Plenty of women these days are choosing to forgo marriage and families to focus on their careers and their own aspirations. You shouldn't feel pressured into doing what your sisters and brothers are doing."

"I don't." She didn't feel pressured, but the more time she spent with Tyler, the more panicky she felt about the deadline she'd put on their relationship. As the end of the year loomed large, she began to wish she hadn't insisted on a time limit.

"People settle down expecting it to be forever, but sometimes it doesn't last and you're left to fend for yourself."

It was as much as Charley had heard her aunt say about her husband's betrayal.

"I'm sorry that happened to you, Aunt Hannah. I can't imagine how difficult it must've been for you."

"No, you can't, especially because I had no idea he was unhappy."

"You guys hadn't been . . . You hadn't had problems?"

"Not that I knew of. One day everything was fine, the next day he was gone."

"And he didn't say why?"

"Nope. What does it matter?" She scrubbed vigorously at one of the few pans Tyler hadn't already washed before he left. "Gone is gone." When the pan was clean and rinsed, she handed it to Charley to dry. "It would be so easy to get caught up in all of this," Hannah said, gesturing to Tyler's lovely kitchen and the rest of his home. "The point is, don't feel you have to jump on the bandwagon just because your siblings are doing it."

"I won't."

"You remind me a lot of myself at your age, Charley. I wasn't in any great rush to settle down and get married, but then I met Mike and let myself get swept away. I don't do regrets, and I love my children very much. But sometimes I wonder what might've been if I'd taken the road less traveled, you know?"

"Yes, I do."

"What's going on in here, ladies?" Molly asked when she joined them, carrying two empty bowls that Hannah took from her to wash.

"Just chatting and washing dishes," Hannah said.

"You should get off your feet, honey," Molly said to Charley. "I'll take over in here."

"I'm okay, Mom. If I don't stop sitting around, I'm going to weigh a thousand pounds by the time this knee is healed."

"You look as fit and trim as you always do," Molly said.

"Maybe so, but I feel flabby and soft."

"If that's flabby," Hannah said, "sign me up."

"No kidding," Molly said. "I want to be flabby like you."

Charley laughed at their commentary. "You two have eighteen kids between you. I think you're due a little extra flesh here and there."

With the dishes done, the three of them returned to the party with fresh drinks to enjoy with the delicious brownies Hannah had baked.

"Are you nervous, Megan?" Lucy asked. Her niece Simone had curled up in Lucy's lap and was on her way to dozing off.

"Not at all," Megan said. "I can't wait."

"When it's right, it's right," Hannah declared, her hand curving over the rounded hump of her pregnant belly.

"What's the deal with this Pig's Belly place you all are taking us tomorrow night?" Ella asked.

"It's where Hunter and I had our first date," Megan said, smiling widely. "It's a special place for us, and we wanted to share it with all of you."

"I can't picture my brother Hunter taking you to a place called the Pig's Belly Tavern for your first date," Charley said.

"It was wildly romantic," Megan said, blushing to the roots of her blond hair.

"*This* I have to see," Charley said.

Megan grinned at her, the picture of happy satisfaction, and Charley experienced an almost painful yearning to experience that for herself. The tingling sensation in her chest was reminiscent of the feelings she'd had in the hospital when the blood had begun to flow to her frozen feet and hands. Only this time, it felt as if blood were once again flowing to her injured heart.

Hannah dropped Molly at the red barn shortly after ten. Molly leaned over to kiss her daughter's cheek. "Get some sleep, honey."

"I'll try, but the little monster is freaking out in there tonight." She took hold of her mother's hand and placed it over her extended belly, where Molly could feel her grandchild doing gymnastics.

"Oh wow," Molly said. "That's amazing!"

"All the times you were pregnant, and you still find the wonder. *That* is amazing."

"I can't wait to meet this little person and watch you and Nolan raise him or her."

"Her," Hannah said softly, revealing previously undisclosed information.

"Oh! Oh, *Hannah!* A little girl." Molly's eyes filled with tears as she hugged her daughter. "I can't wait."

"Neither can I. We weren't going to find out, but at the last ultrasound we couldn't resist, and then we said we weren't going to tell anyone, but you're not just anyone."

"I won't say a word. I promise."

"You can tell Dad as long as you swear him to secrecy."

"I'll make sure no one hears it from us."

"I'm so happy, Mom. I don't know what to do with it all. I'm like a hormonal bundle of joy these days."

"No one deserves that more than you do, Hannah. No one."

"Do you . . . Do you think Caleb knows?"

"I'm sure he does. He's watching over you."

"I think of him every day, no matter what I'm doing."

"You always will, and that's okay. It doesn't take anything away from what you have now with Nolan."

"Nolan is just . . ." She sighed deeply. "He's the best, even when he's furious with me because I'm worried about Fred."

"Fred has been spotted, so go on home to your handsome husband, sweetheart."

"I wonder if Nolan is home yet. He said he wasn't staying up on the mountain because he didn't want me home alone."

"I'm sure he's there waiting for you." Molly hugged her again and got out of the car, waving as Hannah backed out of the driveway. It was thrilling to see her oldest daughter so happy once again after so many years of grief and despair following the death of her first husband.

Molly went inside where she was greeted by their yellow labs, George and Ringo. She let them out in the yard and went to put a kettle on the stove, hoping a cup of tea would soothe the anger that simmered inside her after what she'd overheard her sister say to Charley.

It had taken tremendous self-control not to get into it right then and there with Hannah, but she'd chosen the high road and kept her mouth shut so as not to ruin the evening for Megan and the others. She banged around the kitchen, taking her frustration out on the cabinets and countertop.

How *dare* she say such things to Charley, right when Charley was on the verge of possibly taking a real chance with a man for the first time in her life—as far as Molly knew, anyway. Charley had always been private about her romantic life, and though she dated a lot, she hadn't had a true boyfriend. Until now. Until Tyler came along and inserted himself into Charley's life, refusing to take no for an answer from her stubborn, willful, wonderful daughter.

"Ugh," she said out loud as the dogs came bounding into the kitchen ahead of her husband.

"What's that about?" Linc asked as he put his arms around

her from behind to nuzzle her neck. He smelled of wood smoke and beer.

"I'm furious."

"Uh-oh. What did I do this time?"

"Not you. Hannah."

"*Our* Hannah?" he said, astounded.

"No, my Hannah. I heard her talking to Charley tonight, spewing her bitter shit about men to my daughter when she's on the verge of *finally* taking a chance on a man, or so it seems. I wanted to drag Hannah out of there by her hair and punch her lights out."

Linc rocked with silent laughter.

"Stop! It's not funny. I'm so *pissed*."

"You know how I love it when you get feisty over something."

"This is way more than feisty. This is flat-out furious. I'm stunned that she would have the *nerve* to say such things to Charley. I've watched Charley with Tyler. This is different. She feels something for him, even if she doesn't want to admit it. And now Hannah has filled her head with doubts."

Linc turned her around to face him. "Tomorrow you'll talk to Charley and you'll tell her she shouldn't listen to Hannah on this subject. She's still bitter about what Mike did all these years later, and with good reason. You'll tell our lovely daughter that the only one she needs to listen to is herself and her own heart. You'll take care of it."

"Yes, I will." Molly released a deep breath, trying to calm herself.

"You feel better?"

"I'll only feel better after I talk to Charley."

"You should call her tonight then. Right now."

"You really think I should?"

"From what I've observed, this relationship with Tyler is tenuous at best. It might be better not to let her sleep on a pile of bitterness tonight."

"You're right. You're absolutely right." Molly kissed his cheek, stepped out of his embrace and went to the phone, finding Tyler's business card and key on the desk where she'd put them after he gave them to her. She dialed the number, hoping Charley was still up.

"Hi there," Charley said. "Did you forget something?"

Relieved by the sound of her daughter's voice, Molly said, "I forgot something really important."

"What's that?"

"I heard what your aunt said to you in the kitchen, and I'm so furious about it your father told me I needed to call you tonight before you could sleep on the pile of shit she fed you."

"Mom!"

"What?"

"You don't swear."

"I'm spitting mad right now, Charlotte, and I want you to hear me when I say you should *not* listen to a word she says about men or relationships or marriage or commitment or fidelity or loyalty. She has very good reasons for feeling the way she does, but it's *wrong* of her to inflict that crap on you. Especially not right now."

"Why not now?" Charley asked softly.

"Because! I can see how torn you are about what's happening with Tyler, and you don't need a woman whose husband left her alone to finish raising eight children to tell you all the ways that men suck when you have clearly found a good one in Tyler. He's no Mike Coleman, and I say that without a hint of reservation." Pausing to breathe, Molly said in a calmer tone, "I don't presume to know what's happening between the two of you, but don't you dare make decisions about him based on what your aunt said to you tonight. That would be the biggest mistake you could make."

"I already came to that conclusion on my own. I was so shocked to hear her talk about Uncle Mike in the first place that I just sort of nodded in all the right places at what she said. But I know she's not the best person to take advice from in this situation."

"Good," Molly said, filled with relief. "I'm so glad to hear you say that."

"She loves me, and she doesn't want me or any of us to get hurt. I get that."

"She does love you, and her heart is in the right place, but the only heart you need to follow is your own." Molly glanced at Linc, who was leaning against the counter, arms crossed over his broad chest as he listened to her side of the conversation. "If you're looking for an example of a relationship that works, look at your father and me. Not at her and Mike."

"We all look to you two as an example of what works, Mom. You've set the bar very high."

"Don't worry about our bar. Set your own bar. And though it's absolutely none of my business, I want to say how much I like Tyler and the way he takes care of you. Not to mention, his pulled pork is to die for."

Charley laughed. "Yes, it is. Thanks for calling, Mom."

"Thanks for listening. I was about to explode after I heard what she said to you."

"No need for exploding. It's all good. Love you."

"Love you, too, sweetheart. Sleep tight."

"You, too."

Molly put down the phone and turned to her husband, who watched her with a smile on his handsome face. He pushed himself off the counter and crossed the room to her, eating her up with his eyes. She loved when he looked at her like that, as if she were all he needed in the world.

"What?"

"You. I love the way you still mother our kids."

"They still need mothering."

"They still need *you*. And so do I."

Molly put her arms around him and rested her head on his chest.

"I liked what you said about looking to us as an example of what works."

She held him a little tighter, as grateful today as she'd been nearly forty years ago when he chose her over an Oxford scholarship. "What works better than we do?"

"Not one goddamned thing that I can think of."

"I didn't ask how Hunter's party was."

"Lots of fun, but I was glad to leave the young fools to their cold-weather camping. Those days are over for me."

"I'm glad you came home. How'd you get here?"

"Tyler brought me, Hunter, Nolan and Will."

"I guess you're not the only one who's put those days behind him."

"My boys are smart men. Why would they want to sleep in the cold when they've got a warm woman at home in their bed?"

"Good for them. It's nice to see them domesticated."

"They're thoroughly domesticated. All Hunter could talk about tonight was how Saturday can't get here soon enough for him. He can't wait to marry Megan."

"I'm so happy for him. For all of them."

"Me, too."

"You and my dad do good work," she said of Linc and Elmer's matchmaking efforts.

"I don't know what you're talking about."

"Sure you don't. I have news . . ."

"Are you going to tell me?"

"Only if you swear on a stack of Bibles not to tell another living soul or to let on to anyone that you have a scoop of any kind."

Groaning, he said, "That's a very tall order."

"I know it'll be hard for you, but you have to sit on this one."

Linc took a deep breath and expelled it. "Okay, I promise. Lay it on me."

"Swear to God, hope to die, stick a needle in your eye?"

"Yes!" He laughed. "Yes, to all of it, except for the needle in my eye."

"You'll have my fist in your chops if I hear you telling anyone. You're a terrible gossip."

"I've been well and duly warned. Now spill it."

"Hannah's having a girl."

"Oh," he said on another long exhale. "Oh wow. That's . . . A girl. Well, that's big news indeed, and I promise I won't tell anyone."

She reached up to kiss him. "Thank you. I'm so excited about all these babies."

"All? There're two that I know of."

"Cameron and Will, too."

"*Really?*"

"I'm not one hundred percent sure, but my radar is picking up some signals."

"I'd trust those signals with my life. If anyone knows pregnant, my love, it's you."

"And whose fault is that?"

Laughing, he flipped off the lights in the kitchen and directed her to the stairs with his hands on her hips. George and Ringo followed behind.

After the last of their kids left home, they'd taken down a couple of walls and made a huge master suite for themselves, complete with a fireplace, sitting area and adjoining bathroom that had a bathtub big enough for two. They referred to the room as their reward for surviving the teenage years ten times. The dogs crashed in their beds by the window where they could keep a watchful eye on their best friend Lincoln.

Molly went into the bathroom to get ready for bed, and when she came out, she saw that Linc had lit the fireplace and turned down the bed. She loved that fireplace and the cozy glow it cast over the room. Snuggling up to her husband, she knew a moment of pure gratitude for the life she'd had with him, especially when she thought of what her sister's husband had done.

She and Linc had had their ups and downs, their struggles, their sorrows, especially after losing their beloved son-in-law in Iraq. But through it all, they'd remained steadfast in their commitment to each other, their marriage and their big family.

There was nowhere else Molly would rather be at the end of a long day than wrapped up in his arms.

"Big weekend coming up around here," Linc said.

"Wait till you see the rehearsal dinner spot they chose."

Molly had gone with Hunter and Megan to make the arrangements and had thrilled in their excitement. "It's unique. Not what you'd expect for him at all."

"I'm sure it'll all be great. He's smiled more in the last few months than he has in his whole life. She's perfect for him."

"And vice versa. I had my doubts where she was concerned, but she's overcome them all."

"Your dad is crazy about her."

"Apparently, the feeling is mutual. Did you hear she asked him to give her away in addition to presiding over the ceremony?"

"No! Oh wow. He must be delighted."

"He is. She's a special girl."

"Indeed she is."

"Hunter is getting married," Molly said with a sigh. "Our little boy is all grown up."

Linc chuckled. "So I've heard."

"They're dropping like flies all of a sudden."

"It happens."

"Especially with you and Dad running interference." She ran her hand over his chest and the belly that was still flat when other men his age had gone soft. Not her man. "We should have another one."

He stopped breathing.

Molly laughed at his reaction. "Just kidding."

"Jesus, woman! Don't scare me like that. Whenever you said those words to me in the past, I was holding a new baby a few months later."

Molly couldn't stop laughing.

He turned over so he was on top of her, pinning her down with the weight of his body and his playful scowl. "Only *grand*babies for you, Mrs. Abbott."

"Awww, you're no fun at all. Remember all the hard work that went into making babies?"

"I remember."

"Nothing says we can't still do the work . . ."

"I do love the way you think, Molly Stillman Abbott."

Smiling up at him, she wrapped her arms around his neck and brought him down to her, wanting him as much today as she had the sweltering hot summer day she met him. And she was still hot for him all these years later.

# CHAPTER 20

◄◆►

C harley was wiping down the counters and putting away the last of the dishes when Tyler came in through the garage, the door banging behind him and startling her. She was still getting used to the noises of this house.

He came into the kitchen and stopped in the doorway when he saw her holding a dishrag. "What're you doing? I would've done that."

"No need. It's all set. Thank you for letting us borrow your home, and your pulled pork was a huge hit. My cousin Izzy wants to marry you."

Crossing the big room to where she stood by the sink, he kissed her cheek and tossed his keys and cell phone on the counter, bringing the scent of wood smoke with him. "Tell her I'm not available."

"You will be soon enough," she said in a teasing tone.

His deep sigh spoke volumes for him, and Charley wished she could take back the comment.

He cupped her ass and drew her in closer to him. "I'm not

available right now. I have a girlfriend until the end of the year, and she's the jealous type."

"I didn't mean to hurt your feelings by saying that."

"You didn't. Good to know your cousin is interested. I'm expecting a lonely January."

An emotion she didn't recognize started in her gut and flooded her chest at the thought of him with the gorgeous, vivacious Izzy or any other woman for that matter. What the hell? Was she *jealous*? No, she couldn't be. Charley Abbott didn't do jealousy. What right did she have to feel that way? It wasn't like he belonged to her or anything like that.

"What're you freaking out about?" he asked, his voice a low murmur next to her ear.

"I'm not freaking out about anything."

"Tell me."

She pushed at his chest, needing some space and distance from the overwhelming things he made her feel.

"Whatever you're thinking, stop it. I'm not going near your cousin, or anyone else for that matter. You know you have nothing to worry about, and if you don't know that by now, I'm not sure what I can do to convince you."

Aware of his arousal pressing against her belly, Charley relaxed slightly into his embrace. So what if the thought of him with other women made her jealous? She was sleeping with the guy, after all, so she had the right to feel a little possessive. That didn't mean she wanted to marry him or anything.

"I would give every dime I have to know what goes on inside that head of yours," he said in the low, intimate tone that made her bones turn to jelly.

"It's probably better if you don't know."

His low chuckle was as sexy as the gruff words. "I'd probably be crazier than I already am over you if I knew what you were thinking."

"Probably."

"Let's go to bed, the one place where nothing between us is complicated."

Since she could hardly argue that point, she nodded. And when he picked her up to carry her to bed, Charley snuggled up against him, determined to enjoy every minute with him before their time together ran out.

On Friday night, the Abbott family gathered with Megan's family and other friends for the rehearsal dinner at the Pig's Belly Tavern. Charley hadn't known what to expect when she heard the name of the place where the dinner would be held, but Hunter and Megan had assured them that they would love the food and the atmosphere.

In addition to immediate family, Cameron's dad, Patrick Murphy, had been invited as had Lucy's dad, Ray Mulvaney, as well as Emma and Simone, who were all now unofficial members of the Abbott family. A few of Hunter's college friends were there as well as the Sultans, the group of Caleb Guthrie's closest friends, which included Hunter, Will and Nolan.

Attending on Megan's side were her sister Nina and brother-in-law Brett as well as Butch from the diner and many of the patrons who'd become friends over the years.

As he greeted guests and laughed with his friends, Hunter looked as relaxed and happy as Charley had ever seen him. He kept an arm around Megan at all times, and the bride-to-be glowed with the kind of happiness that Charley could only imagine. It had taken, she knew, a huge leap of faith for Megan to end up where she was tonight, and Charley admired anyone who had the courage to take that leap.

"They look really happy," Tyler said in the intimate tone that Charley was becoming accustomed to. They were seated at a table with Ella and Gavin, Gavin's parents and two of the Sultans—Austin and his wife, Debra, and Dylan and his new wife, Sophia.

"I was just thinking the same thing," Charley said to Tyler.

She'd no sooner gotten the words out of her mouth when Jack, one of the perpetually single Sultans, came over to their table to talk to the others.

As he caught up with Dylan and Austin, Charley avoided Jack's pointed stare at the arm Tyler had around her. They'd had a brief fling years ago, right after Caleb died when her emotions had been raw, and she'd been looking for an outlet—any outlet—from the relentless pain of a loss that had left her and the rest of her family flattened by grief.

Though she hadn't slept with him in years, he always flirted with her when they saw each other, and she didn't appreciate the possessive way he looked at her now.

Apparently, Tyler didn't either. The hand he had on her shoulder tightened as Jack continued to stare at them.

"What's up with him?" Tyler asked.

"Nothing," she said. "Now."

"Ah, I see."

"No, you don't see anything, because there's nothing to see."

"But there was? At one time?"

"Eons ago."

"Am I allowed to invite him outside where I'll ask him to keep his dirty eyes off you?"

"You're absolutely *not* allowed to do that."

"I won't, but I want to."

"Thank you for restraining yourself."

He didn't reply but his grip on her shoulder got tighter, and a tingle between her legs took her by surprise. Was she turned on by his possessiveness? Maybe just a little . . .

They ate a delicious meal that consisted of every kind of barbecued meat and all the sides. Despite her worries about gaining weight through inactivity, Charley had a second piece of corn bread. Tyler kept a cold beer in front of her and made sure she had what she needed, the way he always did.

After dinner, a band in the back room started to play, drawing everyone toward the music.

"Who's that dancing with Mary from your office? He looks familiar."

"Cameron's dad, Patrick Murphy."

"*The* Patrick Murphy? The billionaire?"

"Yep."

"How did I miss that he's Cameron's dad? That guy is a legend in my world. Totally self-made and one of the most brilliant financial minds of our time."

"Sounds like someone else I know."

"Aw, baby, I've got nothing on him. You've got to introduce me."

"I will," she said, intrigued by his interest in meeting Cam's dad. The opportunity presented itself an hour later when the band took a break and Patrick led Mary to the table next to where Charley sat with Tyler. "Patrick, I'd like you to meet my friend, Tyler Westcott. He's a big fan of yours."

Patrick reached across the aisle between the tables to shake Tyler's hand. "Pleasure. Why do I know your name?"

"Uh . . ."

"He's a stock market whiz kid," Charley said because Tyler had gone mute.

"That's it! I read about you in *Fortune* a couple of months ago."

"I'm surprised you still read *Fortune*," Tyler said when he recovered his ability to speak. "You wrote the book."

"There's always something new to be learned from others," Patrick said modestly.

He and Mary got up to join Tyler and Charley at their table so the two men could talk without shouting. Mary ended up next to Charley.

"What's the story, Ms. Mary?" Charley asked in an exaggerated whisper. "You and Patrick?"

"We're friends," she said, but her bright eyes and brighter smile indicated there was more than friendship between them. "He'd like it to be more, but so far, we're all about the phone calls."

"Mary! I had no idea. How long has this been going on?"

"Since Will and Cameron's wedding in October, but please don't make it into something it's not, Charley," she said as some of the magic in her expression seemed to dim. "I was sitting at my desk yesterday, and the whole building started to shake. It was *him*. Arriving on his gigantic helicopter." Mary shook her head. "What could possibly come of it? Our lives couldn't be more different."

Regardless of her own thoughts about love and commitment,

Charley found herself wanting to encourage Mary. "You don't know that unless you try, do you?"

"Look at him," Mary whispered. "He could have anyone."

As she said the words, Patrick reached for Mary's hand under the table without missing a beat in his conversation with Tyler.

Mary's face lit up with pleasure—and befuddlement.

"Seems to me that you're the one he wants," Charley said.

"He thinks so now, but what about a couple of months from now? What happens then?"

"I suppose you won't know if you don't try."

"And what about you?" Mary's brow lifted. "Are you prepared to take your own advice?"

"Oh . . . Well . . . That's different."

"Is it?"

"I guess not," Charley conceded.

Mary smiled warmly. "Vivienne is a close friend of mine. I've known their family for years. You simply couldn't ask for better people. She's so proud of Tyler and all he's accomplished."

"So you know then? About the money?"

"I do, and if *you* know about it, that means something. He doesn't talk about it."

"Our situations are not all that dissimilar."

"Except that Tyler lives here, and Patrick's in New York—a place I haven't even visited. He'd like to change that, but there's something holding me back. I don't know. I just don't know."

"I understand that feeling."

Mary looked down at Patrick's hand, which was wrapped around hers. "What if we were to make a deal, you and me?"

"What kind of deal?"

"That if I try—really and truly try with Patrick—you'll do the same with Tyler. We'll hold each other up and take the leap together. What do you say?"

"Oh, I, um . . . I don't know if I can. I've started to feel like I might want to, but I don't know how."

Mary laughed. "Neither do I. I haven't the first clue what I'm doing, but he's worn me down."

"Sounds like he and Tyler have more in common than their financial prowess."

"I'm to the point now where I know if I don't at least try, I'll spend the rest of my life wondering what if. What if I'd had the guts? What if I'd put aside my fears and gone after what I wanted, when it might not be what I need? What if? What if?"

Charley's chest tightened. She glanced across the table and looked at Tyler. Tonight he'd worn one of those pressed dress shirts she used to disdain. His hair had gotten long in the weeks since her accident, and he hadn't bothered to shave in a day or two. His contacts had been bothering him earlier, so he'd worn the sexy black-framed glasses. As her body zinged with awareness of him, she tried to remember why she'd thought he resembled Hunter.

Other than a similar taste in shirts and a bent toward honorableness, there really was no comparison between them.

"What if indeed," Charley said in reply to Mary.

"I don't want to have regrets, Charley. Do you?"

Charley shook her head. "No, I don't."

Tyler glanced over at her and found her staring at him.

His mouth lifted into a small, intimate smile that fanned the fire burning inside her. Then Tyler was shaking hands with Patrick and getting up to come to Charley.

"Let's dance," he said, helping her up and matching her pace on the way to the dance floor.

The band played a slow song that Charley didn't immediately recognize. They walked slowly to the back room, where the dance floor was crowded with couples surrounding Hunter and Megan—her parents, Will and Cameron, Ella and Gavin, Gavin's parents, Lucy and Colton, Hannah and Nolan, Dylan and Sophia, Austin and Debra.

Tyler put his arms around Charley and drew her in close to him, hardly moving as they swayed to the music.

"What song is this? I haven't heard it."

"'Thinking Out Loud' by Ed Sheeran."

"I like it."

His lips found the spot behind her ear that made her go weak in his arms. "I like it, too. It's how I feel when I'm with you."

The song was about finding love right where you are.

"Does your knee feel okay?"

Charley nodded.

"Good, because I couldn't wait another minute to hold you."

"You didn't enjoy talking to Patrick?"

"I loved talking to him, but I wanted to get back to you."

Patrick had lured Mary to the dance floor, and she floated in his arms, her eyes closed as he whispered in her ear.

Charley hoped they'd make a go of it somehow. She liked him for Mary, who'd been single as long as Charley had known her.

One song became two and two became three.

"We should take a break," Tyler said. "You don't want you to overdo it."

Only because her knee was beginning to ache did Charley nod in agreement. But she was nowhere near done with wanting to dance with him.

They were on the way back to the table when Megan waylaid them. "Could I borrow Charley for just a minute?"

"Sure, but make her sit down."

"I will." Megan hooked her arm through Charley's and led her away from the noise.

They sat together at a table.

"What's up?" Charley asked.

"I have something for you, and it may seem kind of weird, but well . . . They have very romantic rooms upstairs, and they gave us keys to two of them as part of the package for having our rehearsal dinner here. Hunter and I are going to take one of them, and I thought you might want the other one."

Charley glanced at the keycard that Megan held in her hand. "Wow, why me?"

"Because you've been through such an ordeal with your knee. And I saw you and Tyler dancing, and you two seem so well suited for each other. Oh, Charley, I don't know," she said with a laugh. "I'm so damned happy, and I just want everyone we love to be as happy as we are. If I'm overstepping, please feel free to say so. I'm sure I can find someone to take the other room."

Charley thought about what Mary had said about regrets and what her mother had said about following her own heart. She took the keycard that Megan offered. "Thank you for thinking of us."

"I hope you enjoy it as much as Hunter and I did the first time we came here."

"I'm sure we will." Charley hugged Megan. "Welcome to the family, Megan. I'm so thrilled for you and Hunter."

"Thank you. I'm rather thrilled for us, too."

Charley laughed at the stupidly happy smile on Megan's face. She bore little resemblance to the grim, humorless woman she'd been before she fell in love with Hunter and found her bliss. "I'd better go find Tyler and tell him the good news."

"You think he'll like your surprise?"

"Oh, I know he will."

"He's really cute, Charley, and he always has you in his sights."

She looked over to where he sat with Will, Cameron, Patrick and Mary to discover that what Megan said was true. He was engaged in conversation but keeping watch over her at the same time.

"Could I say something that may be way out of line, considering we don't know each other all that well?" Megan said tentatively.

"Of course. We're going to be family after tomorrow. I hope we'll also be friends."

Megan blinked rapidly and fanned her face. "Wow, I'm a hot emotional mess tonight, but I hope so, too."

Smiling, Charley squeezed Megan's arm. "What do you want to say?"

Megan sought out Hunter, across the room with his friends, laughing at something Jack was telling them. "I fought it tooth and nail."

"You fought what?"

She brought her blue-eyed gaze back to Charley. "Him. Us. What I felt. All of it. I didn't believe it was possible that something so good could actually be real."

Riveted by what Megan was saying as well as the parallels to her own situation, Charley took a deep breath. "What were you afraid of?"

"*Everything*," she said with a tremulous laugh. "Every damned thing. After I lost my parents, I decided it was easier to avoid feeling anything for anyone. That way nothing could ever hurt me again. I hid behind an impossible crush on Will that kept me from taking a risk with anyone else. With hindsight, I can see I was living half a life by hiding out."

The statement struck perilously close to home for Charley.

"But Hunter . . . He wore me down. One day at a time, one hour at a time. He never wavered in how he felt or in what he wanted from me." Megan looked at him again, and this time he caught her eye.

*You'd have to be blind to miss their intense connection,* Charley thought, feeling as if she were intruding on a personal moment between her brother and his fiancée.

"And then he got hurt so badly that day on the rock, and I realized how easily I could've lost him. That brought everything into focus. I don't know if any of this helps you, but I wanted you to know that I've been where you are, and I know how hard it can be to take a chance."

"You're awfully observant to say you're the new girl around here," Charley said with a teasing smile.

"I hope I haven't said too much."

"Not at all. I appreciate everything you said, and you're more on target than you could possibly imagine."

"I'm still afraid," Megan said softly. "I worry all the time about something happening to him . . . I feel like I could handle just about anything except for that. But I've decided I'd rather be a little afraid than live without him."

Charley hugged her. "Nothing's going to happen to him. He's made of hearty Abbott stock, and it takes a lot to keep us down, even when we fall off a mountain."

Megan laughed, and when they drew back from each other, Charley saw tears in the other woman's eyes. "Thank you for that. It means a lot."

"I hope you have the most wonderfully magical day of your life tomorrow. You certainly deserve nothing less."

"It'll be magic because I get to marry him. That's the only part that matters to me."

Hunter came across the room to them. "What're you two up to over here? You're not trying to talk her out of marrying me, are you, Charley?"

"As if that's even possible. For some strange reason, she's totally into you."

Megan laughed at their sibling bickering.

Hunter squeezed Charley's shoulder. "I'm glad you're feeling better and able to be here with us this weekend."

She covered the hand he'd left on her shoulder. "I wouldn't have missed it for anything."

"I need to dance with my soon-to-be wife." As they exchanged another of those heated looks, he helped Megan up from her chair and guided her to the dance floor.

# CHAPTER 21

Charley watched as Hunter took Megan into his arms and closed his eyes. Then someone was tapping on her shoulder, and she looked up to find Tyler giving her the same sort of look Hunter had given Megan—needy, desperate, affectionate, loving. He conveyed so much with one heated stare.

"How you doing?" he asked.

"I'm good. You?"

"This is a great time. Your family is awesome."

"I know."

"And Hunter and Megan . . . They're so happy."

"They really are." She crooked her finger at him, and he bent down so she could talk only to him. "I have a surprise for you."

"Oh yeah? What's that?"

"From what I'm told, there're rooms upstairs. Megan gave me a key to one of them."

"Really? Well . . ." He cleared his throat as he sank down into the chair next to hers. "And you had to tell me that when we're surrounded by your family?"

She glanced at his crotch, found him fully erect and began to laugh.

"It's not funny."

"Yes, it really is."

"How soon can we check out this room upstairs?"

Charley took a good look around, taking inventory of family and friends. "I'll go to the ladies' room and then go upstairs. You come in a few minutes."

"I'll come all right."

"Tyler," she said, laughing. "Stop."

"That's not what you'll be saying in a few minutes." He leaned in to kiss her neck. "Can you handle the stairs on your own?"

Flustered by his words and the kiss to her neck, she said, "I think so."

"Take your time and don't hurt anything."

"I will. I mean I won't. I mean . . . I don't know what I mean."

Her befuddlement made him laugh. "Go on then."

She looked down at the keycard. "Room Three."

"Got it."

Charley got up and hobbled toward the lobby, feeling like everyone was watching her and knew what she was up to, when in fact only Megan and Tyler knew, and maybe Hunter. She started up the stairs, taking them one at a time, aware that with every step she took, she was becoming more involved with Tyler, not less.

And that was okay. She was safe with him. He'd do anything for her and had proven as much over the last few weeks. He would never do to her what Michael had done. He simply wasn't made of that kind of stuff.

With each step she took, she felt lighter, less burdened by the pain of the past and more determined to face the future with an open heart. There was no place for her usual brand of skepticism in her relationship with Tyler. And yes, she was thinking of it now as a relationship rather than a situation to be managed before she extricated herself.

They were down to eleven days before their deal was up, and suddenly that wasn't nearly enough. Her heart should've been beating fast and furious after the arduous climb up the stairs, but it beat slowly. Her blood felt hot and thick inside her veins, and the low throb between her legs required her full attention. The surface of her skin prickled and her nipples tightened in anticipation.

All that from knowing he'd be following her up those stairs, that he'd enter the room they were to share and put his hands on her. He'd touch her and kiss her and make love to her until they both were weak in the aftermath. By the time she reached the second-floor landing, she was fully aroused. The keycard didn't want to work in the door, making her dread the idea of going back down to get it fixed.

Then the green light came on and the door swung open, revealing a gorgeous room with a king-sized bed covered in white eyelet, wide-plank wood floors, a fireplace and candles scattered throughout the room. "Oh my God," she whispered, venturing deeper into the room as the door clicked shut behind her. The bathroom was huge and contained an enormous clawfoot tub. She opened the doors to the armoire and found a basket full of sensual products—condoms, massage oil, lubricant, toys in cellophane wrappers.

Next to the basket was a note from the management.

*Welcome to our Fantasy Suite. We hope you'll enjoy your evening with us and feel free to make use of any of the available products. In exchange, send your friends to the Pig's Belly Tavern for dinner, dancing and pleasure.*

"Holy shit," she whispered.

A soft knock on the door startled her. Charley felt like she'd been caught with her hand in the cookie jar or something equally ridiculous. She limped to the door to open it.

Tyler stepped into the room. "Um, wow. Not at all what I expected for a place called the Pig's Belly."

"I know! Wait until you see the rest." She took him by the hand and led him into the bathroom.

"This is awesome. Look at that tub."

"It's bigger than the one at your house, and that's pretty big." She released his hand. "Check out the armoire."

As she watched him walk to the armoire and examine the contents, her heart finally began to beat hard and fast.

He looked over his shoulder at her before returning his attention to the basket, rifling through the items and making her body heat in anticipation. Holding up one of the cellophane packages, he said, "I'm liking this place more by the minute."

Taking the item with him, he went over to sit on the bed, patting the spot next to him.

She went to him, wanting him as much as he seemed to want her. Charley lowered herself to the mattress, her leg brushing against his. Just that slight contact reignited the wildfire that burned so brightly in her when he was near. Though she'd begun to anticipate her reaction to him, nothing could prepare her for the reality of it—every damned time.

"Did I tell you how absolutely gorgeous you look tonight?" he asked.

She'd worn a cranberry-colored wrap dress in a knit fabric that clung to all her curves, such as they were, and she'd made an effort with her hair and makeup for the first time since the accident. "Um, I think you did. Before we left the house."

"You're stunning, Charley. All the time, but tonight . . ." His lips on her neck fanned and flamed the fire. "Tonight you take my breath away." He tugged at the bow at her hip. "Is this the secret to unwrapping you from this sexy dress?"

"Uh-huh." She began to unbutton his shirt as he untied her dress.

His lips found hers, sparking a frenzy of need to get rid of the clothes that stood between them and what they both wanted. She marveled at his ability to multitask, undressing them both while kissing her with deep thrusts of his tongue. When she was down to only the small black knee brace she'd "graduated" to, he broke the kiss, eased her down onto the bed and leaned over her, gorgeous and sexy with that lean, muscular body on full display.

She flattened her hand on his chest. "I like to look at you."

His eyes flared, and he sucked in a sharp deep breath as his cock lengthened before her eyes. "I fucking *love* to look at you."

Cupping her breasts, he dragged his thumbs over her nipples, which were hard and tight and sensitive to his touch. "And I love to taste you." He took her nipple into his mouth and laved at it with his tongue. "Put your hands over your head," he said gruffly. "Keep them there. I want to feast on you."

Charley trembled from head to toe as she followed his direction, eager to see what "feasting on her" entailed. Like he had the other night, he focused his attention exclusively on her breasts until she was to the point of begging him to do something to relieve the pressure that threatened to boil over at any minute. But like before, he refused to be rushed, even when she raised her hips, straining her good leg, to rub her sex against his cock.

"Stop trying to take over my seduction."

"Your seduction has been successful. I'm thoroughly seduced. Now do something about it, will you?"

"Don't rush me. I'm enjoying myself right here." He squeezed her nipples between his fingers to make his point—literally.

"I'm going to start swearing at you in about two seconds."

"Oh, please do. Swear at me, Charley."

"You fucking bastard. I want your cock right now, and you'd better fucking give it to me." She made herself laugh with the foolishness of the statement, but he didn't laugh.

"God, that's hot." He sucked hard on her nipple. "Don't stop. Keep talking."

"Tyler . . . fucking *hell*."

"Call me names. Tell me how much you hate me."

She laughed again as she moaned from what he continued to do to her poor, abused nipples, which were enjoying every bit of sensual torture he doled out. "I don't hate you yet, you rotten fiend. But I will soon."

Rocking against her, his hard cock pressing against her clit, he said, "Tell me how you really feel, and I'll give you what you want."

Oh God, was he asking her for what she thought he was? She writhed on the bed, trying to get closer, but he backed off right when things were getting interesting. "Goddamn you."

His low rumble of laughter infuriated her. "You had something you were going to tell me . . ."

"What do you want me to say?"

"I want you to admit you're hot for me, that you're falling for me the way I'm falling for you. I want you to tell me this time limit you've set for us is ridiculous because we're not going to be nearly done with each other when the clock strikes midnight on New Year's. Tell me, Charley. Tell me what I want to hear."

Again, his cock bumped against her clit, testing her resolve to keep her hands over her head. "That," she whispered urgently. "What you said. All of it."

"You are such a cheater," he said, laughing softly even as he gazed at her with unabashed affection.

"It's a big deal for me to give you that much."

"I know, honey." He pressed a kiss to her sternum and then rested his forehead on her chest, seeming to gather himself.

Charley couldn't resist the need to offer comfort, so she lifted one of her hands and brought it down on the back of his head, sliding her fingers through his hair. "Are you okay?"

"Yeah, it's just a big deal to hear you admit that stuff. I wondered if you ever would."

"I'm sorry if I've put you through hell. It's not—"

"Me," he said with a sweet grin. "It's you, or so you say. But there's absolutely nothing wrong with you that can't be fixed with time and patience and perseverance."

"You make me sound like a mountain to be climbed."

With his chin still on her chest, he looked up at her, amused. "It's a fitting metaphor when you think about how we came to be."

She smiled because how could she not when he was so damned cute? "If I recall correctly, promises were made if I copped to certain confessions. I'm not saying you're reneging on our deal or anything, but . . ."

As expected, he pounced, making her laugh when he went from somewhat relaxed to anything but in the scope of two seconds. But when she expected him to pick up right where they left off, he didn't. He started all over again with potent kisses that drugged her senses and made her lips burn from the intense workout they were getting. Then his lips were on her neck and his hands cupped her ass as he opened her to his cock.

They'd had sex that morning, but she still felt like she'd been waiting forever for him by the time he slid into her. Maybe she had been. Maybe he was what she'd been waiting for without even knowing she'd been waiting. "I wish . . ." She stopped herself when she realized she'd said the words out loud when she hadn't intended to.

"What do you wish for, Charley?"

"I wish I could be on top."

"Hold on tight to me, and don't let go."

There was so much she could read into that, but for now, she put her arms around him and held on as tight as she could. He turned them so she was on top of him.

"Don't move yet," he said.

Her body burned from the effort to remain still as he throbbed and expanded inside her. "I take it you like this, too."

"I love it all, baby. Every single thing we do." With his hands on her waist, he lifted her, sliding out of her in the process and making her groan from the loss. "Easy. I'll be right back. Bend your good leg. That's it. Now keep this one straight and come down slowly so you don't hurt anything."

"Including you?" she asked dryly.

"Including me." He bit his lip as she came down on him, taking him in slowly but surely.

"God, Charley, that's so hot. Look at you. I've never seen anything sexier than you on top of me."

With her hands flat against his chest, she moved as best she could with one leg sticking straight out. "All that time in the gym doing squats is coming in handy now."

He grasped her ass and squeezed. "Yes, it certainly is." Releasing his tight hold on her right cheek, he reached for the package he'd left on the bed. The crumple of cellophane was the only warning she got before a low hum filled the air.

"What the . . ." A vibrator pressed against her clit, nearly sending her into orbit. *"Ahhhh."* Anticipating her reaction, he'd anchored an arm around her waist so she wouldn't jar her leg with jerky movements. Being held still only made the vibrations more intense.

"Too much?" he asked.

She shook her head and rode the vibe and his cock until her body was racked with spasms that went on for what felt like an hour. When it was finally over, she fell forward onto his chest, and he caught her. He always caught her, and Charley was beginning to accept that he always would.

"I take it you like the vibe?"

"What was your first clue?"

His low chuckle rumbled through him. "I could feel it, too. I'd say that one's a keeper."

"Since we can hardly give it back now that we've used it, the least we could do is recycle and reuse."

His hand caressed the back of her head, his fingers sliding through her hair. "I do like the way you think."

The next night, as Charley stood with Tyler's arm around her and watched Megan come toward Hunter, she remembered what Megan had told her about overcoming her fears to find love and happiness. After their night together at the Pig's Belly, Charley had floated through the day drunk on sensual bliss. Tyler had been insatiable during the night, and they'd hardly slept at all until they got home to his house and crashed for hours.

Snuggled up against him now, it no longer felt weird to be "with" him in front of her friends and family. He'd worn a sharp-looking gray suit with a crisp white shirt, a festive red tie and those glasses that made her crazy. She wasn't sure how he did it, but the more time they spent wrapped up in each other, the more she wanted him.

As if he knew what she was thinking, his arm dropped from her shoulders to encircle her waist, drawing her in tight against him.

Charley leaned back, letting him take the weight off her injured leg. She couldn't wait to be able to wear heels again.

As Charley watched her grandfather escort Megan through her parents' huge great room, her eyes filled with tears, the emotional reaction unexpected. But knowing what Megan had endured to get to this day filled her heart to overflowing. Her every emotion was hovering close to the surface these days, which was another thing to "blame" on Tyler.

Charley had never seen her oldest brother as overcome as he was the moment he extended his hand to Megan, offering her everything he had to give. The family and friends gathered around them sniffled as Hunter and Megan came together to join their lives. Megan was beautiful in a strapless cream-colored silk gown with a small train that pooled at her feet. She'd worn her long blond hair in an elaborate updo that made her look sweet and sophisticated at the same time. Judging by Hunter's reaction, she'd scored a grand slam with her groom.

Her attendants, Nina and Hannah, wore red silk that matched the red silk tie Hunter wore with a charcoal suit. Standing beside him, Will served as his best man and Megan's brother-in-law, Brett, was a groomsman.

Molly had gone all out with flowers, Christmas decorations and candles that gave the big room a cozy, intimate feel as Elmer led the bride and groom through the recitations of traditional vows and exchange of rings before declaring them husband and wife.

Hunter wrapped his arms around Megan and looked down at her for a long moment, cradled her face in his hands, and then kissed her while their guests applauded.

"It is my very great pleasure," Elmer said, beaming, "to introduce for the first time, Hunter and Megan Abbott."

Charley realized tears were spilling down her cheeks.

Tyler tightened his hold on her, his lips finding the sweet spot behind her ear that made her shiver every time.

Lucas and Landon, both wearing suits without ties, were in charge of the music and played "In My Life," the song

Hunter and Megan had chosen for their first dance as husband and wife.

Tyler sang along softly, squeezing Charley at the "I love you more" lyric.

His message was received loud and clear. And whereas her inclination a few weeks ago would have been to try to get free of his embrace, the overwhelming interest in her, the eyes that saw far too much, now . . . Now, things were different.

She wasn't ready to make the kind of commitment Hunter had just made to Megan, but she was no longer actively planning her exit strategy either.

The caterers circulated with champagne, and when everyone had a glass, Will stepped up to toast his brother.

"Hunter, you and I go way back," Will said to laughter. "One of my earliest memories is of sharing bunk beds with you and having flashlight wars when we were supposed to be sleeping."

"Uh-huh," Molly said. "No statute of limitations on these things."

Will smiled at their mother. "Why did I know you were going to say that? Megan, you and I have had an interesting history as well . . ."

Megan laughed and blushed at his reference to the crush she'd once had on him. That seemed like a long time ago now that she and Hunter were so madly in love.

"But tonight we're focused on the future, and I'd like to officially welcome you to the Abbott family. I've never seen my brother as happy as he's been since you two got together, and I wish you both a lifetime of love and happiness. To Hunter and Megan." After everyone had raised their glasses in toast, Will said, "Nina, your turn."

Megan's sister dabbed at her eyes with a tissue. "I'm a disaster tonight. My baby sister is a bride—and a beautiful bride at that."

"Couldn't agree more," Hunter said, pressing his lips to Megan's temple.

"On this joyful occasion," Nina said, "I'd be remiss if I

didn't tell my wonderful sister how proud our parents would be to see her married to a wonderful man who truly loves her. They wanted nothing more than our happiness, and they'd be thrilled with your choice of a husband, Meggie. Hunter, I want to thank you for making Megan so happy. I've never seen her smile more than she has recently, and that's all thanks to you. Every so often two people get it exactly right, and I'm so very happy for both of you."

As everyone raised their glasses again, a shout rang out from across the room.

Charley looked over to see Cameron fall to the floor in a dead faint.

Will dropped down next to her. "Cameron, baby, oh my God! *Cameron!*"

Patrick joined Will on the floor, caressing his daughter's face. "Sweetheart, open your eyes."

Cameron's eyes fluttered open to find everyone looking down at her. "Oh Lord. What happened?"

"You fainted," Will said. "Give her some room."

Molly handed him a wet washcloth. "Bathe her face."

"I'm so sorry, Megan," Cameron said. "Stealing the bride's thunder is a wedding felony."

"I don't care about that," Megan said. "As long as you're all right."

Cameron looked up at Will, a small smile occupying her lips. "I'm all right, and I'm pregnant."

As a cheer went through the gathering, Will helped her sit up, leaning her against him.

"A baby?" Patrick asked, his voice filled with wonder.

"So it seems, although this wasn't how I'd planned to tell you."

Patrick hugged her, holding her for a long moment. By the time he released her, some of the color had returned to Cameron's pale cheeks.

Will and her dad helped her to her feet, and Will lifted her into his arms to carry her from the room, with Patrick, Mary, Molly and Lincoln following right behind them.

"Holy shit," Charley said to Tyler.

"Congratulations. You're going to be an aunt again."

She glanced across the room to where Max was showing off Caden to some of their Coleman cousins. "It's a regular baby boom."

"I wonder who'll be next," Tyler said.

He was making conversation, but the innocuous comment struck a note of fear in her heart. He wanted a family. She didn't think kids were in the cards for her. That was no small difference, and before things progressed any further with them, they needed to talk about that. Again.

# CHAPTER 22

—◄►—

W ill carried Cameron into the den and sat on the sofa. Her dad was right behind them, concern etched into his face as he gazed down at his daughter.

"Go on back to the party, everyone," Cameron said. "I swear I'm fine."

"You're sure?" Patrick asked.

"Absolutely sure. I was standing too close to the fireplace and overheated. That's all it was. I promise."

"Do you think we should call a doctor?" Linc asked.

"No, no," Cameron said. "I just need a minute, and then I'll be fine."

Molly handed her a glass of ice water. "Cold water used to be the cure for a lot of my ailments when I was pregnant."

"Thank you," Cam said with a warm smile for Molly.

Over the roaring in his ears, Will could barely hear what they were saying. He was completely focused on the precious bundle he held in his arms and trying to get his heart to return to a normal beat.

"Let's give them a minute," Molly said, taking Patrick and Linc by the arms to lead them from the room.

Mary had a tight grip on Patrick's hand as she followed him.

"Check out my dad and Mary," Cam said when they were alone. "I told you something was going on with them. I need to get him alone to ask him about it."

"Stop." Will's tone was harsher than he'd intended. "Just stop. I'm dying here, and you're playing matchmaker."

Her hand landed on his face in a tender, soothing caress. "I'm sorry I scared you."

"You did more than scare me. You nearly gave me a heart attack when you dropped like that when I was across the room and couldn't catch you. You can't ever do that to me again."

Cameron laughed softly. "I'll try very hard never to faint again."

Will ran his hands over her reverently. "You didn't hurt yourself anywhere when you fell, did you?"

"Not that I know of. I'm really fine."

He flattened his hand over her abdomen. "This little person is already causing us a world of trouble, between the constant puking and now the fainting. I fear we're in for a hell-raiser."

She smiled, her eyes sparkling with joy. "I can't wait to meet our little hell-raiser."

Cupping her face he held her still for a kiss. "Neither can I."

"So much for our plan to wait a while to tell everyone."

"I think some of them had already guessed anyway."

Cameron rested her head on his shoulder. "Do you ever think about where you were and what you were doing a year ago?"

"All the time, and what I'm doing now—and who I'm doing it with—is so much better."

"Who were you doing it with then?" she asked, raising her head off his shoulder.

Laughing at her indignation, Will took his index finger to her chin. "My whole life began the night I rescued you in the mud last spring. There was nothing before that. And now there's only you and the hell-raiser."

She smiled brightly. "Nice save, William."

"It was rather good, wasn't it?"

"The best." She kissed him. "I love you so much."

"I love you, too. You have no idea how much."

"I think I have some idea."

"No, baby," he said, nuzzling her soft blond hair as he settled her once again on his shoulder. "You have no idea at all. They haven't invented a word big enough to describe it."

She sighed with pleasure at his words and burrowed deeper into his embrace, their quiet interlude interrupted a few minutes later by raised voices coming from the kitchen.

What the hell?

"I need to see Max. Right now! Please get him for me."

Grayson Coleman had been alone in the kitchen, sent by his aunt Molly to retrieve a chafing dish, whatever that was, when Chloe came in from the mudroom, her eyes wild and rimmed with red. Still wearing her coat, she clutched a sheaf of papers in her hand.

"Please go get him."

"He's at his brother's wedding, Chloe. Maybe this could keep until tomorrow?"

"It won't keep. I need to tell him . . . Right now. I need to or . . . Please, Grayson. Please get him for me."

"Are you all right?"

"I will be once I speak to him." Tears fell from her eyes, leaving tracks on top of others already on her face.

Though Grayson was almost afraid to leave her alone when she was in such a fragile condition, he said, "Stay here. I'll be right back." He cut through the dining room to the great room where he found Max with Gray's sisters Izzy, Vanessa and Ally, who were taking turns holding baby Caden. All around them, other guests were eating, talking, drinking and dancing.

"Max, could I have a word, please?"

"Um, sure. You guys have him?"

"We've got him," Vanessa said of Caden. "And I might just keep him."

"You can't have him," Max said with a teasing grin for his cousin. To Gray, he said, "What's up?"

Grayson took him by the arm and led him to a quiet corner. "Chloe is here, and she's really upset about something."

Shocked, Max said, "She's here? *Now?*"

"Yeah, and something's up."

Max took a deep breath and released it slowly. "Come with me?"

"Of course." Grayson followed Max to the kitchen where Chloe was pacing as she continued to cry.

"Chloe?"

"Oh, Max! I needed to see you. I'm so sorry. I know it's your brother's wedding, but I couldn't . . . I couldn't wait until tomorrow to tell you . . . I . . . I can't . . ." Her stammering words were interrupted by deep, wrenching sobs that had Max looking to Grayson for help.

But Gray had no idea what to do either.

Max went to her, put his hand on her shoulder. "Chloe, take a deep breath and try to calm down. Whatever is wrong, we can figure it out."

"No." Shaking her head, she choked on another sob. "We can't figure it out. I-I can't figure it out. I can't do this, Max. I'm . . . I'm not ready to be a mother." She thrust the papers at him. "I signed the paper that gives you full custody."

"*Whoa!*" Max said, sounding panicked. "No. No, you can't just do that. He needs you, Chloe. *I* need you. I can't do this by myself."

Molly came into the kitchen and stopped short at the sight of Chloe and Max, locked in an odd standoff. "What's going on?"

Grayson quickly brought his aunt up to speed.

Molly's mouth set with displeasure as she approached Chloe. "Do you understand what you're doing here? Do you really understand?"

Chloe's chin quivered, but she nodded. "I can't do it, Mrs. Abbott. I wanted to, but I can't. I love him, but I'm not ready."

"If you do this," Molly said, "there's no undoing it. There's no coming back a year from now, two years from now and upending Max's life and Caden's with custody demands because you've decided it's time to become a mother. Do you understand what I'm saying to you?"

"Yes," Chloe said softly. "Ma'am."

Molly looked up at her son, who wore a shell-shocked expression on his face. "Max?"

He blinked a few times and looked down at his mother. "Take the paper from Chloe."

"Mom, I can't do this by myself."

"You'll never be by yourself. Ever. Take the paper."

Reluctantly, or so it seemed to Gray, Max took it from Chloe's outstretched hand.

To Grayson, Molly said, "Is there anything more that has to be done or signed to give Max full custody?"

"It'll need to be notarized, but I can do that."

"All right then," Molly said. "Chloe, do you wish to see your son before you go?"

Chloe bit her lip and shook her head. "It would probably be better if I don't. I packed up his stuff. I got as much as I could into my car."

"Grayson, Max, go help Chloe bring in Caden's things," Molly said.

Since Max seemed frozen in place, Gray gave him a push to get him moving. The two men stepped into the freezing cold night without coats and went to retrieve boxes and bags of baby items from the back of Chloe's car. They made two trips each, depositing the items in the mudroom.

Molly oversaw the operation, and when they were finished, she said to Chloe, "Is there anything else you'd like to say before you go?"

"I'm sorry," she said softly. "I'm so sorry, Max. I wish I could be someone different, but . . . I loved you, and I love him. I'm just . . . I'm sorry."

Max's jaw remained rigidly set as he listened to her.

"Are you able to drive safely?" Molly asked.

"Yes."

"Then I think you ought to go now."

Chloe turned her tearful gaze toward Max, who was now expressionless. "I'm so sorry, Max." She turned to leave.

"Chloe." Max went after her. "You'll always be his mother. There'll never be a time that I'll turn you away if you want to see him."

Sobbing softly, Chloe said, "That's more than I deserve." She reached up to kiss Max's cheek. "Take good care of him for me." And then she was gone, into the dark night, out of their lives, leaving Max to raise his son alone.

It was almost too much for Grayson to process. He couldn't imagine how Max must feel.

Reeling, Max watched her go, wishing he could somehow redo the last fifteen minutes and change the outcome.

His mother's hands on his shoulders drew him out of the shock to find her looking up at him with concern. "I know this has to be overwhelming right now, but you're not alone. We'll help you. We'll all help you."

Max knew that he needed to say something, to at least thank her for how she'd stepped in to manage the situation with Chloe, but there were simply no words as the enormity of it settled in like an elephant stepping on his chest and stealing the air from his body.

Bending at the waist, hands to knees, Max closed his eyes as he tried to breathe through the panic. He was twenty-two years old and in no way ready for any of this himself, but what choice did he have when a beautiful, helpless baby boy was relying on him for everything?

Caden . . . He needed to see his son. Standing upright, he walked through the kitchen and dining room, to the great room where the wedding reception had carried on, the guests none the wiser to the fact that his life had just been permanently altered in the scope of a few minutes. His cousin Ally was holding Caden when Max approached them.

"May I?" he asked, holding out his hands for the baby.

"Awww, Daddy ruins all our fun." Ally kissed the baby's forehead before she handed him off to Max.

"Thanks." He took the baby and left the room, heading for the stairs to the room he still used whenever he was in Butler, which was going to be all the time now, he supposed. Other than his mother's sewing machine on the desk that used to be his and the bassinet by the bed, not much had changed in this room since he moved to Burlington for college.

Sitting on the bed and holding the sleeping baby tight against him, he rocked him back and forth. "I'll take care of you. I'll always be there for you. I promise." Tears burned his eyes and slid down his cheeks. He buried his face in the baby's soft blanket.

After knocking on the door, his parents entered the room. They closed the door behind them and came to the bed to sit on either side of him, putting their arms around him and Caden and making Max feel less alone.

"We're right here with you, son," Linc said gruffly. "We'll do this together."

Max wiped his face with the sleeve of his suit coat, embarrassed by the tears. "You guys have already raised ten kids."

"So what's one more?" Molly asked with a cheerful smile. "We love him, we love you and we'll figure it out together one day at a time."

The tears continued to come faster than Max could wipe them away. "I'm so sorry to do this to you."

"You have no reason to apologize to us," Linc said. "It's been a little too quiet for our liking around here anyway. You two will stay here with us until you figure out what you want to do, and we'll help you. We'll all help you, Max."

"Despite how it seems right now, it's going to be okay." Molly wiped away some of his tears. "If Chloe's heart wasn't in it, she did you and Caden a favor by bowing out now rather than waiting until he was old enough to know her. That would've been much worse."

Leave it to his mother to find the bright side in an otherwise dismal situation. "Thank you," he whispered. "Thank you both so much. I've always known how lucky I was to be part of this family, but after the way Chloe's family abandoned her, I'm even more aware of how fortunate I am."

"We're the lucky ones to have such a wonderful son and grandson to love," Linc said.

"You guys should go back to the wedding," Max said. "It's Hunter's big night, and you should be with him. I'm going to stay here with Caden for a little while longer."

"You come down whenever you're ready," Molly said, kissing his cheek as she got up.

Lincoln squeezed his shoulder and then followed his wife from the room.

Long after they were gone, Max gazed down at his son, vowing to be the kind of parent to him that he'd been lucky enough to have. Nothing less would do for his son.

"What's going on?" Charley asked her parents when they came downstairs after following Max up there earlier. Several of her other siblings stood with her, equally curious about what had happened.

"Chloe came to see Max and signed over full custody to him," Molly said. "She brought the baby's things."

"So this is like *permanent*?" Ella asked, sounding as shocked as Charley felt.

"Yes."

"Holy shit," Wade muttered. "Is he okay?"

"He will be," Molly said, "but needless to say he's a bit shocked and overwhelmed."

"We'll all help," Ella said. "Of course we will."

"And I told him that," Molly said, "but I'm sure it would mean a lot for him to hear it from you guys, too."

"We'll tell him," Charley said as the others nodded in agreement.

"What we all need to do now is get back to this joyous celebration," Molly said, forcing a smile, "because, as Max said, it's Hunter's big night."

Charley took a look around the big room for Hunter, who was blissfully oblivious to the drama playing out behind the scenes as he and Megan visited with friends and drank champagne.

Tyler approached carrying two glasses of champagne. He handed one to her and drew her away from the others. "Everything okay?"

"Um, well, Caden's mother showed up and signed over full custody to Max, and I guess he's kind of freaking out."

"This just happened?"

"Uh-huh. She came here and brought the baby's stuff." Charley's stomach ached when she thought of the challenge her brother now faced in raising his son alone—or as alone as anyone ever was in the big Abbott family.

"God, Max has got to be reeling."

"I think he is, but we'll support him. We'll help. It'll be okay."

Tyler put his arm around her and kissed the top of her head. "Still, it's rather upsetting, to say the least."

"Yeah. I mean who does that to their own kid?"

"Let's dance." He took their glasses, put them on a nearby table and led her to the area that had been designated for dancing, sweeping her into his arms and making her forget all about the anxiety she felt on her brother's behalf. When he held her this way, she could only think of him.


Grayson poured three fingers of his uncle's best scotch and took a seat in the corner, away from the wedding fray. The first sip traveled through him like liquid fire, heating him from the inside and giving him something to think about other than the rage that Chloe's decision had resurrected in him.

It had been twenty long years since his father walked away from his wife and children, leaving Grayson and his mom to pick up the pieces for the others. Until then, he'd loved being the oldest in his family and had wallowed in the privileges that went along with being the eldest. Until he became the man of the family almost overnight, responsible for his distraught mother and seven younger siblings who were looking to him to make sense of something that still didn't make sense all these years later.

Here he was now, a man of thirty-six, an accomplished

lawyer, and the scene in his aunt Molly's kitchen had taken him back to the long ago night that marked the official end of his childhood. He could still remember the panic, the despair, the fear, the rage . . . all of it congealing into a hot knot of anxiety in his gut that he'd carried with him for years afterward.

How anyone could walk away from their own kid, let alone eight of them, was beyond him. He actively hated Chloe, a woman he barely knew, for what she'd done to her son tonight. For someday, in the not-too-distant future, Caden would find out that his mother had rejected him, and he'd never be the same.

Grayson had never been the same. He took another deep sip of the scotch, letting the searing heat soothe him.

"What's that stuff?" a little voice next to him asked.

He looked over at the girl with the red curls who'd sat next to him in his quiet corner that wasn't so quiet anymore. "It's scotch. You ever had it?"

She wrinkled her adorable nose. "Of course not. I'm a kid. Kids don't drink scotch. My grandpa likes it, though, so that's how I know what it is."

"What do you drink?"

"I like apple juice, but Mommy says it has too much sugar, so it's a special treat."

"Your mommy is very wise."

"She's very pretty, too." Pointing, the girl said, "That's her right there."

He followed her finger to the blonde he'd met the night before, and had to agree that Lucy's sister, Emma, was indeed gorgeous. Her daughter took after her aunt Lucy with her red hair and pale white skin, whereas her mom was a willowy blonde with big blue eyes.

"Do you have a girlfriend?"

"Who wants to know?" he asked, amused by the girl's blatant matchmaking.

"I do."

"And what's your name?"

"Simone."

"That's a pretty name. Do you have a boyfriend?"

"No! I'm nine. Nine-year-olds don't have boyfriends. You're like Colton. He knows *nothing* about kids."

Grayson knew more about kids than any childless man his age, but he didn't share that information with the girl. "What kind of stuff should I know?"

"Well, you should know that nine-year-old girls don't drink scotch and have boyfriends."

"I guess you don't smoke then either, do you?"

She lost it laughing, and he lost a tiny piece of his heart to her. What a cutie. "*No!* I don't smoke. Smoking is gross and it kills you."

"That's exactly right. Stay away from that stuff."

"What do you want for Christmas this year?" she asked.

God, what a sweet question, and what did he want anyway? How about some peace and a whole new life? That'd be a great place to start. "I want a pair of socks. What about you?"

"Socks? Who wants socks for Christmas?"

"I do, and it's my Christmas list, so you don't get to make fun of it."

"That's true. Sorry."

He nudged her with his elbow. "I was only kidding. You can make fun of me. Socks are a dumb thing to want for Christmas. What's on your list?"

"I asked for a new American Girl doll, but they're kind of expensive. Not sure that'll happen. But it's okay if it doesn't. I always get lots of cool stuff."

"I'm sure you're spoiled rotten."

"Not really. It's just me and Mommy, so we have to watch our pennies. That's what she says anyway."

Grayson wanted to buy her the doll and any other damned thing she wanted to make up for the fact that her father wasn't in her life. He was drawn out of that thought by the arrival of Emma, who'd come to claim her daughter.

"Are you bothering Grayson?" Emma asked.

"Your name is *Grayson*?" Simone asked, giggling. "What kind of name is that?"

"Simone!"

"It's a smart, distinguished name, I'll have you know."

Simone covered her mouth, as if that could contain her laughter, and he was utterly beguiled by the glee in her mischievous eyes.

"I'm sorry about her," Emma said. "The charm school wouldn't have her, so I'm doing the best I can on my own."

"I'd say you're doing a pretty great job," Gray said, looking up at her. She had a body that wouldn't quit and absolutely stunning blue eyes.

"You should ask my mom to dance," Simone said. "She loves to dance, and she doesn't get to very often 'cuz of me."

"Simone, honestly."

For Gray, however, the thought of dancing with Simone's sexy, embarrassed mother was far better than sitting in the corner drinking scotch alone while old memories resurfaced to prove they could still hurt him all these years later. "That's about the best idea anyone's had all day," Gray said.

Simone's expressive eyes widened with joyful pleasure. "Really?"

Gray stood and extended his hand to Emma, who blushed madly. "Really."

"Oh, um, you don't have to," Emma said haltingly.

"I'd love to. Shall we?"

As she looked up at him and took hold of his hand, Grayson felt like he'd been struck by lightning or gut-punched or something equally unpleasant, except there was nothing at all unpleasant about it. In fact, it was the best feeling he'd had in longer than he could remember.

# CHAPTER 23

——◄•►——

"Let's get out of here," Hunter whispered to Megan after they'd eaten and cut their cake and she'd tossed her bouquet right into Lucy's outstretched hands.

"We can't go yet," Megan said. "Everyone is here for us."

"They expect us to go as soon as we possibly can. Let's get this honeymoon started."

"Our honeymoon doesn't start for six days yet." They were leaving the day after Christmas for Bermuda.

"Baby, our honeymoon starts right now. I want to be alone with my wife."

"Your wife," she said with a sigh. "I do like the sound of that."

"I love the sound of it, and that other sound you make, you know the one when you—"

She squished his lips with her fingers. "Stop it."

"Take me home where I can talk dirty to you all I want."

"If you're going to be that way about it."

"I'm going to be that way. I absolutely am."

"What've I gotten myself into here?"

He smiled and waggled his brows at her. "You know exactly what you've gotten yourself into."

"The best thing ever."

"Glad you think so. Now take me home and make a decent husband out of me."

"If you insist."

"I do. I insist, and I'm the husband."

The withering look she gave him only made him laugh. Nothing could get him down on the best night of his life. Their simple wedding at his parents' home had been everything they'd hoped it would be, and now he was ready to get on with the rest of their lives together, beginning with the all-important wedding night.

Hand in hand, they went around the room to say their good-byes and took the expected ribbing about leaving early from his siblings, cousins and friends. Whatever. Let them have their laughs. He got to sleep with the exquisite Megan Abbott every night for the rest of his life. The last laugh was all his.

He'd never in his life seen anything more perfect than she'd looked tonight, glowing with happiness and smiling nonstop. Hunter loved her like that, free from the sorrow of the past and looking forward to the future with him. And he planned to make sure that she never again had reason to be sad about anything if he had anything to say about it.

His mother hugged and kissed him. "So proud of you tonight, my love," she said. "Such a handsome groom and what a stunning bride."

"Couldn't agree more about the bride."

"Love you, son," Lincoln said when he hugged him. "And we love you, too, Megan. Happy to have you in the family."

"Thank you both so much for letting us do it here, especially this week when there's so much else going on," Megan said. "But I pictured it here, and it was exactly what I wanted."

"We loved doing it," Molly said. "Our home is your home."

Megan hugged them both. "It's so nice to have parents again. I'd forgotten how lovely it is."

She reduced his parents to tears with her sweetness.

"You okay to drive, son?" Linc asked, brushing at his eyes.

"I'm fine. I quit drinking hours ago." To Megan he said, "Ready, sweetheart?"

"Ready." They put on coats and hustled into the cold winter night to discover his brothers had decorated his Lincoln Navigator with strings of cans and had written *Just Married* in foam on the back window. Good thing they didn't get any of the foam on the paint or he'd have to kill them.

Megan laughed at the spectacle they'd made of his vehicle.

"It's not funny," Hunter said, though he was deeply amused. He expected nothing less from his moronic brothers, especially Lucas and Landon, who were no doubt the ringleaders.

"Yes, it is."

He held the door for her and helped her—and her dress—into the car before seat-belting her in and stealing a kiss. Lingering was not an option, however, because it was freezing and he didn't want her to get cold. So he put his desire for his new wife on ice for the moment.

Megan giggled uncontrollably at the racket they made as they drove through the sleepy town of Butler on the way home. He'd wanted to take her somewhere special for their wedding night, but she'd said their home was special to her and that was where she wanted to go.

He loved that she was easy to please, and the happy sound of her laughter was a huge turn-on for him. When he thought about the edgy, distrustful woman she'd once been, it was hard to reconcile that woman with the joyful person he'd married tonight. She'd changed a lot in the time they'd been together, had rediscovered her joy and her ability to laugh, both of which had been stolen by the deaths of her parents her senior year of high school.

Hunter had changed, too. She'd lightened him up and shown him what really mattered in life. Though he'd been crazy about her for a long time before they ever went out, he'd discovered the reality of her was even better than he'd expected. He took hold of her hand and held it tightly as he drove them home.

"The neighbors are going to think they're being attacked when we drive up," he said.

She laughed again, harder than ever.

"I'm going to kill those stupid idiots," Hunter muttered. "I should've done it years ago when I had the chance."

"You love those idiots."

"Not right now, I don't."

"Yes, you do."

Hunter squeezed her hand and let her win this round, because she was right. He loved all his siblings—even Lucas and Landon when they were being idiots. They arrived at home and he killed the engine, thankful to quiet the clattering racket behind the car before it woke the whole neighborhood.

"Hi, honey, we're home," he said.

"I think everyone in a one-mile radius got the memo that we're home," she said with more helpless laughter.

Maybe his brothers weren't total idiots if their hijinks had given Megan such a good laugh. "Stay there. I'm coming around for you." Hunter jogged around the front of the car, watching out for black ice as he went. Ice and dress shoes did not make for a good match.

Megan had removed her seatbelt and was waiting for him.

"Come to me, my love."

"Always."

With one word she made his heart beat faster and his body tighten with the kind of desire he'd only ever felt for her. He lifted her into his arms and carried her to the porch.

She punched in the code that opened the front door and he swept them over the threshold in keeping with tradition.

"Ahhh, home sweet home," she said.

In the months since she moved in with him, she'd made subtle changes that had made his home theirs. Throw pillows and blankets to snuggle under on the sofa, her prized antique typewriter on the mantel, candles and new lampshades, her books mixed in with his, some of her favorite art on the walls. He loved every change she made because it meant she was there to stay.

Hunter put her down only long enough to shed their coats and then picked her up again to carry her upstairs. Their puppy, Horace, was spending the weekend with Aunt Hannah and Uncle Nolan, so Mommy and Daddy could have some time to themselves, as Hannah had said when she made the offer. The house was eerily quiet without the little guy to welcome them home.

"If you injure yourself toting me around, you won't be any good to me on our honeymoon."

"I'm not going to injure myself, and I'm going to be so good to you on our honeymoon."

She sighed and rested her head on his shoulder. "Did today really happen?"

"It really did, and we've both got rings to prove it."

"Best day of my life."

"Mine, too, honey. Best ever."

"Every day that I'm with you is the best day ever."

In their room, he put her down but kept his arms around her. "I love you more than life itself, Mrs. Abbott."

"I love you more than that, Mr. Abbott."

"No way."

Smiling up at him in the darkness, she said, "Yes way."

He kissed her nose and then her lips. "Hang on for one second." Hunter went around the room, lighting the candles they kept on every available surface because she loved them so much. "There," he said when he was finished. "That looks more like a wedding night." Returning to her, he placed his hands on her shoulders. "Now tell me how I get you out of this gorgeous dress that bowled me over the first time I saw it."

"Did it really?"

"Oh, baby, you have no idea. I almost lost it when you came in with my gramps. I've never seen anything more beautiful."

"I hoped you'd like it. I wanted so badly to ask your opinion. You have better style sense than any woman I know."

"Should I be offended by that? And P.S., I *loved* it."

"You should not be offended because that was a compliment, and P.S. I'm thrilled you loved it."

"About getting you out of this gorgeous dress I loved so much . . . What's the secret?"

Smiling, she raised her arm and pointed to the zipper.

"Ahhh, thank you." He unzipped her slowly, taking his time now that they had the rest of their lives to spend together. The zipper went all the way to her hip, and when it was open, he slid his fingers over the skin he'd uncovered, making her shiver in response. Nuzzling her neck, he said, "Take your hair down."

She reached up to remove the pins that had held it in place and it dropped to her shoulders in sheets of fragrant golden silk. Then she went to work on his tie, unknotting and removing it. Her fingers moved over the buttons of his shirt with determination. She spread the two sides apart and pressed her lips to his throat, making him tremble.

Hunter pulled off his suit coat, his dress shirt and the T-shirt he'd worn under it. He helped her out of the dress, which he placed on a chair while his own clothes landed in a heap on the floor. He didn't care in the least about the suit he'd had made just for tonight. How could he when his gorgeous, sexy wife was standing before him in the most scandalous lingerie he'd ever seen.

"I thought you might like this, too," she said, dragging a finger over the plump tops of her breasts that were contained by a lacy, sheer strapless bra.

Hunter took a step back to take in the full view of equally lacy panties, garters and sexy-as-hell stockings. "Dear God, woman. Are you trying to give me a heart attack?"

"Hardly," she said.

"Let me see the back side."

Turning, she looked at him over her shoulder as he took a long perusing trip down her back, swallowing hard at the sight of the thong that disappeared between supple cheeks. "Holy Christ," he whispered. "I've got to be the luckiest guy to ever live." He placed his hands on her hips and drew her ass in against his hard cock. Then he raised his hands to cup her breasts, teasing her nipples through the bra.

"Hunter," she said breathlessly.

"What, baby?"

"I want you. Now."

"Are you going to be a needy, demanding wife?"

"Yes," she said, laughing. "A very needy, demanding wife."

"Excellent. That's just the way I want you." Keeping one hand on her belly, he released his belt and unfastened and unzipped his pants, letting them join the growing pile on the floor. His boxers followed, and his cock snuggled into the valley between her cheeks.

Kissing her shoulder and the curve of her neck, he smoothed his hand over her flat belly down to cup her intimately, reveling in the shudder that gripped her and the moan that escaped from her lips.

"You're not a very obedient husband," she said gruffly. "Torturing your wife this way."

"My wife loves this kind of torture."

"Two can play at the game," she said, reaching around grasp his erection in her tight little hand.

Hunter saw stars when she began to stroke him. "Maybe you're right. We ought to move things along here."

Her laughter went straight to his heart. "I like when you see things my way."

With his hand over hers, he extricated himself from her grip and turned her to face him. She was so pretty and so damned sexy, especially with arousal heating her cheeks and her lips already swollen from the many times he'd kissed her during their wedding.

Reaching behind her, he released the clasp on her bra and watched with desperate desire beating through him as her breasts sprang free. "So beautiful," he whispered. "And all mine." He put his arms around her and brought her in tight against him for a deep, passionate kiss. While he kissed her, his hands moved over her, touching her with the kind of reverence required for a wedding night, but the reverence only amped up the desperation for both of them.

She tugged on him, drawing him down over her on their bed, her legs opening to welcome him.

He pulled back, only to remove the garter belt, stockings and thong, leaving her bare to his ravenous gaze.

"Hunter," she said, reaching for him. "Make love to me. Please."

He could deny her nothing, especially when she asked in such a pleading tone for something he wanted more than his next breath. They both wanted a baby as soon as possible, so they'd stopped trying to prevent pregnancy a while ago. He'd hoped she'd already be pregnant by now, but it hadn't happened yet.

Sliding into her with nothing between them but raw desire and love was like finding paradise on earth. He had to take a minute to get himself together or risk this being over way before he wanted it to be.

Megan held him close, caressing his back and running her fingers through his hair. "You feel so good. So, so good."

"Mmm, you do, too. Best thing I've ever felt is your skin against mine. And to know I get to have you in my bed every night forever . . ." He raised his head to meet her gaze. "There's nothing else I could ever want as long as I have you."

"Me, too." Lifting her legs over his hips, she arched into him, asking for more.

Hunter was more than happy to give it to her, surging into her until they both came with sharp cries of pleasure. Every time they made love, he wondered if it would lead to the child they both wanted so badly. He kissed a path from her neck to her lips, kissing her softly in the calm that followed the storm.

"Thanks for marrying me, Megan."

"It was a tremendous hardship, but somehow I'll cope."

Smiling at her witty reply, Hunter dropped his head to her shoulder, as content as he'd ever hoped to be in this lifetime.

# CHAPTER 24

T he days between Hunter's wedding and Christmas passed in a whirl of work and holiday parties and long hours in bed with Charley. Tyler had never neglected his business as much as he had since Charley had been staying with him, but he figured it was a small price to pay to spend hours lost in her.

She'd been quieter than usual since the drama with Max and Chloe at the wedding, and he'd wanted to ask her what was on her mind, but he'd held back, afraid of what he might hear. Despite all their many steps forward, he knew it wouldn't take much to send her spiraling backward.

On Christmas Eve, they wrapped the last of the presents that had been delivered to his house from her rash of online shopping.

"I've got to admit there's something to be said for having it all show up in the driveway instead of slogging through malls in the cold and snow," she said late in the afternoon.

Wearing only a Dartmouth T-shirt of his, she sat on the

sofa and he was on the floor as they used the coffee table to wrap. He knew there was nothing under the shirt because he'd put it on her when he dragged her out of bed earlier to attend to the wrapping that had to be done before the gathering at his parents' home later.

"I won't tell anyone you said that."

"Please don't. I'll get run out of the family."

"Who would manage their systems if they ran you out?"

"Systems administrators are a dime a dozen. They'd find someone."

Tyler studied her intently, one of his favorite pastimes. There was so much insight to be found in her many expressions, her tone of voice and the things she *didn't* say. "Do you think Hunter would be as easily replaced because CPAs are a dime a dozen?"

"He's way more than a CPA. He manages the whole show. We'd be lost without him."

"How about Will? Couldn't just anyone run the Vermont Made line?"

"Will knows this state better than the governor does. He'd be hard to replace."

"How about Ella and Wade?"

"Ella is magic with the employees. They absolutely love her. And Wade, as our resident healthy living fanatic, is ideal for running the health and wellness line. They're all really good at what they do."

"And you're not?"

"I am, I guess. I've spent a lot of time building the systems and making them talk to each other. But that doesn't mean someone else couldn't come in and take over for me."

"If you ask me, you're selling yourself short. You're as essential to that business as any of your siblings are."

"Dad's making noise about a catalog and distribution center after the first of the year. That'll make for a nice juicy challenge."

"And you love nothing more than a nice juicy challenge."

She smiled, flattening him with the punch of emotion that hit him when she looked at him that way.

"Don't look now, but I think we're done wrapping," he said.

"Thank God. I don't know how the ladies in the store wrap all day at work and then go home to do their own. They must see dancing Santas in their sleep."

He stood and stretched, working the kinks out of his back from an hour sitting on the floor. Wearing only boxer briefs, he tried not to think about all the keys he'd handed out to her family and how often they'd made use of them. Then he opened his eyes to find her staring at him. "What?"

"You."

"What about me?"

"I like to look at you."

Taken aback by the statement and the blatant invitation in her eyes, he said, "You can look at me any time you want, free of charge."

She held out her hand to him and brought him to lie next to her on the sofa.

"You rang?"

Charley laughed and flattened her hand on his chest, stopping his heart. He was still getting used to what it felt like to be touched by her. "I wanted to tell you that I think that having a boyfriend is . . ."

Tyler died a thousand deaths waiting to hear how that sentence would end.

". . . pretty nice."

"Pretty nice, huh? I suppose that's better than pretty awful but not quite as good as pretty awesome would be."

"You never give up, do you?" she said, her lips curved in amusement.

"No, I'll never give up on you, unless you tell me I have to. But please don't do that." He ran a finger over the furrow that had frequently marked her brows since the wedding. "What's this about? You're stewing over something, and you have been for days now."

"I've been thinking about Max and the baby and what Chloe did—and how hard it must've been for her to decide that motherhood isn't for her."

"She probably should've thought about that before she had a baby."

"He wasn't planned. Accidents happen—and they happen to people who don't want to be parents."

"True, and I don't mean to be judging someone I don't even know, but I can't help but feel sorry for Caden. Someday he's going to learn that his mother didn't want him, and that's going to be tough."

"He'll have plenty of people who love him and want him."

"But his mother isn't one of them, Charley. Whenever he figures that out, he's going to have a lot to deal with."

"I know," she said with a sigh. "You're right."

"So what else is bothering you about this? I know it's more than Max and Chloe."

She rolled her lip between her teeth and glanced up at him with huge brown eyes gone liquid with emotion.

"What is it? Just tell me and we'll figure it out. Please don't cry." He kissed her cheek and lips.

"You want kids someday, right?"

"I guess. I like being an uncle. I like that a lot, but I've never even come close to having my own kids. Of course, there's no comparison between an occasional visit and a daily commitment that lasts for eighteen years. Why do you ask?"

"Because I don't think I want them. I never have. While my sisters and cousins were playing with babies, I was shooting baskets or wrestling with my brothers or skiing. While they were babysitting, I was waitressing. I've never been into babies and kids, and at thirty, I'm not expecting to change my mind about that."

"Okay."

She eyed him skeptically. "That's it? Just okay?"

"What do you want me to say?" He twirled a strand of her hair around his index finger. "I'd never try to talk you into something you don't want, especially something as important as a baby."

"You built this house for the family you hope to have someday. Those are your words."

"If my family were you and me and Rufus, I'd be pretty damned happy about that."

"That's a lot of empty bedrooms, Tyler."

"Who says we'd have to stay here?"

"You love this house."

"I love you more." The words were out of his mouth before he took the time to weigh the pros and cons of telling her that.

Her eyes went wide with surprise—or maybe it was shock. "You . . . You . . ."

"I love you, Charley. I've loved you for a while now, even when you were pushing me away and shooting me down." He leaned in close enough to kiss her, forcing her to make eye contact with him. "I. Love. You."

"Oh," she said on a long exhale. "Well . . ."

Laughing at her befuddled reply, he said, "No need to panic or freak out or run away or do any of your usual things. It doesn't change anything." Even as he said that, however, he knew it wasn't entirely true. It actually changed everything.

"Yes, it does," she said softly.

"If I get to have you but I don't have kids, I'd be just fine. I'd be better than fine. I'd be fantastic because I had you."

"Your parents would hate me if I kept you from being a father."

"They won't hate you. They'll love you because I do." Now that he'd said those three powerful words out loud, he couldn't seem to stop saying them. "And they'd never know anything other than *we* decided not to have kids."

"This conversation is getting pretty far down the road seeing as how you're my temporary boyfriend."

"I thought we decided deadlines were silly."

"We did and they are, but still . . . Nothing has been decided, and we shouldn't even be talking about this stuff." When she would have pulled away from him, he stopped her by tightening his arm around her.

"Don't, Charley. Don't run away from me because it's gotten intense between us." He moved ever so slightly to position himself on top of her, looking down at her as he spoke. "Don't run. Stay here with me and freak out. I'll hold you until you get it out of your system."

"What if I never get it out of my system?"

"I'd hold you forever if you'd let me."

"You're too good for me, Tyler. You deserve someone who can give you everything you want and need."

"I already have her. I have what I want and need. The question is, Charley, what do *you* want?"

*What do you want?* Tyler's question stayed with Charley as she showered and changed for the gathering at his parents' home. It stayed with her when she met his brothers, Rob, Chris and Dave, as well as his sisters, Cheryl and Paula, and their husbands and children. It stayed with her while she chatted with his dad and watched Tyler on the floor wrestling with his nephews and later, allowing his nieces to paint his nails a bright shade of pink.

*What do you want, Charley?* Her heart melted at the sight of his littlest niece, Violet, asleep in his arms while the family chatted in their big family room after dinner. The tiny girl's face was flushed with holiday excitement. Tyler ran his fingers through her blond curls while talking football with his brothers.

*I love you, Charley. I've loved you for a while now, even when you were pushing me away and shooting me down.*

He caught her eye and sent her a private smile that warmed her all the way through.

She thought about everything he'd done for her since her accident, the nights he'd spent by her side in the hospital, bathing her face with cold cloths while she burned with fever, carrying her around those first painful days at home, helping her in the bathroom, setting up his bedroom for her, holding hands in the dark with her night after night, encouraging her through physical therapy and cooking delicious meals. Even when she was cranky from the pain, he'd never lost his sense of humor or his ability to cheer her up.

*I want him*, she thought with sudden clarity that left her breathless. *I want to always feel the way I do when he looks at me. I want to stop being so afraid and take everything he's offered me.* The decision sent her reeling, which of course he noticed, his brow raised in inquiry. That he could be so attuned to her in a room full of people validated her life-changing decision.

On the verge of overheating, she got up and hobbled into the kitchen in search of a glass of ice water.

Vivienne, who'd been unloading the dishwasher, stopped what she was doing when Charley entered the room. "You shouldn't be on your feet, honey. What can I get for you?"

"Just some water, please, and I'm fine. My knee is feeling great."

"I'm so glad to hear it." Vivienne filled a glass with ice and poured water from a pitcher. "Here you are."

"Thank you." Charley took a greedy drink of the cold water and felt her nerves begin to settle ever so slightly. "And I've never gotten the chance to thank you for what you did to help Tyler get his place ready for an invalid."

"It was my pleasure to help you—and him. He was out of his mind after you got hurt."

"So I've heard. He's been really great helping me get back on my feet."

"He cares for you very deeply."

"I know."

Though Vivienne smiled and began to wipe the counter, Charley could tell there was more she wanted to say.

Charley went to her, put her hand on the other woman's arm. "Don't worry. I think it's going to be okay."

"Oh, honey . . ." Vivienne took a deep breath and blinked back tears. "I'm so happy to hear you say that."

"What's going on in here, ladies?" Tyler asked when he joined them.

"Just girl talk," Vivienne said with a smile for Charley. "None of your business."

Charley laughed at her saucy reply. She glanced up at Tyler, who was looking sexy in a gray cashmere sweater and dark jeans that hugged his muscular body in all the right places.

His eyes heated with awareness of her. "*My* girl and I need to head out. I don't want her overdoing it."

"And he thinks I buy that," Vivienne said, rolling her eyes.

Charley cracked up laughing as Vivienne hugged her. "Thank you for a lovely evening."

"It was delightful to have you here with us, Charley. I hope you and all the Abbotts have a very merry Christmas."

"Same to you."

Tyler hugged and kissed his mother. "Thanks for a great night, Mom. I'll call you tomorrow."

"You enjoy your time with Charley and her family."

"I will."

They said good-bye to the rest of the family and went out into the frigid night.

Tyler kept his arm tight around her as they walked to the Range Rover. "Look up."

"Oh wow," Charley said of the stars that filled the night sky. She brought her gaze down from the heavens to find he'd been looking at her while she looked at the stars. And then he was kissing her with hours of pent-up desire.

She curled her arms around his neck and lost herself in the kiss—and in him. The kiss was so hot she could barely feel the cold.

He pressed her against the car and destroyed her with deep sweeps of his tongue and soft bites of his teeth on her bottom lip. "Charley," he whispered when he finally broke the kiss many minutes later. "I've been dying for you for hours. How do you do that to me?"

"The same way you do it to me, I suppose."

"Let's go home."

When, she wondered, had his home become *their* home? When had she stopped thinking of her apartment as home and started thinking of the spacious home on the hill as theirs rather than his? Maybe it was when he brought home a huge Christmas tree and she helped him decorate it. Or perhaps it was when she tried to cook for him and burned pancakes beyond recognition, forcing him to open windows to let in fresh, freezing air while praising her efforts. It could've been the many times they'd stayed up all night talking and laughing and making love.

How was it that tearing up her knee could've led to some of the best times of her life?

She stared out the passenger window on the way home, fully aware that at some point over the last few weeks she'd stopped pushing Tyler away and had begun to actively pull him closer. And now he was closer to her than any man had ever been, and she was actually okay with that.

Charley pulled off her glove and reached over to put her hand on his leg.

He looked at her, smiled warmly, and covered her hand with his.

When they got home, he took her coat and hung it next to his in the mudroom. When she was growing up, her coat had hung between Ella's and Wade's and now it was next to Tyler's as if it belonged there.

She went into the kitchen, as if it were hers, and put a kettle on to boil while Tyler lit the Christmas tree and the fire. Instead of her usual bedtime cup of tea, tonight she made hot chocolate with shots of Baileys that she found in the liquor cabinet above the fridge. She topped it off with whipped cream and chocolate sprinkles.

Tyler came into the kitchen to see what she was up to.

"I've made myself right at home here, rifling through your cabinets."

"You're more than welcome to rifle through anything of mine. You know that."

She handed him one of the mugs. "How do you do that so easily?"

He took a sip of the hot chocolate. "Oh, that's good. What is it that I do so easily?"

"Cede your personal space and make me feel like I belong here."

"You do belong here. That's what I've been trying to tell you for weeks now."

"You really believe that, don't you?"

Tyler put his mug on the counter and slid his arms around her. "When I was building this place . . ." His voice trailed off and he looked away, as if he'd thought better of whatever he was going to say.

"Tell me."

He looked down at her, handsome, adorable and sincere, like always. "I pictured you here."

Shock reverberated through Charley. "That was years ago! Before you ever even asked me out the first time."

Shrugging, he said, "I pictured you here."

"Tyler—"

He kissed the words right off her lips, keeping her pressed tightly to him as he devoured her. Tasting of chocolate and Baileys and Tyler, he thrust his tongue into her mouth. He kissed her until she forgot what she'd been about to say, until his hands were under her sweater and his lips were on her neck, clearing her mind of every thought except for one. He'd pictured her here years ago.

"Let's go in the other room," he said when he finally released her.

It took a second or two for her brain to unscramble enough to take her mug as well as his outstretched hand and follow him into the living room.

When they were settled on the sofa, he turned to her and caressed her face while gazing at her lips. "Do you want your present tonight or tomorrow morning?" he asked.

"Oh. We're doing presents?"

"I got you a little something."

"I got you something, too," she said with a teasing smile.

His fingers slid through her hair. "Tonight or tomorrow?"

"Right now."

"Okay then." He got up and went into his office, returning with a big box that was wrapped in gold foil paper with a huge bow on top.

"That is not a *little* something."

"I could always send it back if you don't want it."

"Gimme," she said, making him laugh. Knowing he did nothing halfway, her hands trembling ever so slightly, she removed the top lid to find a box full of smaller presents. "You said a *little something*. This is a *lot* of little somethings."

"Can still send it all back . . ."

"Stop that foolishness." She dove into the box, her excitement trumping the anxiety. Each gift that she opened proved how closely he paid attention to what she loved—some of the sexiest lingerie she'd ever seen, high-end bath oil and body lotion and a new pair of running shoes that were lighter than air.

"You'll be needing them again before you know it."

"I hope you're right about that," Charley said, examining the pink sneakers in detail.

"Is that color okay?"

"I love them. Thank you for all of this. You went way overboard."

"There's one more in there, at the bottom."

She sifted through tissue paper to find the small remaining box. "Tyler . . ."

"It's not what you think, so don't panic," he said, laughing. "Just open it."

"Don't make fun of me. This relationship business is all new to me, and I'm at a serious disadvantage here. You're excellent at it, and I suck."

"You most definitely do *not* suck at it. You're much better at it than you think, and you know how I know that?"

Charley shook her head.

"Because I've never been happier in my life, so you must be doing something right."

She smiled at him. "See what I mean? That, right there. A plus."

"Sorry. I'll try harder not to be so good at this."

"Now that would just be silly. As long as you're aware of who you're dealing with, it's all good."

His fingers continued to slide through her hair, making

her want to purr from the pleasure he gave her with even the simplest of touches. "I've never been more aware of anyone. Ever. Now open your present."

Charley slid the bow off the small package and opened the box from a jewelry store. Inside was a platinum charm bracelet. "Oh, that's beautiful." She held it up for closer scrutiny, taking note of the various charms he'd chosen—a runner, first aid, crutches, snowflakes, a Christmas tree and a heart with his name engraved on it. "Tyler, this is amazing and so sweet!"

"It's our story—so far—but there's room for more. Much more."

"I love it." Charley hugged him. "Thank you."

"I'm glad you love it."

"I really do." As she watched him put the bracelet on her arm, she wanted to tell him she loved him, too, but the words were frozen on her tongue. Saying them would change everything, and as much as she wanted to give him what he'd already given her, she couldn't. She wasn't ready to change everything. Not yet anyway. "Do you want yours now, too?"

"Whatever you want."

Charley got up and limped into the bedroom where she'd hidden the presents she'd gotten for him, hoping he'd like them as much as she'd liked his. What did one get for the man who had two hundred million dollars? That question had kept her awake on more than one night recently. He'd done so much for her that she wanted to get it right. But as always where he was concerned, she questioned herself and her judgment.

The Baileys and the fire had her feeling overheated, so she removed her sweater and tossed it on the bed. When she returned to the living room, Tyler immediately homed in on the tank top she wore. His attention made her nipples tighten with awareness. Naturally he noticed that, too.

Making the slow walk across the room with two wrapped packages in hand, Charley's nerves went berserk as she second-guessed one of the presents. Quadruple-guessed, she thought grimly. She'd rethought the wisdom of one of these gifts for days since the idea first came to her.

"Why do you look like you're walking to a firing squad?" he asked as she approached.

"Because I'm quintuple-guessing the wisdom of one of these gifts."

"Do you think I won't like it?"

"Oh, you'll like it. I'm just feeling a little . . . self-conscious, I guess."

"After everything we've done together, you still feel self-conscious around me?"

She nodded. "About this. Yes."

"Now I'm crazy with curiosity. As you would say, gimme."

Charley handed him the first one and watched him unwrap the video game version of Risk that she'd found online.

"This is awesome! I didn't even know there was a video game."

"Do you have that game console?"

"Yep, I've got all of them. Boys and their toys," he said with a sheepish grin. "I really love this, and I look forward to kicking your ass on the video version."

"The way you haven't yet on the board version?"

"Exactly. Gimme the other one." He tugged on it and she held back, her face burning as she imagined his reaction. "Oh this must be good if your face turns bright red."

"First some backstory. Remember the day you went to help your brothers get a Christmas tree for your parents' house?"

"Yep."

"My cousin Izzy came over to see me that day."

"She's the photographer, right?"

"Yes, and she brought her camera so she could take some pictures of your view. While she was here, I asked if she might take a couple of photos of me, and well, she had a few ideas and we sort of got into it a little and well . . ."

"Give me that gift, Charlotte. Right now."

The sexy, gravelly tone of his voice made her heart leap wildly as she handed over the package.

He tore the paper off it and stared at the black-and-white photo of her, wearing a sexy black push-up bra and nothing else, wrapped up in the rumpled sheets on his bed. While the photo was tastefully done, it left the curve of her ass on subtle display. She'd worn smoky, sexy eye makeup and her hair was messy. She looked as if she'd just been thoroughly ravished.

"Charley . . ." He continued to stare at it while his Adam's apple moved in his throat. "Holy fuck," he whispered. "Except for the real you, this is the sexiest thing I've ever seen."

"You like it?"

"I *love* it." He put his arm around her shoulders and drew her into a lusty kiss that set her on fire for him.

Charley broke the kiss. "You won't let anyone else see that, will you?"

"Never. For my eyes only. Are there others?"

"Maybe . . ."

"I want them. I want all of them."

"I might be able to work out something with the photographer," she said with a coy smile. "I know it's not much, but what do you give the man who has everything?"

"You gave me the one thing I want that I don't completely have. You gave me *you*, Charley. What could be better than that?" He studied the photo again, as if he couldn't get enough of it, running his fingers over the glass. "I love that you did this for me."

"I wanted you to see me without the leg brace and the ugly scar and the limp."

"I don't see any of that when I look at you. That's all temporary anyway."

Charley took the frame from him and put it on the coffee table. Then she took hold of his hands and tugged on them as she lay back on the sofa.

Tyler willingly followed. "What's on your mind, honey?"

"You are. We are. I'm thinking a lot about what you said before."

"I hope that didn't make this harder on you."

She squirmed against his erection. "It seems to have made it harder on *you*."

His bark of laughter drew a smile from her. "Baby, I'm always hard for you. All you have to do is breathe for that to happen, or walk into the room wearing this sexy shirt." He dragged his finger over the tops of her breasts. "Are you ready for me?"

"Always, it seems. I'm not quite sure how you do that."

"It's magic between us. I feel it. Do you?"

She nodded, unable to deny for another second the magnitude of what she felt for him. "Make love to me, Tyler."

He released a slow, shuddering breath and captured her mouth in a savagely passionate kiss. Her request had undone something in him, something wild and untamed, and she loved it.

Clothes came flying off, pillows fell from the sofa, hands and lips and tongues aroused to the point of madness before he pounded into her and took them both on a crazy ride that ended in simultaneous cries of completion.

"Jesus," he whispered.

Charley laughed at the astounded tone of his voice as he said the single word. She was feeling rather astounded herself at the moment.

"We didn't even get our pants off." His jeans were down around his thighs. Hers were tangled around her left leg.

"Your knee . . ."

"Is fine. Everything is fine."

"Good," he said, sounding relieved. "I didn't mean to be so rough."

"I loved it." Her fingers slid through the perspiration on his back while his chest hair tickled her breasts, making her squirm under him.

He groaned, and his tongue touched the spot behind her ear, and just that quickly, she wanted him again.

They began to move together, slowly this time. He gazed down at her, seeming to memorize her every expression, her every reaction.

Day by day, hour by hour, minute by minute he had chipped away at her defenses until all her walls had fallen, leaving her fully exposed to him in every possible way. A few weeks ago, the realization would've had her running from him as fast and as far as she could, injured knee or not.

But now . . . Now things were different, and she had no desire to run. No, she wanted to stay forever, and that was far scarier than running had ever been.

# CHAPTER 25

—◄►—

Christmas at the Abbott barn was madness. Tyler had thought his family was loud and boisterous, but the Westcotts had nothing on the Abbotts, who were joined this year by several additional extended family members who'd stayed in town after the wedding. Patrick Murphy spent the whole day glued to Mary's side.

"Are they dating?" Tyler whispered to Charley after dinner left most of the Abbotts in a turkey coma. Bodies were scattered throughout the great room, on every piece of furniture and the floor while a Christmas movie that no one was watching played on the TV.

"I don't know. I have to ask Cam."

Lucy's dad, Ray, had spent much of the afternoon chatting with Charley's aunt Hannah, while Emma and Grayson were huddled together on one of the sofas with her daughter Simone between them. Lucas Abbott was out cold in the middle of the living room floor. His twin was asleep on the floor of the den, where Hunter and Megan were snuggled in front of one of the two fireplaces that Colton had kept fed with wood all day.

Gavin's parents had come for dinner and were still at the dining room table with Molly, Lincoln and Elmer long after the others had headed for sofas and floors and other horizontal surfaces.

Stepping over bodies, Max walked the floor with Caden, who'd been fussy all day. Molly said the baby was overstimulated by the noise and chaos of the holiday, so Max was trying to soothe him. Tyler wanted to offer to help the poor guy but didn't feel it was his place. Not yet anyway. Maybe someday he'd be an official member of the Abbott family and Max would be his brother-in-law and Caden his nephew. Then he could offer to relieve the tired dad for a while, but for now, he held back, not wanting to overstep.

Last night, on the sofa, he'd felt Charley's surrender. He'd actually felt her let go and give in to the relationship she hadn't wanted until it happened, but their accord was still fragile, and he had a long way to go in convincing her that his love for her would last a lifetime.

He couldn't wait for their trip to Boston tomorrow where he'd have her all to himself for a night—maybe two if he could talk her into staying longer. Tyler had spent hours planning their night away down to the last detail, and he couldn't wait to leave in the morning.

"Poor Max," Charley said softly from their perch on the sofa. "He's so exhausted."

"I was going to offer to relieve him for a while, but I didn't know if that would be weird."

"That would be really nice. You should."

"Oh, okay." Tyler kissed her cheek, got up and stepped over Lucas to cross the room to where Max was standing in front of the biggest Christmas tree Tyler had ever seen.

"Hey, Max, you want to take a break? I'd be happy to help. I've got lots of niece and nephew experience."

Max seemed surprised by the offer, but the surprise was soon replaced by gratitude. "Wouldn't say no to that, Tyler. My arms are asleep, but he's wide awake."

"Let me take a whirl. My sister Paula used to call me a

baby whisperer because I was the only one who could get her older daughter to sleep."

"Work your magic," Max said as he carefully transferred the tiny bundle into Tyler's arms.

"Go get a drink. You look like you need one."

Max laughed. "I need about ten."

"Start with one. We'll be fine."

"Thanks."

"Any time." After Max had walked away, Tyler looked down at the big eyes looking up at him. "Hey there, little man. I'm Tyler, your aunt Charley's boyfriend." He walked through the big rooms that made up the first floor of the Abbotts' barn, talking softly to the baby as he went, ending up in the mudroom where each of the ten Abbotts had a hook with their name on it. The hooks were laden with coats today.

"I hope maybe someday I'll be your uncle, but I shouldn't say that out loud. Your aunt Charley isn't like other women. She's very, very special, and I have to be really patient with her. Someday you might love someone the way I love Charley, and you'll know what I mean."

"So it's love, huh?" a voice behind him said.

Tyler turned and found Elmer smiling widely.

"You heard that?" he asked, embarrassed to have been caught when he thought he had found the one unoccupied corner of the house.

Charley's grandfather smiled broadly. "I heard it, and I'm delighted. I had a feeling about you two kids."

"I know that feeling. I've had it for a while myself." Tyler kept watch over Caden, whose eyes were beginning to get heavy.

"So I've noticed, but our Charley . . . She hasn't made it easy for you, has she?"

Tyler suppressed the urge to laugh out loud so he wouldn't disturb the baby. "You could say that, but she's worth it."

"I couldn't agree more. Ever since she was as tiny as this fellow, she's marched to the beat of her own drummer. Couldn't tell her anything when she was a kid, so she had to learn every lesson the hard way. Used to pain me to see her hurting, but after a while I realized that's just how it's meant to be for her."

"I picture her with skinned knees and elbows and tear tracks on her freckled face," Tyler said.

"You're not that far off," Elmer said with a chuckle. "It took a lot to make her cry."

"Still does."

"And when it happens, it breaks your heart because you know she has to be really hurting."

"Yeah."

"I want to let you in on a little secret that has to stay between us."

"Sure," Tyler said, intrigued.

"Before Charley started talking about training to run a marathon, Vivienne told me you were in training with a local running club. So when Charley told me about her plans to train over lunch one day, I told her about the club. I might've forgotten to mention that you were already a member."

Astounded by Elmer's confession, Tyler said, "I've heard you were good, but wow. That's . . ."

"Shameless?"

"A little bit," Tyler said with a laugh.

"Did it work?"

"Hell yes, it worked. Although we both could've done without the plunge off the side of the mountain."

"That was not part of my plan, in case you were wondering."

"Good to know you're not completely diabolical."

Elmer snorted with quiet laughter. Placing his hand on Tyler's shoulder, Elmer said, "You, my friend, have stepped up admirably for my granddaughter. We all appreciate what you've done. But I have to ask what your intentions are where she's concerned."

"Isn't that rather old-fashioned?"

"You may not have noticed, but I'm rather old."

"Don't play that card. You're old like I am."

"I'm young at heart, but old-fashioned just the same, and I want to see all of my grandchildren happily settled before I go."

"Where're you going?"

"Don't get smart with me, young man, or I'll have no choice but to report you to your mother."

"You wouldn't dare."

"Try me," Elmer said, his eyes twinkling with delight. He clearly lived for this shit.

"My intention is to spend the rest of my life with your granddaughter, if she'll have me. And that's still the great unknown. We've made progress, but we're not quite there yet."

"Does she know you love her?"

"She does."

"And how does she feel?"

"Your guess is as good as mine. I think she feels the same way, but she's not ready to say so, which is fine. I'm not going anywhere."

"That's good," Elmer said, nodding in approval. "That's what you've got to do. Show her you're in it for keeps, no matter what."

"That's the plan."

"And when it all works out, you'll be sure to tell my son-in-law that I was instrumental in bringing you two together, right?"

"You two are *competing* against each other?"

"I'd call it more a friendly wager than a competition."

"You really are diabolical."

"And you're really good with babies."

Tyler looked down and saw that Caden was asleep.

"You'll make a fine father someday, Tyler."

The compliment was bittersweet for Tyler, who'd meant what he'd said to Charley about being fine with her not wanting children. But he was still getting used to the idea that if he married her, he wouldn't be a father. Kids had been something way off in the distant future, like an idea of what might happen rather than anything definite. If the choice was a life with her and no kids or kids with someone else, he chose her. He'd always choose her.

"I'd better get him back to his dad."

"I'm glad we had this chat. If I can be of any help to you, I hope you'll let me know."

"You already have, Mr. Stillman. More than you know."

"Call me Elmer, son. I have a feeling we're going be family before too long."

Though Charley's grandfather's words gave him hope, Tyler wouldn't relax until he was hearing them from Charley.

Hours after everyone else had gone to bed on Christmas night, Grayson lingered at his aunt Molly's because he'd yet to run out of things to talk about with the beautiful, shy and funny Emma Mulvaney. They sat on the sofa closest to the fire in the den that he'd kept stoked for hours while they chatted about their lives in Boston and New York, her adorable daughter, her sister's romance with his cousin and their jobs.

He learned that she worked as the office manager for a dentist, and the rest of her life was devoted to Simone. Until recently, his had been devoted to work. That had led to their current conversation about balance and how to find it.

"So what made you decide to make the move now?" she asked.

He'd discovered she was an excellent listener, which made him want to tell her things he normally kept private. Most of the people in this world were accomplished talkers. Few were as good at listening. Emma was a true exception. "I had this case assigned to me . . . We have these A-list clients, you know? The ones we pander to, no matter what disgusting thing they might've done. The senior partner calls them the 'gravy' clients. So this guy, a bigwig in the local business community, beat the shit out of his wife, and it was my job to get him off even though we all knew he did it. He put her in the hospital with broken ribs and a broken jaw—and it wasn't the first time."

Emma gasped and her hand covered her heart. "Dear God."

"I couldn't do it. I couldn't make myself defend him when I knew he was guilty. All the money in the world just isn't worth it. I submitted my resignation, my partners bought me out and here I am."

"You did the right thing."

"This time. There've been other times when I successfully defended the scumbags, and I'm not proud of that. But after a while, it gets harder to wash off the scum. It stays with you. I made a lot of money in that job. The kind of money I used to dream about having back when we were scrambling to make ends meet after my dad left. But when I saw the police photos of the injured wife, something in me just said, *Enough of this crazy shit. I can't do it anymore.*"

Her hand on his arm was intended to be comforting, but it stirred something else he hadn't experienced in far too long—pure desire.

"I'm sure you'll make a very nice living here, without having to sell your soul to the devil to do it," Emma said.

"I hope so. It won't be the living I was making in Boston, but I worked so much I didn't have time to spend half of what I made there. It'll be okay. Anything is better than what I was doing there."

"What did your partners say when you told them you were leaving?"

"They tried to talk me out of it. A few said I was making a huge mistake, committing career suicide by moving home to the boonies." He shrugged. "Nothing they said convinced me to change my mind."

"Your gut was telling you it was the right move at the right time. I'm a big believer in following my gut."

"What kind of things has your gut told you to do?"

She thought about that for a second, which gave him time to study the sweet face and the cheeks made rosy by the heat of the fire as well as several glasses of chardonnay. "It told me not to marry Simone's father or allow him to be in her life."

Grayson immediately sensed from her hesitation that this was not something she talked about often. "How come?"

"He wasn't always nice to me."

"Did he . . . Did he hurt you?"

"Once."

How was it possible, when he'd only just met her, that he wanted to find the guy and kill him for hurting her even once?

"When I told him it was over between us, he . . . he didn't take it well."

"What happened?"

"It was a long time ago. A lifetime ago."

"But you've never forgotten it."

As she stared into the fire, all the life in her eyes seemed to go dull. "No, I haven't."

Grayson didn't think before he reached for her, wishing he could take away the pain of someone he barely knew. That was certainly a first. She flinched, ever so slightly, but he saw it and realized the damage ran deep from the one time the man she'd loved hurt her.

"Do you want to talk about it?"

"I've never talked about it," she said with a shaky laugh. "Are you sure you're a lawyer and not a shrink?"

"Quite sure," he said with a chuckle, "although sometimes I think the two professions aren't all that different."

Emma took a drink of her wine and continued to stare at the fire. "When I told him we were done, he flipped out. He . . . He held me down and forced me to . . ." She blew out a deep breath. "When it was over, I told him to leave or I'd call the police. I said if I ever saw him again, I'd report what he'd done to me."

"Christ, Emma. You've never told *anyone* that? Not even Lucy?"

Shaking her head, she said, "No one knows how Simone came to be. Except for you now."

"Emma," Grayson said on a long exhale. Though he had no right, he drew her in closer to him, needing to hold her.

"My dad was so mad when he found out I was pregnant. He didn't speak to me for the longest time. I hated that he was so disappointed."

"Why didn't you tell him, sweetheart?"

"Because I didn't want Simone's life to be colored by how she was conceived. I couldn't bear that for her. As soon as I knew she was coming, I was in love with her. I didn't care how she came to be. Somehow I've managed to keep those two things very separate in my mind. There's him and what he did, and then there's her—perfect in every way and no reflection whatsoever of the man who fathered her. In fact, she's a perfect reflection of my sister. I love that." Emma wiped away a tear that had slid down her cheek. "I love that she looks like Lucy. I thank God every day that she doesn't look like him." She released another of those shaky laughs. "What is it about you that has me spilling my guts to a total stranger?"

"I'm not a stranger. Not anymore. I'm a friend, and I'm glad you finally told someone. What he did to you, Emma . . . It was a crime. You know that, right?"

Nodding, she said, "I've had counseling, and I've come to terms with what happened that night. As much as one ever accepts such things."

"And he doesn't know about her?"

She shook her head. "I've never seen him again, thank God. I used to be so afraid of him coming back and doing the math . . . But she looks nothing like him, and she's always looked young for her age. There would be no reason for him to suspect she's his."

If he were thinking like a lawyer, Grayson might have something to say to that. But he was thinking as a man who'd been profoundly moved by a woman for the first time in his thirty-six years. "You're amazing."

"Don't say that. I did what any mother would've done to protect her child."

"At tremendous personal expense."

"The payoff has been the most wonderful little girl that anyone could hope for. I'll never regret a thing because I have her."

"She's very lucky to have you, too."

"We're both lucky. We've made a nice life for ourselves, and I never think about this stuff anymore."

Grayson didn't know if he totally believed that, but he wasn't about to question her. "You must be beating the men away with a stick."

"Right," she said, laughing. "Between work and home-work and dance class and birthday parties and soccer, I'm a regular dating machine."

"So there's no one special in your life?"

"Just Simone, my dad, Lucy, Colton and a few very good friends, including Cameron."

"Do you ever want more for yourself?"

She shrugged. "I've learned to be very satisfied and thankful for what I have."

"I want to see you again, Emma. I want to spend more time together." The words were out of his mouth before he decided to say them because the thought of her getting away, of never seeing her or Simone again except for at family events, was unacceptable to him. Here he'd just taken steps to simplify his life, and one night with her had made everything complicated again. And that was fine with him.

"Oh, um, you do?"

"I really do. I haven't talked to a woman the way I've talked to you tonight in, well, ever. I don't want to stop talking to you, even though I should let you get to bed so you're not exhausted tomorrow. Something tells me Miss Simone won't be too forgiving of an exhausted mother."

"You're right. She'll take full advantage. But I'm not quite ready to go to bed just yet."

"No?"

She shook her head as she returned his gaze, never blinking as they drank each other in. Once again, Grayson acted before thinking, leaning in to kiss her. He was careful not to move too fast or take too much, but he could not let this night end without tasting her. As soon as he processed that first taste, he knew it wasn't going to be anywhere near enough.

The slight mewling sound that came from her throat made him instantly hard. He drew back to look at her, slightly stunned by his reaction. Her eyes were closed, her lips parted and damp. He dragged his fingertip over her bottom lip.

"You're beautiful, Emma."

Her eyes opened slowly and she took a long look at him, as if trying to gauge his sincerity. He'd never been more sincere.

"How long are you here?"

She cleared her throat. "Molly invited us to spend the week since Simone is on vacation."

"Could Lucy watch Simone so I could take you to dinner tomorrow night?"

"I . . . I think they'd both love that."

"How about you? Would you love it if Simone went with Lucy so you can go out with me?"

"Yes, Grayson, I believe I'd love that, too."

# CHAPTER 26

———— ◄ ► ————

In the morning, Charley and Tyler were up early for breakfast before hitting the road to Boston. The day was sunny and cold, the sky a bright blue and the trees frosted from overnight snowfall.

"I love winter days like this," Tyler said. "Take away the snow, and you can almost fool yourself into thinking it's summer."

"Until you step outside in a bathing suit and freeze your ass off."

"Why would I do that on the twenty-sixth of December?"

"It's your metaphor," she said teasingly. She'd been awake before dawn, excited about their trip and to spend more time with him. While they were in Boston, she wanted to find the courage to tell him she'd fallen for him, too. She wanted him to know that she was no longer looking for an exit strategy.

It'd been more than ten years since she told a man she loved him, and that man had run roughshod over her heart and soul. Even knowing there was no chance of that happening this time, Charley was still nervous about saying those words to Tyler. But she wanted to. More than once in the last few days since he'd first said them to her, she'd come close to uttering those three magical words.

Something had always stopped her. Tonight, she'd decided, nothing would stop her. Charley loved him. She loved everything about him, from the tender way he'd cared for her to his obvious devotion to her to his love for his family. She loved that he was brilliant at his work and humble about his success. Over the last couple of weeks, she'd fallen in love with his beautiful home on the hill, too. She could see herself living there permanently.

Taken on their own, any of these realizations would be life changing. Taken together, they left her feeling as if an emotional tsunami had roared through her life, changing her forever. In the early predawn light, she'd begun to understand that she would never again be the woman she'd been before her accident, before Tyler had loved her.

And that was okay, because she liked who she was with him, who they were together. She was comfortable in the new skin of this relationship because he'd handled it—and her—just right.

He turned on the radio and reached for her hand.

Charley cradled his hand between both of hers. "Wait. Is this the Beatles channel?"

"Yeah, why?"

"Noooo, no, no. No Beatles."

"Why not? I love the Beatles."

"*Noooooo*. You can't. No, no, *no*."

He laughed at her vehemence, which made her dig in deeper.

"I can't be with a man who listens to the Beatles channel. I was weaned on the Beatles. My father is insane for them. We have dogs named Ringo and George. Please, I beg of you, no Beatles."

"Baby, come on. You can't do this to me. They're my favorite band ever."

"*Noooooooooooooo*. I knew you were too good to be true. There had to be something wrong with you. Better I discovered this now rather than later." She tried to pull her hand free of his grasp, but he held on tighter.

"I'm not letting you go. I'll change the channel for you."

Holding the wheel with his knees, he used his other hand to flip the channel. "Do you have anything against Nirvana?"

"Nothing at all."

"I may keep you around then."

"The Beatles and Nirvana. There's an interesting combo."

"I'm an interesting kind of guy."

"If my dad didn't already love you, he would after hearing you love the Beatles. That's all it takes to win him over."

"That's good info to have. Might come in handy someday if I want to kiss up to him."

"Why would you want to do that?"

He glanced over at her, seeming to gauge whether he should say what was on his mind. "You know. In case . . ."

"Of what?"

"If I maybe want to marry his daughter, it would be nice if I asked his permission."

Hearing him use the M word hit her like a punch to the heart.

"Should I not have said that?"

"It's okay."

"If it's okay, why is your voice all high and screechy?"

"My voice is not screechy."

"You aren't hyperventilating, are you?"

Charley laughed at the genuine concern in his tone. "No, Tyler, I'm not hyperventilating at the thought of marrying you."

"Really? You're not?"

"You sound disappointed."

"I'm . . . I'm not sure what I am. This is a good thing, right? That you're not hyperventilating?"

"I've heard hyperventilation isn't good for one's health, so yes, it's a good thing that I'm not hyperventilating."

"That's not what I meant, and you know it."

"You're sounding a bit screechy."

"Charley! Stop torturing me and quit talking in circles. I'm getting dizzy."

"What was the question again?"

"I haven't asked you the question, but if I did, what would you say?"

"You want like an answer now?"

"A gist would be good. Are we in the maybe zone or the hell-no zone?"

"Definitely maybe."

"Definitely maybe," he said, grinning widely. "Those might be my new favorite words."

"You're easy to please, Tyler."

"Not always, but you please me, Charlotte. You please me very much."

They got to Boston in plenty of time to attend a matinee of *Beautiful*, the Carole King musical, which Charley absolutely loved. After the show, they checked into an elegant suite at the Ritz-Carlton, and Charley was appropriately dazzled. At the floor-to-ceiling windows that looked out over the Boston Common, Charley took in the view of the park and the city and the water in the distance.

Tyler slid his arms around her from behind. "Good?"

"Fantastic."

"I'm glad you like it." He kissed her neck and the hot spot behind her ear that made her go weak. "I was thinking about seeing if the bed lives up to the hype before our dinner reservations. Unless you want to go shopping or something."

Smiling at his shameless flirting, she turned in his arms and hooked hers around his neck. "We really ought to make sure the bed is comfortable before we're stuck with it for the night."

"It would be the responsible thing to do." He slid his hands down her arms to link their fingers, walking backward as he led her into the bedroom. The blinds had been lowered but not completely drawn and candles flickered on the bedside table.

"I've been set up," she said.

"Guilty as charged."

"I like being set up by you."

He put his arms around her and hugged her in close to him. "Sometimes I still can't believe you're saying stuff like that to me. You have no idea how long I've wanted you."

"How long?"

"I don't remember a time when I didn't want you. You were so untouchable though." As he spoke, he continued to kiss her neck and his hands moved restlessly over her body, setting her on fire. "So aloof and out of reach."

"I wasn't."

"Yes, you were. You weren't ready for this. I get that now."

"You intimidated me with your intensity. Pushing you away was easier than letting you in."

He gathered up the skirt of the dress she'd worn for their trip to the big city and had it up and over her head in a matter of seconds, leaving her wearing the red-and-black lace bra and panties set he'd given her for Christmas.

Watching the bob of his Adam's apple and the flare of heat in his eyes as he took in the sight of her was madly arousing. And knowing he loved her made it possible for her to give herself to him completely, letting him sweep her under into the sea of emotion and desire he aroused in her.

He guided her to sit on the bed and then began unbuttoning the dress shirt he'd worn untucked with dark jeans. As he revealed his body to her, it was Charley's turn to stare at the play of muscles, the trail of dark hair that led into black boxer briefs, the thick bands of muscle that curved around his hips and the hard cock that sprung free when he removed the briefs.

She reached for him, but he stopped her from stroking him.

"Not yet," he said. "First you." With his hands on her hips, he tugged her gently to the edge of the mattress, supported her healing leg on a stack of pillows and then dropped to his knees beside the bed.

Charley's heartbeat was a wild, untamed thing as he removed her panties and used his big hands on her inner thighs to open her to his gaze. For the longest time, he only looked while she incinerated from the anticipation that grew and multiplied until her breathing became choppy and uneven. She was on the verge of begging him to do something when he dropped his head and exhaled against her sensitive flesh.

Was she really going to come from only his warm breath against her tingling clit?

"You're so beautiful, Charley. You have no idea what you do to me, or what it feels like to finally be able to touch you this way and to tell you how much I love you." Using his thumbs to hold her open, he punctuated his words with deep strokes of his tongue over her, into her.

She grasped the soft fabric of the comforter, holding on for dear life as he took her up so fast she barely had time to register what was happening before she detonated. That was the only word she could think of to describe the full-body orgasm that ripped through her.

He brought her down slowly, with light strokes of his tongue over her quivering flesh.

Charley had only begun to regain control of her senses when he pushed two fingers into her, rolling one orgasm into another as he sucked on her clit and stroked her from the inside. Before him, she'd suspected sex like this only happened in movies and romance novels. It didn't happen to real people. It had certainly never happened to her.

His fingers were slick with her wetness when he slid one of them into her anus, with no advance warning, no fanfare, nothing more than the casual press of flesh against flesh until she was crying out from the dark, shocking pleasure that blasted through her like an out-of-control skier careening downhill at full speed.

Charley had never felt anything that could compare with that third orgasm as she bucked against his tongue and contended with the tight squeeze of his finger in a place where nothing had ever been before. By the time he brought her back down to earth and withdrew from her body, she was a trembling, needy mess of raw nerves and emotions that were all new to her.

He kissed her tenderly. "Don't move. I'll be right back."

As if she could move when her muscles and bones had gone liquid. She heard the water running in the bathroom, and then he was back, hovering over her with his huge cock stretching above his navel.

"You okay?" he asked, his brows knitted with concern as he looked down on her.

She could only imagine how she must look after being thoroughly ravished—and apparently he wasn't done with her yet. "Mmm. Think so."

"Think so? You're not sure?"

"I don't think I could move if the place were on fire, but otherwise, I'm good. I'm great in fact. Do you mind if I sleep for the next eight to twelve hours?"

His smile unfolded slowly, making his eyes sparkle. "No way. I've got lots of plans for you, and I need you *wide* awake."

"That thing you did . . ."

"This?" He reached beneath her to press again on her back door, setting off a riot of sensation that she felt everywhere. "You liked it?"

"You couldn't tell from the nuclear orgasm?"

Chuckling, he nuzzled her cheek and continued to press rhythmically against her tight opening without breaching her.

Charley couldn't believe that she was about to beg him to do it again.

But he had other plans, she realized, when that imposing cock pushed against her tender flesh, entering and withdrawing repeatedly.

"Tyler! Stop teasing me."

"Is that what I'm doing?"

"You know it is."

His cocky grin told her he knew exactly what he was doing to her and was enjoying every second of it, the sadistic bastard.

"Tyler . . . Please."

"Is this what you want?" he asked, thrusting into her before withdrawing once again.

"*Yes*," she said on a gasp as her internal muscles stretched to accommodate him and then contracted after his abrupt departure.

"How about you give me something I want first?" Reaching

behind her, he released the clasp of her bra and was tossing it across the room a second later. Lowering his head, he caressed her left nipple with his tongue before moving to the other side for more of the same. The sensations traveled from her nipple to her clit, making her burn with desire even after coming three times.

"What? What do you want?" At that moment, she'd give him just about anything if it meant relief from the sweet torture.

Propped on his elbows, he gazed down at her, his fingers sweeping the hair back from her face. "I love you, Charley. I really and truly love you. I want to know if you love me, too. I want to know if I'm going to have forever with you. I want you to tell me you're here with me to stay, that you're not thinking anymore about how best to leave me when it's so fucking *good* between us. You have to feel it, too. You—"

She raised her fingers to his lips to quiet him. "I do feel it, and I do love you, too, Tyler."

When the time was right and the person was right and the pieces had come together to form a picture you'd never imagined for yourself, it wasn't all that hard to say the words, Charley discovered. And the deep sigh that escaped from him as he closed his eyes and rested his forehead on hers told her everything she'd ever need to know about how invested he was in her.

"I'm sorry if I put you through the wringer to get here."

"You, this . . . It was worth everything you put me through and then some." Taking himself in hand, he entered her slowly, reverently, taking his time probably because she'd told him they'd have the time—all the time in the world. "Tell me again. I need to hear it again."

"I love you, Tyler. I love everything about you."

"Fuck, Charley . . . You're killing me."

Amused by his reaction, she tightened her muscles around him, drawing a low groan from him before he began to move faster, pounding into her as he gripped her ass cheeks in his big hands, giving her everything he had to give and more than she'd ever dreamed possible.

They came together, straining, sweating, gasping, fingers digging into dense muscle and cries of completion shattering the quiet.

"Charley," he whispered after he'd collapsed on top of her. "God, Charley . . ."

She stroked his back in small circles with one hand, while running the fingers of her other hand through his hair soothingly.

"Say it again. I'm still not sure if I dreamed it."

Smiling, she said, "I love you, Tyler. I love you, I love you, I love you. And you're not dreaming."

"I have to be." Cupping her breast, he touched his tongue to the tight tip and began to harden inside her once again. "Nothing this astonishing could possibly be real."

"It's real."

"And you're not going to leave me at midnight on the thirty-first?"

"I'm not going to leave you for as long as you still want me—masochist stalker perv that you are."

"I'm always going to want you."

"Then I guess you're stuck with me."

He wrapped his arms around her and squeezed so tight she could barely breathe. "Thank Christ for that."

They dined at a fabulous Italian restaurant in the North End and drank a full bottle of champagne over dinner. Tyler was euphoric after the afternoon in bed with her, during which so many questions had finally been answered. She loved him. She had no plans to leave him. He was stuck with her, and that was all he'd wanted to hear.

As he fed her a bite of chocolate mousse after dinner, he watched her face, memorizing the happy glow, the flushed cheeks, the swollen lips. He couldn't wait to get her back to the hotel to pick up where they'd left off before dinner.

"Could I ask you something?" he said between bites of decadent mousse.

"Uh-huh."

"Did I blackmail you into saying something you weren't ready to say earlier?"

"Not at all. I was ready. In fact, I was planning to tell you sometime during our trip, so thanks for making it easy on me."

"When did you know?"

She eyed him coyly, smiling in that secretive way she reserved only for him. "Like you want the exact minute?"

The best sex of his life had already turned his blood to liquid fire, but Tyler topped off their glasses with the last of the champagne anyway. Tonight was for celebration. "The exact minute would be good."

Charley appeared to give his request considerable thought while he fed her more bites of mousse. "If I'm being honest . . ."

"I wouldn't want you any other way."

"The first day at your house, when you helped me in the bathroom and were a perfect gentleman. I think it might've happened then."

Tyler stared at her, agape. "*That* long ago?"

"That was the first time I felt something happen here," she said, rubbing her breastbone for emphasis. "It took a lot longer for me to accept it for what it was."

"And what was it?"

She rolled her eyes. "You've already gotten me to say it like a hundred times."

"I still won't be satisfied when you've said it a million times."

"It was *love*, you knucklehead. For such a smart guy, you sure can be dense sometimes."

Tyler laughed at the comment and fed her more of the mousse.

"It'll take a really long time to say it a million times, you know. Years."

"Decades," he said. "I'm not going anywhere, and you're not either, so feel free to get started on that million any time now."

She crooked her finger, drawing him close enough for her to whisper in his ear. "I love you, Tyler."

The words, the heat of her breath skirting over his ear . . . That was all it took to make him hard. While Charley giggled at his befuddled reaction, he signaled for the waiter. "Check please."

He was all over her in the cab back to the hotel, his hand inside her coat and flat against her inner thigh, creeping up, up, *up*, until she stopped him from going any further.

"Not here," she said against his wet lips.

Despite the anxious glances from the cabdriver in the mirror that she noticed out of the corner of her eye, Tyler never stopped kissing her, touching her, arousing her.

"We're here," the cabbie said with annoyance when he'd brought the car to a stop outside the Ritz.

Tyler pulled himself away from her to take a fifty from his wallet. "Keep the change."

"Hey, thanks, man."

Tyler got out and then helped her, holding her until she got her bearings.

"The last thing I want is for you to reinjure yourself while tipsy from champagne," he said into her ear, making her squirm against him shamelessly. His black overcoat was unbuttoned, giving her an unfettered view of his smoking hotness in the dark gray suit and creamy white dress shirt that he'd worn without a tie.

"I'm not going to fall. Don't worry."

Taking her hand, he led her into the hotel.

"I have to pee," she whispered—or what she considered a whisper.

"We'll be upstairs in a minute."

"Can't wait that long." A bellhop pointed her toward the lobby restroom, and she left Tyler with her coat at one of the sofas, kissing him before she walked—or hobbled—toward the long corridor that led to the restrooms. She was approaching the ladies' room when a man came out of the men's room and nearly crashed into her.

"So sorry," he said, taking her elbow to keep her from falling over.

The voice was familiar so Charley looked up at his face and gasped at the sight of Michael Devlin—older, heavier, balder, but definitely him. She recoiled from his touch, her skin seeming to shrivel on her bones.

"*Charley?* Charley Abbott? Is that really you?"

"No." She felt like a wounded, trapped animal as she tried to send the message to her legs to get her out of there, away from him. "No." Walking backward, afraid to take her eyes off him, she stumbled, wrenching her surgically repaired knee. The pain was massive and required her full attention as she stumbled into the ladies' room, praying he wouldn't follow her.

"Charley, wait! It's been too long. I can't believe it's you. What're the odds?"

What were the odds indeed? Someone up there must surely hate her to put him, of all people, in her path on this of all days.

He actually followed her into the bathroom.

"Go away," she growled, "or I swear to God I'll have you arrested." Where her ability to form words was coming from, she couldn't begin to imagine. All she knew was that she had to get away from him and the threat he posed to her physical and emotional well-being. She lunged for a stall and fumbled with the lock, her sweaty hands slipping over the cool metal twice before she was able to secure it. With tiny beads of light dancing before her eyes, Charley realized she'd been holding her breath. She took deep greedy gulps of air as tears flowed down her cheeks.

"Charley, come on. I just want to talk. You have to come out of there sometime."

Tyler would come for her. If she was gone long enough, he would come. Her hands shook uncontrollably, and the pain in her knee was agonizing, but there was no way in hell she was leaving that stall with him still out there waiting for God knows what.

"Look, I know you're probably mad about what happened, but that was a long time ago."

Why didn't someone else come in to use the facilities? How was it possible she was actually trapped in the bathroom with *him*? *Please, Tyler, please come find me* . . .

The dinner that had been so satisfying and delicious now churned like an angry sea in her belly, threatening to come back up at any second. But she couldn't give Devlin the satisfaction of knowing he'd actually made her sick, so she fought it back, the effort bringing more tears to her eyes and sweat to her brow.

"Charley," he said in a softer voice. "I'm sorry for what I did. I'm not that guy anymore. I wish you'd let me tell you—"

The door slammed open, and Tyler's deep voice rang out. "What the hell is going on? Who are you and where's Charley?"

"Tyler," she cried, the single word ripped from her throat. "Get him out of here. Please."

From her post inside the stall, she heard the sounds of a scuffle—grunts and groans and flesh connecting with flesh. She flinched at each sound. If that monster hurt Tyler, she would kill him the second her hands stopped shaking and her knee started working again.

Then she heard the door to the room crash open again, and Tyler called for security. More scuffling, more grunts, new voices.

"This guy was hassling my girlfriend in the ladies' room," Tyler said.

"He was *in* the ladies' room?"

"All the way in, and she's locked in a stall."

"I just wanted to talk to her," Devlin said. "We're old friends."

"You're no friend of hers if she had to lock a door to keep you away from her," Tyler said.

"We can take it from here, sir, but we'll need a statement from your girlfriend."

Charley leaned against the wall inside the stall, taking deep breaths and trying to calm herself, but the rush of adrenaline drained from her system, leaving her shaking violently and crying hysterically. She deeply resented the tears, but the shock of the encounter had rocked her to the core.

"Charley, baby," Tyler said softly from outside the stall. "Let me in."

She eyed the lock and tried to get her arms to cooperate with her desire to see him, to hold him, to let him fix what was wrong inside her, but she couldn't bring herself to do it.

"Charley, it's okay. He's gone. Security's got him, and he won't get near you again." To Tyler's credit, he didn't ask who the man was or what he meant to her, but he'd probably already figured that out for himself. "Sweetheart . . . Please, I love you. Let me in. Let me help."

The desperation she heard in his voice finally cut through the numbness. Her arms moved jerkily, her fingers clumsy until the lock finally opened with a click of metal against metal. Tyler stepped around the door, closing it and locking it behind him as he reached for her. "It's okay," he whispered into her hair. "I've got you, and everything is okay."

She shook her head.

"Did he touch you?"

She shook her head again. Devlin's grasp to her elbow didn't count because he'd been trying to stop her from falling.

"Jesus, you're shaking violently."

"T-Tyler . . . My knee. I hurt my knee."

"*Fuck,*" he said on a long exhale. "I'll fucking kill him."

"No," she said, clawing at him, terrified of him leaving her alone for even a minute. In her entire life, she'd only ever felt this way once before—and she'd been alone then. Thank God she wasn't alone this time.

"Baby, I'm not leaving you for a second, but we've got to get you to the hospital."

She whimpered at the thought of another hospital, but the pain was bad enough that she couldn't disagree.

"Would it be okay if I lifted you?"

"I-I need to use the bathroom first." The urgent need to pee had nearly been forgotten in the chaos.

"I'll hold you while you do."

"Tyler . . ."

"This is no time for modesty, Charley," he said through gritted teeth. "Let me take care of you."

Since she didn't have much choice in the matter, she said, "Okay." Working together, he positioned her over the toilet without jarring her leg and pressed his lips to her hair as if she were the most precious thing in his world.

She took care of business, and he helped her to right her clothes before lifting her gingerly into his arms.

"Okay?"

Grimacing from the pain, she nodded.

He carried her from the room into a crowd of people outside the restrooms. "She's injured," Tyler said. "Let us through."

"We called for police and rescue," one of the security guys said.

Charley kept her face pressed against Tyler's chest so she wouldn't have to look at anyone.

"The police are going to want a statement," the security guy said.

"Tomorrow," Tyler replied tightly.

The ambulance ride, the emergency room, the antiseptic smells and the fear on Tyler's face were all eerily familiar. After being put on an IV to deal with the pain, she was taken right to X-ray for a scan of her knee, and then they waited for the doctor in the tiny ER cubicle.

Through it all, Charley could not stop crying at the thought of having to relive the ordeal with her knee, not to mention the aftershocks of her encounter with Devlin.

After shedding his suit coat and rolling the sleeves of his shirt, Tyler paced the small space, anger coming off him in waves.

"Tyler."

He came right to her.

"Sit with me."

He did as she asked, sitting on the narrow bed and putting his arms around her. "Who was he, Charley?"

"Michael Devlin, the guy I fell for in college until I learned he was running a scam on me and a dozen other girls at school."

"Of all the freaking people to run into on an overnight getaway."

"As he said, what're the odds?"

"Baby, I'm sorry this happened. I'm so filled with rage that he scared you that I want to punch a hole through the wall."

"Don't do that," she said, running her thumb over the knuckles he'd bruised dealing with Devlin. "It won't change anything."

"Maybe not, but it would sure feel good right about now."

She put an arm around his waist, keeping him from acting on the impulse.

"He's the reason you've never had a real boyfriend, isn't he?"

"Yes."

"Did he hurt you back then?"

She knew he meant physically. "Not the way you think. What he did was so much worse in some ways. It was like psychological warfare. He said everything I wanted to hear, made promises he never intended to keep, and I fell for every word he said. I fell so deep I almost couldn't find my way out of the hole when I found out it was all a bunch of shit."

His body trembled from the rage he tried so hard to contain for her. "I want to kill him for doing that to you. I've never before wanted to kill another human being, but I wish I had those five minutes in the bathroom to do over again."

"I was never so happy to hear your voice in my life, except for maybe that day at the bottom of the ravine when you came back with help."

"I'll always come for you, Charley. No matter what, you can count on me. Don't ever, *ever* lump me in with that piece of shit in your overactive imagination, you hear me? I'd rather cut off my own arm with a bread knife than ever cause you a second of pain or heartache or—"

"Tyler."

"What?" he asked, sounding annoyed that she'd interrupted his tirade.

"Kiss me, will you?"

Tyler did more than kiss her. He devoured her, pouring every bit of his love for her into that one kiss, and Charley felt it slide through her veins, comforting and calming her after the trauma of the encounter with Devlin.

He was her long-ago past. Tyler was her present—and her future.

"Don't let what happened tonight take this away from us, Charley. We've worked too hard to get where we are to let that scum derail us." Tyler laid his hand flat against her fast-beating heart. "Promise me, you won't let him get to you."

"If you weren't here, I'd be losing it."

"I'm here. I'll always be here because there's nowhere else in this world I'd rather be than with you. You have to promise me, Charley. You won't let him hurt you any more than he already has."

"I won't. I promise."

Tyler kissed her again, caressing her tongue with deep strokes of his.

A throat clearing brought them up for air.

"Pardon the interruption," the doctor said with a grin, "but we have the results of your scan, and everything looks good. We don't see any new tears or damage to the surgically repaired area. You probably just jarred the incision site, which would account for the pain. I'm going to write you a script for some pain meds and send you home, if that's okay."

Filled with relief and gratitude, Charley smiled up at Tyler when she said, "That would be perfect."

Charley spent the entire first weekend in January in bed with Tyler—and Rufus, who'd moved in with them a week ago and made himself right at home in their bed. Last weekend had been dedicated to helping Ella move in with Gavin. This one was all theirs. Tyler had skipped the weekly workout with the running club, and they didn't even bother to get out of bed for Sunday dinner at her parents' home. With a howling snowstorm going on outside, they were perfectly content to hunker down in bed with nowhere to be and nothing to do except make love, sleep, shower, eat, let Rufus out and then do it all again.

"This is beyond ridiculous," Charley said on Sunday night as she lay facedown on the bed while Tyler kissed his way down her back. "I've never been so slovenly in my entire life." Because he hadn't shaved in days, he had the starting of an actual beard, and Charley loved how it looked on him.

"I love you when you're slovenly." He cupped her cheeks and took a gentle bite of each one, waking her body to the drumbeat of arousal that had become so familiar to her in the last few glorious weeks.

Charley had gone back to work after the holidays, but returned to Tyler's bed every night. Rather than drive a wedge between them, the encounter with Devlin had brought them closer together. Tyler had refused to allow her to retreat into a pit of painful memories. Rather he had forced her to stay focused on the present, which he said had nothing at all to do with the past.

And thank God for him, because she didn't like to think about what would've happened if he hadn't been there to remind her that Michael Devlin no longer had any power over her and couldn't hurt her unless she let him. At Tyler's urging, Charley had pressed charges against him for the incident in the bathroom. Because of his criminal record and the circumstances of his encounter with Charley, the prosecutor had assured Charley that he would be charged with disorderly conduct.

Charley tried her best not to think about him, and with Tyler demanding all her attention it was easier than it would've been otherwise to keep the past where it belonged. She sighed with pleasure as he ran his hands over her, stimulating every nerve ending with the reverent way he touched her.

"So when are we going to make things official around here?" he asked.

His question brought her out of the contemplative state she'd slipped into. "I thought we already were official?"

"I guess I mean when are you going to move in with me and make it super official?"

"Oh, um, like you want me to *live* here with you?" Charley kept her smile hidden behind her arm.

He bit the back of her shoulder, making her squeal. "Don't mess with me, Charlotte. You know exactly what I mean by 'live together.'"

"That's kind of a big step."

Before she knew what was happening, he'd picked her up and turned her over effortlessly and without jarring the leg that had recovered quickly from the events in Boston. "Are you screwing with me?"

"Yes, I think maybe I am."

His attempt at a sinister frown was so comical that Charley started laughing and couldn't stop. Grasping her hands, he held them over her head as he pushed into her, filling her with one deep stroke that made her sigh with pleasure.

She waited for him to move the way he always did, but he stayed lodged deep inside her, throbbing and expanding as she squirmed beneath him, trying to spur him to action.

"You're moving in with me," he said.

She looked up at him, memorizing every detail of his fierce expression as he gazed at her. "Okay."

Her easy capitulation made him stagger. "Really?"

"Really."

"And you're staying forever once you officially move in."

"Okay."

"How did the most difficult girl in the world become so easy?"

"She fell in love with you. Does that count as number three hundred?"

"I think it's three hundred and one," he said before he sealed the deal with a kiss. "I love you, Charlotte Abbott. You've made me so happy."

She reached up to place her hands on his face, loving the scrape of his whiskers under her palms. "I love you, too."

"Three oh two. It's gonna take ages to get to a million."

"I'm not doing anything the rest of my life. Are you?"

Surging into her, he said, "I hope to be doing *you* for the rest of my life."

"Such a gentleman to the rest of the world and such a dirty, dirty boy with me."

"You love when I'm dirty."

"Mmm, yes I do, but then I love you all the time."

"Three oh three," he said, drawing a smile from her as he picked up the pace, taking them both to the stars and then back to earth where he caught her, giving her a warm, soft, safe place to land.

# EPILOGUE

KIND HEARTED

E lmer Stillman laid the sheets of paper he'd brought with him flat on the table at the diner while he waited for his son-in-law to arrive for lunch. Tanned and rested after her honeymoon, his new granddaughter-in-law Megan glowed with happiness that made Elmer's romantic heart sing with joy. Never in his life had he seen two people better suited for each other than Megan and his grandson Hunter.

While he took pride in all the matches each of his precious grandchildren had made in recent months, he was particularly proud of Hunter's. For many years before Hunter worked up the nerve to actually ask out Megan, she'd held a special place in that romantic heart of Elmer's. After losing her parents the way she had during her senior year of high school, the sweet girl greatly deserved the kind of happiness she had now with his beloved grandson.

She topped off his coffee cup. "What're you up to today, Elmer?"

"Oh this. And that."

"You're looking awfully cagey."

The thing about seeing someone every day for ten years,

they got to know you quite well, and Megan knew him as well as anyone did.

"I have no idea what you're talking about, sweetheart. Tell me about your trip. How was Bermuda?"

"It was incredible. So beautiful."

"You look rather well rested for a woman just back from her honeymoon."

Megan laughed. "You're not getting the details, so don't even try it."

"You used to be so nice to me before I fixed you up with my grandson," Elmer said mournfully.

Megan leaned over to kiss his forehead. "I'm still nice to you, and you're still not getting the dirt."

"Oh well. You can't blame an old man for trying." Elmer loved her spunk and her spirit, but more than anything, he loved the way she loved Hunter, who also deserved nothing but the best life had to offer. Elmer took hold of her free hand and gave it a squeeze. "Thank you for making him so happy. That's all I've ever wanted for him."

Blinking furiously, she said, "Are you trying to make me cry?"

"Would I do that?"

"Yes, I believe you would, and P.S., it's my pleasure to make him happy." Smiling, she winked at him and moved on to tend to other customers.

Ah, yes, he'd chosen well for Hunter. Now where in the heck was Linc? He'd no sooner had the thought when his son-in-law came rushing into the diner. "So sorry I'm late." Linc hung his coat on a hook and slid into the bench seat across from Elmer. "I got stuck on a phone call that I couldn't get out of."

"I can forgive that since you do such a great job of running the family business."

"You think so? Really?"

Elmer stared across the table at the man who'd been family to him since the day he married Molly nearly forty years ago. "Have I never said so? Have I never told you how proud I am of what you've done with my parents' little country store?"

"You have, but it's still nice to hear you approve. Your voice is always in my head, no matter what we're doing."

"Ahhh, I like that," Elmer said with a big grin. "It's like I'm haunting you."

Linc's bark of laughter had others looking over to see what was so funny. "The meeting was about the catalog and distribution center. I'm gathering information before I go to the kids with it."

"Keep me posted on that. You know you have my support. I think it's a brilliant idea, and something we probably should've done a long time ago."

"We agree on that." Linc smiled up at Megan as she ran by, putting a glass of ice water on the table for him as she went. "What's all that?" he asked of the papers spread out on the table.

"It's an accounting of our efforts on behalf of the kids."

Linc took a subtle look around to see where Megan was. "You're sure it's a good idea to do this here?"

"No one needs to know what we're talking about." He shuffled the papers around so Linc could see them. "Now that I've successfully got Charley about to move in with Tyler—"

"Wait just a minute. You're taking credit for that one, too?"

"You bet I am. Whose idea was it to tell Charley about the running club?"

Linc glowered at him. "Yours," he said begrudgingly.

"And what brought those two happy kids together? Oh wait, was it an accident while they were *running* together?" Elmer put his hand to his ear so he wouldn't miss Linc's reply.

"All right, all right." Linc scowled, acknowledging he'd been bested yet again in their little competition.

The poor boy had no idea that he was up against the master.

"I took the liberty of making a list of who's left and who's available. I'm a little concerned about Wade, who seems to have his heart set on a woman he can't have."

"And how do you know *that*?"

"I'm not at liberty to reveal my sources."

"You do know that Wade is *my* son, and as such, I have a right to know these things."

Elmer howled with laughter that drew more attention from other diners. This was too much fun. "You have a right. Whatever. As much as I'd like to say I know everything I need to know about the situation with Wade, I don't. So I propose we both try to find out a little more about what's going on there. I made lists for Lucas and Landon, but I think we'd both agree that they're not ready to be set loose on the world quite yet."

"Totally agree. They're like a couple of untamed circus animals ninety percent of the time."

Elmer chuckled at that description, but didn't disagree. "They're hilarious circus animals."

"Granted, but they're not ready for prime time. Not yet."

"And Max . . . Our poor boy has been dealt a blow that he's still reeling from. But between you and me, it's sort of a relief to know that Caden will grow up here with us to help guide him—and his dad."

"Totally agree, although I hate to think of Chloe not being in the baby's life at all."

"Maybe she'll come around in time."

"I hope so."

"That leads me to Grayson." Elmer pushed forward a sheet of paper that had Grayson's name printed across the top of the page with just one name written below it—Emma Mulvaney. To emphasize his point, Elmer had put a series of stars before and after her name.

"Subtle," Linc said.

"You saw it as much as I did over the holidays—there was a spark between those two, and I like that gal. She's quieter than Lucy, but she's every bit as strong and lovely. And that little girl of hers melts my heart."

"Mine, too. Molly and I loved having them stay with us for Christmas. It was so nice to have a little one around on Christmas morning again."

"They have something in common, too, although it's an

unfortunate thing. His father left. Simone's father apparently isn't in the picture from what Ray tells me."

Linc hesitated before he said, "But once again we're looking at significant geographical challenges with this pairing."

"Did that stop us with Will and Cameron or Colton and Lucy? It did not." Elmer loved to answer his own questions. "I see no reason whatsoever why we'd let it stop us this time."

"So Grayson and Emma, huh?"

"That's my proposal. Are you game?"

"What do you have in mind?"

Elmer leaned in closer so he couldn't be overheard. "Here's what I'm thinking."

# AUTHOR'S NOTE

Thank you so much for reading *Ain't She Sweet*! I hope you loved Charley and Tyler's story as much as I loved writing it. Charley was a tough nut to crack, as we knew she would be, but I like that she got her happy ending without sacrificing the things that were important to her. Now I know you're all going to say you're dying to know what happened on Grayson and Emma's first date. So am I! Their story, *Every Little Thing*, will be next up for the Green Mountain Series, coming in 2017. Keep reading for the first look at chapter one of *Every Little Thing*.

Between now and then, I hope to write a novella featuring Patrick and Mary, because I'm also dying to know what's up with those crazy kids. Join my newsletter mailing list at marieforce.com (left side where it asks for your name and e-mail) to hear more about plans for future books and novellas.

As always, a huge thanks to the incredible team that runs my business so I can do *almost* nothing but write: Julie Cupp, CMP, Lisa Cafferty, CPA, Holly Sullivan, Isabel Sullivan, Cheryl Serra, Nikki Colquhoun, Ashley Lopez and Courtney Lopes. What a blessing it is to have each of you in my life and part of this wild ride. It's so much more fun to ride the roller coaster with friends and family holding my hand as I scream my head off. ☺ Major kudos to my husband, Dan, who keeps things relatively under control on the home front so I can write, and to my kids, Emily and Jake, who keep me humble with their sarcasm and wit. Love you guys so much!

Thanks go to my fabulous team at Penguin Random House

and the Berkley Publishing Group, led by my friend and editor Kate Seaver. Kate, you're the best. That's all there is to it. Erin, Erica, Jeanne-Marie, Jessica (does your arm still hurt from the loud slap heard round New York last summer?) and everyone on the Berkley team—I appreciate your hard work so much. My agent, Kevan Lyon, has been with me for so long and has become such a great friend and supporter. Thank you for all you do, Kevan, and for being on that roller coaster right along with me. Special thanks to my beta readers, Anne Woodall, Ronlyn Howe and Kara Conrad, for all you do to help me.

To my readers—I say this all the time, but I never get tired of telling you how much I truly love you all and your amazing support of my books. I'm always happy to hear from you at marie@marieforce.com, and please make sure you join the Ain't She Sweet Reader Group at facebook.com/groups/AintSheSweet6/ when you finish the book to dish about the details with spoilers allowed and encouraged. You also want to make sure you're a member of the Green Mountain Reader Group at facebook.com/groups/GreenMountainSeries for updates about upcoming books and other series news.

Happy reading!

xoxo
*Marie*

Read on for an extract from the next gorgeous
book in the Green Mountain series . . .

*Every Little Thing*

Coming soon from Headline Eternal.

How was it possible to *forget* to breathe? Emma was going
to pass out if she didn't remember to breathe. It was that
simple. All day, she'd relived the magical few hours in the
Abbotts' den, sitting by the fire sharing confidences with the
supremely handsome, sexy and successful Grayson Coleman.

Emma had told him things she'd never told another living
soul, even Lucy, her sister and closest confidant. Waiting for
the clock to move forward today, Emma had expected to feel
regrets, recrimination or something negative for spilling the
biggest secret of her life, a nearly ten-year-old secret that
involved the most precious person in the world—her daughter,
Simone.

Something about the way Grayson had paid such close
attention to her, listening to every word she said as if they
were the most important words he'd ever heard, had her telling
him things she never talked about—and rarely thought about
anymore. It had been such a long time ago, and Emma was a
big believer in looking ahead rather than back. Nothing good
ever came from looking back.

It had been so nice of the Abbotts to invite her, her dad, Ray and Simone to spend the week with them so they could attend Hunter and Megan's wedding and then spend Christmas with Lucy and Colton in Vermont. And what an incredible week it had been, complete with sledding and snowman building and even a ride for Simone on the back of Lucas's snowmobile.

Her daughter would be talking about this week for months.

Simone was spending today and tonight with Colton and Lucy at their home on the mountain. She was so excited to have alone time with Auntie Lucy and Uncle Colton and their dogs, Sarah and Elmer. When she left with Lucy earlier, Emma heard her asking if they might see Fred the moose, and Lucy said you never knew when he might come by for a visit.

Since Simone and Lucy left, Emma had felt sort of aimless as she whiled away an unusually quiet afternoon at the Abbotts' lovely home. Her dad had gone into town for lunch with Lincoln, and Molly was at her daughter Hannah's helping her with something.

Emma finally settled on the same sofa where she'd sat with Grayson last night and tried to lose herself in a book she'd been enjoying. But her mind kept wandering to silly things—like the way the fire had turned his dark blond hair to a burnished gold, the twinkle in his eyes when he was amused, the furrow of his brow when he was concentrating or listening to her, and how he'd shown just the right amount of empathy and outrage when she told him about Simone's father.

He'd been forced to step up for his younger siblings after their father left when he was sixteen, but he spoke of his brothers and sisters only with love and affection. None of the burden he must've felt at having so much responsibility at such a young age was apparent in him now.

It had been a very long time, if ever, since she'd been as intrigued by a man as she was by him, thus the breathing trouble. Since he asked her to have dinner with him tonight, she'd been left breathless, winded—and nervous. Really, really *nervous*. She hadn't been out on a proper date in well . . . years. Unless she counted her good friend Troy Kennedy, who'd been her plus one in the city while she served as his. But Troy didn't count. There'd never been anything other than platonic friendship between them, despite the desire of Lucy and Cameron to see them together.

It wasn't happening with Troy, but something had definitely happened last night in front of the fireplace with Grayson.

Emma touched her fingers to her lips, reliving the soft, sweet kiss he'd given her before suggesting they call it a night. If it'd been up to her, he'd still be here and they'd still be talking—and maybe kissing, too.

She'd been so wrapped up in taking care of Simone, working and handling all the parenting and household duties alone that there hadn't been anyone serious since her relationship with Simone's father ended in a spectacular—and violent—fashion.

"Don't think about that," she whispered. "Not today when you have a lovely guy taking you out for dinner." Her mind wandered once again to that brief fleeting kiss and how it had made her yearn for so much more. Another of her deep dark secrets was one she planned to tell no one, especially Grayson. She hadn't had sex since the night she conceived Simone.

"Ugh." She dropped her head into her hands, disgusted with herself for hiding behind the cloak of motherhood as an excuse to keep her distance from men. One year had become two and two became three and three had become a decade while she was busy raising her beautiful daughter, who was now nine.

She hadn't planned to put her own life on hold when she had her daughter. It had just worked out that way. When you were the single mother of a young child, you didn't spend your evenings out at bars or clubs or any of the other places women her age met men.

After her sister finally accepted that Emma was never going to think of Troy in a romantic way, Lucy had wanted her to try online dating. But there was something so inherently frightening about the anonymity of the Internet, especially living as she did in New York City. She had a child to think about, so even if the idea of meeting a guy interested her, online dating did not.

Grayson Coleman interested her.

The Abbotts' dogs, George and Ringo, who'd been sleeping on beds in front of the fire, jumped to their feet and bolted for kitchen. Emma heard Molly talking to the dogs, who barked happily at the return of their loved one. Molly came into the great room a few minutes later.

"Hi there."

"Hi. How's Hannah?"

"Feeling ungainly, but that's pregnancy for you."

"I remember that stage, and thinking I could've been one of the hot-air balloons in the Thanksgiving parade."

Molly laughed and threw some wood on the fire before taking a seat in an easy chair. She put her feet up on the ottoman. The woman was a dynamo. She'd given birth to ten children, but you'd never know it to look at her slender frame and unlined face. The only sign of her age was the mane of gorgeous gray hair that she wore mostly in a braid, but even that did nothing to detract from her otherwise youthful appearance.

"I love the day after Christmas. Back when the kids were little, I used to take to my bed for the entire day, and one of Linc's gifts to me was handling kid care for the entire day while I lolled about being lazy."

"That's a brilliant idea."

"I thought so, too, and the best part? Linc bowed down to me, *every year*, after one day alone with the hellions."

Emma laughed at the picture she painted of ten unruly kids running roughshod over their dear old dad.

"Christmas is one heck of a production for the moms," Molly said. "Still is, and my kids are all grown. But I do love having all the family here—the noise, the presents, the bickering, the chaos. And I love today when they all go home and leave me to my wallowing."

"Sorry to intrude on your peace and quiet."

"Oh please! You're no trouble at all, and Linc and I are in *love* with Simone. We want you to come back every year."

"That would be lovely. Christmas in Vermont is my new favorite thing."

"I love to hear that. Look at this big empty barn we're rattling around in. We've got plenty of room, and we'd love to have you."

"Simone would never speak to me again if I didn't say we'd love to."

"Then it's settled. Please think of our home as your home, Emma. You and Simone and your dad are family to us now. There will never be a time when you won't be welcome here."

"That's so nice of you, thank you."

"Linc and I are going to our favorite Italian place in St. Johnsbury tonight if you'd like to come along."

"Oh, um . . ." She and Grayson hadn't spoken about what, if anything, they would tell other people about their plans for the evening. Would he not want her to tell his aunt they were going out? She made a split-second decision. "Thanks for the invite, but I'm going to stick around here tonight and take advantage of my night off."

"I don't blame you at all. There's a huge tub in our room that you're welcome to if you'd like to take a nice bath."

"That sounds lovely."

"Go ahead. Indulge. I'm going to sit right here and take a nice little nap until Linc gets home. Enjoy."

"You, too."

"Oh, I will."

As she went upstairs, Emma decided she wanted to *be* Molly Abbott when she grew up. What an amazing woman—and mother. Her kids were all great people, even the twins, Lucas and Landon, who'd flirted shamelessly with Emma at both Will's wedding and Hunter's until Colton told them to back off or deal with him—and his axe. They were adorable and hilarious, but far too young for her. Their attention, however, had not been unwelcome. It had served as a reminder that despite how she felt sometimes, she was still only thirty, not sixty.

Molly had handled a wedding in her living room five days before Christmas and a mob scene for the holiday with nothing but grace and humor and mad skill that had left Emma dazzled. It was official. Emma had a full-fledged girl crush on the woman, and being invited back for next year was the second best thing that had happened this week.

By the time Grayson drove to his aunt's house to pick up Emma, he'd already had a full day. His cousin Ella had brought him to see the apartment she'd soon be vacating, and he'd immediately snapped it up, along with the bed and sofa she'd given him. She was moving in with Gavin and didn't need either item. He was happy to check three things off his to-do list. She'd even suggested turning over her landline number to him. He hadn't had a landline in Boston in years, but in Butler, the place where cell service went to die, it was a necessity.

Even though he'd been busy apartment hunting, shoveling snow and doing odd jobs around his mother's house, he'd kept a close eye on the clock, which seemed to be moving in reverse today.

*Emma.*

His first thought that morning had been of her, of the secrets they'd shared, the stories they'd told and the spark that had burned so bright between them. That spark had him more intrigued than he'd ever been by a woman. Sure, he'd heard about it and even seen it happen to some of his cousins and friends, but it had never happened to him, until Emma.

And Simone . . . For it was not possible to consider one without the other. He already knew Emma well enough to understand that there would be no such thing as a relationship that included only Emma. For a guy who'd never had the urge for a family because he'd already helped to raise one family, it was rather startling to realize he was glad Simone was part of the package. She was adorable, smart, funny, sweet and respectful to her mother.

Pulling up to the big red barn, Grayson cut the engine in his Audi SUV but left the headlights on so he could get to the door without falling on the ice. His uncle's Range Rover was gone, so they must have been out for their usual Friday night dinner. He was secretly glad that he wouldn't encounter his beloved aunt and uncle when he picked up Emma.

Grayson was nervous enough without adding a family inquisition to the agenda for the evening—and it would be an inquisition with his uncle Linc involved. Serving as a surrogate dad to the Colemans, Linc was always interested in whatever they were up to. Normally, Grayson welcomed his uncle's interest. Tonight, he was grateful for a little privacy. The light over the back door helped to guide him as he made his way, carefully, to the door.

He let himself in and greeted George and Ringo, who gave him a thorough sniffing before allowing him to proceed into the mudroom, as if to say *He's one of us.* This had been his second home growing up, and he felt every bit at home here as he did at his own mother's house.

"Hello?"

"Hi there," Emma called from upstairs. "I'll be down in a minute."

"Take your time." As Grayson leaned against the counter in his aunt's tidy kitchen he tried to remember his last first date, and his stomach immediately soured at the memories of Heather, his ex-girlfriend. He'd been so blown away by her beauty and captivated by her charm as well as the best sex of his life that he hadn't seen that she was really a stone-cold bitch until he'd already been completely sucked into her web. Extricating himself had been nasty, and he hadn't been with anyone in the year since he ended it with her.

Hearing Emma's footsteps on the stairs, he shook off those memories to put himself in the right frame of mind to spend this evening with her. It was high time he got back to the land of the living after the debacle with Heather.

She came into the room, and Grayson could only stare at how lovely she was in a black turtleneck sweater that she'd paired with sexy jeans and boots. Her hair was down around her shoulders, and she'd done something to her big blue eyes with makeup that made them stand out. "You said casual, right?"

"I did, and you look great."

"So do you," she said with a shy smile.

He liked that she was shy, that she hadn't dated in years, that nothing about her was fake or fabricated. And he really liked that the spark of attraction from last night flared between them, still vibrant and vivid after they'd both had a day to reconsider. He hadn't changed his mind, and judging from the way she looked at him, she hadn't either.

"I should leave a note for Molly so she doesn't worry," Emma said. "I didn't know what to say to her about my plans for tonight, so I didn't say anything."

"You could've told her where you were going."

"I didn't know if you'd want me to."

"One thing you'll quickly learn about this family—and this town—is that there're very few secrets."

Emma smiled and dashed off a quick note to Molly, leaving it on the counter where his aunt was sure to see it.

Over her shoulder, he saw that she'd written, *Went to get dinner with Grayson. See you in the morning. Emma.*

"You're planning on an all-nighter?" he asked in a teasing tone.

"What?" He hated that she sounded and looked stricken by his comment. "No, of course not. I was just thinking they'll be asleep when we get home."

"I was teasing, Emma. Sorry."

She laughed. "Wow, call me out of practice. I missed that completely."

He chuckled at her adorable befuddlement, loving that she was out of practice when it came to men and dating. What a breath of fresh air she was. In the mudroom he held her coat for her and waited for her to zip up and put on gloves. "Ready?" he asked, extending his hand to her.

She took hold of his hand. "Ready."

He led her out into the night, excited to spend time with her, to start over with her, to simply *be* with her.

———

**Read *Every Little Thing*, Emma and Grayson's story, coming soon from Headline Eternal.**

Keep reading for a preview of the spellbinding first book
in Marie Force's Green Mountain series . . .

*Your Love Is All I Need*

# CHAPTER 1

------◄►------

*A hard job is like forty miles of rough road.*

—The gospel according to Elmer Stillman

"What the heck is a frost heave?" Cameron asked Troy, who'd briefly been her boyfriend until they realized they made better friends than lovers.

"Searching," Troy said, indulging her as he had on and off during her long journey from Manhattan to the end of the earth.

"Well?"

"I need a freaking PhD in geology to understand these explanations, but if I'm reading it right, it's what happens when water freezes under the road and the pavement heaves upward."

"Apparently, there're a lot of them around here. Signs every two minutes." Cameron's stomach tightened along with her fingers on the wheel of her gleaming cherry red Mini Cooper, purchased yesterday with this trip in mind. "What do you suppose I do if I happen upon one?"

"Um, I guess you hit the gas and jump it?"

"Thanks. That's really helpful."

His loud yawn had Cameron choking back one of her own. What should've been a leisurely five-and-a-half-hour trek up the scenic Taconic Parkway had turned into seven tense hours as her paltry driving experience had proven no match for the twists and turns of mountain roads.

"Are you almost there? I'm getting tired."

"The GPS says twenty more minutes." All at once, the phone made a series of weird clicking noises. "Troy? Hello? *Ugh!*" Colleagues had warned her that mountain cell phone reception was spotty at best, but she'd refused to imagine a scenario in which she didn't have the world at her fingertips. It didn't bear thinking about.

Cameron hit Redial on the smart phone and reached Troy's voicemail. At least he was trying to call her back.

She put down the phone and focused on driving. In addition to the frost heave signs, the frequent moose-crossing warnings were also unsettling. What were the rules of the road when it came to moose? Who had the right of way? The questions reminded her that she had lots more research yet to do about her destination.

When the phone rang, she pounced on it. "Are you there?"

"I'm here."

"Good," Cameron said, relieved to hear his voice. "Reception sucks up here."

"How long do you have to be there anyway?"

"If they hire us, and that's a huge if at this point, hopefully just a week, maybe two. I'll pacify my father, and then get back to civilization." Cameron didn't like to think about what was riding on her landing this big job.

"Sounds like a plan," he said, yawning again.

"Stop that, will you?"

"Sorry."

Cameron had never driven on such a dark road and had visions of missing a turn and pitching off the side of a cliff. Her fingers ached from gripping the wheel so tightly. "Talk to me," she said.

"What do you want to talk about?"

Over the course of their ten-year friendship-that-defied-definition, they'd covered every subject under the sun. "I don't know. Think of something."

"You never did tell me much about the project."

She released a rattling deep breath, seeking to calm her nerves. "The Green Mountain Country Store needs a website. From what I hear, they're still living in the early-twentieth-century dark ages. My dad went to school with the majority partner, and they ran into each other at their Yale reunion. Dad told him what I do, and one thing led to another."

"You mean one thing led to frost heaves and moose crossings."

Despite her tension, Cameron laughed. "God, Troy, what am I *doing* here?"

"Taking one for the team the way you always do."

"Yeah, I guess." Her father was one of her weak spots, and he'd taken full advantage by all but ordering her to meet with his old friend. But since her website development company was still recovering from the economic downturn a few years back, any new business was welcome—even if it required a trek into the wilderness. "It's so dark I can barely see where I'm going."

"You're talking hands-free, right?"

"Since both my hands are surgically attached to the wheel at the moment, yes."

"I should've driven you up there," he said, sounding regretful.

"You've got court this week." Her friend was an up-and-coming attorney in Manhattan, and Cameron was proud of all he'd accomplished—and appreciative of the pro bono work he did for her company.

"Still, we could've gone up yesterday. I would've been back in time."

"That's sweet of you, but I wanted to do this on my own."

"Had something to prove to yourself, huh?"

"Well, when was the last time I drove? Or even left Manhattan? I'm almost thirty, and until yesterday I'd never *owned* a car."

"I'm proud of you, Cam. You could've said no or sent one of your employees. It says something about you that you decided to take this on yourself."

Touched by what he'd said, she released a nervous laugh. "We'll see how proud you are of me after I'm here a week and going through ugly city withdrawals." Her eyes darted from the dark road to the GPS. "Only five more minutes. I guess I can take it from here."

"You sure?"

"Positive. Thanks for keeping me company."

"Anytime, kiddo. Call me tomorrow?"

"I will. Good luck in court."

"Thanks."

Cameron looked down long enough to end the call. When she returned her attention to the road, something large and black was in her path. A shriek escaped from her clenched jaw as she jammed on the brakes. The tiny car skidded perilously, and she was certain she'd be spiraling into the abyss at any second.

Instead she smashed straight into the immovable object, deploying the car's airbags. That was the last thing she saw before everything went black.

DISCOVER MARIE FORCE'S
*Green Mountains.*

*A place to lose your heart –
and find your home.*

Your Love Is All I Need
Let Me Hold Your Hand
I Saw You Standing There
And I Love You
You'll Be Mine (novella)
It's Love, Only Love
Ain't She Sweet

Available now from

**headline**
ETERNAL

*We hope you've fallen in love with*
# MARIE FORCE

Discover more of our books and authors by visiting our website
www.headlineeternal.com

For exciting news, competitions, and to chat to us and other fans

Follow us on Twitter
 @eternal_books

And like us on Facebook
/eternalromance

**headline**
ETERNAL